D1606540

Martin Amis: Postmodernism and Beyond

Martin Amis:
Postmodernism and Beyond

Edited by Gavin Keulks

palgrave
macmillan

First published 2006 by
PALGRAVE MACMILLAN
Houndmills, Basingstoke, Hampshire RG21 6XS and
175 Fifth Avenue, New York, N.Y. 10010
Companies and representatives throughout the world

PALGRAVE MACMILLAN is the global academic imprint of the Palgrave
Macmillan division of St. Martin's Press, LLC and of Palgrave Macmillan Ltd.
Macmillan® is a registered trademark in the United States, United Kingdom and
other countries. Palgrave is a registered trademark in the European Union and
other countries.

ISBN 13: 978–0–230–00830–4   hardback
ISBN 10: 0–230–00830–5   hardback

This book is printed on paper suitable for recycling and made from fully
managed and sustained forest sources.

A catalogue record for this book is available from the British Library.

Library of Congress Cataloging-in-Publication Data

Martin Amis : Postmodernism and beyond / edited by Gavin Keulks.
    p. cm.
  Includes bibliographical references and index.
  ISBN 0–230–00830–5 (cloth)
    1. Amis, Martin–Criticism and interpretation. 2. Postmodernism
(Literature)–Great Britain. I. Keulks, Gavin.

PR6051.M5Z75 2006
823'.914–dc22   2006045216

10   9   8   7   6   5   4   3   2   1
15   14 13 12 11 10 09 08 07 06

Printed and bound in Great Britain by
Antony Rowe Ltd, Chippenham and Eastbourne

For
R.S.B. & E.C.R.

Contents

Acknowledgements   ix

Notes on the Contributors   x

Introduction   1
Gavin Keulks, Western Oregon University (USA)

1 **"My Heart Really Goes Out to Me": The Self-indulgent Highway to Adulthood in *The Rachel Papers***   9
Neil Brooks, University of Western Ontario (Canada)

2 **Looking-glass Worlds in Martin Amis's Early Fiction: Reflectiveness, Mirror Narcissism, and Doubles**   22
Richard Todd, University of Leiden (the Netherlands)

3 **The Passion of John Self: Allegory, Economy, and Expenditure in Martin Amis's *Money***   36
Tamás Bényei, University of Debrecen (Hungary)

4 **Money Makes the Man: Gender and Sexuality in Martin Amis's *Money***   55
Emma Parker, University of Leicester (UK)

5 **Martin Amis and Late-twentieth-century Working-class Masculinity: *Money* and *London Fields***   71
Philip Tew, Brunel University (UK)

6 **The Female Form, Sublimation, and Nicola Six**   87
Susan Brook, Simon Fraser University (Canada)

7 **Martin Amis's *Time's Arrow* and the Postmodern Sublime**   101
Brian Finney, California State University, Long Beach (USA)

8 **Under the Dark Sun of Melancholia: Writing and Loss in *The Information***   117
Catherine Bernard, University of Paris 7, Denis Diderot (France)

9 **Mimesis and Informatics in *The Information***   137
Richard Menke, University of Georgia (USA)

10 **W(h)ither Postmodernism: Late Amis**   158
    Gavin Keulks, Western Oregon University (USA)

11 **J.G. Ballard's "Inner Space" and the Early Fiction of
    Martin Amis**   180
    James Diedrick, Agnes Scott College (USA)

12 **A Reluctant Leavisite: Martin Amis's "Higher
    Journalism"**   197
    M. Hunter Hayes, Texas A&M University-Commerce (USA)

13 **Nonfiction by Martin Amis, 1971–2005**   211
    Bibliography, compiled by James Diedrick and M. Hunter Hayes

Index   235

Acknowledgements

This collection is the product of more than two years of correspondence, thought, and effort. I thank my contributors for their dedication to the project, their generosity of spirit, and their collegial enthusiasm. It has been an honor to work with each of them as this book – and our professional relationships – evolved.

I also thank my wife, Preeti, for so patiently enduring the emotional economy of scholarship.

Notes on the Contributors

Tamás Bényei is Senior Lecturer at the Department of British Studies, University of Debrecen, Hungary. He has published widely on contemporary British fiction (ranging from Angus Wilson and Iris Murdoch to Graham Swift and Jeanette Winterson), Latin-American fiction, and literary theory. In addition to his five books in Hungarian, he is the author of *Acts of Attention: Figure and Narrative in Postwar British Novels* (1999).

Catherine Bernard is Professor of English literature at the University of Paris 7, Denis Diderot. She has published extensively on English contemporary fiction (A.S. Byatt, Peter Ackroyd, Graham Swift), on contemporary art, and on Modernism, and has co-edited several volumes of essays on Virginia Woolf, including *Virginia Woolf: Le pur et l'impur* (2002). A monograph on Mrs Dalloway is to come out with Gallimard in 2006.

Susan Brook is Assistant Professor in English at Simon Fraser University. Her monograph on Angry Young Men, Women and the New Left is forthcoming from Palgrave. Other work includes articles on Lynne Reid Banks, John Osborne, and Hanif Kureishi. Her current research focuses on suburbia in postwar British literature, film and television.

Neil Brooks is Associate Professor and Chair of the Department of English at Huron University College, University of Western Ontario. His main areas of research are African-American literature and the contemporary novel. His recent publications include articles on Thomas Pynchon, Julian Barnes, Walter White, and James Weldon Johnson. He is co-editor of *Literature and Racial Ambiguity* (2002) and of the forthcoming volumes *Attending the Wake of Postmodernism* and *Reading at the Wake of Postmodernism*.

James Diedrick is Associate Dean of the College and Professor of English at Agnes Scott College in Atlanta, Georgia. He is the author of *Understanding Martin Amis* (1995, 2004) and the co-editor of *Depth of Field: Stanley Kubrick, Film, and the Uses of History* (2006). He has also written essays on Martin Amis, Charlotte Brontë, Charles Dickens, George Eliot, and John Ruskin.

Brian Finney is Associate Professor in English at California State University, Long Beach. He taught at London University from 1964–87 and since emigrating to the US at UCR, UCLA, USC, and CSULB. He has published *Since How It Is: A Study of Samuel Beckett's Later Fiction* (1972); *Christopher Isherwood: A Critical Biography* (1979), which won the James Tait Black Memorial Prize; *The Inner Eye: British Literary Autobiography of the Twentieth Century* (1985); a critical study of D.H. Lawrence's *Sons and Lovers* (1990); and, most recently, *English Fiction Since 1984: Narrating a Nation* (2006).

M. Hunter Hayes is Assistant Professor of English at Texas A&M University-Commerce, where he specializes in contemporary British literature. He has published articles on British fiction and poetry and is completing a book on Will Self. *Martin Amis: An Annotated Bibliography and Critical Checklist*, by James Diedrick and M. Hunter Hayes, is forthcoming from the University of Michigan Press.

Gavin Keulks is Associate Professor of English at Western Oregon University, where he teaches contemporary British and Irish literature. He is the author of *Father and Son: Kingsley Amis, Martin Amis, and the British Novel Since 1950* (2003), and in 2006 he succeeded James Diedrick as the online administrator of the Martin Amis Web. He also recently completed his first novel, tentatively titled *Flight*.

Richard Menke is Assistant Professor of English at the University of Georgia. He has published essays on nineteenth- and twentieth-century literature in *ELH*, *PMLA*, *Modern Fiction Studies*, *Critical Inquiry*, and elsewhere, and is completing a manuscript on realism and information in Victorian fiction.

Emma Parker is Senior Lecturer in English at the University of Leicester and a founding member of the Contemporary Women Writers Network. She has published essays on Margaret Atwood, Toni Morrison, Angela Carter, Jeanette Winterson, Michèle Roberts, and Graham Swift, and is the author of *Kate Atkinson's Behind the Scenes at the Museum: A Reader's Guide* (2002) and the editor of *Contemporary British Women Writers* (2004).

Philip Tew is Professor of English at Brunel University and Director of the UK Network for Modern Fiction Studies. He is the author of *Jim Crace: A Critical Reading* (2006); *The Contemporary British Novel: From John Fowles to Zadie Smith* (2004); *B.S. Johnson: A Critical Reading* (2001); and the editor – with Richard Lane and Rod Mengham – of *Contemporary British Fiction* (2002).

Richard Todd received his PhD from University College London. In 1976 he moved to The Netherlands and in August 2004 was appointed Professor of British literature after 1500 at the University of Leiden. He has authored *Consuming Fictions: The Booker Prize and Fiction in Britain Today* (1996), *Iris Murdoch* (1984), and *Iris Murdoch: The Shakespearian Interest* (1979), as well as a short monograph on A.S. Byatt (1997). He has also published widely on sixteenth- and seventeenth-century lyric verse, with emphasis on Anglo-Dutch cultural relations in the period ca. 1540–1672.

Introduction

Gavin Keulks
Western Oregon University

Spanning three decades, ten novels, six works of nonfiction, two short story collections, and nearly 400 reviews and essays, Martin Amis's career already testifies to a lifetime devoted to literature. From the appearance of his first novel, *The Rachel Papers* (1973), to his most recent novel, *Yellow Dog* (2003), roughly 30 years later, Amis has inspired some of the most controversial literary debates of the contemporary era. His work has prompted new considerations of realism, postmodernism, feminism, politics, and culture, and his personal life has provided fodder for gossip and tabloid journalism. As is true of anyone whose life has veered into celebrity, such evaluations have not always been civil or reciprocally welcomed. However, they have always been lively, always been edifying, and they continue to confirm Amis's status as one of England's most important living writers.

From the leveling satires of his early period, through the mature flourish of the 1980s, to the ongoing evolution of his latest publications, Amis's career has garnered international attention. His awards include the Somerset Maugham Award for best first novel and the James Tait Black Memorial Prize for biography, and his work is routinely shortlisted for other awards, most notoriously the Man Booker Prize, which he has yet to claim despite his numerous literary achievements. Formal commendations aside, few writers can match the spectacle of Amis's literary ascension during the 1980s. After establishing his name with a series of early comedies and satires that centered upon hip, sarcastic, urban youths – *The Rachel Papers*, *Dead Babies* (1975), *Success* (1978), and *Other People: A Mystery Story* (1981) – Amis expanded his stylistic and thematic repertoire to produce his masterpiece, *Money: A Suicide Note* (1984). Twentieth-century literary history stills bears the imprint of this work, which represents for many scholars the commencement of Amis's middle – and decidedly major – period. Following a collection of essays (*The Moronic Inferno and Other Visits to America*, 1986) and a book of short stories (*Einstein's Monsters*, 1987), *London Fields* appeared in 1989, joining *Money* as two of the decade's most incisive portraits of apocalyptic anxieties, nuclear fear, and bristling individualism. Indeed, Amis considers these works to form – with *The Information* (1995) – an informal trilogy. Literary scholars have largely agreed, ranking this triptych of novels among Amis's major achievements, a showcase for his distinctive themes, influences, and techniques. Of course such classifications obscure the intervening *Time's Arrow, or, The Nature of the Offense* (1991), a taut yet forceful novel that examines Nazi atrocities through the structural lenses of reverse chronology and split consciousness. Such a work also exemplifies the grounds upon which Amis's detractors have often congregated: some readers objected to Amis's subjugation of history to style, labeling his efforts artistically callous or indulgent. Like *Money*, however *Time's Arrow* is a technical *tour-de-force*, a forum for Amis to re-imagine literary frameworks and forms.

A highly influential, often imitated stylist, Amis has engendered more than his share of literary rivalry, and as is true of most authors, he has struggled to maintain the momentum of his major period. Literary history features relatively few W.B. Yeatses or Saul Bellows, perennial producers of exceptional work, literary longevists. Indeed the author of *Yellow Dog* bears little resemblance to the author of *The Rachel Papers* – as one would expect or hope, given the rigors of experience. After refining his trademark characteristics and summiting the pinnacle of literary celebrity, Amis took a semi-hiatus from fiction after 1995, inaugurating a transitional period that would ultimately produce his best nonfiction writing. Although two works of fiction appeared – *Night Train* (1997) and *Heavy Water and Other Stories* (1998) – the highlight of this most recent period remains his memoir, *Experience* (2000), a poignant rumination upon the most pressing relationships in his life: those with his father, his mentors and friends, wives and children, and – perhaps most important – his own aging. Significantly, his authorial perspective is divided in this book. Often he peers at the specter of literary immortality, surveying fame; other times he languishes upon lower terrain – mortality, celebrity, feuds. Of course, there remains only one unsettled feud in *Experience*, and that is Amis's quarrel with death.

Besides *Experience*, the early years of the twenty-first century witnessed the publication of two additional nonfiction books: a collection of previously published work – *The War Against Cliché: Essays and Reviews, 1971–2000* (2001) – and the controversial political memoir *Koba the Dread: Laughter and the Twenty Million* (2002), a companion text in many ways to *Experience*. Solidifying his reputation as a Man of Letters, Amis also composed some of his most forceful essays during this period, especially following the 2001 terrorist attacks in the United States. In 2003 he returned to fiction with *Yellow Dog*, an ambitious novel that many people consider his least successful work. Fueling the controversies that his work always seems to inflame, the novel has spawned new debates concerning the evolution of Amis's career, his prodigious talent, his literary reputation and legacy. In 2006 and 2007 Amis is scheduled to publish two new books: *House of Meetings* and *The Pregnant Widow*. The first couples two of the political stories that emerged from the events surrounding September 11, 2001 – "The Last Days of Muhammad Atta" and "In the Palace of the End" – with a novella about two brothers and a Jewish girl in the "pogrom-poised Moscow of 1946." *The Pregnant Widow* is scheduled to be the first novel in a new four-book contract for Amis.

Now that Amis has assumed his position amid the established orders, the "older guard," of contemporary literature, abdicating his vanguard throne, it has become easier to regard him as a literary father in his own right, someone against whom younger writers are compelled to react or – as has recently become more common – to inveigh. It has also become easier to contextualize his achievements within literary genres and movements. After more than three decades of controversial, critically acclaimed, and popular work, Amis remains a writer in transition, one who has never failed to captivate readers' interest and imaginations. Beneath the noise of controversy and the triumphalism of prizes, that interest alone ensures an audience and possibly fame.

This volume emerges from, and consequently resides within, each of these contexts. It offers the first collective assessment of Amis's career. The essays that follow extend the critical dialogues surrounding Amis's work and shed new light upon the status and stature of Amis's work – a scholarly field that seems destined to grow, rather than contract, as Amis evolves his subsequent periods. Three features in particular distinguish this volume and separate it from extant scholarship. First, the 12 invited contributors are experts on Amis's work and contemporary British literature. They also form an impressive international cast, hailing from six different countries. Far better than any monograph or more streamlined collection, this volume displays the vital cross-section of Amis's worldwide influence and reception, an often overlooked appeal in discussions about Amis's relation to literary London or contemporary English society.

As editor, I have also endeavored to compile a volume that avoids such extra-literary issues as biographical subtexts, literary rivalries, or celebrity. There is nothing wrong with such approaches; indeed many of the contributors, including myself, have published on such subjects before. However, these subjects require devotional monographs for sufficient coverage and are notoriously expansive, thwarting essayistic limitations. Only one casualty derives from this conviction: *Experience*. The decision to bracket this work was not lightly made, and ultimately I determined that the extensive treatment it has received – and the complex biographical issues it raises – justified its omission. It has been analyzed most recently as well: in countless reviews and interviews as well as scholarly monographs by James Diedrick and myself. Too often, as Amis himself has lamented, analysis of his work has swerved into his relations, whether familial, literary, or romantic, and this collection seeks to return discussion, for the time being, to his literary contributions.

Finally, this collection features essays devoted to Amis's talents as an essayist and reviewer, a previously neglected subject in Amis scholarship. It also provides a comprehensive, authoritative bibliography of Amis's nonfiction from 1971–2005. Long before he became a novelist, Amis excelled at composing lively, incisive reviews and essays, some of which appeared anonymously or under pseudonyms. Readers of all levels will be impressed and intrigued by the numerous subjects that Amis has surveyed in newspapers, magazines, and journals. This bibliography and the essays on Amis's nonfiction appear at the end of the collection, which is otherwise chronologically structured. This structure is by no means limiting, however; individual essays may, and in some cases do, tend toward non-chronological configurations. As the following paragraphs clarify, the essays in the collection also form natural thematic clusters.

Neil Brooks commences the volume, exploring the ways that Amis's first novel, *The Rachel Papers*, reworks the "coming-of-age" tradition. Emphasizing the novel's distinctive narrative voice, Brooks analyzes the interplay between identity and textuality, portraiture and self-fashioning that culminates in Charles Highway, one of Amis's most memorable narrators. In contrast to the *bildungsroman* or *Künstlerroman* traditions, however, Charles arguably fails to evolve. He subordinates lived experience to textual representation and remains disconnected, both from himself and other people. For Brooks, this is the basis of the novel's – and Amis's – social message.

The next essay comes, appropriately, from Richard Todd, who was among the earliest commentators on Amis's work. In an illuminating analysis of "mirror narcissism" and "reflectiveness" in Amis's early novels, Todd analyzes Amis's use of doubles, one of his signatory narrative strategies. Imaginatively working backward to reveal how *Money* helps us reconsider, or reread, Amis's first four novels, Todd clarifies the ways that mirror imagery functions as a structural framework. These essays by Brooks and Todd – coupled with James Diedrick's later in the collection – comprise the first scholarly cluster, surveying Amis's early period, which had, until now, remained under-examined. They therefore function as companion pieces as well as necessary critical correctives – two common rhetorical strategies in this collection.

Tamás Bényei follows next with a sophisticated, in-depth analysis of *Money,* Amis's most complex novel. Comprehensively annotating the work's extensive use of allegorical frameworks, Bényei unmasks how the narrator, John Self, is equally conditioned and constituted by metaphors of commerce, shame, and exhibitionism. Excess and surplus – both textual and performative – are crucial to Bényei's reading, and his essay is the most authoritative examination to date of the shifting levels of allegory within this seminal contemporary text.

Joining Bényei on *Money* is Emma Parker, who turns attention to the most controversial dynamic in Amis's oeuvre – gender portraiture. Informed by queer theory, her reading counters charges that Amis's novel should be seen as sexist or misogynistic and argues instead that its transgressive sympathies are inherent in its critique of hegemonic masculinity. Challenging "heteropatriarchal" assumptions, the novel privileges dissidence and disruption to register a taxonomic crisis rooted in same-sex desire. Despite Self's homophobic and pornographic attitudes, the novel revels in the dissolution of gender and sexual boundaries.

Philip Tew continues this controversial debate, exploring how the male protagonists of *Money* and *London Fields* struggle for definition under the often suffocating weight of class and urban angst. Coupling gender to class, he cautions against programmatic attempts to theorize such issues separately. He concurs with Emma Parker that Amis's characters often elude and therefore undermine systematic rubrics, and his analysis strives to contextualize the interlinked material and ideological underpinnings of masculinity, a masculinity that ranges in class and character from John Self to Keith Talent but uncovers common ground in its treatment of working-class masculinity.

Susan Brook completes this collection's tripartite analysis of Amis's gender schematics. Her essay explores the relationship between Nicola Six, the heroine of *London Fields*, and a series of oppositions that Amis invokes and problematizes: between mediation and the real, the unnatural and the natural, the text and the body, creation and destruction. On one hand, she contends, Nicola is pure form and order, a "shapely" moral aesthetic standing in contrast to masculine amorality and formlessness. On the other hand, she thwarts representative control through her performative engagement with fantasy and transgression, both sexual and authorial. She thereby expresses an anxiety common to Amis's work: the anxiety that literature, in assuming form and shape, also sanitizes, mediates, or evades the real. In many ways, *Money* and *London Fields* pose questions about gender that are as historically significant as those in works by Virginia Woolf or D.H. Lawrence, and the companion essays by Parker, Tew, and Brook not only expand the debate about Amis's gender portraits but will no doubt figure prominently in future examinations of the subject.

Brian Finney next adopts *Time's Arrow* as his subject, exploring how the novel filters history through the lens of the "postmodern sublime." Since the mid-1980s, controversy has saturated the subject of postmodernism – whether perceived as historical period or descriptive label. The historical background for *Time's Arrow* is mid-century Nazism, of course, and Finney elucidates how Amis both engages and dissents from this problematic, subordinating history to aesthetics in order to revitalize morality and humanism. Accentuating the importance of irony to narrative perspective, Finney provides a method for reconciling stylistic experiment and historical horror, tracing Amis's figurative war not only against cliché but against all ideologies that would rationalize atrocity.

Turning attention to *The Information* – the work which concludes Amis's major period as well as his self-described "informal trilogy" – essays by Catherine Bernard and Richard Menke elevate scholarship on Amis's most significant novel of the 1990s. Along with the essays by Finney and Keulks (below), these essays form another important scholarly cluster, highlighting Amis's shifting relations to realism and postmodernism, two modes whose representational strategies demarcate much twentieth-century literature. Bernard theorizes these dynamics through *The Information*'s opposition between nostalgia and satire, showing how Amis "fetishizes emotion" in a complex gamble that unveils the "failed promise of universality" within contemporary culture. Focusing upon tropes of melancholy, writing, and loss, her essay convincingly charts the novel's stratagems for depicting vulnerability and negativity, contingency and realism, universality and the culture industry.

Richard Menke subsequently decodes the novel's sophisticated presentation of "informatics." Exploring how information not only "resists assimilation" but also mediates "mimetic play," Menke unravels how the novel thwarts revelation, whether theorized in terms of character rivalry or more comprehensive depictions of informational saturation. Crucial to his discussion is the significance of pixelation – strategies of blurring, filtration, interpolation, and compression – which relate to the entropic epistemology of the novel. What emerges, he concludes, is an account of culture as "mediated information" rendered increasingly powerful because of its relation to "modern informatics."

Concluding the cluster on Amis's relation to realism and postmodernism, my own essay speculates how the novels *Night Train* and *Yellow Dog* – the inaugural texts of his "late" phase, I theorize – potentially foreshadow a recuperative form of "sanitized postmodernism." Rather than dismiss these works as derivative missteps, as some have done with *Yellow Dog*, I explore how Amis embeds a dialectic between realism and postmodernism within their plots and polarized characters to express his dual discomfort with radical postmodernism as well as any wistful retreat to realism. The questionable success of these novels within Amis's corpus confirms the tentative, exploratory nature of his efforts to chart a period after – or beyond – postmodernism, the trend that solidified his fame in earlier decades.

The collection culminates with two essays on Amis's essays and reviews – although James Diedrick's essay comments also upon Amis's early novels. As Diedrick and M. Hunter Hayes document, Amis's nonfiction writing deepens readers' understanding of his novels and artistic concerns. Whether writing about other authors or books, television programs or sporting events, royalty or celebrities, Amis repudiates simplistic distinctions between "popular" and "high" culture. Especially during the 1970s and early 1980s, Amis often approached his subjects with iconoclastic exuberance. As his career assumed form, and his subjects became more serious, Amis consciously evolved a more authoritative persona to pontificate about politics and society. Focusing upon the science fiction reviews that Amis published under his first professional pseudonym – Henry Tilney – Diedrick proves that

Amis's assessment of J.G. Ballard's work provides a key to his "self-mythologizing" and "increasing literary status anxiety." He then traces the effects of these changes, especially on *Dead Babies* and *Other People*, recovering the connections between Amis's nonfiction persona and his early novels. Diedrick's essay thereby links thematically with Brooks's and Todd's, concluding the collection's survey of Amis's early career.

M. Hunter Hayes tracks this conflict between mainstream fiction and high art – or populism and pontification – onto new terrain, concentrating on Amis's anxiety of influence with F.R. Leavis, the Cambridge don who popularized the "Great Tradition" and was the leading critic of his age. Elucidating Amis's own form of emergent, rival "Leavisism," Hayes chronicles Amis's alternating adoption and subversion of Leavisite values through numerous reviews, including two written under Amis's other pseudonym, Bruno Holbrook. These reviews strove to broaden literary tradition and to authenticate a space for Amis's own satiric forms and his American literary mentors. The essays by Diedrick and Hayes are accompanied by a comprehensive bibliography of Amis's nonfiction writing from 1971–2005. The majority of these entries appear here in print for the first time, and their essays and bibliography will undoubtedly illuminate numerous avenues for subsequent scholarship.

Analysis of any living writer always poses unique challenges: new works appear, modifying traditions; styles and interests change; artistic habits recede. This collection presents the first extended analysis of Martin Amis's career from diverse nationalities and critical perspectives. These 12 articles stand equally as individual contributions or as representative clusters or thematic constellations. Amis's authorial evolution remains far from concluded, and as he continues to publish new work, and as readers and scholars continue to assess those achievements, it will remain exciting to track his significance and influence. This collection testifies to his already distinguished and celebrated career, and it has been an honor to bring it to print.

1

"My Heart Really Goes Out to Me": The Self-indulgent Highway to Adulthood in *The Rachel Papers*

Neil Brooks
University of Western Ontario

> My next encounter with Rachel was on the Friday, three days after the Tea Centre incident.
>
> It couldn't have been more spontaneous if I had planned it. All the more startling because I had resigned myself to dumping the entire Rachel opus. (65)

In the passage above, Charles Highway, narrator of Martin Amis's first novel *The Rachel Papers*, recounts his chance meeting with the titular character. Each of his sentences reveals aspects of the ways he fictionalizes his life in order to avoid the vulnerability associated with authentic emotional response. Charles's reference to the "Tea Centre incident" immediately places his experiences into the realm of story; his need to appear spontaneous betrays his obsession to control every situation; and his reference to "dumping the Rachel opus" conveys his egocentrism and predilection to see events in terms of literary value rather than empathic emotion. Charles's constant attempts at self-aggrandizement ultimately disconnect him from his own experience and even his own body. He becomes so immersed in a world of texts that he becomes uninterested in finding any validation outside the written word. He can therefore be seen as a quintessential representation of the postmodern subject whose perceptions are so mediated that, despite his seemingly likeable nature, he is not only unstable but also frighteningly dangerous, both textually and ideologically.

Charles's egotism and self-aggrandizement appear early in the novel, when he extensively analyzes his own name, immediately establishing the labeling power of words as well as his role as the ultimate arbiter of signification. He assures the reader that "it isn't that I like or love myself. Rather, I am rather sentimental about myself (I say, is this normal for someone my age?)" (16). Later, in reflecting upon his sexual prowess, he confesses to being "jealous of myself" (23). Clearly, Charles has an inflated notion of his self-importance; however, this aggrandizement is logical because he perceives his solipsistic way of *writing* the world to be a superior form of understanding – far surpassing mere lived experience. For Charles, such self-importance is entirely justified because in the absence of any compelling external morality he feels empowered to generate his own version of reality. In *The Postmodern Condition*, Lyotard argues that "the grand narrative has lost its credibility" (37), yet optimistically he posits that although "consensus has become an outmoded and suspected value ... justice is neither outmoded nor suspect" (66). In opposition to Lyotard, however, Charles filters all responses through the prism of his self-serving rationalizations. *The Rachel Papers* catalogues his need for a master narrative through which to ground himself. In the absence of such socially-derived moorings, he charts his own egocentric universe.

Any gestures Charles might make towards empathy fail because of his stunted emotional life. Later, discussing Charles's family, I will suggest how his childhood may have contributed to this emotional vacuum, but Amis certainly seems to define Charles's condition as endemic to his generation, not merely personal failing. However, Charles separates himself from his generation. Whereas his peers are immersed in shallow, youthful, media-inspired pursuits, Charles imagines himself as looking back to an earlier time. His is a retrospective perspective. Rather than being a stereotypical disengaged, late-twentieth-century man, Charles's egotism leads him to identify with highbrow authors and erudite scholars. Significantly, Charles defines himself in almost direct opposition to Amis's later protagonist John Self (of *Money*), about whom Amis has commented: "I do mean him to be a consumer, and he is consumed by consumerism, as all mere consumers are. I also mean him to be stupefied by having watched too much television – his life is without sustenance of any kind – and that is why he is so fooled by everyone" (Haffenden, 7). Self has become merely a product, utterly defined by the hollow culture around him. Despite all of Charles Highway's sophisticated trappings, he too becomes entombed in cultural productions. Self seems to wander from event to event with an utter lack of agency; Charles only avoids a similar fate by making his "papers" the mark of his identity. The very way Charles textualizes his existence renders him unable to move outside of the artificiality of society he seeks to escape. For all his highbrow references he too has a "life without sustenance of any kind."

In his interview with John Haffenden, Amis remarks that the *The Rachel Papers* contributes to the genre of the "coming of age novel" in that it deters from the convention of the aspiring artist, offering instead an aspiring literary critic who exhibits "all the faults of the literary critic – that comfortable distance from life" (10). However, Charles is not a mere literary critic; he is too aware of his own posturing to maintain that comfortable distance, despite striving for it, as in passages such as when Charles muses, "What will that mind of yours get up to next? I said, recognizing the self-congratulations behind that recognition and the self-congratulations behind recognizing that recognition" (96). His own reflections and, more importantly, his reflections *upon* his reflections render him unable to view any situation objectively – except with himself at the center. When Rachel reveals personal details of her relationship with another man, for example, Charles tries to empathize. However, he only can conclude that her internal thoughts must wonder why she was "so unruffled discussing him with this strange, oddly compelling young man, this Charles Highway?" (85). Gavin Keulks notes that Charles "embraces egotism as a redemptive virtue" (125) and describes the character as "compulsively cerebral, willfully controlling, maniacally precocious" (126). This very embrace of intellectualism and egotism leads Charles to create elaborate fictions to control his sphere of existence and reduce people to mere papers, as the novel's title suggests.

Indeed, at one point he vaguely contemplates suicide as an appropriately romantic response to his life but dismisses the idea because he worries where he would find a "responsible literary executor for the notebooks" (135). Such privileging of his notebooks over his actual physical existence demonstrates his valuation of reflection over experience itself. Even from the grave, it would seem, his controlling nature would require satisfaction. Through such psychology Amis simultaneously skewers both elitism and the philistine nature of contemporary culture. Charles's responses seem justifiable on one level, given that his egotism does separate him – redemptively – from his more dissolute associates. More importantly, however, and despite Charles's smug self-satisfaction, Amis exposes a narrator who is partly derivative – merely another alienated, self-centered emblem of late-twentieth-century man. Charles may be even more pathetic *because of* his delusion that he controls the external forces that restrict him.

Much of the novel's humor derives from the extent to which Charles tries to control all aspects of his life. The day before his first date with Rachel, for instance, he sees the movie by himself, then rehearses "an amusing commentary to be whispered at Rachel in the dark" (49). His use of preposition is telling – "whispered *at* Rachel, rather than *to* Rachel. He spends evenings "drinking sherry and making diagrammatic plans" (133) for telephone conversations; he prepares for a date by reading "two early Edna O'Briens and annotating my sex techniques handbooks. Horlicks at nine o'clock" (70). His desire for routine and order becomes extreme during the consummation of his relationship with Rachel, when he becomes aware that he "really wants a cup of tea" (148) – much like he wants the Horlicks, his comfort drinks, in the planning stages. Indeed, when Charles graphically describes his most intimate moments with Rachel, his descriptions read like a pilot's checkdown routine rather than the exaltations of a passionate man. While removing her panties, he recalls that his head became "a whirlpool of notes, directives, memos, hints, pointers, and random scribblings" (155). Indeed his physical arousal often seems predicated on moving his hand over her body, something that perfectly parallels the authorial movement of his hand over paper. Although he thinks compulsively about sex, the experience remains insufficiently transcendent or liberating. In an interview with Will Self, Amis notes that the world of his novels "presents very few opportunities for healthy Lawrentian sex," and indeed for many of his characters it remains a necessary bodily function. For Charles, however, it remains a different kind of necessity: raw material utilized primarily for the transcendent and liberating effects it can lend to his journals.

The journals are where Charles effectively brings order to chaos and offers a corrective to the messy vital world. However, unlike the "angry young men" characters of a previous generation, Charles seeks neither to expose the flaws of his corrupt society nor offer any optimistic, youthful alternatives to current social conditions. Rather, he simply feels he can avoid being implicated if he can set himself apart in his own self-created world. This also in no way mirrors a return to the ideal of a new "aesthetic order" espoused by modernist writers; rather, for Charles the ugly is more appealing than the beautiful: "surely," he states, "nice things are dull, and nasty things are funny" (88). The nice has been pre-defined and appropriated within society whereas the nasty allows him to order and arrange perceptions himself. This quotation also leads to the common thread of what little criticism has been written on *The Rachel Papers*. Repeatedly, critics have sought to understand Amis through examining the work of his father, Kingsley Amis, and specifically to compare *The Rachel Papers* with Kingsley Amis's *Lucky Jim*. James Diedrick was the first to note how Charles re-writes Jim Dixon's "favorite maxim" that "'nice things are nicer than nasty ones'" (35), and Gavin Keulks's full-length study of the two Amises does an excellent job in examining the relationship between their oeuvres. Instead of continuing this dialogue, I would like to examine how this context affects Charles rather than Martin.

Like many late-twentieth-century adolescent narrators, Charles exhibits a sardonic attitude towards the cherished beliefs of the adults around him. In "Teenage Wasteland," Kirk Curnutt writes that "up through the 1970's, teenage resistance to social authority was such a pervasive motif.... In contemporary novels, however, youth's disaffected disposition is credited not to the oppressiveness of adult authority, but to a lack of it" (95). Charles mocks or dismisses every adult character in *The Rachel Papers* – with the possible exception of an Oxford tutor who abrogates his authority. In particular, it seems that the absence of moral authority in Charles's family greatly contributes to his development of an amoral autonomy. Early in the novel he claims that "hatred is the only emotionally educated reaction to a sterile family environment" (11). But he never seems to be able to generate any feelings as strong as hatred. Indeed, he is emotionally uneducated and gets this belief from reading D.H. Lawrence rather than any reaction to his own situation. His unfinished letter to his father is constantly referred to, but it remains unwritten – a "virtual letter" representing the way in which emotions remain less than real to Charles. At one point he almost has a sincere conversation with his sister Jenny but instead merely reflects, "we had both wanted to talk, I think. I don't know why we didn't" (70). This is as close as he gets to any meaningful connection with his family. He is appalled at the way his younger brother and others are bullying and mistreating another boy, but when Valentine defends his actions, claiming that everyone does such things, Charles responds, "I could think of nothing to say, so I caught hold of his shoulder and boxed him on the side of the head. But without much conviction" (124). Charles can muster no greater conviction in the novel. Near the end of the novel he has a final confrontation with his father, which culminates in reconciliation. However, as Diedrick notes, "Charles's emotional freight is so quickly unloaded, and his expression of solidarity with his father so pat, that it seems another verbal pose" (38).

Indeed, verbal poses comprise the basis of Charles's identity – an identity that threatens to be subsumed by textuality. As John Dern notes, "his character is not fixed, but rather a collection of caricatures he employs as necessary" (57). Thus, the very situation of the novel mirrors Charles's character. The novel is set the night before Charles's twentieth birthday, and he tells his reader "I confess that I've been looking forward to this night for months" (8). The night marks not only a significant date on the calendar but, more important for Charles, a night he can spend alone with his papers. It would seem that the overlooked central conceit of the novel is Charles's belief that he will enter his maturity *only* when he has completed his papers. Maturity therefore remains subordinate to composition and genre. As in many novels, a woman introduces the male narrator to adulthood. However, in an ironic twist, Rachel does so *not* by taking Charles's virginity or by helping him establish his first adult relationship; rather, she gives him the fodder for his first publishable set of papers. Crucially, she enables him to reach an audience – but not herself – which Charles does through his "Rachel Papers." Charles's egotism not only provides the opportunity to control events but also leaves him little more than a diarist, one whose inadequacies cannot be hidden through his narrative suppressions.

Now would seem an appropriate time to examine my own conceit throughout this analysis of treating Charles Highway as though he were a human being rather than a fictional character. The book gives Charles such narrative authority that to read him as a mere creation diminishes the central messages of the text. Amis has claimed "I have enough of the postmodernist in me – although I hope that I'm on the humorous wing of postmodernism – to want to remind the reader that it is no use getting het-up about a character, since the character is only there to serve this fiction" (Haffenden, 19). However, no such overt reminders exist in his first novel, simply because they would run counter to the novel's central movement: Charles Highway shaping his own world through his papers. Unlike in Amis's other novels, where an authorial presence is often foregrounded (most directly, of course, in *Money*) the author – or any related trickster figure – remains absent in *The Rachel Papers*. Amis has suggested that the tutor could be "an author figure" (Haffenden, 10), but to use his own analysis against him, surely the tutor functions more as the figure of a literary critic rather than an author. This lack of authorial voice is necessary for Charles to assert his authority, both textually and personally. But one could also argue that the absence of the author is *exactly* what Amis is criticizing in contemporary society. In narrating the text through Charles's self-inflating autobiographical voice, Amis succeeds in hiding his own position as creator and thus succeeds in making the "author function" appear reduced to Charles's selfish exhibitionism. Such tactics also seem significant in the context of postmodern fiction – as though Amis is arguing that postmodernism, with all its self-reflexivity, risks squandering its social authority and value. Asked by Haffenden to reply to the question "Do you think literature has a function?" Amis stated:

> I would say that the point of good art is remotely and unclearly an educative process, a humanizing and enriching process. If you read a good novel, things must look a little richer and more complicated, and one feels that this should eat away at all ills. The only hope is education, and one is vaguely – though not centrally – involved in the process of education. (24)

Charles Highway may be "compulsively cerebral" and extraordinarily clever, but he is ultimately uneducated. His admission to Oxford at the novel's end seems more an indictment of the institution (and higher learning in general) than a victory for Charles. The tutor expresses hope that Charles may become "educated" – or to use Amis's term: "humanized" – but he does not express a great deal of confidence. After asking in an exasperated tone whether Charles even likes literature, the tutor proceeds to chastise him that "Literature has a life of its own [...] You can't just use it ... ruthlessly, for your own ends." Ultimately he admits Charles, but this may only serve to confirm the exhaustion of traditional value, especially as it is accompanied by the deprecating words, "I'm going to take you anyway; if I don't somebody else will and you'll only get worse" (211). Charles's interview, then, should stand as the moral climax of the novel, but coming on the heels of his indefensible liaison with Gloria and followed by his callous treatment of Rachel, no moral lesson seems to have been learned. And that is precisely Amis's point: moral lessons, comeuppances, closure, and structure – these appear more frequently in literature than in life. The irony goes even deeper because, as the tutor lectures Charles that "literature has a life of its own," a subtle shift occurs. The actual recipients of this lecture become Amis's readers, not simply Charles: readers who, like Charles, have been conditioned by a society that no longer respects art as anything other than – at best – a distraction or – at worst – something that can be manipulated for nonliterary ends.

The instances of Charles manipulating art for selfish or dishonorable ends are manifold throughout the novel. He constantly wants to appear sophisticated and uses books, visual art, and music to help conjure this image. He repeatedly details which books and records he has arranged in his room to generate an appearance, or effect, of emotional engagement. In perhaps the least subtle imagery of the novel, Charles plays *Sgt Pepper's Lonely Hearts Club Band* as the soundtrack for an intimate encounter with Rachel. He takes time to observe that "the gnomic George Harrison [was singing] about the space between us all, about those persons who willfully conceal themselves behind a wall of illusion and so on" (97). Charles, of course, in no way relates the lyrics to his own illusions or to the clear space between himself and others. Instead, the dismissive "and so on" and the adjective "gnomic" suggest a smug superiority to the lyrics. Similarly, when Charles watches cricket, he haughtily observes the racist commentary of the announcers but lacks the conviction or social consciousness to confront such racism himself.

For all his self-righteousness and intellectual elitism, Charles is not a mere creature of the mind. Indeed, given the lengthy descriptions of, and observations about, sex, one could see the novel as more of a sex romp than a serious analysis of a disaffected youth in a thoroughly mediated culture. However, it is this very disconnection between mind and body that allows Charles to become a more sympathetic character than his amoral behavior might otherwise suggest. His alienation from his own body serves as a synecdoche for his alienation from the human race. Much of the novel is devoted to Charles's sexual adventures, but each erotic encounter only further drives Charles to become a creature of the mind. The descriptions of the physical encounters – from disrobing to consummation – seem to follow an inverse arc with ever-increasing dispassion. Charles has "read widely in prophylactic literature" (152), "knows from a variety of sources" that kissing her head "will do more for you than any occult caress" (155), and observes while beginning an encounter that the floor was "bare boards so it must have seemed pretty spontaneous" (147). All of these evidence Charles's hyperanalytical dislocation from his own body. Not only does he refer back to past reading, but events in the present simply become fodder for future literary delving. When Rachel and Charles discuss her impending departure for France, Charles feigns emotional engagement but admits, "even then as memo pad 3A clearly states part of me wasn't thinking of that. Part of me was thinking how well I'd do on exams with Rachel in France ... and what florid letters I could write to her" (166). He derives greater satisfaction from the possibility of adopting a new genre – epistolary fiction – than from the promise (or potential loss) of a physical encounter.

Indeed, actual encounters only become valuable *after* they are documented, as Charles confirms when he writes, "I saw Rachel only twice in the six days before she was due to come and stay [...] a good deal of clerking was necessary to keep The Rachel Papers up to date, what with all these new emotions to be catalogued and filed away" (168). Needless to say, "filing away emotions" is what Charles Highway does best. Unlike earlier "coming of age" narrators whose authentic emotional response seems to be the antidote to what Holden Caulfield in *Catcher in the Rye* (1951) calls the "phoniness" of the adult world, and unlike later protagonists like Clay in Brett Easton Ellis's *Less than Zero* (1985), who try to anesthetize themselves from feeling, Charles's emotional responses serve ultimately to pad his files. Perhaps this stems from a lack of trust. Yet Charles does not even trust his own body to order experience in a sensible manner. His society, his peers, and his own body all suffer from a tendency towards chaos and confusion; only in his papers can he perhaps maintain order and control. Amis the novelist seems to offer the book as hope: that by annotating the breakdown in value and meaning everywhere except in literature, one gleans direction to overcome the morass of meaninglessness. However, at the same time Amis the satirist makes Charles the object of ridicule, symbolizing that such idealized optimism may be equally misplaced, even delusional – a byproduct of literature, not life.

Perhaps the "coming of age" novel that can best be compared with *The Rachel Papers* is John Fowles's *The Magus* (1965). Charles would almost certainly prefer this parallel to those novels mentioned above because he condescends towards Americans and American culture, dismissively observing that "every American over 8 and under 25 looks like a middle-aged sportswriter" (51). Moreover, the comparison with Fowles's university-educated and hyperliterary Nick Urfe would flatter Charles, who prides himself on his precociousness. Fowles's novel was widely embraced as an expression of youthful liberation from the restrictive British society, but it also contained the warning that such liberation comes with responsibility: the novel repeats the message that "the better you understand freedom the less you possess it" (526). Nicholas Urfe travels to Greece and learns of his responsibilities through experiences that cause him to question the elitist and chauvinistic attitudes with which he has governed his life

Similarly, Charles's parents arrange for him to travel to Spain to gain the experiences necessary to usher him into adulthood. For Charles, however, even this act of escaping has become merely another literary cliché: a rite of passage, a way of meeting expectations, orchestrating a happy ending. Rejecting this structure, he instead arranges for prewritten postcards to be posted from Spain; he then spends his time experimenting with drugs and prostitutes in London, as though emulating Lord Byron rather than Nick Urfe. While Nick ultimately learns that, stripped of his prejudices, sexual intimacy culminates in greater understanding – both of himself and of others – Charles never evolves beyond his constant need to analyze and annotate his bodily responses.

This dislocation from his body can perhaps best be seen in a jarring transition Amis makes – a transition made more disconcerting by the fact that the reader is generally guided scrupulously from scene to scene. After intercourse with Rachel, Charles feels self-satisfied and naturally turns immediately to contemplating his papers. He reflects:

> Perhaps The Rachel Papers aren't in such a mess after all. With some interleaving of *Conquests and Techniques: A Synthesis*, and an index …? When I'm twenty this will be a thing of the past. The teenage boy is entitled to a certain amount of disorder, and, anyway, I'll mellow tomorrow. (159)

Charles clearly allows the sex act to calm him but, significantly, he only locates that comfort in the context of his papers. Minutes before he had silently mouthed the words "I love you" to Rachel, but he quickly retreats from any confusion this bodily/emotional response might cause. Thus, his immediate reduction of Rachel to her place and role in *Conquests and Techniques*. Even more telling is the next paragraph, which begins by asking whether "Something particularly revolting" had "gone wrong" (159). We then move from Charles's mouthed expression of love to a scene in his dentist's office. Charles's dental dilemmas serve to underscore his discomfort with his body in general as well as the spoken word. His physical pain often interferes with his ability to think, and he privileges writing as a form of discourse where it is less likely that "something particularly revolting" will go wrong.

Despite Charles's obsessively controlling nature, much of the novel addresses those areas of existence that he cannot control. As I mentioned earlier, Charles seems to lack social conscience, but the "dread" witnessed in other contemporary novels seems paralleled here by an

"anxiety" to which Charles repeatedly refers. Consistent with his character, Charles uses such anxiety as fodder for his prose rather than to
define his identity or his generation. Indeed, he suggests that his
anxiety is "something to take an interest in" (45) and weekly compiles
an "Anxiety Top Ten," which reveals he has no concern about the
dangers facing humanity. By contrast, issues such as "boil on back,
loose molar, and rotting feet" (93) all secure a place on the list. This
continued obsession with physical ailments seeks to hide Charles's real
anxieties. Buried at number 7 is "being friendless," but Charles never
elaborates. Each pimple and boil, however, receives graphic description. Charles's obsessive response to his body is not vanity but rather
an elaborate defense mechanism to protect him from obsessing over
his stunted emotional growth. By providing such explicit physical
descriptions, Amis reveals a youth culture that has escaped the shackles
of "polite society" but has not evolved to address the gaps that
indicted that society in the first place. Charles can frankly address the
fact that his father has a mistress, but he cannot deal with the emotional consequences of this fact. Despite his claims to the contrary,
Amis shows that neither Charles nor contemporary youth-culture
really advances beyond "sixth-form cleverness and fifth-form nastiness" (8). Similarly, Charles's fixation on Rachel's bodily functions
serves as a convenient distraction, sheltering him from addressing their
growing emotional intimacy. Further, and in keeping with Charles's
comic motto about nastiness, his sardonic wit helps reduce the threat
of the "nasty." In so doing, however, Charles incorporates the nasty
equally with the "nice," erasing any distinction between the two.
By rendering everything disturbing as merely "funny" Charles avoids
confronting anything upsetting.

    After temporarily losing control of his emotions, Charles asserts that
"irony and blood returned to my features" (73), as though the two
together form his essential life-force. Irony is an effective mask for
Charles, and masking his public thoughts and expressions keeps his
private papers pristine. I suggested at the beginning of this essay that
Charles's behavior is frighteningly dangerous. He is dangerous because
– mirroring his misunderstanding of literature, which the tutor corrects
– he acknowledges no perspective other than his own. However, his
redeeming qualities are manifest in the omissions within his narrative,
the places where the reader can see the distinction between Charles's
role as compiler of "The Rachel Papers" and his true reaction to the
events the papers detail.

Despite Charles's privileging of his notebooks and his obsessive planning, his greatest courtship success comes not from well-scripted encounters but from a serendipitous meeting: "I didn't have a single note-pad on me. So I ad-libbed" (65), he writes, oblivious to the fact that this revelatory ad-libbing is what impresses Rachel. Later, he finds himself surprised by his attraction to her, observing, "I gazed at Rachel's profile. Goodness me, I really did like her. A novel turn in our relationship" (111). After their breakup he even admits that he cannot read the nicely worded paper he has written and has to "slap his hand over the telephone" (156) so she does not hear him cry. Of course, he immediately moves on, providing no commentary on this loss of control. The need to relinquish control and indulge in authentic emotional response may be the ultimate moral lesson the book has to offer.

I mentioned earlier that Charles's interview with the tutor should have provided the moral center of the story but that the tutor's cynical admission to "take [Charles] anyway" (216) in order only to prevent his further moral degeneration undercuts his authority. To find a moral tutor, perhaps, one needs to look to Charles's earlier interview with his friend Geoffrey. Geoffrey advises Charles not to "get too wanky" with Rachel: "And cut out all this intellectual shit. Chicks don't want to be over-awed ... if you make it cool, if you don't then don't sweat it" (77). Geoffrey does not seem to be a teacher of morality – like Conchis in *The Magus* – but compared to Charles, Charles's father, the Oxford tutor, or even Rachel, he is the most honest. His parting words are, "With me, it's not all part of some great ... scene" (79), but for Charles, and to a lesser extent everyone else in the novel, it would seem that playing a part in "some great scene" has become more important than authentic human contact. The novel exposes a society that has lost all sense of coherence – not because of technological change but rather because of a cultural revolution that witnessed the ascension of individuality. As individualists, Amis contends, we run the risk of isolation and solipsism, like Charles Highway.

Ultimately, Charles decides that he cannot remain with Rachel but that he should still attend Oxford. He sees their breakup as another necessary romantic adventure and conceptualizes her feelings only in terms of their effectiveness in the notebooks. Clearly, he has chosen the path of avoiding life, immersing himself in the world of textuality where emotional connections can be controlled and structured. In fact, Charles decides to leave Rachel soon after he is forced to confront her humanity – not just his romanticized or textualized projection of her. Accidentally witnessing evidence of her bodily functions, he writes that "our relationship until that moment had been so straightforward and idealized, so utterly without candour" (178). The "Rachel Papers" – both Charles's and Amis's – could be similarly described. Charles seeks to mature by improperly losing all trace of vulnerability. At the end of the novel, his entrance to adulthood is symbolized not only by his turning 20 but, more importantly, by the conclusion of his version of "The Rachel Papers," a version that now differs dramatically in outlook from Amis's own. He has organized his notebooks but given up on Rachel, chosen her "papers" over her body or soul. Consequently, his entry into adulthood remains tragically flawed by textuality: the novel's final words are, "I refill my pen." Charles has resigned himself to life as a disembodied scribe.

The contribution of *The Rachel Papers* to "the coming of age" genre is not merely as Amis suggests: the shifting of the protagonist from a budding artist to a budding literary critic. Rather, in that shift a greater cultural swing can be understood. As literary critic, Charles embodies the late-twentieth-century individual who finds himself struggling in the absence of transcendent moral authority. He finds comfort and distraction from anxiety only by mediating experience through the cultural productions with which he is inundated. Art becomes for Charles a mere diversion, not the "humanizing and enriching process" Amis believes art can be. This dehumanizing mediation of the individual has remained one of Amis's central concerns in the three decades since *The Rachel Papers* first appeared. And this novel could be seen as his own artistic "coming of age," even if his protagonist remains incapable of maturity, as rigidly imprisoned in *The Rachel Papers* as those he incarcerates within his own "Rachel Papers."

Works cited

Amis, Martin. *The Rachel Papers*. 1973. London: Penguin, 1984.

Curnutt, Kirk. "Teenage Wasteland: Coming of Age Novels in the 1980's and 1990's." *Critique* 43.1 (Fall 2001): 93–112.

Dern, John. *Martians, Monsters, and Madonna: Fiction and Form in the World of Martin Amis*. New York: Peter Lang, 2000.

Diedrick, James. *Understanding Martin Amis*. 2nd ed. Columbia: U of South Carolina P, 2004.

Haffenden, John. "Martin Amis." *Novelists in Interview*. New York: Methuen, 1985. 1–24.

Keulks, Gavin. *Father and Son: Kingsley Amis, Martin Amis and the British Novel Since 1950*. Madison: U of Wisconsin P, 2003.

Lyotard, Jean-François. *The Postmodern Condition: A Report on Knowledge*. Trans. Geoff Bennington and Brian Massumi. Minneapolis: U of Minnesota P, 1984.

Self, Will. "Interview with Martin Amis." *Mississippi Review* 7 (Oct. 1995). <http://www.mississippireview.com/1995/07amis.html>

2

Looking-glass Worlds in Martin Amis's Early Fiction: Reflectiveness, Mirror Narcissism, and Doubles

Richard Todd
University of Leiden

Casting a retrospective eye over the insouciant and prodigious early fiction of Martin Amis, we may detect the emergence and development of a cluster of preoccupations. The period in question is 1973 through 1984, spanning the publications of Amis's first book, *The Rachel Papers*, through *Money: A Suicide Note*, the first novel of what has come to be termed "the London triptych." After *Money* this cluster is still discernible – in such novels as *Time's Arrow* (1991) and *The Information* (1995) – but has gradually become etiolated, making way for other concerns. Of the two major tasks I have set myself in this essay, one is to attempt to unpack this cluster of preoccupations, while also applying a sharper focus on individual and interrelated elements to which other commentators have previously drawn attention. A full-scale examination of the totality of these elements does not, however, seem to have been attempted. I shall argue that matters such as plot and characterization, about which Amis has tended to speak lightly, are in fact subordinate to, or even the result of, a central obsession with aspects of doubleness. In advancing this argument, I find that it involves a refiguring of the first part of the Amis *oeuvre*. One cannot of course dispute the validity of a chronology of publications, and to try unavailingly to do so is not a purpose of this essay. But to try to view particular preoccupations from another perspective than the chronological is, surely, justified.

In most of Amis's early novels the plot pivots around two male protagonists, one ostensibly successful and one the reverse. But such a relationship is not always central to or stable in a given novel, and in reality it often varies from novel to novel.[1] Nonetheless, all such protagonists were as early as 1985 perceptively being termed "doubles" by Karl Miller. Miller's account commences with *Success* (1978), a novel he views as "the first of three fictions [...] in which orphan and double meet" (409). It will further go without saying that many, possibly all, of these double relationships in Amis's fiction are metafictional in nature (although this is not to be thought of – in this essay – as their primary function): one or more characters attempts explicitly to control the fate of other characters, or allow themselves to be so controlled. This aspect of Amis's fiction has been extensively discussed and will not be central to my argument. Moreover, Miller's beautifully-written account of Amis's doubles perceives the phenomenon as originating from *Success* onwards and depending on an ontological connection between the orphan and the double. Here I shall not be concerned with the orphan, but will argue instead that doubles – interpreted in what I call "mirror narcissism" and "reflectiveness" – have been a constant, brooding presence in Amis's work from the beginning, culminating in *Money*.

In what follows, then, I argue that the theme of doubles is quintessential to Amis's earlier work, rather than subservient to it, and that all aspects of the novels I discuss are themselves subservient to this theme. Where Miller and I perhaps meet is that he, whose Scottishness is purer than mine, presents a remarkable survey of the presence of doubles in Scottish fiction.[2] Several times Amis appears to make use of Robert Louis Stevenson's *The Strange Case of Dr. Jekyll and Mr. Hyde* (1886), which has become a *topos* for the gothic use of the double.

In this opening section I shall briefly make the case that a morphology underlies and informs the theme of doubling in Amis's early fiction. (I am not the first to do so.) Having argued this case, I will then examine the more obvious systemic doubling in terms of an identification of that theme's hidden roots. Later we will see that doubling is expressed in the trope or binary of persecution and victimization. The more complex the canvas of characters in a given novel, the harder it becomes to discern doubling under a disturbed surface of forms involving mimetic inversion or hyperbolic "irrealism." Perhaps this is truest of *Dead Babies* (1975) and *Money*. Yet while these textures might seem to draw attention away from systemic doubling, they nevertheless present us with a looking-glass world in which the form of "irrealism" does reflect what we see in the mirror.[3]

Had *The Rachel Papers* inaugurated another literary career altogether, the theme of doubles and doubling might have been hard to detect, since it was the novel's sexual insouciance that seemed to be the hallmark of this debut, with its ironic take on the "coming-of-age" genre. But in Amis's second novel, *Dead Babies*, the genre is deeply gothic – a version of the quintessential doubling of Dr Jekyll and Mr Hyde – and the plot disturbingly is ensnared in a swirl of lethal rivalries. Whereas *Dead Babies* may be the most violent and sadistic of Amis's fiction to date, doubles are almost always encountered in the presence of violence and sadism. Because one of the purposes of this essay is to refigure Amis's early work by offering a thematic challenge to a chronological survey, the case I make in its first section depends on developing a conception of "mirror narcissism." This conception affords a comparative account of Amis's debut *The Rachel Papers* with *Money*, the first of the London triptych novels.

**

Reflectiveness imbues *The Rachel Papers*. This novel is, apart from *Success*, the only wholly first-person narrative until *Money*, and despite the other features of *Success*, no novel between the debut and *Money* features narcissistic reflectiveness so prevalently. It therefore makes sense to examine this aspect of each novel first: briefly in the case of *The Rachel Papers*, at greater length in the case of *Money*. Probably the most palpable contrast between *The Rachel Papers* and *Money* is that although the figurative language is equally if not more striking, it is pressed into service in the latter novel to present cityscapes and urban visions that invert the "normal" or mimetic worlds of London and Manhattan. In other words, the mirror narcissism in *The Rachel Papers* applies to, or is conscripted into, Charles's own self-reflectiveness.[4] The mirror narcissism in *Money* operates around the narrator John Self and the doubles Martin Amis and Martina Twain, among others. But the environment in which the action unfolds is consistently and hyperbolically "irreal" and anti-mimetic. Commentators have noted Amis's bizarre naming of automobiles and credit cards in the London triptych above all: *The Rachel Papers* shows from the beginning of his career Amis's alternative world in all its squalid glory.

Charles Highway, the narrator, surveys the dossier that gives the book its name on the eve of his twentieth birthday. From the start he presents himself as physically unattractive, and for a young man with what turns out to be a sexually active teenage life behind him, this seems an important disjunction. We are told that he wears glasses – to the true myope this rings as false as does the use of glasses as a fashion accessory – but the glasses do act as an interesting subliminal metaphor in refracting Charles's world. His opening self-description, though unflattering, is nonetheless tinged with narcissism:

> my medium-length, arseless, waistless figure, corrugated ribcage and bandy legs gang up to dispel any hint of aplomb. [...] But I *have* got one of those fashionable reedy voices, the ones with the habitual ironic twang, excellent for the promotion of oldster unease. And *I imagine* [emphasis added] there's something oddly daunting about my face, too. It's angular, yet delicate; thin long nose, wide thin mouth – and the eyes: richly lashed, dark ochre with a twinkle of singed auburn ... ah, how inadequate these words seem. (7)

Indeed, this portrayal exhibits considerable rhetorical skill, building from torso through voice to face to eyes. Later in the novel we will hear more of Charles's face: there is no doubt that he considers it his most valuable attribute. But like Narcissus, he cannot see his face except in a mirror.

Writing of *The Information* two decades later, Adam Mars-Jones perceptively observed that one of Amis's stylistic skills is "to separate verbal beauty from the cause it has traditionally served, to detach lyrical language from the lyrical impulse" (19). Customarily taboo subjects are thus retrieved from the censor's red pencil. The effect is to release the entire experiential spectrum of Charles's reflective dossier, which he titles "The Rachel Papers." Charles's frequent contemplation of his own image accentuates the narcissism and self-reflectiveness that his major assets – his face and above all his eyes – bring about. Thus his chief use of the mirror remains secondarily one of admiration; primarily he scrutinizes his face for blackheads, boils and other blemishes. The immaculate face of Charles's imagination – his mental vision enhanced by his glasses – confronts its Dorian Gray-like portrait in the mirror. Charles and his mirror-double are avatars for many characters in the later work. We see the process again in *Money*, when a wrecked John Self first checks into his Manhattan hotel: "The mirror looked on, quite unimpressed, as I completed a series of rethinks in the hired glare of the windowless bathroom. I cleaned my teeth, combed my rug, clipped my nails, bathed my eyes, gargled, showered, shaved, changed – and still looked like shit" (11). It is, however, the mirror that tells Self he looks like shit. Musing on whether his girlfriend Selina Street is fooling around with his friend Alec Llewellyn, Self consoles himself:

> I don't think Selina Street is fucking Alec Llewellyn. Why? Because he hasn't got any money. I have. Come on, why do you reckon

Selina had soldiered it out with me? For my pot belly, my bad rug, my personality? She's not in this for her health, now, is she? ... I tell you, these reflections really cheered me up. (28)

Whether Self deliberately chooses that word "reflections" for consolation must remain a matter for debate. And is it coincidence that our first view of Fat Vince – "beer crate operative and freelance bouncer at the Shakespeare," who has "been in and out of this place for thirty-five years" (140) – once Self has returned to London is (together with his son Fat Paul) "[i]n the booze-lined defile under the bendy mirror" (55)? John Self will later learn that it is Fat Vince, not the slim and well-preserved Barry Self, who is his biological father. Fat Paul is thus his half-brother, and it is surely appropriate that we first perceive Fat Vince and Fat Paul in the presence of a "bendy mirror." They represent one kind of double – an illegitimate one – for Self.

It is also worth drawing attention to a passage susceptible of metafictional interpretation that occurs in the locked and bolted Shakespeare pub:

We heard the sounds of chains shaking. We turned: a small shadow bided its time behind the locked glass doors.
"Fuck off out of it!" said Fat Paul in his youthful way.
"No, it's all right," I said. "This must be my writer." (55)

The primary interpretation we might give to this scene is that a customer is trying to get into the pub; in the present context, however, another interpretation discloses itself. Self is indistinctly seeing one of his doubles – the most manipulative because authorial – through the glass, as the wording ("a small shadow"; "[t]his must be my writer") indicates. This is an exact reversal of Charles Highway's mirror narcissism. The reflectiveness is obscure: Self does not yet realize how much and how nearly fatally he will be exploited.

This thought suggests the more obvious pair of doubles in *Money* – the duo Martina Twain and Martin Amis, whom Self's encounters inauspiciously. Martina and Self make a breakfast appointment that Self arrives at 12 hours too late, having overslept and forgotten Martina's original suggestion that he come to a dinner party attended by numerous writers, including Martin Amis. Self muses: "A writer lives round my way in London. He looks at me oddly in the street. He gives me the fucking creeps" (42). Self eventually meets two more versions of this double: in London he finally meets the writer named Martin Amis, whom he coerces into rewriting the script of *Money*, and in New York he is pursued by Martina Twain, who introduces the uncultured Self to such works as *Animal Farm* and *Nineteen Eighty-Four* and takes him to see Verdi's *Otello*. Despite Self's philistinism, he is an excellent chess-player, although he is "zugzwanged" by Amis after a cliff-hanging game. The mixture of thuggish philistinism and almost hypertrophied intelligence is emphasized by Self's having used the chess term earlier in the novel (117): now, at the end of it, he has to ask Amis for a definition. The Amis character replies: "Literally, *forced to move*. It means that whoever has to move has to lose. If it were my turn now, you'd win. But it's yours. And you lose" (353). Earlier Martin had told Self: "The further down the scale [the hero] is, the more liberties you can take with him. You can do what the hell you like to him, really. This creates an appetite for punishment. The author is not free of sadistic impulses" (233). This comment seems to sharpen a sense of Amis's treatment of his first-person narrator Charles in *The Rachel Papers* – a sense not immediately palpable from that novel alone.

In the end, Self discovers that he has been tricked into financing an elaborate operation. During swathes of his own narrative, Self's memory proves faulty, either through blackouts or because he simply fails to remember information. For whatever reason – after all, he does share some DNA with the images he first perceives under the "bendy mirror" (55) – Self is not in control of his narration. If we question who *is* in control of his narrative, the answer can only be one or more of those who are watching – and exploiting – him. Self's self-reflectiveness is blotched and blurred – surely no first-person narrator spends so much of his narration out cold. In the presence of Martina Twain, he reflects: "Actors are paid to pretend that they are unaware of being watched, but they of course rely on the collusion of the watcher, and nearly always get it. There are unpaid actors too (I thought): it's them you really have to watch" (128). All Self's doubles – and *their* corresponding doubles – are complicit in his exploitation. This question casts its perspective back on *The Rachel Papers* and allows us to identify a sense of sadism in Amis's portrayal of Charles Highway. Perhaps Charles Highway's mirror narcissist double, too, is complicit in the exploitation of *his* self-portrayal, an effect that becomes possible only through the author's ironic deployment of the first-person narration, a deployment that only seems clearest when juxtaposed against John Self's treatment in *Money*.

**

The trope (or binary) of victimization and persecution emerges, by the end of *Money*, with increasing clarity as all the potential doubles are seen to have played their part in exploiting John Self. Part of this realization emerges from our increasing understanding of Self: he becomes the object rather than the subject of his narration, and is thereby reified. In the current section I shall focus on the theme of reifying victimization in Amis's earlier fiction, where it becomes possible to link Mary Lamb in *Other People* (1981) with Keith Whitehead in *Dead Babies*. These two novels, in contrast to *The Rachel Papers* and *Money*, are largely third-person narrations.[5] Moreover, Mary Lamb and Keith Whitehead can both be seen as respective victims of the character-worlds around them. Striking differences exist between them, however. Keith is a solitary figure, about whom the Martin Amis character in *Money* might say: "The author is not free of sadistic impulses." Mary is an *ingénue* whose innocence, we shall see, is not always harmless in its effects.

Although this section is primarily devoted to *Other People*, it seems incontestable that Keith Whitehead in *Dead Babies* is the most sado-masochistically portrayed character in Amis's canon, partly because the "suavely degenerate" (Haffenden, 13) and sexualized nature of the country-house environment exaggerates his social, physical, and psychological "shortcomings" to degrees of comic hyperbole. He can offer no acceptable rival perspective or reflection, and is deeply aware of his physical appearance. In this sense, of course, he differs completely from Mary Lamb or Amy Hide and resembles Charles Highway. Keith Whitehead is such a complete misfit, such an extreme type, that the sadomasochism of *Dead Babies* is palliated by the narrator's obvious sympathy for him. Frequently he is referred to as "little Keith" – hardly an exaggeration, as he is frequently described as a dwarf. Readerly sympathy is manipulated with great skill and unpredictability. On one hand, it is pitiful to see Keith, the obese and ugly victim of a congenital glandular disorder that obliges him to wear makeshift platform shoes to rise above his three-foot height. This ludicrous attempt at DIY prosthesis is bound to fail, as it does: the attempt should be seen as Keith's attempt to mirror both normality as well as the physical appearance of the other guests at Appleseed Rectory. On the other hand, Keith's grossness is manifest, particularly in his involuntary farting, belching and halitosis. His failure at any kind of sexual allure consigns him to chronic masturbation (when he is potent).

Reacting to his own victimization, Keith spends much of the novel victimizing – or at least attempting to humiliate – the tenants of

Appleseed Rectory, Mr and Mrs Tuckle. A distilling quotation sums up much of Keith's life prior to the weekend of the narrative. Keith has earlier been confined to the Research Wing of the St Pancras Hospital for Tropical Diseases: "For the time being, Whitehead lies in pulsing, hot-faced, glandular silence by day and at night is the weeper of *unreflecting* tears" (30, emphasis added). This solitariness depends on a striking rhetoric that emphasizes Keith's need for company, however alien (or even his own), against which to construct or reflect himself. The portrayal of Keith in a hospital bed is not only grotesque but also specifically stresses how – even as one of life's undesirables – he needs to have a mirror held up to his nature.

By contrast, Mary Lamb in *Other People* is not similarly "solitary," despite early intimations. The novel in fact opens on an existential cusp. We are to imagine that the character Amy Hide, who has apparently been murdered, starts a new life as a *tabula rasa*, thus furnishing Amis an amnesiac model to which he will return in *Time's Arrow*. The entire process of murder, resurrection after death to a deadened world, and return to an original world of ambivalent moral value, is supervised by John Prince, who acts as narrator, policeman, murderer, and metafictional guide. In Mary Lamb's initial perceptions we find a kind of Martian *Verfremdungseffekt*:[6]

> There were six kinds of people outside. [...] People of the second kind were less worrying; they were shrunken, compacted – mysteriously lessened in some vital respect. They limped in pairs, with such awkward caution that they hardly made any progress at all, or else whirled about with a fluttery, burst, directionless verve. Some were so bad now that they had to be wheeled round in covered boxes, protesting piteously to their guides, who were people of the third kind. (16)

An Amy Hide would recognize that the second kind will in fact grow into the third (and the first and possibly other) kind or kinds; Mary Lamb's perception of the world, on the other hand, is a mirror of reality, as the narrative reveals in its opening, when she glimpses herself in the hospital:

> She steadied herself and turned to face the room, catching the eye of a shiny square of steel on the wall; through this bright window she briefly glimpsed a startled figure with thick black hair who looked at her and ducked quickly away. Is everyone frightened, she wondered, or is it just me? (14–15)

This inverse mirror narcissism reveals a more complex world than Charles Highway's: Charles's exists primarily to seduce, Mary's to commence the painful process of self-identification. Indeed, Mary is actually *deprived* of the enjoyment of mirror narcissism: it is withheld until the end of the novel (185). She must make the journey from object to subject – from reified victim to self-reflecting autonomous being – in what Amis *in propria persona* has suggested will be a recurrently cyclic process (Haffenden, 17–18). The suggestion here, then, will be that behind the glass into which Mary looks – and again foreshadowing *Time's Arrow* – there will be horrors too dark to contemplate:

> No news came. Mary looked for news in the mirror. *She played the mirror game.* Mary Lamb was getting to know Amy Hide quite well now.
> Was Mary Amy, or had she at some point been Amy, and to what extent? Amy had done things. To what extent, and how automatically, had Mary done them too? Did it matter? What authority was there? God? Prince? Who minded?
> Mary did. She minded. She locked herself in the bathroom and looked into the mirror. She wanted to be good, and she didn't believe that Amy could have been all bad if Mary had in some sense come out of her. Perhaps every girl was really two girls ... Mary looked into the mirror. She didn't look too bad. On the contrary, she looked quite good. [...] As she turned away from the mirror she saw the ghost of a smile from the knowing genius that lived behind the glass. The image flickered: there was chaos in there somewhere. Mary stared on. Her eyes *fought with all their light* until they had subdued whatever hid behind the glass. But as she turned away she knew that whatever was hiding there would now coolly reassemble and go on waiting for whatever it was waiting for. (75, emphasis added)

There are various allusions throughout *Other People* to the inverted mirror-identity of Mary and Amy. One of the most striking involves one of the girls in Jamie's squat, where Mary resides. Augusta has once been Janice, but this renaming seems different from the spooky existentialism that characterizes Mary/Amy; rather, Augusta is simply an alias for a runaway. Augusta/Janice asks Mary whether her "real" name is Amy. Mary's affirmative answer leads Augusta to tell her that Amy was "doing some strange things. With heavy men and ethnic guys and that." Augusta proceeds to say:

> "But really you had this one guy. This strange guy. For years and years. You said you'd never leave him. You ... I liked you more then.

[...] I remember now what you said. You said you loved him so much you wouldn't mind if he killed you. Something like that. I'll never forget that." (172)

If we accept that Mary is a *post-mortem* reflection or double of Amy, we must also accept that she is a faded, washed-out example. Pastels dominate: the innocent terms *white*, *pink*, and *pale* are often applied to her; her passiveness is not just that of the "newly born" but of the social *ingénue*.[7] Here we might note again that Mary's *post-mortem* world, of all those under consideration, is the *least* irreal, and the most drably mimetic. Her journey through such a world is (by definition) picaresque. Significantly, mimesis is *not* inverted here: Amis's vivid, figurative style has, as it were, been bleached out. In yet another rival male-protagonist episode, Alan and Russ compete for Mary. She does not know how to play to such a scenario, which proves destructive. Alan – balding, depressed, gentle, wimpish – does have mild and placid sex with Mary, but it is brief, and when she finally tells him she cannot continue their relationship, he hangs himself. Russ is macho, boastful, illiterate, and despite his repeated claims, recounted by the narrator Prince, possessed of diminutive genitals. This exterior is unwittingly damaged by Mary. Unlike in many of Amis's other novels, this rival male episode plays a faint role in *Other People*. Instead, the climax to this novel – a climax to which doubling is central – is brought about through a confrontation with Jamie over food as their domestic life falls apart:

[Mary] could not control her face or the extraordinary sounds that came from her mouth. These sounds would have frightened her very much if it hadn't been Mary who was making them. It was lucky Mary was making them. She wouldn't want to deal with anyone who could make sounds like these. Some time later she was in the bathroom, standing before the mirror in thick darkness, listening to laughter. The instant she threw the switch a face reared out of the glass, in exultation, in relief, in terror. She had done it. She had torn through the glass and come back from the other side. She had found her again. She was herself at last. (185)

This extraordinary passage – with a characteristic temporal blip that signals a form of Amis censorship, analogous to John Self's blackouts – is the last we see of Mary. She herself is Amy; she has come back from the Sartrean hell that is "other people" into the world she knows. But the mirror has played – and continues to play – with light and dark, and if there is an allusion to Jekyll and Hyde inscribed in Amy's last name, it is not incontrovertibly the site of a straightforward battle between good and evil. Indeed, and on the contrary, Amy may have to undergo a further incarnation, as the last pages of the novel intimate.

**

This final section focuses more briefly on *Success* and *Dead Babies*. The former would seem to be, among Amis's early novels, the one that quintessentially examines, interrogates, even dances around the theme of the double, as Karl Miller saw 20 years ago. *Dead Babies* is the only one of Amis's early books not to be set in an urban landscape. Indeed it engages, and often parodies, the country-house genre of English fiction, so that the opportunities it offers to showcase Amis's talent for anti-mimetic irrealism and comic hyperbole – what might be termed the "Amis voice" – are different. In *Dead Babies* the focus falls less on the anti-mimetic urban frameworks or settings of the other novels; instead, Amis's irrealism is targeted more sharply upon character portrayal. Paradoxically, the "pure" portrayal of doubleness in *Success* produces an effect whereby the corresponding portrayals of mirror narcissism and doubleness are more distilled and intense than in the other novels under discussion. The urban landscape is largely subordinate in *Success*, dwelling as it does on spatial interiors and human behavior.

The explanations for such a refocusing certainly relate to narratorial unreliability and the metafictional use of the intrusive author, but it must be emphasized that these things do not in themselves serve as explanations. Earlier I described *Success* as a first-personal narration: I am now in a position to qualify this description by pointing out that it is in fact two antiphonal first-person narrations, each narrated by the other's double. I also earlier mentioned that *Dead Babies* is probably the most violent of Amis's fiction: the apparently careful construction, the symmetrical use of character in this book is destroyed at the end by what might be termed a metafictional intervention by the most psychopathic of all Amis's doubles – Johnny, described in the *dramatis personae* as "a practical joker." James Diedrick has perceptively pointed to a symmetry in the structure of *Success* that we do not encounter in this novel's predecessors. He describes:

> a rigorously controlled narrative consisting of parallel dramatic monologues spoken by feuding foster brothers: Gregory Riding and

Terrence Service. Taken together, these monologues form an "X" whose intersection marks the death of Greg's sister Ursula, which both men have contributed to. It also represents the crossing point in the fortunes of each: while one brother falls in the world, the other ascends. (47–8)

The clarity of this analysis is slightly blurred by a constellation of ingenious "intertextual doublings." Amis's use of the dramatic monologue means that in no other early novel is the reader so apt to distrust each narrator. As Diedrick explains: "*Success* expects a great deal of the reader, who is left to construct the truth from the gaps in and between each narrative" (49). The challenge to the reader is perhaps most evident in the different versions of the episode in which Greg contemptuously narrates his apparent seduction (or fantasy rape, depending on which version we are reading) of Terry's platonic girlfriend Jan. The episode is made repellent precisely because of the ways in which these versions reflect off each other. Greg's fantasy version cannot even get Jan's name right, and this fact, more than the fantasy itself, distresses Terry. If the morphology of *Success* seems like a well-constructed fable – with pride being unseated and humility being rewarded – this is not finally what the novel is "about." It would be more accurate to say that the device of the double *enables* the fable-like morphology, and it seems that this is how we should regard early Amis fictions that have often – insufficiently in my view – been described as satires, urban or not. Of course it would be foolish to deny that there is satiric or fable-like content, but unlike in Jonathan Swift's prose, often conscripted into discussions of Amis's, these things are served by another, deeper obsession – the obsession with doubles, self-reflectiveness, and inverted mimesis.

Near the publication of *Money*, in a now-famous answer to John Haffenden's question about "stylistic sheen," Amis remarked:

> I would certainly sacrifice any psychological or realistic truth for a phrase, for a paragraph that has a spin on it: that sounds whorish, but I think it's the higher consideration. Mere psychological truth in a novel doesn't seem to me all that valuable a commodity. (16)

These words strike at the essence of Amis's art. The point is that Amis's writing will never be fully admired by those whose primary line of questioning relates to meaning, asking "what is it *about*?" Those who are prepared to admire the swirl of transgressive language – to accept with Adam Mars-Jones that the core of Amis's fiction is the separation of verbal beauty from the cause it has traditionally served, the detachment of lyrical language from the lyrical impulse – have in effect accepted that Amis's writing is, in no pejorative but rather a virtuoso sense, self-reflective and narcissistic. The uses of mirrors and doubles – from their metafictional to their gothic and even *noir* effects – is absolutely inherent to Amis's style and his aesthetic. Indeed they *define* that aesthetic, which is one of realistic or mimetic absence and detachment. At times readers will be offered the *frisson* of the thriller, or enjoy sophisticated recognition of the author as metafictional construct, but even the theme of the thriller, or the device of the metafictional author, should be seen as subordinate to style. Equally as important, that phrase or sentence with a rhetorical "spin on it" often involves the double and usually – especially when it contributes to a *denouement* – comes with a chill of horror, as in an exchange towards the end of *Dead Babies* between Celia and Marvell, while Quentin reclines in an adjoining room:

> Quentin's eyes opened. He sighed, and a great weight seemed to slide upwards from his body. Then it hit him. Like newly-fallen snow, all the blank wrong yesterdays.
> "Quentin?" Celia called. "Quentin."
> "Yes?" said Johnny. (219)

Notes

1   One is reminded of Amis's admiration for Iris Murdoch, who used to remark that the main theme of her work was "the artist" *versus* "the saint": the shallow prolific producer of second-hand words versus the thinker so weighed down by articulacy that he remains silent. Just as Murdoch occasionally parodied her own theme, Amis inverts the terms in which we should perceive his protagonists.

2   Miller's account offers other intertextual thematics, involving Hermann Hesse, Saul Bellow, and Vladimir Nabokov. The latter two have particularly influenced Amis.

3   Though I shall not discuss it further here, the most extreme example of what I am alluding to can be found in the "reverse narrative" of *Time's Arrow*.

4   I elect for "self-reflectiveness" (rather than Diedrick's "self-reflexiveness") to emphasize the mirror narcissism I am arguing.

5   Although strictly speaking *Other People* is a third-person narration, that narration is interrupted by first-person commentary from John Prince.

6   On the novel's Martian qualities, see Diedrick, 58–63.

7   Another kind of doubling is therefore justified: between the innocent whiteness of Mary and the Manichean identification between John Prince and the Prince of Darkness (see Diedrick, 64).

Works cited

Amis, Martin. *Dead Babies.* 1975. London: Penguin, 1984.

——. *Money: A Suicide Note.* London: Jonathan Cape, 1984.

——. *Other People: A Mystery Story.* 1981. London: Penguin, 1982.

——. *The Rachel Papers.* 1973. London: Penguin, 1984.

——. *Success.* 1978. London: Penguin, 1985.

Diedrick, James. *Understanding Martin Amis.* 2nd ed. Columbia: U of South Carolina P, 2004.

Haffenden, John. "Martin Amis." *Novelists in Interview.* London: Methuen, 1985. 1–24.

Mars-Jones, Adam. "Looking on the blight side." *Times Literary Supplement* 24 March 1995: 19–20.

Miller, Karl. *Doubles: Studies in Literary History.* Oxford: Oxford UP, 1985.

3

The Passion of John Self: Allegory, Economy, and Expenditure in Martin Amis's *Money*

Tamás Bényei
University of Debrecen

A title such as *Money: A Suicide Note* (1984) triggers a doubling of meaning that may itself entitle divergent, even incompatible strategies of reading, a discussion of which will inevitably echo Derrida's speculations about Baudelaire's title "Counterfeit Money" in *Given Time*. On one hand, these titles may be read referentially (as part of their texts): like the main body, the title is *about* money. Conversely, they may be read as extrinsic to the text, naming it figuratively and performatively, equating it with money: in buying *Money*, that is, the reader is buying money.[1] Amis reinforces the latter possibility through his subtitle, which invokes the ambiguity of "note." In the light of the novel's textual dynamics, "suicide note" sounds like a coupon or specialized banknote that stands for suicide – a refund for it or possibly its opposite: money is that which staves off suicide. "Money is the only thing we have in common," says John Self, *Money*'s narrator-protagonist. "Dollar bills, pound notes, they're suicide notes. *Money* is a suicide note" (116). To entertain both of these possibilities simultaneously requires seeing the text as involved in a performative folding: "money" will speak about "money," about, that is, itself. This paradox resembles the financial transactions in which the novel's dubious "moneyman" Ossie Twain is involved: working "in the cracks and vents of currencies, buying and selling on the margin, riding the daily tides of exchange" (120). This structure also recalls Marx's definition of interest-bearing capital as an "automatic fetish," a self-begetting and self-propelling force. Value valorizes itself, Marx suggests; money breeds money and "no longer bears any mark of its origin. The social relation is consummated in the relationship of a thing, money, to itself" (*Capital*, v3.516).

Such doubling is crucial to the financial maneuvers on which the plot of *Money* turns. Supposedly filming his life-story, Self becomes the victim of a transatlantic hoax. He believes that making *Money* will translate to making money but inadvertently pays for everything via his double signature (as "co-signatory" and "self"): "I signed some contracts, directing more and more money my way" (24). The money is Self's own, and because he repeatedly defines himself as made of money, his expenditure equates with self-depletion, erasure.

It is in the interstices of this paradoxical circulation, the folds and vents of figurative capital, that my reading of the novel resides. Instead of reiterating the critical clichés concerning the homologies between money and language, I am interested in the uniqueness of this text's "excessive self-reflexiveness" (Keulks, 177), the ways the verbal universe of this "Sado-Monetarist" (Brantlinger, 208) novel performs the feat of self-enfolding. Rather than simply observe the way *Money* conceives "the correspondence between the mode of economic exchange and the mode of signifying exchange" (Goux, 96), I will discuss the role of monetary metaphors in the novel's textual strategies, or textual "economy." I am therefore concerned with the homologies, rifts, and spillings between the textual and rhetorical, the monetary and economic, the cultural and psychological levels or orders of the book.

The "allegory deal"

My chief premise is that *Money* performs the feat of self-enfolding, the collapsing of disparate levels, within the mode of allegory. If allegory, as defined by Maureen Quilligan, is "a narration peopled by personified abstractions moving about a reechoing landscape of language" (163), then *Money* – full of characters with blatantly allegorical names and personified abstractions – is clearly allegorical. The presence of the allegorical substructure, and its role in the novel's textual economy, is indicated by two episodes. John Self receives two presents on the same day, an interesting fact because the logic of the gift violates the logic of exchange. The second gift is a plastic lady (143), the par excellence pornographic object – what Baudrillard calls a "poupée sexuée," a sexualized puppet (235). It is an allegorical object signifying objectification, a bodying forth of abstraction. The other gift – "a proper present" (136) – is a book from Martina Twain: Orwell's *Animal Farm*, arguably the best-known allegory of the twentieth century. Not a bookworm, Self struggles to read it; even after finishing, he cannot understand it because he overlooks the political allegory.[2] Orwell's allegory is everything that a consumer's good is not, and Self, whose desires are largely pornographic, is not equipped with the strategies of consumption the text requires. Orwell's text insists on its otherness from the reader by setting up interpretive obstacles: it demands work, interpretative investment, to render its yields, conceived as surplus meaning.

It is not accidental that the two gifts are an allegorical object and an allegorical text; nor is it accidental that Self's first venture into what he calls the "bookish, the contemplative life" (136) occurs through allegory. Because Self immediately reinscribes the logic of allegory into the order of financial transaction – referring to the "allegory deal" (212) – this episode can be seen as a *mise en abyme*: as Self fails to perceive the allegorical world of *Animal Farm* so too does he fail to read his own world. Because he is a "pornographic person" (187), he sees things in terms of price and value. His inability to decipher – or even notice – allegory therefore parallels his inability to form relationships that are not based on economic exchange. "You know where you are with economic necessity" (24), he states, referring to his lover, Selina Street.

Besides these two parallel episodes, the novel abounds in other signals of allegory, including numerous instances of personification allegory. This allegorical mode is announced early by two conspicuous instances of personification allegory, the more extensive of which appears below:

> Fear walks tall on this planet. Fear walks big and fat and fine. [...] One of these days I'm going to walk right up to fear [...] and say, *Okay, hard-on. No more of this. You've pushed us around for long enough. Here is someone who* would not take it. *It's over. Outside.* Bullies, I'm told, are all cowards deep down. Fear is a bully, but something tells me fear is no funker. Fear, I suspect, is really incredibly brave. [...] Now I come to think about it, maybe I'd better let fear be. When it comes to fighting, I'm brave – or reckless or indifferent or just unjust. But fear really scares me. (4)

In this hypertrophied allegory, the narrative creates a second-order reality of its own, so that the tautological phrase "fear really scares me" seems to make sense. It also reattaches the allegorical diversion to the primary reality of the novel. The doubling or "folding back" performed in this tautological phrase is repeated in the phrase "just unjust," a juxtaposition which creates excess or surplus meaning from difference. The circular structure of this passage recalls the structure of double disavowal that Slavoj Žižek identifies in commodity fetishism. First, the commodity is deprived of its bodily autonomy and reduced to a medium which embodies social relations. Then this network of relations is projected onto a commodity as its direct material property, as though a commodity possessed value in itself, or as though money itself were a universal equivalent (Žižek, 306).

Seen as an allegorical text, with Self as a reincarnated Everyman, the novel becomes an "allegory of money" in which the production of meaning depends on the role of money in the allegorical process. This is indicated by the many instances of prosopopoeia and personification that allegorize money (55, 153, 165, 238, 270). Rather than cite additional examples, I want to question what this expression – this "allegory of money" – means within the novel's textual economy. On the most general level, the allegorization of money might work from opposing directions: it may represent money as a physical object substituting for some abstraction (power, wealth) or as an abstraction that assumes phenomenal shape in objects or persons. This distinction is reinforced by the dual role money has played in cultural theory debates regarding fetishism, where money is either allegorized from above or below. In the former – as in the treatise of Georg Simmel – allegory relates to an unrepresentable, transcendental entity (Value). In the latter – as in Marxist and Freudian discourses – money is a fetishized object invested with imaginary properties, a symbolic representative substituted for the indescribable, ineffable reality of social relations (Pietz, 125).

Monetary allegory assumes many forms in *Money*. "Money is freedom. That's true. But freedom is money," Self says (270). In this Orwellian apothegm, money – which at first seems to be physical, an object embodying an abstract notion – easily slides into another level, reversing the expression as well as its implied hierarchy. In many cases, money seems to possess transcendental powers: "You cannot hide out from money. You just cannot hide out from money any more" (153). In other instances, money seems material but also diffuse, quasiallegorical. Trying to resist Martina's human and humanizing look – a relationship that Self identifies as "perversion" (215) – Self says: "I'm in no kind of shape for the love police. Money, I must put money round me, more money, soon. I must be safe" (222).[3] Throughout the novel money remains physically visible as an object, sustaining the possibility that it occupies the lower level of allegory: on the last page Self is mistaken for a beggar (394). But the most important physical appearance of money occurs when Self receives his ultimate Oedipal injury – a blow by Fat Paul inflicted by "two tubes of bank-packed coins" rolled into a sock that mockingly reminds Self of a "scrotum" (371).

There is something disturbingly inconsistent in all these allegories of money, an uncertainty concerning allegorical levels and, by extension, the levels of physical existence and abstraction, which also confuse John Self. Perhaps it is precisely the presence of money in the allegorical process that affects and disturbs allegoresis, just as money underlies Self's fetishism, disturbing his ability to distinguish between the physical and the abstract. To understand this dynamic, it helps to consider different aspects of money in philosophical texts.

The philosophy of money

Money's status in allegorical language is at least dubious: not simply because it is both object and concept – Marx called capital a "sensuous supersensuous thing" (Pietz, 130), echoing Shakespeare's oxymoronic "visible God" – but also because it is the metaphor for allegorical transactions, an exchange between levels.[4] For Georg Simmel, money performs a distinctly allegorical function in representing an abstract and fundamental sphere that cannot be represented. Thus, money cannot equate simply with language but, like *allegorical* language, must name something linguistically unattainable and is therefore doomed to failure. Simmel contends that money approaches a Platonic ideal of Value, always falling short because of its contamination by a residue of material value (167). Yet, by being the sign of unsuccessful representation (naming), it becomes the only connection with what it fails to name: it becomes a metasign signifying its own failure.

The other aspect of this allegorical sense of money is indicated by Simmel's definition that:

> money is simply a means, a material or an example for the presentation of relations that exist between the most superficial, "realistic" and fortuitous phenomena and the most idealized powers of existence.... The significance and purpose of the whole undertaking is simply to derive from the surface level of economic affairs a guideline that leads to the ultimate values and things of importance in all that is human. (55)

Within the space of two sentences, money is called "means," "material," "example," and "guideline," four ontologically incompatible things. Crucially, three of these metaphors are relationships or connections. If such interchangeability is homologous to allegory, then Simmel's definition of money as "interchangeability personified," representing "pure interaction in its purest form" (124), identifies money as a double-allegory. In Simmel's discourse, money is allegory – the naming of something abstract, unreachable – *and* meta-allegory, the representation of "pure interaction," the empty form of exchange and interaction.[5] It is a metasign of relationality, a metatrope; it is what it does.

Money's ascension to the level of transcendence, whereby it occupies an abstract position besides the physical and the allegorical transfer, is explained by Simmel through reference to money's emptiness. Lacking content, it becomes the pure form of exchange. Whereas other objects derive value from content, money derives content from value (121). This void incites allegorization, urging us "to talk about it, to fill it with language" (244). Seen as infinite valency, emptiness can therefore be theorized as the ability to stand for anything, making money a "general equivalent," a standard measure that strives to make things equal by making them "commensurable" (Goux, 2). Money's infinite interchangeability excites feelings similar to those excited by the concept of God as *coincidentia oppositorum*, the unity of disparate and opposing things (Simmel, 236). John Self would agree: "Money is very versatile. You really have to give money credit for that," he claims in one of his superbly tautological, enfolding statements in which economic expressions double as meta-rhetorical tropes. Unlimited interchangeability makes of money a divinity – what Self calls a "money god" (361).[6]

Understanding how John Self's unique fetishism informs the novel's portrait of late capitalism mandates that we see money's transcendent power as deriving from its "meta-allegorical" nature as the *agent or form of transformation*. For Marx, money transforms the essential powers of man into mere abstract conceits" ("Economical", 370). Yet Simmel calls money the *absolute means*: it provides unlimited potential for enjoyment yet leaves enjoyment untouched, its "ownership" unused (242). Money is therefore like power: a mere potentiality, possibility. It requires that other conditions be fulfilled before enjoyment arrives.

This feature of money accounts for its fetishistic nature in Self's world. He is a money fetishist, declaring in one instance of prosopopoeia, "Money, I love you." He does not hoard money, or, like Sade, *whore* it either, masturbating before it. He is, as it were, a meta-fetishist: his enjoyment is displaced onto "money" as the *possibility of pleasure*. He craves desire itself, the endless metonymic postponement of enjoyment. In capitalism, Goux suggests, "the general exchange-value, or liquidity, rather than limited particular use-values, *must* become the fetishized object, the imaginary cause of satisfaction" (208). We could extend this to contend that Self does not fetishistically desire money as *money* – or as the promise of pleasure; rather, he desires money in the abstract – as the *form* of pleasure, a financial transaction, a matter of economy. This is the heart of his characterization.

The structural similarities between money and fetishism are relevant to the interconnections, displacements, and transfers between the rhetorical, psychological, and economic levels in Amis's novel. First, as the trope of the inadequacy of naming – the trope that arrives late and becomes a memorial for its own failure – allegory mirrors the double-logic of fetishism, its mixture of acknowledgement and disavowal. Self's fetishized objects – especially his car – are sites of displacement and lack, dream-surrogates for improved value. As William Pietz says, commenting on Slavoj Žižek's rereading of fetishism: the fetish converts "the experience of objects lacking adequacy as expressive signifiers into the experience of them as objective signifiers of that very lack" (127).

In the novel, fetishism acts as pure perversion in that the object of desire normally precedes satisfaction: it is the abstract form of satisfaction, the possibility of attaining on every occasion the same quantity of satisfaction. John Self's largely pornographic desires are defined by solitary gratification, repeatability, and abstraction. Pornography is necessarily fetishistic in that its object is by definition inadequate, reducing people to objects. Yet Self's perversion is both unique and universal. It is unique in its atypical nature: Self is not addicted to rare, sophisticated forms of pleasure; he wants fast food rather than expensive delicacies, space games rather than Russian roulette, "handjobs" rather than exquisite sadomasochistic scenarios. In a porn emporium he muses upon the multitude of specialized perversions without expressing any particular interest (158, 323–4). He is addicted to vulgar, *ordinary* fare: he wants more of the same, the abstract pleasure guaranteed by money, which reduces and converts each transaction into a business deal. Self's perversion therefore approximates the *opposite* of pleasure. As he tellingly remarks: "With business I'm usually okay. It's pleasure that gets me into all this expensive trouble" (2).

His pornographic taste becomes perceivable if we note the allegorical structures of money and pornographic desire: in pornography, the fetishized object embodies the failure of satisfaction – the surrogate, abstract, empty form. Self's pursuit of pleasure amounts to a quest for deferral, an avoidance of jouissance, the traumatic pleasure that threatens the consistency of his desire. His fetishism also isolates him from human relationships. If capitalism, as Goux argues, has produced an unprecedented rift between intersubjective and economic relations (129), then Self's perversion equates with the compulsion to translate relationships into money. His business is pleasure, just as his pleasure is business: he even refers to masturbation – one of his chief occupations – as a "handjob."

Money therefore resembles allegory in several senses. Its "work" is the work of allegory, connecting the physical with the abstract, desire with its object, although always in deferral. It is not only a metatrope signifying signification itself, but also a hopeless, or disabused trope, attempting to name the ineffable: Platonic "value" in Simmel, real social relations in Marx. As a metatrope, its naming is exposed as figurative, but it successfully names this lack and, from that, builds a narrative. It is the jetlagged, belated trope, always arriving late. Thus, an "allegory of money" is inevitably an "allegory of allegory," a turning back upon itself. In Amis's novel, money and allegory are equally contaminated: allegorical signification is stained by its complicity with money.

There remains one final aspect of this knot made by allegory, money, and fetishism that needs to be discussed in order to understand the symbolic "work," the double allegory, of Amis's *Money*. According to Walter Benjamin, the meaning of things has been displaced by modernity, both as an intrinsic quality and as something guaranteed by a transcendental agent. Objects therefore are already allegorical, allegorized by their commodity exchange value: they are hollowed out, rendered meaningful only by the arbitrary assignation of price (370). "The allegories stand for that which the commodity makes of the experiences people have," says Benjamin (328), before calling the commodity form "the social content of allegory" (335). This social or cultural allegoricity is distinguished as a conscious strategy of representation. The allegorical gaze (and representational strategy) of the artist exists on a second-order of allegory – a demystified, disabused practice of writing, having abandoned illusions of meaning and accepted the arbitrariness of value. For the allegorist, anything can stand for anything else; objects receive their temporary, arbitrary meaning through writing, and the allegorical narrative lacks genuine, organic temporality. Allegory therefore acts as social critique: seeing things as fragments and ruins recalls the process of commodification and destroys the illusory unities of the mythical mode of perception (Pensky, 114, 168).

Repetition and usure

This twofold allegory urges us to take another look at the microstruc-
tures of the novel's explosive, ugly, and beautiful language. In what
remains of this essay, I will examine how the verbal structures,
processes, and transactions of the text interact with the structures,
processes, and transactions of the fictional world. These elements will
lead to a deeper understanding of the allegorical/representative nature
of John Self.

One of the most striking features of Amis's text is the proliferation of
catalogues, lists, and series. Excessive, Rabelaisian, carnivalistic enu-
merations occur frequently, including the items in Self's modest library
(66–7); the purchases acquired during a shopping binge (191); the
endless list of Selina's unsavory suitors (14); Lorne Guyland's previous
roles (111); or the smells of Self's tuxedo (300). We can better understand the economic and rhetorical functions of these catalogues by
noting that they often concern Selina, cataloging her phobias, acces-
sories, and attributes (72, 244). Selina, for Self, acts as an object of
detail: we are never allowed to glimpse her face, and her body is
revealed in glimpses, as Self lingers over details with fetishistic rapture.
Yet the peculiarity of his fetishism is also evident in these lists. A store-
house of fixations, Self has no privileged objects (lingerie, make-up,
breasts); instead, he is an all-round fetishist, a "fetish-artist," as he
might say, deriving pleasure from the structure of desire. A sense of dispersal lurks in the synecdochic logic of his catalogues, as in his account
of movie auditions, a session that instructs him in voyeurism and
humiliation.

> [A]fter a while, during that sun-bleached, snowblind vigil of booze
> and lies and pornography, the girls tended to mangle and dismem-
> ber in my mind [...] Across the floor they came, edgy as hell but
> mortally excited, the nerves spiraling to the ends of their hair, each
> with her special details of shape and shadow, of torque and thrust.
> [...] They talked about their careers, their crack-ups, their prongs,
> their shrinks, their dreams. (197–8)

Self is patently aware of the compulsive nature of such "breaking
down." Besides the conspicuous, bulging catalogues, the novel is
syncopated by mini-lists and syntactic triads. The actor Nub Forkner,
for instance, is described through his "cave shave, primal jeans, noble-
savage beerbelly" (220). Self talks about the "daily sky of empty

eggtrays, full sinks, kitchen mists" (249). Occasionally the text wallows in proliferating triptychs, including cadences of syntactic structures, adjectives, and phrasal parallels, as when Self describes how the streets

> darkened despite *the sun, the juicy air, the innocence of the covering blue*. Three blocks back there were *canopied doorways, wealth-guards in livery and vistas of brownstone*. Now the lanes were carless, lawless. We skirted the spreading sponge of split mattresses and jaw-busted suitcases facedown in the gutter, [...] – this was *no-money country, coldwater, walkup*. [...] And I also sensed – *perversely, unnecessarily, wastefully* – how gay Fielding and I must look, him in his *sneakers and strontium rompers and flyaway hair*, me with my *butch suit, thin jekylls and proud-rounded shoes*. (113–14, emphasis added)

These series function as miniature replications of the repetitive plot: congeries, accumulations without progress, blatantly simulated for rhetorical effect. Conversely, they produce surplus value, exceeding the sum of their parts, and pleasure derives from their seriality. From the viewpoint of textual economy, they are verbal waste, exceeding the logic of rational exchange. The affective investment is directed less at details or objects *themselves* but, first, upon the (sadistic) *process* of detailing and, second, upon the excessive verbosity. Like Nabokov's grandiloquent Humbert Humbert, Self is a fetishist of language, acquiring an added pleasure from linguistic accumulation.

In addition to the strategy of listing, Amis's novel strives to revitalize clichés through repetition or chiasmus. Such repetition reconstructs meaning, as in the lines, "Something is waiting. I am waiting. Soon, it will stop waiting – any day now. Awful things can happen any time. This is the awful thing" (3–4). Sometimes, repetition leads to the enfolding of meaning, an allegorical rift within similar words, as in the perfectly succinct phrase "painful, like pain" (289). This strategy recalls another aspect of Quilligan's conception of allegory. Disagreeing with the traditional vertical hierarchy of ontologically different levels, Quilligan advocates a model where allegory never hovers above the text, but exerts an inherent polysemy on the page. "Allegory works horizontally, so that meaning accretes serially, interconnecting and crisscrossing the verbal surface long before one can accurately speak of moving to another level 'beyond' the literal," she explains (28). Seen as the repetition of sameness that generates difference, allegory thus repeats the work of money: Self dreams of creating something out of nothing, *making money* by sleight of hand or figurative signature, circumventing the laws of circulation.

The other major source of this surplus is the novel's narrative mode, identified as *skaz* by several interpreters, including Diedrick, Lodge, and Keulks. This Dostoevskian identification, although appropriate, raises interpretive questions. Self certainly represents the allegorical fragmentariness, cretinization, and irreality of the subject of late capitalism: he is "made up of time lag, culture shock, zone shift," a "salty slipstream thinning out and trailing down over the black Atlantic" (264). Nevertheless, *skaz* suggests that on the level of voice, allegory strives to recuperate a coherent subjectivity. Thus the novel could be seen as an allegory (in Paul de Man's sense) where the primary narrative attempts to name the subject referentially. When, in the allegorical superstructure, this proper name is revealed as metaphoric, the self-identity of the subject is salvaged or recuperated by voice. As Leo Bersani puts it: the "self implicit in modern literature is an ordered and ordering principle; what we 'hear' in listening to its voice is a guarantee of wholeness, of totality, and therefore a negation of the fragmentariness which that voice may even be explicitly documenting" (258).

Self's voice does not work in such ways. As has been frequently noted, Self's monologue is profoundly dialogic, Babelian in tone, resembling the strange noises of foreigners ("turks, nutters, martians") in a London pub, who speak "stereo, radio crackle, interference [...] sonar, bat-chirrup, pterodactylese, fish-purr" (87). Numerous voices inhabit Self's head: his tinnitus joins the distinct voices of money, pornography, the weather, and something strangely undefined (107–8). This list recuperates the speaking voice as something outside Babelian confusion, a voice that is able to account for multiplicity and fragmentariness and thereby contain such things. This radical self-difference resides not in such intrusions but in the fact that Self's monologue is traversed by another voice – an educated, poetic one. This imposed voice remains unpredictable. Self's words thereby emerge simultaneously from two places (as in free indirect discourse). The site of enunciation itself is revealed as divided and plural. This unpredictable doubleness produces the semantic excess – the allegorical effect – in the narrative. Since individual expressions might derive from separate "places," their semantic value is suffused by self-difference. In rhetorical terms, this could be called syllepsis – a word's possession of different, even incompatible meanings – or simply irony, which has been nominated as the supreme trope of fetishism for its duplicitous structure of acknowledgement and disavowal, where the cited discourse remains rejected *and* interjected, negated and preserved

(Schor, 97) – although Amis's novel complicates the identification of "cited" and "host" discourses.

As my opening identified, a frequent strategy of such enfolding is the treatment of titles. Every title in the novel is tainted by Self's inability to recognize these expressions as "titles," segregated from common words. Goodney praises "the sound and the fury" (219), and Self believes the guests at Martina's party will include "the two gentlemen of Verona" (133). The irony is revealed in all its cruelty: by exposing Self's ignorance, the text reminds its readers of their superiority. The readers, correctly perceiving the titles, become complicit in such sadism, not unlike the aesthetic speculations between Martina and the Martin Amis character (132). The text's excessiveness seems to derive equally from vertical doubling (the duplicity of the voice, a lurking difference within its sameness) *and* horizontal doubling/repetition.[7]

This repetition-economy functions not unlike the paradox suggested by the French word *usure*, which means – first – a "using up" or loss of value. Instead of a progressive, teleological plot, *Money* provides an entropic seriality or repetition that subjects the reader to attrition. "That's my life: repetition, repetition" (25), says Self, betraying a textual logic that enacts (or performs) its referential content. Diedrick contends that repetition is "Self's favorite rhetorical strategy" (77), but it also forms the basis of the novel's (non-)narrative logic, its compulsion to repeat. The economic significance of repetition is loss (friction, loss of energy). On another level, however, the "automatic fetish" performs its work: the repetition and enfolding of the text results in surplus, excess energy.

But *Usure* also means "usury," the self-breeding accumulation of value through interest. This is the second-degree allegory that functions as "critique" – the allegorical gaze of the satirist. The textual economy of *Money* therefore resembles money: surplus resides in circularity, doubling, repetition, the difference within the same. This production can act as a register of pleasure, as Derrida suggests, explaining how metaphor yields a "dividend of pleasure" ("White", 239). Roland Barthes concurs, writing that a word "can be erotic on two opposing conditions, both excessive: if it is extravagantly repeated, or on the contrary, if it is unexpected, succulent in its newness" (42). In *Money*, words are eroticized in both of these ways, creating an excess that defies the logic of economic transactions. And excess, as Georges Bataille explains, "indicates the attraction of everything that is more than that which is" (*Visions*, 268n).

The big spender

There exists one final aspect of *Money*'s repetitive logic – the lack of teleology, progression, or final discharge. For Self, action can be dangerous, as in the allegorical chess game in which he becomes zugzwanged (119, 379), unable to move without self-destruction. That is also why Self experiences form as threatening – it implies change. The well-known Freudian thesis teaches that the pleasure principle meets the death principle through repetition: in order to spare itself from trauma, an organism selects repetition over change. Repetition is thus movement that prevents change, the activity of inertia. Self's inertia is so massive that his proliferation of pseudo-activities verges upon passion: his passion is the opposite of "action," however – a cosmic passivity.

Self is not a capitalist, not even an entrepreneur.[8] Despite being a director, he is rendered helpless by the circulation of money. Instead, he is a *consumer*, like the Baudrillardian "heroic consumers" he invokes (326; Baudrillard, 53). According to Keulks, Amis's characters "thrive on their excesses" (78), and Self's excesses reside in compulsive spending. He is the ultimate allegorical figure of consumer society, a figure of waste. For Baudrillard, the waste of consumer society is that which "defies scarcity and, contradictorily, signifies abundance. It is not utility, but that wastage which, in its essence, lays down the psychological, sociological and economic guidelines for affluence" (48). Affluence is not defined by sufficiency of commodities but by overabundance (49). Consumption is synecdochic: one buys the part for the whole and therefore buys into abundance itself. As Baudrillard suggests, in words that recall the textual logic of *Money*: "this metonymical, repetitive discourse of consumable material, of commodities, becomes once again, thanks to a gigantic collective metaphor, thanks to its own excess, the image of the *gift*, of that inexhaustible and spectacular prodigality which is that of the feast" (19).

Self is the self-conscious, self-hating, monstrously allegorical representative of the economy of waste, a golem of consumption, as his hyperbolic lists indicate. Additionally, the novel presents him as an ironic representative of a sovereign individual. He is an ironic reincarnation of the feudal lord, the subject of "dissipated wealth, of impetuous and unproductive consumption [who] recognizes himself as transient, fleeting" (Goux, 203). Through Self, consumerist society is portrayed as a demonic, mass-produced version of the "non-economic" significance of waste, as in the practice of the potlatch, the ritual destruction and wastage of possessions.

Only in one sense can Self's unproductive expenditure be reinterpreted and redeemed. In light of "his" language, Self's will to loss assumes heroic qualities, and one is inclined to credit his claim that he is "consuming myself" (207) or his metaphor in another zeugmatic list that "Life is all losing" (272). "The need to lose oneself," writes Bataille, "goes beyond the need to find oneself": Lovers "search for a measureless annihilation in a violent expenditure whereby the possession of a new object, of a new woman or a new man, is only a pretext for an even more annihilating expenditure" (*Eroticism*, 252). Given the apocalyptic or terminal overtones of Amis's novel, Self becomes a sacrificial victim or ritualized scapegoat.

Ritual scapegoating takes us to the final consideration of the psychological and ethical stakes of the novel's textual economy – its crucial connection to shame. Early in the narrative, Self meets a pregnant prostitute. He gives her money and departs, feeling noble. "She was like me," he says; "she knew she shouldn't go on doing it. But she went on doing it anyway. Me, I couldn't even blame money. What is this state, seeing the difference between good and bad and choosing bad – or consenting to bad, okaying bad?" (26). Self's condition does have a name: Aristotle called it *akrasia* (VII.1145b), which means "weakness of will" and etymologically signifies "lack of mastery," "lack of command," or "bad mixture." This passage suggests a moral consciousness in Self: even though he is unfamiliar with ethical philosophy, he accurately defines *akrasia* and ironically provides an acute self-diagnosis. In the "Babel" section of *The Pleasure of the Text*, Barthes discusses an imaginary person, a quasi-Monsieur Teste in reverse:

> who abolishes within himself all barriers, all classes, all exclusions, not by syncretism but by simple discard of that old specter: *logical contradiction*; who mixes every language,... who silently accepts every charge of illogicality, of incongruity.... Such a man would be the mockery of our society: court, school, asylum, polite conversation would cast him out: who endures contradiction without shame? (3)

Barthes's (and Self's) questions establish a relationship between "bad mixture," self-contradiction, and shame. Apart from money, shame features in perhaps the largest number of personification allegories in *Money*, often in tandem with fear. In one instance, the suggestion of "shameless shame" forms another tautological repetition and surplus meaning: "Shame is a chick who blew you in the can that time. Ooh, she is so shameless" (272).

The ubiquity of shame and its involvement in the novel's allegorical economy confirm the text's moral discourse, implicated in the interplay of the rhetorical, libidinal, and economic dimensions previously discussed. For Sartre, shame suggests an ontological consciousness: "I recognize myself as the other perceives me; I have my foundation outside myself, in the Other" (302, 349, 358). Because it involves the totality of one's existence, shame is always "shame of self" (350). It affects the quality of one's person – what Self calls his "private culture" (*Money*, 373). Steve Connor translates shame into rhetorical terms, confirming its synecdochic nature: "Whereas I am guilty of a crime, I am always ashamed of myself. Shame is therefore immeasurable, untellable" (218).

Two aspects of such discussions relate to John Self. The first addresses the relationship between shame and guilt. As opposed to the exorbitant nature of shame, guilt attempts to reduce shame to expression and quantification. Possessing recognizable units of currency, guilt can be accounted for; it is a symbolic *cashing* of shame, of "the excessiveness, the immeasurability against which guilt protects" (Connor, 217–20). This clearly mirrors Self's compulsive spending, not only in the progressively larger figures he gives to Felix,[9] but also in the episode where he offers money to prostitutes after insulting them (232). Shame makes Self pay, but these "serial humiliations" (261) cannot reduce the shame that induces them. Self's visits to the shrines of shame and his obliging compulsion to give money symbolize his attempts to pay for his shame, to insert excessive expenditure into the rational economics of penitence. Even the pervasive imagery of hell might be seen as Self's rhetorical attempt to view shame as guilt, thereby transform it, and – this is the crucial element – to see events as punishment. "Punishment, that's what this is. Punishment is what I'm taking here" (18), he says, welcoming not only his body's pain but Frank the Phone's harassment. A symbolic installment plan for his shame, Self labels these calls "punishment by boredom" (290), and the sadistic impulses of the author (and reader) are, in this sense, welcome additions to his tortures.

Thus, much of *Money* is indeed money – indemnities, a wad of suicide notes and suffering. Shame suffuses Self's being, making it inexpiable: "To speak of shame is to prolong or exacerbate it. I am ashamed of being a man; I am ashamed to speak of this shame, and ashamed of the need I feel to do so" (212). This is a self-perpetuating, self-propelling structure that juxtaposes shame and endless irony as the ever-present possibility of self-transcendence. *Speaking* of shame only produces more language, culminating in an endless spiral: "I am ashamed of what I am," says Self; "And is that anything to be ashamed of?" (324). We can now see his attitude to pornography in a new light: his compulsivity seems like a course of humiliation, performative exercises in masochism. The economy of masochism implies a psychic split, a simultaneous experience of suffering and enjoyment. Its libidinal investment defines the role of shame in the novel's textual (and psychic) economy as far from unequivocal, indicated by shame's lack of exemption from the rhetorical logic of excess, repetition, and usure.

In the closing, italicized section of the novel, Self attempts to reevaluate his situation after his unsuccessful suicide: "My life has been a fight between shame and fear. In suicide, shame wins. Shame is stronger than fear, though you still fear shame. [...] In the finished suicide, shame wins, but you wouldn't want anyone to see it winning" (386). This passage echoes the famous Marion episode of Rousseau's *Confessions*, which discloses a grievous sin from Rousseau's youth. Paul de Man comments on the "obvious delight with which the desire to hide is being revealed" (285), and his words help to clarify the implications of shame to Self's confessional narrative. On one hand, shame continues to function as the unnarratable source of Self's guilt, proliferating discourse in a spiraling movement. On the other hand, the textual excess generated by shame can also be seen as a source of pleasure in the perverse dynamics of Self's text. In suicide, Self says, "shame wins," but no suicide takes place. He attempts to become a romantic protagonist, and the narrative delights in the revelation of his shameful habits and general ugliness. *Money*'s masochism is thereby colored by exhibitionism.

Because shame is "primarily exhibitionistic" (de Man, 285), the text of the novel becomes an excess-producing machine, generating text purely for exposure: the repetitive logic of the text represents this obscene pleasure.[10] Self's inability to discuss certain episodes in his life is another textually produced sin requiring revelation and exculpation. In this sense, the logic or "economy" of the text prevails over the narrated story: the shameful things are committed solely to provide Self with a text in which to parade his disgrace. In the register of libidinal economy, this process of doubling and redoubling unfolds accordingly: pleasure is allegorically reinterpreted as impossible and therefore interminable payment. Punishment is transformed by sheer excess – according to the logic of masochism – into pleasure on the level of the text. Similarly, shame – Self's object-cause of suffering – becomes an ambiguous but endless source of textual pleasure in the economy of exhibitionism.

The text is generated by the inability to name the source of shame and by a desire to produce additional material for exposure. This involves the reader in the economies of pleasure and pain. To see such shameless, obscene self-exposure is unbearable, yet one cannot help to crave more. This might be the most important comment *Money* makes about contemporary culture: in a reversal of Ruth Benedict's famous distinction, consumer society is revealed as a "shame culture" that revels in exposing abjection and obscenity. Self's narrative is a one-man reality show before its time. The novel remains so disturbing because, against our better intentions, we *are* involved in an act of voyeurism. We feel outrage over Self's vulgarity, but his voice yields a pleasurable dividend.

This returns us to the "allegory deal" and concludes this essay. What does the reader buy by buying *Money*, we again ask. The title identifies the novel as allegory, requiring the semantic transaction whereby we see the characters' essences displaced into allegorical meaning: John Self as the exemplar of consumer culture, cretinization, and so on. However, the transaction – and this is the towering achievement of Amis's novel – cannot work perfectly, that is, without residue or excess. Self overflows his allegorical significance, and an excessive affection exists in the transaction of our reading.

Readers are solicited into the textual economy of the novel in ways that exceed what they expect. The reader's "surplus" derives – first – from the repetitive, duplicitous language, which libidinally creates surplus through the sadistic impulse identified in Benjamin's allegorical gaze. However, a second, potentially ethical, aspect of this surplus emerges from the narrative, which by definition is always "pure transference" (377) and includes an element of gift, an excess hinted at by Self's frequent asides and appeals. Even though the libidinal excess of the language compels us to read Self entirely – and sadistically – in terms of allegory, we cannot help relating to him on an affective level, violating the allegorical contract. Ironically, this vindicates Self's simplistic abilities as a reader. Although he overlooks the entire idea of allegory in *Animal Farm*, we might say he does so because he has invested so much into the empirical level of the text, personally relating to the animals. In other words, he does precisely what we do when reading him: pulled towards an allegorical reading – and thereby a hollowed-out Self – we are left, in the end, with a sense of his excessive, inadmissible life.

Notes

1 Brantlinger discusses the symbiosis between money, realism, and credit (86, 143–4). Although *Money* is clearly not a work of Victorian realism, the parallels between text and money are maintained. Significantly, Self's grandfather was an "oft-busted counterfeiter" (253). Amis's title also suggests the novel is an intertextual "redo" (as Self says) of Zola's novel *Money* (1891).
2 As Diedrick remarks (87), Self relates genuinely to the book, trying to place himself among the animals, before concluding, "I think I might have what it takes to be one of the dogs. I *am* a dog" (207).
3 See also 335, 354, 383, and especially 263: "Money softens the fall of life, [...] Money breaks the fall."
4 In *The Decline of the West* (1954), Oswald Spengler defines money as a category of thought (482) rather than a material object. Modern (or "Faustian") money is not minted but conceptualized as an efficient center emerging from life.
5 Goux calls money "the crystallized reflection in one special commodity of the relations among all other commodities" (94). Simmel defines it as the purest reification of *means*, a concrete instrument that is absolutely identical with its abstract concept (211) and identifies it – here we arrive to the core of the allegorical and non-allegorizable nature of money – as a member of a set as well as the set itself.
6 In Zola's novel, money is also posited as a God (218, 223). For a different allegorical account, see D.H. Lawrence's "John Galsworthy" (1927), in which Man, terrified by his Fall and divorce from Physis (Nature, the cosmos), turns to money for consolation. Like Self, Lawrence's fallen, "castrated" man tries to protect himself through money: "Money, material salvation is the only salvation. What is salvation is God. Hence money is God."
7 This doubleness produces the language's visceral, elemental qualities, where everything is experienced as sensuous density. The narrative also mobilizes the physical, acoustic dimensions of language, as in the celebrated cityscapes (24–5, 150, 159) and character descriptions. Phonetics and alliteration saturate many of Self's lists, and symbolic violence exists in the manipulation of verbs as nouns, an acoustic ugliness that subordinates meaning.
8 This contrasts Saccard, Zola's hero, who embodies the romantic hero whose downfall is his illimitable desire. *Money* debunks several romantic myths, including desire, the body, and suicide, as repositories of authenticity in an inauthentic world. A fourth myth is art: still a valid sphere in Zola but undermined in *Money* through the Martin Amis character.
9 These increase from one dollar (13) to one hundred (142–3) before dwindling to 20 (181) and five (351). The name Felix might allude to Nabokov's alter-ego tramp in *Despair*.
10 See de Man, 283 – "I feared shame more than death, more than the crime, more than anything in the world" – and 285: "The more there is to expose,

the more there is to be ashamed of; the more resistance to exposure, the more satisfying the scene, and especially, the more satisfying and eloquent the belated revelation ... of the inability to reveal." The latter recalls Self's suppressions, all announced with gusto.

Works cited

Amis, Martin. *Money: A Suicide Note*. 1984. Harmondsworth: Penguin, 1986.
Apter, Elizabeth, and William Pietz, eds. *Fetishism as a Cultural Discourse*. Ithaca: Cornell UP, 1996.
Aristotle. *Nicomachean Ethics*. Trans. Roger Crisp. Cambridge: Cambridge UP, 2000.
Barthes, Roland. *The Pleasure of the Text*. Trans. Richard Miller. New York: Hill and Wang, 1975.
Bataille, Georges. *Eroticism: Death and Sensuality*. Trans. Mary Dalwood. San Francisco: City Lights, 1986.
——. *Visions of Excess*. Trans. Allan Stoekl. Minneapolis: U of Minnesota P, 1985.
Baudrillard, Jean. *La société de consummation*. 1970. Paris: Denoël, 1990.
Benjamin, Walter. *The Arcades Project*. Trans. Howard Eiland and Kevin McLaughlin. Cambridge: Harvard UP, 1999.
Bersani, Leo. *A Future for Astyanax*. New York. Columbia UP, 1984.
Brantlinger, Patrick. *Fictions of State: Culture and Credit in Britain, 1694–1994*. Ithaca: Cornell UP, 1996.
Connor, Steve. "The Shame of Being a Man." *Textual Practice* 15.2 (2001): 211–30.
de Man, Paul. *Allegories of Reading*. New Haven: Yale UP, 1979.
Derrida, Jacques. *Given Time I: Counterfeit Money*. Chicago: U of Chicago P, 1992.
——. "White Mythology: Metaphor in the Text of Philosophy." *Margins of Philosophy*. Trans. Alan Bass. New York: Harvester, 1982. 207–71.
Diedrick, James. *Understanding Martin Amis*. U of South Carolina P, 1995.
Goux, Jean-Joseph. *Symbolic Economies: After Marx and Freud*. Ithaca: Cornell UP, 1989.
Keulks, Gavin. *Father and Son: Kingsley Amis, Martin Amis, and the British Novel since 1950*. Madison: U of Wisconsin P, 2003.
Marx, Karl. *Capital: A Critique of Political Economy*. 3 Vols. Trans. David Fernbach. London: Penguin, 1991.
——. "Economical and Philosophical Manuscripts." *Early Writings*. Harmondsworth: Penguin, 1975.
Pensky, Max. *Melancholy Dialectics: Walter Benjamin and the Play of Mourning*. Amherst: U of Massachusetts P, 2001.
Pietz, William. "Fetishism and Materialism: The Limits of Theory in Marx." Apter and Pietz 119–51.
Quilligan, Maureen. *The Language of Allegory*. Ithaca: Cornell UP, 1979.
Sartre, Jean-Paul. *Being and Nothingness*. Trans. Hazel E. Barnes. New York: Pocket, 1966.
Schor, Naomi. "Fetishism and Its Ironies." Apter and Pietz 92–100.
Simmel, Georg. *The Philosophy of Money*. Trans. Tom Bottomore and David Frisby. London: Routledge, 1978.
Žižek, Slavoj. *The Ticklish Subject: The Absent Centre of Political Ontology*. London: Verso, 2000.

4
Money Makes the Man: Gender and Sexuality in Martin Amis's *Money*

Emma Parker
University of Leicester

If, as the proverb states, money makes the man, then the denouement of *Money* (1984) calls the gender of its protagonist, John Self, into question by leaving him penniless. In this context, Amis's assertion that Self's financial downfall constitutes a "happy ending" suggests that the novel's critique of capitalism is entwined with a critique of patriarchy (Haffenden, 14). Such a reading contradicts existing interpretations of the text that propose that it endorses male hegemony. Although it is possible to counter the charge that Amis is a masculinist writer by arguing that *Money* offers a critique of masculinity, this essay contends that the novel goes further than highlighting the need to redefine dominant modes of manhood. Offering a queer reading of the text that focuses on the unstable borders of identity and desire, this essay demonstrates that *Money* subverts the ideology of its bigoted protagonist by deconstructing the heteropatriarchal concepts "woman" and "man" and creating what Judith Butler terms "gender trouble."

Feminist fury

Amis's gender politics have inflamed controversy since his first novel, *The Rachel Papers*, appeared in 1973. He writes from a distinctly male perspective, draws on male literary influences (principally Nabokov and Bellow), and, as Charles Michener's *Esquire* article suggests, has a strong male appeal. He is, in Michener's words, a "big-cocked novelist" (109), and the "testosterone-driven narrative" of *Money* (Miracky, 143) is the most frequently cited example of his alleged misogyny (Keulks, 165). A racist, sexist homophobe, John Self is an unsavory figure addicted to junk food, television, cigarettes, alcohol and sex. He is the apotheosis of what critics find objectionable about Amis's male protagonists, whose pornographic encounters with women have ignited indignation. Shanti Padhi describes Amis's early portraits of women as "indecent" and "callow" (39), and Neil Powell accuses his first three novels of "gratuitous, knowing obscenity" (45). Protesting Amis's tendency to sexualize his female characters or reduce them to body parts, Sara Mills denounces Amis as "a quintessentially sexist writer" (207). James Diedrick avers that patriarchal assumptions inform his work (4), and Adam Mars-Jones argues that he "defends the sexual status quo" (8). Reviewing *Money*, R.Z. Sheppard declared that "Amis' new novel should have feminists calling for blood" and, as Laura Doan's critical response illustrates, they soon were. According to Doan, Amis fails to extend his critique of the economic system to gender and class. Thus, his "restricted focus hinders a critique of the gender system which is, instead, upheld and reified (i.e. maintained)" (70). Amis, she concludes, "elects to stay within the patriarchal gender boundaries by upholding the pattern of dominance and submission" (78).

Critiquing masculinity

Countering charges of misogyny, Amis's defenders have claimed that *Money* exhibits "feminist energies" (Keulks, 180). Amis himself has stressed his feminist sympathies, contending to Claudia FitzHerbert: "I think I am [...] one of the feminist writers of my generation. And I'm on the point of declaring myself an outright gynocrat." Moreover, he told James Naughtie, "I was a feminist when I wrote *Money*" and has elsewhere stated, "I consider *Money* my feminist book" (Morrison, 101). The novel's self-conscious feminist agenda is suggested through an allusion to Tolstoy when Self takes Selina to dinner at "Kreutzer's" (73). Like *Money*, *The Kreutzer Sonata* (1889) was initially condemned as indecent and misogynistic because – like Self – the protagonist Pozdnyshev has a penchant for prostitutes, is subject to jealous rage, and treats his partner abominably. However, Tolstoy's novel has come to be considered a sensitive exploration of inequality that links women's oppression to their status as sexual objects and, in her introduction to the Modern Library edition (2003), Doris Lessing defends it as a feminist text.

Amis's claim to Naughtie that *London Fields* (1989) satirizes "certain male illusions," and his assertion that "maleness has become an embarrassment" (*War*, 5), further suggest that *Money* can be read as a critique of masculinity. An intertextual reference to Saul Bellow invites the reader to consider the novel in this way. Fielding Goodney, Self's producer, orders him a "Rain King" from the bar (20), and like the rich, alcoholic narrator of Bellow's *Henderson the Rain King* (1959), Self's poetic thoughts contrast his demotic speech. However, the allusion to Bellow also suggests that Amis shares his interest in masculinity. As Gloria Cronin explains: "The Bellow text simultaneously enacts traditional gender ideologies, protests them, exploits their comic dimensions, explores their intellectual and social origins, deconstructs them." Similarly, Elaine Showalter conceives *Money* as an example of "Ladlit" – a genre that exposes the "insecurities, panic, cold sweats, performance anxieties, and phobias" lying beneath male bravado (60) – and includes *Money* in her discussion of novels that offer "a masterly examination of male identity in contemporary Britain" (60).

Lorne Guyland, one of the stars of Self's film, is the target of the novel's most pointed satire on masculinity. As his surname suggests, he represents masculinity incarnate: throughout his career, Guyland ('guy-land') has played "bigshots" and "heroes" (111, 247). However, as his first name suggests (*lorn* meaning *lost*), he is an aging actor and fading sex symbol whose career is in terminal decline. He responds to anxieties about the loss of male power with hypermasculinity and continually exaggerates the patriarchal signifiers of manliness (aggression, virility) to stave off fears of weakness and redundancy. He demands nude sex scenes in Self's film *Good Money* and insists that the script be revised to allow him to thrash his son – 40 years his junior – and seduce his daughter-in-law. As he explains to Self, "I got to have some beef in that role....it's got to be like big, you know?" (110). However, Guyland's insistence that he is in "great shape" and "up half the night screwing" (120) is cast in doubt by Goodney, who claims that "Lorne hadn't had a hard-on for thirty-five years" (183).

As Guyland develops his narcissistic vision of the film, his amusing delusions of grandeur transform his character from humble publandlord into millionaire, athlete, poet, professor of art, and part-time archeologist who "has the world in his hands" (184). The correspondence between his name and those of the characters he invents – "Gary," the original character, becomes "Garfield" then "Sir Garfield" and finally "Lord Garfield" (186) – indicates that Guyland projects his fantasy-self onto this fictional character. In so doing he reveals the fictiveness of his own masculinity. Even Self, blinded as he is by various addictions, repressions, and delusions, recognizes that Guyland is fake. Informing Self that Guyland has called, a hotel desk-clerk inquires, "Would that be the real Lorne Guyland, sir?" Self responds, "Oh, I wouldn't go that far" (10). Self also highlights the construction of masculinity when he compares Guyland to a robot: "this isn't a man, I kept thinking, it's a mad old robot, all zinc and chrome and circuitry coolant" (185).

It is through Self, however, that Amis most clearly subverts a patriarchal model of masculinity. Self is addicted to sex and relates to women only as sexual objects, but the novel exposes how thoroughly pornography and prostitution impoverish human relations. After watching a pornographic film, Self wonders, "hard to tell, really, who was the biggest loser in this complicated transaction – her, him, them, me" (47). His relationship with his girlfriend, Selina, reveals the part that pornography plays in stabilizing patriarchy and capitalism through the commodification of women. As her surname "Street" suggests, Selina's relationship with Self aligns her with a "street-walker" or prostitute. The distorting and dehumanizing effects of pornography are epitomized by Self's preference for fantasy over reality, which creates his need to fantasize about the very woman with whom he is having sex (Butch Beausoleil). Self also acknowledges that images of women produced by male sexual fantasy are unrealistic and that pornography misrepresents female sexuality: "That's the thing about pornography, that's the thing about men – they're always giving you the wrong idea about women" (236). He demonstrates pornography's damage when his relationship with Martina Twain – whom he is forced to recognize as a "woman" (335) rather than a "girl" (131) – renders him impotent. Underlining pornography's antithetical relationship to eroticism, Self's sexual escapades are passionless. His description of sex is impersonal and mechanical: "here comes her hand"; "I'm on my knees"; "she's turning over" (275). Such dehumanization also means that, despite his numerous sexual liaisons, Self constantly craves "the human touch" (235).

Illustrating Karl Miller's observation that Amis "punishes excessive or delirious machismo" (412), Self himself becomes the object of the male gaze to which he submits women when Goodney places him under surveillance. Self is also troubled by a bad conscience. At points his conscience – the uncontrollable thoughts that come from "squatters and hoboes who hang out in my head" (267) – fills him with disgust for women's sexual exploitation: "I'm finding myself more and more reluctant to face up to the fact that all women's mouths have at some point played hostess to a man's..." (267). His inability to finish the sentence, and reluctance to employ one of his favorite terms – "dick" (268) – suggests shame and revulsion. He expresses sympathy for women and laments relations between the sexes: "I'm not shocked, just disappointed. My tone is not angry. My tone is concerned, tender, grieving" (267–8). Thus, although *Money* is sexually explicit, it is not casually crude or obscene because it raises awareness of the ways in which men use sex to exert power over women. As Padhi notes, although the content may be repellent, it is not irresponsible (41).

Furthermore, Self's poor physical and emotional state suggest that Amis does not champion his protagonist's model of masculinity. Indeed, Amis makes his central character literally and metaphorically unattractive. Self frequently notes that he is fat and finds both his face and his life ugly. A shambolic rather than heroic figure, Self is, like his car (the aptly named Fiasco), a wreck. He has toothaches and tinnitus, and is losing his hair: "I am a rug retard, a gut bum, a gum gimp. I have ticker trouble. I know nothing. I am weak, wanton, baffled, faint" (303). He confesses feeling "weak and scared" at night (26), and senses his own decline: "Every hour you get weaker" (184). His constant "crying jags" suggest his unhappiness and confusion (108). When Guyland seeks reassurance about the nature of his cinematic role (conflating his filmic and male roles), Self's response reveals his own crisis in masculinity: "Me too, pal. Lorne, I sympathise" (182). Self's powerful response to *Prehistoric*, a caveman movie starring Spunk Davis (who also plays a character based on Self in *Good Money*), suggests that Self intuits the outdated redundancy of his own model of manhood: "Moved? I had a nervous breakdown" (128). If money makes the man, Self's longing to "leave this moneyworld" (363) communicates a desire to escape the conventional confines of masculinity or even manhood itself. His repeated preoccupation with "turnaround" registers an interest in revolution. Indeed, he admits the need for change – "I need a new dimension" (303) – and implores the reader, "Don't be like me, pal. Sister, please find another way" (380). Spunk Davis even selects a quotation from the Book of John that suggests the signficance of change to Self's salvation – "Unless a man is born anew, he cannot see the kingdom of God" (141) – and Self's need for salvation is confirmed by the number of his first flight to New York: 666, the symbol of the beast (or anti-Christ) in the Book of John.

Formal aspects of the novel likewise suggest that Amis opposes what Self represents. The use of unreliable narration undermines Self's authority and perspective, as tinnitus, blackouts, and repression limit Self's awareness. Rather than constituting "lifeless vehicles of an ideology of macho behaviour" (Mills, 207), characters like Lorne Guyland and John Self are vehicles for a critique of masculinity that exposes and undercuts patriarchal power. Certain passages may be uncomfortable to read, but Amis strives "to vex and disturb" (Ryan, 204), employing shock-effects purposefully. He offers an exaggerated or extreme portrait of masculinity to counter the normalization of patriarchal ideology that makes sexism invisible and to affect what Kiernan Ryan terms a "redemptive defamiliarization," enabling readers to perceive the world anew (216).

Ultimately, however, attempts to recoup *Money* by reading it as a critique of masculinity are limited if the novel simply inverts the positions of men and women in a gender hierarchy. In *The War Against Cliché* (2001), Amis charts the emergence of the post-1970 New Man, one who believes that "the female is not merely equal to the male but is his plain superior" and who regards the cultivation of his feminine side as "a kind of homage to a better and gentler principle" (4). According to Mars-Jones, Amis himself can be classed among "men of goodwill and imperfect conscience" who "try to find an existential niche in the traditional realm of female values" (39). *Money* also exhibits what Mars-Jones punningly terms "venus envy" through Self's absent mother and Martina Twain, who both represent potentially redemptive feminine values. Showalter is one of the few critics to comment on the significance of Self's mother, who dies when he is young and whom he hardly remembers. While Showalter identifies the mother's death as the source of Self's loss and pain (71), one could also argue that her death represents the repression of the feminine principle in the masculinist culture of the 1980s, epitomized by the *Spitting Image* caricature of Margaret Thatcher, which depicted the Prime Minister in a pinstripe suit, smoking a cigar. The death of his mother forces Self to grow up in a male-dominated environment, producing a problematic sense of masculinity. Spunk's film *Prehistoric* – in which a woman teaches him "how to dress, eat, speak" (128) – endorses this theme of women's civilizing influence and mirrors Self's relationship with Martina. Encouraged by Martina, Self undertakes a program of physical, moral, and cultural self-improvement. Although he falters in his attempt to change and betrays Martina by sleeping with Selina, Martina nonetheless offers Self salvation: "Martina makes me strong" (297). Often associated with light, she represents enlightenment and an enlightened set of values. While the novel's celebration of women as redeemers may seem pro-feminist – presenting women as superior and identifying redemptive principles as feminine – Amis's critique of patriarchy is constrained by the gendered binary oppositions and hierarchical structures it maintains.

Queer possibilities and John Self

However, a rich, subtle, and ambitious novel, *Money* challenges male hegemony with more than a critique of masculinity that reifies patriarchal structures. By destabilizing the binary categories of gender and sexuality, the novel privileges a queer perspective. Amis revels in the dissolution of boundaries and nearly all the characters in the novel have an ambiguous gender identity that generates "gender trouble": the subversive performance of gender that troubles, or confounds, the patriarchal belief that separate and discrete genders correspond to a subject's sex and naturalize heterosexuality. Amis attributes his interest in traversing gender boundaries to Gloria Steinem's *Outrageous Acts and Everyday Rebellions* (1983), as he told James Naughtie: "Gloria Steinem turned me into a feminist by the simple means of transposing the sexes. She asks you to put yourself in a position across the gender divide." Nonetheless, Amis's ventures into queer territory began (however unconsciously) much earlier, when he took a role in the film *A High Wind in Jamaica* (1965). This film features cross-dressing pirates, but its queerness is amplified by Amis himself: because his voice broke during filming, his speeches had to be dubbed by an actress, as Amis explains: "On the screen you see me but hear her" (Michener, 111). His ambiguous public image also suggests the persistence of a queer persona. Despite a reputation for being a "sneering little tough guy" (Morrison, 96), Amis has been called a "wimp" by Norman Mailer and a "cute little thing" by Gore Vidal (Michener, 109). Although he told Laura Miller that he once believed that "there are huge differences between men and women," he revised his position when writing *Night Train* (1997), which features a female protagonist named Mike Hoolihan. Discussing the novel's first-person narration, Amis informed Miller that "becoming" a woman was "a breeze": "It turns out that when your creative energies are in play, there doesn't seem to be any difference at all."

Money consistently presents gender as unfixed and fluid, and the novel's feminist sympathies can be located in its queer deconstruction of the heteropatriarchal concepts "man" and "woman." According to Mills, sexism "constitutes, promotes or exploits an unfair or irrelevant marking of distinctions between the sexes" (209). As Amis subverts the clearcut distinctions between men and women upon which discrimination depends, charges of sexism clearly require reconsideration. Although Miracky claims that Self is an "intensely masculine protagonist" (143), his masculinity is constantly compromised in ways that render his gender deeply ambivalent. Keulks describes Self's television commercials as "campy" (174), and aspects of his clothes and behavior are equally camp. For example, at various points in the narrative Self drives a "purple" car (62), consumes a "crimson" drink (93), wears a "pink" cummerbund (299), and dishes out haircare tips: "The second wash...can be a big mistake. It expands the follicles and then the cleaning agents dry and harden" (99). Furthermore, he is overemotional and frequently weeps. Self's femininity is also underscored by the name of an actor who auditions to play Self's character in *Good Money*: Christopher Meadowbrook. Although Self rejects him on the grounds that he is not sufficiently manly – "He looked like a weakie, unmanned, pure victim" (129) – his heavy drinking and tears confirm their similarity.

Self's ironic rejection of Meadowbrook is consistent with his general state of delusion but also indicates a desperate attempt to repress feminine characteristics that threaten his masculinity. Significantly, Self also fends off femininity by constantly claiming to be butch: "I was lying on the bed, hugely, malely, in my winded Y-fronts. Boy am I butch" (38). Faced with a difficult situation, he repeatedly strives to "butch it out" (65, 98, 235, 370). Ironically, however, his masculinity is undercut by the fact that, in *Money*, "Butch" is a woman – the actress, Butch Beausoleil. Self even admits to feeling like a woman on occasion. When his shopping bags are delivered to his hotel room, he states, "After a while I felt like Lady Diana would no doubt feel on her wedding day" (191). Having sex with Butch, he declares, "oh man, some girls – they make you feel like a real chick" (277). Hosting moneymen makes him feel "like a mother-hen or an orchid-fancier" (332). Self's transatlantic flights underscore the motif of boundary crossing, and his dual nationality (he is half-American) reflects a dual gender identity. His ambiguous gender is epitomized by his boil – "I've had some boils on my ass before, but this mother has to be the daddy of them all" (210) – and reflected in the cityscape of New York, which is equally queer, unstable, and plural. Self traverses "masculine Madison" and "feminine Park Avenue" (19, 96); "On bucking Broadway the cabs all bitched and beefed" (193). By employing gendered words such as *bitch* and *beef* that share the same meaning (to complain), Self subverts difference even as he invokes it.

Intertextual allusions to classic literary texts echo the novel's concern with crossing and confounding gender boundaries. Self is aligned with Hamlet through his commercial for "a new kind of flash-friable pork-and-egg bap or roll or hero called a Hamlette" (69), which features an actor dressed in black holding a skull. *Money* reverberates with the same Oedipal tensions that suffuse Shakespeare's play (Self sleeps with Vron, his step-mother), but Self also echoes the uncertainty of Hamlet's status as a man. Claudius tells Hamlet that his grief is "unmanly" (I.ii.94), and the prince's femininity led one critic to specu-late that Hamlet was not only a "womanly man" but "in very deed a woman" (Vining, 59). Performances of the play have emphasized the plurality of Hamlet's gender: women have occasionally taken the part (most famously Sarah Siddons and Sarah Bernhardt), and in the 1921 film version Asta Nielsen characterized Hamlet as a woman attempting to pass as a man.

Self's queer-ness applies to both his gender and his sexuality: his homoerotic desires call the naturalness of heterosexuality into question and disturb binary categories of sexual identity. However, as his rejec-tion of Christopher Meadowbrook indicates, Self refuses to acknowledge his homosexual proclivities. If Meadowbrook's surname highlights his femininity, his first name (which alludes to Christopher Isherwood's memoir *Christopher and his Kind* (1976), a text adopted by the Gay Liberation Movement) indicates his homosexuality. Having internalized patriarchal ideology, Self believes that manhood is aligned with, and affirmed by, heterosexuality. He seeks to establish his heteronormativity through homophobia and frequently employs the derogatory term "faggot" to locate homosexuality elsewhere. He calls his stalker a "faggot" and a "no-man," equating the two (310). His penchant for pornography and his desire for marriage and fatherhood can also be read as products of heterosexual anxiety: "I must marry Selina and settle down and raise a family," Self states, before adding, "To become a husband and a father: no you can't get much butcher than that" (173). As Amis demonstrates in his wry review of Robert Bly's *Iron John* (1990), however, assertions of masculinity easily slide into what the logic of heteropatriarchy labels as their opposite: ironically, Bly's title sabotages his own attempt to celebrate manly men because, in Britain, *iron* (short for "iron hoof") is Cockney rhyming slang for *poof* (*War*, 4).[1] In a simi-larly deconstructive moment in *Money*, Self senses that his "butch suit" makes him look "gay" (114).

While Self submerges same-sex desire in the struggle to establish heteronormative masculinity, his repressed homosexuality finds expression at the level of subtext. For example, the delayed revelation that Roger Frift is his dental hygienist suggests a sexual frisson in their relationship: the man that Self introduces as "a dinky 26-year-old and a hyperactive homosexual" complains about the state of Self's tongue and tells him to "lie back and relax" while Self implores him to "Just do it" (74–5). Sexual innuendo is enhanced by the fact that, in Britain, *roger* means "to penetrate sexually." Likewise, comparing himself to Martina, who runs on "true lines," Self asks, "Who's straight?" before responding, "I'm not" (119).

Self's delusion is so grand that he manages to deny his homosexual tendencies even as he alludes to same-sex encounters. During a "handjob" Self laments that his fantasy about Selina is disturbed when "all these guys came walking in on the act" (17). Similarly, discussing his boil, Self comments, "I thought that these characters had gone out of my life along with circle-jerks and slipped octaves" (210). He can neither repress nor acknowledge his attraction to Goodney: strolling on Ninety-Eighth Street, he suddenly realizes "how *gay* Fielding and I must look" (114). Elsewhere, he seems to adore his friend: "Christ, what a goodlooking guy" (223). Having blanked out the memory of his steamy evening with Goodney – aka "Frank the Phone" (118) – at Zelda's, Self is bemused by the message he finds in a book of matches: "Frankie and Johnny were lovers" (219).

Self does, however, gain self-knowledge as the novel progresses and comes to recognize and accept the polymorphous nature of his desire. Still using homophobic language, he tentatively acknowledges the fluidity of sexuality: "The world wavers. Who's straight? Are you? Is Martina Twain? [...] Me I have no faggot history whatever. I have no faggot past. But who knows these days? Maybe I have a big faggot future. As a faggot, I might be a roaring success" (202). Later, he entertains the possibility of sexual relations with a man. Thinking about fellatio from a woman's point of view, he remarks: "Pretty soon, most of the guys will have done it too, and we'll be in the same boat, along with you girls. I suppose I might even get round to it myself one of these days – I wouldn't put it past me" (268). Not long after this admission he develops "some kind of gay thing for Spunk" (325) and admits his attraction to Goodney: "Sometimes, among all the fever, the wayward thoughts, I start facing up to the fact that I've probably been deeply in love with Fielding Goodney from the moment we met" (326). He also confesses to incurring a "minor hard-on" during his chess game with Martin Amis (378). Although Self is involved with a woman at the novel's end, her name – Georgina, a femininized "George" – suggests the persistence of homoerotic desire that renders his sexuality far from straight(forward).

Self's homoerotic desire for Goodney is also articulated through a plethora of allusions to queer texts and authors other than *Hamlet*. Hotel names suggest literary classics that not only echo the novel's critique of capitalism and American imperialism but, importantly, allude to themes of sexual transgression. Self first meets Goodney at the "Carraway Hotel" (19), invoking the narrator Nick Carraway in F. Scott Fitzgerald's *The Great Gatsby* (1925), the quintessential indictment of the American Dream of self-made success. However, *The Great Gatsby* is also "a sexually ambiguous novel" in which a heterosexual narrative is shadowed by a homoerotic subtext that centers on Carraway's unconscious homoerotic attraction to Gatsby (Tyson, 345). Self and Goodney meet in the "Dimmesdale Room" (20), and the allusion to Hawthorne's *The Scarlet Letter* (1850) invokes themes of deception, betrayal, and same-sex desire through the homoerotic possibilities that reside between Dimmesdale and Chillingworth. As Gregory Woods points out, their relationship offers an example of what Eve Kosofsky Sedgwick calls an erotic triangle, in which desire between men is mediated through a woman, in this case Hester Prynne (161). When Goodney and Self become the leasees of the "Blithedale Projects" (317), Amis summons another Hawthorne text, *The Blithedale Romance* (1852), which depicts a utopian, anti-capitalist community destroyed by its members' self-interest. Blithedale is a place of queer desire and queer gender, a place where the discrete categories of man, woman, heterosexual and homosexual are set up to be undermined (Grossberg, 7). Goodney's suggestion that Self take a floor of the "Bartleby" or a suite at the "Gustave" invokes additional texts that emphasize the dangers of capitalism (142): Herman Melville's *Bartleby the Scrivener* (1853) and Gustave Flaubert's *Madame Bovary* (1857). The expression of repressed homosexuality in Melville's work has received considerable critical attention (most notably from Sedgwick) and, as Woods notes, *Bartleby* underlines Melville's interest in masculinity (163). Flaubert's famous statement, "Madame Bovary, c'est moi," suggests he possessed a transgendered sense of self. Naomi Schor even identifies Flaubert – who enjoyed an intimate friendship with the lesbian George Sand and once declared, "Lesbos is my homeland" – as a male lesbian (394). Despite Goodney's insistence, Self remains at "The Ashbery" (142), referencing the poet John Ashbery, who, like other literary precursors in the text, writes about homosexuality indirectly, despite being queer.

Fielding Goodney and other queer characters

Self is not the only queer character in *Money*. Several other characters contribute to the dissolution of established boundaries of identity and desire, most notably the cross-dressing Fielding Goodney. As his ironic surname suggests, Self's producer is not who he claims to be: "good-ney" turns out to be a "baddie" who tricks Self into bankruptcy. According to Marjorie Garber, transvestism illustrates that identity is not fixed and that there is no underlying "self"; it suggests identity as self-fashioning (32). Cross-dressing thus challenges the idea of an original and stable identity (16), and illustrates that all gender is impersonation (40). Although Goodney looks like an All-American Boy, the end of the novel exposes him as the woman who has followed Self around New York. Goodney's queer status is signaled by his "ginger" hair, which is Cockney rhyming slang for *queer/ginger beer* (*War*, 4). Unaware that he is being followed by Goodney, Self describes the "gingery" figure sitting next to him in a topless bar as "hermaphroditic" (7). Although the woman who haunts Self is "square in the ankles, more than six feet tall on her high heels" and has a chin that is "low and stubborn and insane" (192), Self does not identify her as a "him," even when Martina points out this fact. Self finds it hard to accept that his stalker is a man: "The figure backed off with a hesitant confusion that could only seem womanly to me." Doubting his conviction, he adds, "but would a *woman* back off like that?" (310). Self's confused use of pronouns confirms Goodney's evasion of binary gender categories: "she stepped nimbly out of her shoes, crouched to collect them, and lifting her dress with one hand ran fast and purposefully towards Seventh Avenue. I stood there and watched him run" (310).

Goodney's sexuality is equally difficult to pinpoint. He arranges fake auditions in which women are gratuitously asked to strip and shares Self's interest in pornography and sex clubs (where women are on display). Yet his heterosexuality is rendered suspect by the homoerotic nature of his attack on Self: "he started to jounce me up and down, his pelvis stirring my rump" (349). Allusions to *Othello* suggest an undercurrent of homoeroticism in their relationship. When Goodney whispers "inhuman dog" in Self's ear (377), he quotes Roderigo condemning Iago. However, as Amis points out, Goodney plays the part of Iago in the novel and Self is Roderigo, the betrayed friend who becomes a pawn in Iago's power games (Haffenden, 23). *Othello* thus underscores the theme of betrayal. However, drawing on Sedgwick's concept of erotic triangles, Robert Matz establishes Iago as a queer figure by suggesting that Desdemona mediates his desire for Othello. Finally, Self's discovery that Goodney is sleeping with Doris Arthur, a lesbian, frustrates any correspondence between gender, sex, and sexuality through the suggestion that Goodney is a male lesbian. As Doris explains: "In bed he's a woman" (353). Goodney's status as a male lesbian is also suggested by the location of his first sexual encounter with Self – Zelda's, an allusion to Zelda Fitzgerald, who identified herself as a latent lesbian. Schor defines male lesbianism as the "imaginary identification of men with lesbians" (391), which entails a "psychic process whereby men imaginatively divest themselves of their male attributes" (397). Thus the categories *homosexual* and *heterosexual* cannot adequately reflect the complexity of Goodney's dispersed and fluctuating desire. As a transvestite, Goodney exemplifies Garber's contention that cross-dressing is disruptive and destabilizes categories, engendering "a crisis of 'category' itself" (32). As Self notes, thinking about his anonymous caller: "Sometimes he sounded big, sometimes he sounded small" (38). Likewise, he comments, "As threatening telephone calls go, these threatening telephone calls seem comparatively friendly" (290). The nickname that Self bestows on his anonymous caller – Frank the Phone – underlines the threat that Goodney poses to fixed boundaries by suggesting that he is simultaneously frank (honest) and phoney (false).

Nor is Fielding the only queer character to frustrate Self's attempt to affirm sexual difference. Throughout the narrative Self's responses are governed by clear demarcations of gender boundaries: "the first thing I wonder about a woman is: will I fuck it? Similarly, the first thing I wonder about a man is: will I fight it?" (238). Ironically, his use of the gender-neutral pronoun "it" subverts the very difference he asserts. Although Self insists, "women, they're different from us, about as different as the French are, say," he contradicts himself when he adds, "but they are Earthling, and very like ourselves" (331). The queer figures that Self encounters also contradict him. Doris Arthur's name and clothes suggest gender ambiguity – "Her manly white shirt...glistened in its silk" (60) – but, even naked, Self mistakes her for a "boy" (225). Self's dentist also subverts gender boundaries: "Boy is she butch. She makes me feel like a starlet. Martha McGilchrist – she's a *bloke*" (172). Self's comment that Martha feminizes him (makes him feel "like a starlet") not only challenges the view that gender is innate but also destabilizes the discrete categories "man" and "woman," reclassifying them as relative terms. Elsewhere Self muses, "A man is womanish without a woman, and vice versa" (258), a statement that undercuts his previous assertion that prison is a "manworld" (254). Self wonders if the character Thursday – who greets him at Guyland's apartment – is a transvestite or a transsexual, and his inability to decode Thursday's gender further negates his claims about difference: "I think she's a bloke" (320). The topless dancer's "tomboy face" (7), Martina's "tomboy smile" (134), and Ella Llewellyn's "boyish bob" (365) likewise erode gender boundaries. Even Selina, the epitome of femininity (Selina was the Greek goddess of the moon, a traditional symbol of femininity), has a mannish torso characterized by "erect triangularity" (129). Nub Forkner's masculinity is reflected in his name (*nub* signifies *knob*, slang for *penis*) but qualified when Self declares him a "bearded lady" (220). Additionally, Self's Manhattan taxi driver possesses a face that is "barnacled and girlish with bright eyes and prissy lips" (2), and as their names suggest, Martina Twain and Martin A(mis) are doubles (*twain/two*), suggesting they share a dual gender identity that transcends sexual difference.

Amis rejects the notion of a singular and secure gender identity from the outset of the novel; however, towards *Money*'s end he suggests the possibility – or indeed the necessity – of transcending gender altogether. The Martin Amis character's inability to distinguish between chess pieces accentuates the novel's deconstruction of sexual difference. Selecting a piece at random he asks, "What's this? A king or a queen?" (372). Because the piece in question is a gender-neutral pawn, it becomes as queer as Self, who is a "pawn" in Goodney's game (377). Although pawns have the least value of all chess pieces, Self affirms the importance of the queer subject by unwittingly quoting Philidor: "pawns are the souls of chess" (376). Moreover, by the end of the novel, Self has begun to transcend binary categorization. From the outset, he addresses the reader in gendered terms – "Oh it's true man. Sister, don't kid yourself" (4) – but the penultimate paragraph closes with his declaration, "Humans, I honour you" (394). His use of "humans" rather than gender-specific terminology indicates a subtle but significant shift in his perspective that offers the tentative promise of change.

Although feminist criticism has generated valuable debate about the representation of gender in Amis's work, a queer reading of *Money* offers a useful way of rethinking feminist readings of the text. By focusing on the instability and plurality of gender and sexuality, a queer reading prompts a reconsideration of the view that *Money* is a sexist text that "does not transgress the established boundaries of the patriarchal order" (Doan, 76). Focusing on the novel's deconstruction of "man" and "woman," such a reading also illustrates that *Money* escapes the binary structures that its critique of masculinity appears to uphold. Arguably, Amis anticipates the emergence of queer theory in the early 1990s but, unlike queer theory, does not overlook that formations of gender and sexuality are shaped by capitalism. Through the elaboration of a queer perspective, *Money*'s powerful critique of capitalism is vitally combined with an equally powerful and previously unacknowledged critique of heteropatriarchy.

Note

1   Had Margaret Thatcher – instigator of homophobic legislation that criminalized the "promotion" of homosexuality – been more familiar with this slang, she may not have been so flattered by the moniker "Iron Lady."

Works cited

Amis, Martin. *Money*. 1984. London: Penguin, 1985.

——. *The War Against Cliché: Essays and Reviews 1971–2000*. 2001. London: Vintage, 2002.

Butler, Judith. *Gender Trouble: Feminism and the Subversion of Identity*. London: Routledge, 1990.

Cronin, Gloria L. "An Introduction to Saul Bellow." 26 July 2005. <http://www.saulbellow.org/NavigationBar/LifeandWorks.html>.

Diedrick, James. *Understanding Martin Amis*. Columbia: U of South Carolina P, 1995.

Doan, Laura L. "'Sexy Greedy Is the Late Eighties': Power Systems in Amis's *Money* and Churchill's *Serious Money*." *Minnesota Review* 34–5 (Spring–Fall 1990): 69–80.

FitzHerbert, Claudia. "Amis on Amis." *Daily Telegraph* 12 Nov. 2001.

Garber, Marjorie. *Vested Interests: Cross-Dressing and Cultural Anxiety*. 1992. London: Penguin, 1993.

Grossberg, Benjamin Scott. "'The Tender Passion Was Very Rife Among Us': Coverdale's Queer Utopia and *The Blithedale Romance*." *Studies in American Fiction* 28.1 (Spring 2000): 3–25.

Haffenden, John. "Martin Amis." *Novelists in Interview*. London: Methuen, 1985. 1–24.

Keulks, Gavin. *Father and Son: Kingsley Amis, Martin Amis, and the British Novel Since 1950*. Madison: U of Wisconsin P, 2003.

Mars-Jones, Adam. *Venus Envy*. London: Chatto & Windus, 1990.

Matz, Robert. "Slander, Renaissance Discourses of Sodomy, and *Othello*." *ELH* 66.2 (Summer 1999): 261–76.

Michener, Charles. "Britain's Brat of Letters." *Esquire* Jan. 1987: 108–11.

Mills, Sara. "Working with Sexism: What can Feminist Text Analysis Do?" *Twentieth-Century Fiction: From Text to Context*. Eds. Peter Verdonk and Jean Jacques Weber. London: Routledge, 1995. 206–19.

Miller, Laura. "The Sadistic Muse." *Salon*.com 10 Feb. 1998. <http://dir.salon.com/books/int/1998/02/cov_si_10int.html>.

Miller, Karl. *Doubles: Studies in Literary History*. Oxford: Oxford UP, 1985.

Miracky, James L. "Hope Lost or Hyped Lust? Gendered Representations of 1980s Britain in Margaret Drabble's *The Radiant Way* and Martin Amis's *Money*." *Critique* 44.2 (2003): 136–43.

Morrison, Susan. "The Wit and the Fury of Martin Amis." *Rolling Stone* 17 May 1990: 95–102.

Naughtie, James. *BBC Book Club.* 5 Aug. 2001.

Padhi, Shanti. "Bed and Bedlam: The Hard-Core Extravaganzas of Martin Amis." *Literary Half-Yearly* 23.1 (1982): 36–42.

Powell, Neil. "What Life Is: The Novels of Martin Amis." *PN Review* 7 (1981): 42–5.

Ryan, Kiernan. "Sex, Violence and Complicity: Martin Amis and Ian McEwan." *An Introduction to Contemporary Fiction.* Ed. Rod Mengham. Cambridge: Polity, 1999. 203–18.

Schor, Naomi. "Male Lesbianism." *GLQ* 7.3 (2001): 391–9.

Sedgwick, Eve Kosofsky. *Epistemology of the Closet.* Berkeley: U of California P, 1990.

Sheppard, R.Z. "Money: A Suicide Note." *Time* 11 Mar. 1985: 70–1.

Showalter, Elaine. "Ladlit." *On Modern British Fiction.* Ed. Zachery Leader. Oxford: Oxford UP, 2002. 60–76.

Tyson, Lois. *Critical Theory Today: A User Friendly Guide.* New York: Garland, 1998.

Vining, Edward P. *The Mystery of Hamlet.* Philadelphia: J.B. Lippincott, 1881.

Woods, Gregory. *A History of Gay Literature: The Male Tradition.* New Haven: Yale UP, 1999.

5
Martin Amis and Late-twentieth-century Working-class Masculinity: *Money* and *London Fields*

Philip Tew
Brunel University

According to Berthold Schoene-Harwood: "Under patriarchy a man's reticence and silence constitute insidious imperatives that safeguard and control his masculine authenticity. For a man to speak about his gender in a critical self-conscious manner already indicates that he has failed to live up to the patriarchal ideal and that, consequently, his masculinity is 'in trouble'" (viii). In both *Money* (1984) and *London Fields* (1989), Martin Amis intensifies the satirical and comic mode found in his previous work, and centers his texts on the exaggerated vulgarities, the demotic impulses, and the literal and verbal frenzy of patriarchal masculinity. In contrast to Schoene-Harwood, such self-consciousness is explicit in Amis's work, not insidious. This self-reflection relentlessly considers the masculine in terms of action, events, and underlying desires, helping to evoke the heterogeneity of elements that impact individuals or groups. In this essay I intend to critique the class perspective inherent in the protagonists of these novels, Amis's crowning achievements of the 1980s. In so doing I do not intend to summarize their plots, indicate overall textual character-istics, or annotate major themes and motifs, because these have been more than adequately represented by James Diedrick, Gavin Keulks, and Anne-Laure Fortin-Tournès. Rather, I will dissect Amis's view of urban working-class masculinity and in so doing interrogate the conflicted and perhaps undermining position of the author in class terms. I therefore seek to detail (or deconstruct) aspects of his relation-ship to that central and very particular masculinity: a white working-class commonality that becomes an archetype for critics. Sara Mills, for instance, has detailed Amis's innate meta-linguistic bias in *London*

Fields, identifying a schemata or "intermediate structure between the language items and the ideology of sexism" (207). In a similar interstitial space, Amis's class prejudices are deeply structured by implicit assumptions that I read similarly to Mills: as the overall outcome of "a complex of statements, which, taken together, combine to form an ideological viewpoint" (214).

The two novels under scrutiny are characterized by their density, complexity, and – most significant to my analysis – masculine perspectives. Their narrators – John Self and Keith Talent – demand close attention. Among their peers they may not be highly regarded, but they are relentlessly visible and discussed. Social interactions create their identities, mirroring R.W. Connell's conclusion that "Masculinities are neither programmed in our genes, nor fixed by social structure, prior to social interaction.... They are actively produced, using the resources and strategies available in a given social setting" (12). Stylistically Amis produces streams of phrases that draw attention to themselves, but he socially contextualizes such matters, relating them to masculine self-images within class frameworks. In *Money*, for instance, John Self recalls, "All my commercials featured a big bim in cool pants and bra. It was sort of my trademark. No one said my ads were subtle. But boy did they sell fast food" (69–70). The humor resides not only in the reader's recognition of a commercialized, commodifying advertising industry, but also in Self's own typology. He is a cultural philistine whose only acuity appears to be a Thatcherite sense of money, which he worships and is ultimately unable to control. Given his class origin, this may be problematic, as it seems predicated upon the worst British class prejudices. In *London Fields*, the writer-narrator Samson Young, reflects:

> Guy had of course been friendly with people like Keith before: in the City. [...] They weren't poor, like Keith. Keith had his fistfuls of fivers, his furled tenners and folded fifties; but Keith was poor. His whole person said it. And this was why Guy honoured him and pitied him and admired him and envied him (and, he sometimes thought, even vaguely *fancied* him): because he was poor. (91)

The sexual ambivalence hints at Guy's problematic self-image, a covert and under-acknowledged desire projected on a quasi-authentic other. Again, however, the underlying class-critique is stereotypical. Despite the novel's plethora of detail, the characters are curiously mono-dimensional. Applying Schoene-Harwood's overly schematic account of reflexive masculinity (as an implicitly singularized category) would neutralize Amis's self-evident class perspective. This has been a tendency in examining Amis's work, however. Critics have interpreted Amis unproblematically in class terms, responding mainly to the topographical rhetoric of his narratives and marginalizing subtler nuances. Such a strategy allows critics covertly to universalize the presence of patriarchy (as though undifferentiated or monolithic) and further permit a self-avowing radicalism such as Lea and Schoene do when they claim to be engaged in an emancipatory project. At best this is posturing. Lea and Schoene do broadly identify one context that is relevant to an understanding of Amis's "bloke" novels – the visibility of masculinity:

> Masculinity has now become visible as a gender, and in many of its flesh-and-blood realizations it appears both ready and suitable. However, as a fixed set of ideologically motivated imperatives and ideals, inscribed and upheld by patriarchal heteronormativity, it still proves to be as markedly resilient and persistent as it is now anachronistic. (8)

Of course their appeals to change imply a radical project and critique, one that fails to differentiate culture and text in class terms. Certainly, cultural and textual nuances of reading and representation determine a period's (or region's) aesthetic: what should be validated, ironized, or dismissed. Neither representing nor critiquing the characterization of working-class males within patriarchy is sufficient or radical unless the complex class ideology is closely examined. Moreover, to talk of a "gradual postmodern dismantling of the patriarchal inscription of masculinity as the one subjectivity that remains forever definitively uncontaminated by 'difference'," as Lea and Schoene do, remains profoundly universalistic and uncritical of the class blindness that haunts contemporary British fiction and academic exegesis. This applies specifically to renditions of the working classes, as can be seen in Amis's fiction. As Ben Knights explains:

> A set of inverse snobberies and ignorance seems to lead to a semi-articulated and widespread belief that working-class men – a grouping itself forged in the struggle against oppression – somehow expresses masculinity in a purer form. They thus become the objects at once of social horror ... and simultaneously a kind of awed admiration. Such fantasies are organized around icons of uninhibited physicality, strength, drinking, male bonding, and a no-nonsense orientation towards the world. (181)

This quotation helps to situate Guy's impulses in *London Fields*, his curious attraction toward an innate working-class masculinity that masks his underlying repugnance. This emerges through his compulsive rivalry, as when he tries to warn Nicola Six about the true nature of Keith Talent, the working-class cheat and darts player who is the locus of his almost fetishistic adulation. Amis stresses the unconscious, involuntary nature of Guy's opinion:

> She shrugged minutely and said, 'I suppose he's rather an attractive character.'
> 'Of course you know,' Guy heard himself saying, 'that in some ways he's little better than a common criminal. Or worse.'
> 'Or worse? Guy, I'm shocked. I think it's so unkind to judge people by hearsay. Or by their backgrounds.'
> 'Just so long as you know. I mean, you haven't found anything missing. Cash. Jewellery. Clothes.'
> 'Clothes?'
> 'Scarves. Belts. He might give them to his girlfriends. He's got lots of girlfriends, you know. Underwear.' (318)

Guy comes off worse in this exchange, manipulated by Nicola. His attitudes are generic rather than individualizing and, in class terms, are conventionally dismissive of his supposed inferiors and deeply entrenched. In presuming Keith might serve as a handyman, Nicola exhibits a similar range of assumptions, affording Amis many opportunities for humor related to the apparent resistance of dumb objects.

For Connell masculinity is always a practice that must be regarded as "necessarily a social construction" (29). Amis reflects such practices humorously. Through football – an enjoyment that Guy and Keith unknowingly share – Amis inverts social expectations, with Guy in the cheaper section, Keith in the more expensive:

> Both men supported Queens Park Rangers, the local team, and for years had been shuffling off to Loftus Road on Saturday afternoons. In fact they might have come across each other earlier, but this had never been likely: Guy stood on the terraces, with his pie and Bovril, whereas Keith was always to be found with his flask in the stands. (90)

Perhaps this mirrors a failed attempt at what Connell calls "the collective construction of masculinities in adult peer groups" (12–13). The characters fail to connect because social behavior remains nuanced and subject to chance, as Amis demonstrates. Additionally, Keith exhibits a curious inauthenticity, mirroring the collective forms of formal communication with regard to sport. His jargonized commentary mimics professional sports reports: formulaic, full of cliché, yet oddly accepted by his peers. Like his obsessive compulsion for Nicola and his cheerleading for Keith's darts matches, Guy hopes football will engage him to the alien world of men. But he objectifies the other as much as his wife. Connell believes desire and emotion are psychologically, sociologically, and therefore ideologically constitutive (25), and he insists that "masculinities" are subject to diversity:

> Issues about masculinity are ... made no easier by the recent influence of a school of pop psychologists who offer a highly simplified view of the problems of men. Their central idea is that modern men are suffering from a deep psychological wound, being cut off from the true or deep masculinity that is their heritage. (5)

Existing outside of a settled pattern of behavior, Guy – who despite his Oxford education is defined by dimness – struggles to cope with the world and his emotions, seeking to overturn the dynamics that underpin British culture.

Guy could be taken to emblematize patriarchy, but only if it is seen as fluid, adaptive – a true product of the ambivalence of modernity and threatened by apocalypse. Consider the conceptual assumptions subtending Berthold-Schoene's covert notion of the "patriarchal *Bildung*" as an "authoritative catalogue of normative standards" (178). Unless one can truly regard the patriarchal as essentially monolithic *and* precisely determining, then such an ideology simply consists of hegemonic tendencies, spaces of possibility (*pace* Bourdieu) within the complexity of masculinities. Even patriarchy itself implicitly acknowledges such heterogeneity in its insistent attempt to avow conformist identities to resist disorder, responding to the challenge of the inchoate. A critique such as Berthold-Schoene's exhibits a tempting self-avowal, since patriarchy structures and curtails behavior within ethical and moral codes. This produces his neglect of class perspective. His tendency is to indulge in the very kind of reification of masculinity that Connell refers to as threatening "a drift away from concern with institutions, power relations, and social inequalities" (23).

Guy Clinch contrasts his wife, who demonstrates no self-doubt, no desire to explore the streets, and no underlying sexual ambiguities. She simply betrays him with an international tennis player. As Keith reflects:

> Some women didn't like otherness; they didn't like the other, when it came to the other. Hope Clinch, now: there was a perfect example of a rich lady who didn't like a bit of rough. They looked right through you and out the other side; for them you were nothing, not even animal – you were nothing. And Keith knew very well that he *was* a bit of rough, relatively speaking, at least for the time being. (112)

The qualifying phrases ironically refer to Keith's desire for transcendence through darts, a clearly delusional social construct given the activity's irredeemable class nature. To Keith, Hope's nullity is unsurprising whereas Guy's patronage is intriguing. Guy appears subject to change, but he remains conventionally patriarchal with regard to Nicola. His class perspective is more complex, and may be regarded as contradictory. This transition may suggest that even a figure who is more than residually patriarchal can be regarded as what Schoene-Harwood describes as a "dynamic *sujet en process*," a category he privileges through application to contemporary, supposedly plural and fragmented subjects (179). But such an orientation essentially dehistoricizes and parodies the past as both un-differentiated and homogenous. Patriarchy is no less an example of the "artificial make-up" (182) of culturally inscribed behavior. Patriarchy might be more outwardly repressive and endemic than other decodes or patterns, but Schoene-Harwood's critique finally depends upon inaccurate self-privileging definitions. Amis's *London Fields* demonstrates that even patriarchal, archetypal males are subject to a "dynamic *sujet en process*" as a state of becoming.

The distance between Guy and Keith demonstrates the plurality of the residue of such mutually exhibited patriarchy. The differences may appear to be submerged in or transcended by the pattern of male behavior, but differentiation remains illusory. In terms of the narrative's parameters, however, Guy can neither be excluded from, nor fully participate in, this otherness, except superficially. He represents sentimentality whereas Keith confirms a vulgarized existence. Nicole perceives this underlying conflict of values, seeing "Two broad fronts: the cloudy trophies of Guy's archaic heart; Keith Talent, and his reptile modernity" (192). However, one could argue that, through this relationship, Amis cannot resist parodying and inverting the mythology of the Angry Young Men referred to by Ian Haywood, who articulates an archetypal "home-grown version of the rebel-without-a-cause [which] is an anti-hero of the lower classes" (94). Amis Jr. would here be subtly mocking his father's first novel. His graduate is upper class and stupid; the working-class protagonist a different kind of "charmless" anti-hero.

Money and *London Fields* cannot be simply regarded as coterminous. Amis resists this linkage explicitly in *London Fields*, paradoxically appealing to ontological realities – especially the universality of death – through the reflections of his novelist-narrator, Samson Young:

> The form itself is my enemy. All this damned romance. In fiction (rightly so called), people become coherent and intelligible – and they aren't like that. We all know they aren't. We all know it from personal experience. We've been there. [...]
> Death helps. Death gives us something to do. Because it's a full-time job looking the other way. (240)

This relational framework, with its universality of finitude, its commonality, and the inter-subjective necessity that grounds both writing and implied readership – all implicit in Samson's view of his craft – confirms that even in apocalyptic worlds one can retrieve Amis's observations about working-class masculinity without assuming they merely represent life. As Samson Young indicates, such socially constructed types are either false literary stereotypes or drawn from the ontological confusion of the world.

In a collaborative volume, Slavoj Žižek responds to Judith Butler's critique of the "hidden bias and exclusion of universality" ("Class Struggle", 102). Chiefly, he contends that however subtle her denouncement of the privileging effect of particular content by the universal (101), such ideas culminate not in absolute, fixed form but rather what Žižek describes as:

> the other, "living", "concrete" universality of the permanent process of the questioning and renegotiation of its own "official" content. Universality becomes "actual" precisely and only by rendering thematic the exclusions on which it is grounded, by continuously questioning, renegotiating, displacing them... (102)

Butler responds in "Restaging the Universal," concurring with Žižek regarding the "incompletion" of reality and reminding that:

> every subject,... is liable to the same postulate of inconclusiveness. The subject which comes into existence through the "bar" is one

whose prehistory is necessarily foreclosed to its experience of itself
as a subject. That founding and defining limit thus founds the
subject at a necessary and irreversible distance from the conditions
of its own traumatic emergence. (12)

Such incompletion and lack of accomplishment (whose meaning I read
as resolution) haunt both Amis texts – formally, rhetorically, and in
terms of characterization. Despite the sheer volume of detail concerning
the key male characters – John Self, Keith Talent, and Guy Clinch – a
Shandyean regress emerges. The overall picture eludes the reader – inten-
tionally so, I suggest. One only comes to know these characters through
their unreliable accounts, retold unreliably in *London Fields*, as Samson
Young – the most unreliable of narrators – continually reminds the
reader.

Money and *London Fields* are not simply witty satires but particularly
inflected dark comedies. Amis's subject matter is somber and transgressive, satisfying the notion of the comedic that he described to
Christopher Bigsby:

> Comedies are full of things that shouldn't really be in comedies, like
> rape and murder and child abuse, real sin and evil. A comic novelist,
> of course, doesn't work things out with the strictness of the tragic
> writer; he doesn't reward and punish and convert. All he can do
> with these evils is laugh them off stage. There are some things,
> though, that can't be laughed off the stage. (25)

Uncomfortable as it has proved for some readers, Amis has persuaded
many that bleakly comic possibilities reside in trauma, buoyed by the
expressionistic mania of his style, a kind of literary Max Wall and
Buster Keaton synthesized with more than a touch of Lenny Bruce and
Johnny Vegas. As John Self says in *Money*: "Recently my life feels like a
bloodcurdling joke. Recently my life has taken on *form*. Something is
waiting. I am waiting. Soon, it will stop waiting – any day now. Awful
things can happen any time. This is the awful thing" (3–4). Self's anti-
cipatory intuition – and his name, of course – are matters of reflexive
humor and the comedy of the human condition. So too is his notion
of his recent "formal" transformation ironic but yet accurate: he
doesn't, after all, assume form until the book is read. Another interpretative imperative exists, however, since all of these comic devices serve
to evoke an authorial presence lurking in the text like some pan-
tomime monster. They reestablish a privileged position based on

authorial tradition and the finely calibrated nuances of the English class-system.

This underlying authorial superiority complicates considerations of the working-class masculinity in both texts when read as a universal category or code, for despite particularities which suggest divergent narrative emphases, common, self-evident features are nevertheless identifiable. Such elements remain central to any informed deconstruction of their multiple layers. The concerns of the working-class characters seem narrow, their analysis of life cynical and blinkered. Both narratives are determinedly reflexive: they are *about* writing and authorship, self-consciously featuring acts of reading and of writing. Both are London novels, centering upon pub culture, street-life, and what might generally be termed "blokishness."

As well as attempting to understand the nature of these "working-class blokes" in terms of their textual framing, one is obliged to consider the author's and narrator's relations with their worlds. However pluralistic the novel becomes, issues of ideological representation and authenticity are suggested by such a relationship. These are intricate and detailed exegetical tasks, and an awareness of the issues of class and economic stratifications is essential to unraveling or deconstructing Amis's aesthetic rendering of masculinity. Questions of literary masculinity are too easily framed in simplistic terms masquerading as gendered rhetoric. The lack of class critique, I contend, is one of the central problems in the apparently reasonable and contemporary questions asked by Daniel Lea and Berthold Schoene in "Masculinity in Transition: An Introduction." Lea and Schoene ask, "How successfully and by what representational means have men begun to contest, subvert, reconstruct, or resuscitate androcentric paradigms of many being?" (7). What men, one feels compelled to ask? Is this a universalizing category, where the notion of the universal is apparently problematized but misunderstood?

The nature of the dark comedy alluded to by Amis may also be multiple, capable of being periodized, affected by the five years that lie between the two novels. *London Fields* and *Money* derive from very different social, cultural, and economic phases, as Lynne Segal comments: "by the close of the 1980s, little seemed to remain but the insatiable profit-seeking force of global capitalism, following the pacification of class struggle, tireless ideological assault on Keynesian social democracy and its belief in public planning, all rendered emblematic with the final collapse of the USSR and its satellites" (142–3). Patrick Brantlinger argues that *Money*'s portrayals of "shady, petty dealings in high finance mirror the supposedly legitimate, grand-scale monetary dealings of Thatcherite Britain, Reaganite America, and much of the rest of the world" (259). The novel's depiction of sex seems periodized by its historicity, for in a pre-Aids world, it threatens to be equally excessive and unbridled. John Self is an archetype of fear and self-loathing, a character Knights sees as deriving from the Dostoevskyan underground man, exemplified by "his fascination with his own degradation" (124). This particular influence is noted by Diedrick (73–4) and summarized as concerning a "manic, profane, [and] perversely perceptive" view (26). In an oft-quoted statement, the Martin Amis character objects to Self's notion of motivation, contending that, "as a controlling force in human affairs, motivation is pretty well shagged out by now" (*Money*, 359). Self is oblivious to the double-irony of the Amis persona. Nevertheless, a poignant scene follows which demonstrates that Self does possess – despite his working-class made-good credentials – a high degree of suppressed self-knowledge. This sensitivity is conveyed obliquely when he visits his "posh" friend, Alec, whose ten-year-old daughter offers an object that symbolizes Self's life – both textually and supra-textually – in the hands of the middle-class author:

> "Hello, will you fix it? It's new," she said, and gave me the dead thing. "I'm ten now," [...]
> The toy umbrella dangled from my hand. It was cheap and knew it wasn't meant to last long. I knew it was meant to break. They say everything wants to persist in its being. Even sand wants to go on being sand. It doesn't want to break. But I don't know. This umbrella looked relieved that it had broken, had broken out of the world of definition and was just a sprig of plastic again.
> "I'll buy you a new one," I said. "But now I've got to run." (366)

Ironically this appeal to "fix" things recurs in Nicola's more sexualized appeal to Keith. In a world of entropy, the male ought to redeem the incurable obsolescent. Perhaps partially it suggests the obsolescent nature of such versions of masculinity. This image of the broken umbrella is poignant because of the cruelty and sentimentality inherent in the image of the child with her broken new toy. (A similar ludic quality is inherent to the depiction of Nicola Six, the monstrous child having grown older and not matured.) The scene ends ironically as they pass the point on the stairs where Self once cuckolded his friend. He confesses this perfidy to Alec, who similarly confesses to an affair – with Self's own lover Selina. The irony lies in the comparison that Self has been manipulated out of shape, or broken; of course, as a fictional character, he has no being to inhabit, and therefore metonymically resembles a toy's vulnerability and inauthenticity. The symbol seems to signify his unconscious knowledge and admission of his fictional status.

In its structure and texture, *London Fields* remains unresolved, fractured, and less mimetically inclined than *Money*, even though the former exhibits a mimetic impulse that is casual and frantic, suffused by stylistic marginalia. Because of its greater disassociation, *London Fields* remains more disjointed in terms of its characterization, and its focus spread wider: an apocalyptic world situated as an insistent and yet unspecified subtext. Its archetypes are rendered through almost pantomimic grotesqueries. Knights regards the novel as fundamentally articulating "collective fears haunting the moment of writing – nuclear war (accidental or planned), the degradation of the city, the emergence of an alienated and violent underclass, escalating environmental and atmospheric degradation" (207). No partial resolution occurs, for at the end of *Money* Self reverts to type, sleeping with a large hairdresser girlfriend, Georgina. In *London Fields*, the entire world remains in crisis – a crisis more fundamental than the Thatcherite-Reaganite excesses of the 1980s – because its continuation is threatened.

Anne-Laure Fortin-Tournès offers a generally perceptive critique that refuses the full implication of literary influence and the fine nuances of social context. She sees the novel as an inversion of hierarchies and traditional humanist values (19), regards its representations of birth, love, and death as expressive within either a burlesque mode or the mock-heroic (19–20), and identifies the novel as a quintessential postmodern text, reflecting both a mode of writing and a broader critique characterized by crisis, both irremediable and immanent (11–12). Despite her acute close reading, however, her overall interpretative position tends to predetermine the text schematically. Importantly, she identifies an aspect of the protagonist to argue that the novel does not judge from a position of authority but affirms the power of literature to interrogate discursive structures (14). She reads Keith Talent as a grotesque con-man and proletarian caricature, enlisted as the "baddy" (19) who demonstrates no remorse for his legal and moral offenses (50). However, she overlooks an important cultural determinant. One ought to wonder whether such parodies of the working-class or proletarian male found in these novels can be sufficiently ironic to be reduced to generic, textual, or postmodern matters, especially when articulated from positions of cultural authority, whether represented by the novel form itself or from Amis's own self-evident class-specific position.

The emphasis on other issues tends to displace this important theme from analysis, and I wish to redress this balance. Scholarship on these novels has largely centered on formal issues: the use of demotic voice and tone, Amis's sexism, or self-reflexivity. Chapters five and seven of Nicolas Tredell's critical guide offer an instructive overview, providing a paradigm of how the text is inflected by critics' covert, assumptive views of working-class male identity and its secondary relation to broader generic concerns. What soon becomes evident is that, despite the innumerable thematic and generic detail, little close scrutiny has been applied to Amis's ironic position toward his working-class protagonists and the implications of his response to masculinity. John Self is for Eric Korn an "upstart" (56); for Karl Miller a "guttersnipe" (66); and for Laura Doan "The epitome of the racist, sexist homophobe" (75), a *"parvenu par excellence"* (76). As far as Keith Talent is concerned, he is for Penny Smith "petty crook, wife-beater, rapist" (101); for Brian Finney "a working class yob" (104); for Frederick Holmes "a womanizing petty crook" (113); and for Peter Stokes an "overgrown Dickensian street urchin, [and] a professional cheat" (120). Both characters are apparently central and yet peripheral, relegated into parody and cliché by the demands of the text.

First is the need to sustain a superior, ironizing voice. Second, Amis frames the demotic and everyday with the structural dictates of elaborate, reflexive narration. Finally, such reflexivity prioritizes an intellectual and aesthetic culture both allusively and schematically. It requires an external perspective of the world-views of these protagonists (given their unreliability), and thus creates an implicit ethical hierarchy. Their elaboration lies elsewhere. It is thematic rather than personal. Keulks concludes that "Regardless of how much money he has, Self is denied the boon of intellect, reason, and logic. Self, however, understands only the rhetoric of consumption, and his ignorance of altruism thwarts his numerous attempts at self-improvement, regardless of whether he craves acceptance by class or by women" (182). In fact, Self turns out to have a facility at chess, but is nevertheless defeated by his creator. The Martin Amis persona reflects on events in the same language as an author pondering his plot, and the text therefore deconstructs Self's reductive masculine identity, revealing its fragility and universalizing ambitions.

"Can you remember," [Martin Amis] asked, "can you remember what Fielding said, in the alley, after the fight? He said something. Can you remember what it was?"

"I don't know. You – new man dog. Something like that. It didn't make sense."

"Could it have been inhuman dog? ... Fascinating. Pure transference. Oh damned Iago. Tell you what. You're better than I thought but this is still money for jam. If you win, I pay up. If we draw, you win – I'll give you the game. If I win – I just take something from you. Anything I want, but just one thing." He pointed to the dice. "The money's sort of a joke, by now anyway, or a symbol. Sex, status, phallic. Have I left any out?"

The cunning bastard, I thought. Oh, I caught that reference to his own little rattletrap. He's definitely after my Fiasco. (377)

This exchange depends upon two modes of masculinity: one archetypal and hegemonically inscribed (Self's); the other reflective, knowing, and informed (Amis himself and the Amis persona). Note the implicit opposition. As Keulks explains, the blackness, the dark humor and cynicism, even the satirical dismissiveness derive from Evelyn Waugh, but Amis abjures Waugh's nostalgia (83–4). Amis even alludes to Waugh parenthetically in Samson's characterization of Guy in *London Fields*, when he imagines the book as a film:

There must be a dozen hot actresses who would kill for the part of Nicola Six. I can think of several bankable stalwarts who could handle Guy (the ones who do Evelyn Waugh heroes: meek, puzzled, pointlessly handsome). As for Keith, you'd need a total-immersion expert, a dynamic literalist who'd live like a trog for two or three years as part of his preparation for the role. (282)

The knowingness in the chess passage above derives partly from Waugh's satirical dynamics and parameters, but also is rooted in a liberal humanist intellectual culture whose most active figure is Martina Twain. She "comes to epitomize what James Diedrick and Tamás Bényei define as the moral center of the novel, its crisis point of value and genuine emotion" (Keulks, 181). Amis the author plays out a relationship much as described by Žižek in "Da Capo Senza Fine," one that is part of a universalizing assumption by a broad new critique that assumes its radicalism in terms of archetypes and gender, and potentially its aesthetic and ethical superiority. "It is not that before, people were 'stupid essentialists' and believed in naturalized sexuality while now they know that genders are performatively enacted," Žižek explains. "[O]ne needs a kind of metanarrative that explains this very passage from essentialism to the awareness of contingency" (6). The setting of this scene is suggestive, as Amis's retreat into his flat could represent a dehistoricizing withdrawal from the world of the novel and indeed from any extensive external reference, however diffuse, to reality. Self – and the self-identity of the other from Amis's authorial/ narrative viewpoint – risks becoming a cipher.

That may well be Amis's point, but this reduction risks reducing Self's self-projection and the comprehension of otherness in two major ways. First by implication: unless it is simplistically privileged, the legitimacy of authorial narrative becomes suspect. Second, Amis appears to contract his fiction to the merely ludic or radically anti-real. A kind of eternal *regressus* detours from meaning and from the contextual realities that animate the laughter, the grotesqueries, and the familiarity upon which the novels depend. As playfulness, the ethical and social position of this maneuver is suspect. I'd prefer to see it as a complex reflection upon the real, mirroring the articulation of hurtfulness and identity described by Žižek when he limits Butler's notion of re-signifying identity, contending that although injurious comments can be assumed mockingly they cannot finally be overcome or subsumed:

> Apropos of what kind of speech acts does the distance between pretending and being ... collapse? Apropos of speech acts which aim at the other in the Real of his or her being: hate speech, aggressive humiliation, and so on. In such cases, no amount of disguising it with the semblance of a joke or irony can prevent it from having a hurtful effect – we touch the Real when the efficiency of such symbolic markers of distance is suspended. ("Da Capo", 223)

By his perverse attacks is Amis reminding us about the vulnerability of humanity to typological reduction, to the archetypal movement of myth and history? If so, there remains a liberal humanist kernel beneath this hard narrative nut. One might wish to exonerate Amis by appealing to the Menippean satire that both Diedrick and Keulks identify, the latter commenting that this allows an "incongruous world [which] deliberately subverts conventional facets of normality and stability, including those of language and verisimilitude," blending "Fantastical, comic, and parodic elements" with "'crude underworld naturalism'" (153). The result, Keulks argues, occurs *"within the novel"* [my emphasis], a contingency and amorality that act as textual markers and narrative co-ordinates. However, satire is either broadly reductive of all dignity (Waugh) or a privileging can reassert itself. I consider the latter to be the case in Amis. Moreover, in terms of overall textual reception – sociologically, ideologically, and aesthetically – such partializing satire creates a context in which the author must carefully calibrate the potential stereotypical and inscribed responses to the character type.

There remains something patronizing about the chess game between John Self and the Martin Amis character, a residue of irremovable reductiveness that derives from the Amis character's voice and echoes the implicitly vengeful God of the Pentateuch. The underlying basis of this elevation of the projected self is intriguing. The problem remains that the parody called Self is Amis's creation, his bauble, his toy. For all its amusing, layered references to authorship and the overall authority of a male, liberal humanist voice, this portrait depends upon both, representing a vision of the unknowable other especially in class terms that rests upon the intellectual power of the middle-class writer. That Amis chooses to talk about the "Self" may be humorous and punning, but that part of the authorial act remains curiously inappropriate as well.

Finally, it is left for me to wonder whether, for all its grotesqueries, the quotidian in Amis can sufficiently rise above the bitter class perspectives, the ranting opinions of occluded world-views and the parodic. I'm not sure I can answer that question, but I will not be enfolded into the limits of vision simply by celebrating rhetorical and formal virtuosity (of which Amis exhibits plenty). Amis does far more than this, teasing his readers with the precocity and ambivalence of masculinity. In so doing, he deconstructs heterogeneity as a concept, demonstrating that even patriarchal, archetypal males are subject to what Schoene-Harwood describes as a "dynamic *sujet en process*," a state of becoming. Those males, or male characters, simply might not become what the liberal reader would prefer to see.

Works cited

Amis, Martin. *London Fields*. London: Jonathan Cape, 1989.
——. *Money*. London: Jonathan Cape, 1984.
Bigsby, Christopher, ed. *Writers in Conversation*. Vol. 1. Norwich: Arthur Miller, 2000.
Brantlinger, Patrick. *Fictions of State: Culture and Credit in Britain, 1694–1994*. Ithaca and London: Cornell UP, 1996.
Butler, Judith, Ernesto Laclau, and Slavoj Žižek. *Contingency, Hegemony, Universality: Contemporary Dialogues on the Left*. London and New York: Verso, 2000.
Butler, Judith. "Restaging the Universal." Butler, Laclau, Žižek. 11–43.
Connell, R.W. *The Men and the Boys*. Cambridge: Polity, 2000.

86 *Martin Amis: Postmodernism and Beyond*

Diedrick, James. *Understanding Martin Amis*. 2nd ed. Columbia: U of South Carolina P, 2004.
Fortin-Tournès, Anne-Laure. *Martin Amis: le postmodernisme en question*. Rennes, France: U de Rennes, 2003.
Haywood, Ian. *Working-class fiction: from Chartism to Trainspotting*. Plymouth: Northcote, 1997.
Keulks, Gavin. *Father and Son: Kingsley Amis, Martin Amis, and the British Novel Since 1950*. Madison: U of Wisconsin P, 2003.
Knights, Ben. *Writing Masculinities: Male Narratives in Twentieth-Century Fiction*. London: Macmillan, 1999.
Lea, Daniel, and Berthold Schoene. "Masculinity in Transition: An Introduction." *Posting the Male: Masculinities in Post-War and Contemporary British Literature*. Eds. Lea and Schoene. Amsterdam and New York: Rodopi, 2003. 7–17.
Mills, Sara. "Working with sexism: What can feminist text analysis do?" *Twentieth-Century Fiction: From Text to Context*. Eds. Peter Verdonk and Jean Jacques Weber. London and New York: Routledge. 206–19.
Segal, Lynne. "Theoretical Afflictions: Poor Rich White Folks Play The Blues." *Remembering the 1990s*. Eds. Joe Brooker and Roger Luckhurst. *New Formations: A Journal of Culture/Theory/Politics* 50 (Autumn 2003): 142–56.
Schoene-Harwood, Berthold. *Writing Men: Literary Masculinities from Frankenstein to the New Man*. Edinburgh: Edinburgh UP, 2000.
Tredell, Nicolas, ed. *The Fiction of Martin Amis: A Reader's Guide to Essential Criticism*. Cambridge: Icon, 2000.
Žižek , Slavoj. "Class Struggle or Postmodernism? Yes, Please!" Butler, Laclau, Žižek, 90–135.
——. "Da Capo Senza Fine." Butler, Laclau, Žižek, 213–62.

6
The Female Form, Sublimation, and Nicola Six

Susan Brook
Simon Fraser University

Critics have frequently taken Martin Amis to task for the apparent relish with which he depicts his misogynistic characters' predilections, which range from pornography and erotic underwear to rape, as well as his portrayal of female characters as the passive victims of male violence. *London Fields* (1989) raises both these issues, featuring a female murder victim or "murderee," Nicola Six, who stars in her own pornographic films and uses an extensive collection of "wondrous frillies and costliest scanties" (321) to fulfill the fantasies of the hapless grotesque, Keith Talent.[1] Critical discussion about the novel's gender politics has focused overwhelmingly on issues of power and powerlessness. Amis and other critics have defended Nicola against charges of passivity and victimization by claiming that she controls the male characters: she not only sleeps with but also manipulates working-class Keith, aristocratic Guy Clinch, and Samson Young, the narrator. This essay will argue that power and powerlessness have been invoked in problematic ways in discussions of *London Fields*, and in feminist analysis more generally. I seek to refocus the debate about gender and *London Fields* by arguing that the symbolic importance of femininity is primarily related to questions of form and authorship.

I contend that Amis expresses his ambivalent attitude towards aesthetic form through his use of female authorial doubles. Martina Twain (in *Money*) and Nicola Six are linked with aesthetic form and betray Amis's anxieties about the power and limitations of such form. Idealized but undermined, Martina embodies fears and anxieties about the moral purpose of art. Amoral, cynical, and shapely, Nicola is both author and text. She is a radically deconstructive figure who embodies the slippery nature of textuality, breaking down oppositions between form and content, the mediated and the real, the natural and the unnatural, language and the body. Operating to undo categories, Nicola can be read through Bataille's notion of the *informe* – that form which is also formless. However, readings that focus only on the way in which texts destabilize the process of signification risk restabilizing and reifying the meaning of these texts into familiar, well-worn signifieds: the uncertainty of signification and the performativity of gender. Such readings can sublimate content into form so that a novel's status as metafiction becomes the trump card. Yet *London Fields* raises questions about form and representation through a specific representational content: it is a novel not only about ontological and linguistic instability but also about the death of a beautiful, seductive, sterile woman. And its deconstruction is undermined by the connections it establishes between femininity and aesthetic form. Its content, and the signifiers associated with Nicola's "female form" (71), work counter to its deconstructive operations, revealing an anxiety about the sublimating properties of aesthetic form itself: namely that form, for all its shapely beauty and parodic energy, leads to sterility and death.

Lifeless characters and femmes fatales

Feminist critics have slapped *London Fields* around. In 1989 Maggie Gee and Helen McNeil objected to its inclusion on the shortlist for the Booker Prize, arguing that Nicola was a sexist figure of male fantasy. More sustained feminist criticism followed in the nineties, notably from Sara Mills, who uses stylistic analysis and narratology to argue that the novel is not only structured around Nicola's passivity but also naturalizes her lack of agency: "it is not simply the case that the female character is acted upon ... but the fact that she wishes to be acted upon and paradoxically strives to bring that about" (216). Underlying Mills's analysis is the complaint that neither Amis's form nor his content accurately represents reality. In criticizing "ideological complexes like sexism" (218), Mills implies that writers should depict the reality that lies beyond ideology, a real world in which women are "strong and active in the public sphere" (214). A similar logic produces Susie Thomas's polemical denunciation of the novel's characters as "dehumanized cartoons" and "exploitative stereotypes" who perpetuate sexism, racism, and classism, and are "flat because [Amis] has no depth to give them." Like Mills, who objects that Amis's male characters are "lifeless vehicles of an ideology of macho behaviour" (208), Thomas longs for fully rounded realist characters.

Yet it is precisely the "lifeless" quality of Amis's characters that helps to destabilize gender identity by revealing it as both fictional and unstable. Amis shows that reality is frequently what Roland Barthes famously describes as a "reality effect" and that gender identity is the effect of a series of physical performances and linguistic iterations, with the result that it can be exaggerated and manipulated.[2] Throughout *London Fields*, masculinity is hyperreal, often hilariously so. Guy relies on outdated chivalric codes and on D.H. Lawrence as a guide for masculine behavior; meanwhile, Keith is "synthetic modernity (man-made)" (202), and his masculinity is constructed from half-digested television programs and darts manuals: "tears at the dartboard, lachrymae at the oché: this was Keith's personal vision of male heroism and transcendence" (314). Similarly, Nicola's femininity is linguistic and performative: she acts out a series of conflicting male fantasy roles (being a fantasy figure "really takes it out of a girl" [260], she tells Samson), but exceeds these roles, just as she exceeds the conflicting allusions which create her identity, including the devil (Old Nick), Machiavelli, the Femme Fatale, and La Belle Dame Sans Merci.[3]

Amis himself has pointed to Nicola's power and control as a sign that his feminist critics are misguided. However, Amis's position raises many problems. Feminist analyses constructed around the presence or absence of powerful female characters are misguided not only because they frequently desire the putative stability and mimetic accuracy of realism: they also often overlook the complex meanings and effects of power and therefore of the representation of powerful women. As early feminist debates around film noir suggested, powerful women can be aligned with the castrating phallic mother, who is both fetishized and devalued. Amis unwittingly suggests such an interpretation when he defends himself against feminist attacks by telling Will Self: "The only aggressive feeling I have towards women is to do with their power over me. I've spent a big chunk of the last thirty years thinking about them, following them around, wanting to get off with them, absolutely enthralled. That's bound to produce a slave's whinny for mercy every now and then." Although Amis's comments are deliberately provocative, they suggest that supposedly positive representations of powerful women can derive from deeply ambivalent attitudes to women and femininity.

Not only does the celebration of "powerful women" overlook this fact, it is also based on a reductive distinction between power and powerlessness. Amis's novels unsettle such a distinction, in contrast to his facile comments in interviews. Significantly, Amis's apparently powerful characters are in fact powerless, because their actions are controlled by the author. The Martin Amis character in *Money* describes the author's power over the character as absolute: "You can do what the hell you like to him, really. This creates an appetite for punishment. The author is not free of sadistic impulses" (247). However, the power of author figures is also undermined: Martina is betrayed by John Self; Martin Amis's own power over Self is foiled by Martina's placebos; Samson is manipulated by Nicola and dies, as does Nicola herself. Amis satirizes the abuse of power, and the plight of his manipulative author figures might be seen as self-punishment for his own authorial abuses. This interpretation further complicates the notion of power by suggesting that moral power might be gained through weakness or self-punishment. Martin Amis (or "Martin Amis") may be both a sadist and a masochist, and since Freud masochism has been understood as a means to exert or gain power through powerlessness. Certainly, masochism complicates a simple distinction between these categories, as recent critical work on masculinity has demonstrated. Sally Robinson and David Savran suggest that representations of wounded masculinity in postwar American film and literature use masochism to assert a new kind of power: either the power of the male victim, as Robinson argues, or the revitalization of phallic masculinity through the masochist's ability to "take it like a man," according to David Savran.

Beyond power and powerlessness: Nicola as form's dangerous structure

Savran and Robinson question the nature and effects of power and powerlessness and the relationship of power to cultural constructions of masculinity and femininity. Their work implies that the signifiers of – and relationship between – power and powerlessness are unstable. As both dominatrix and victim, Nicola herself illustrates this instability, and she ceaselessly undermines other binary oppositions as well. She is associated with the labile, liminal properties of writing and art. However, while Nicola is writing as deconstruction, she is also writing as sublimation. On one level, *London Fields* deconstructs the distinction between the shapely cunning of aesthetic form, illustrated in its elaborate plot, and the chaotic, naïve energies of formlessness, embodied in its digressive narrative structure. Yet the novel also invokes a polarity between Nicola as sublimating aesthetic form and Keith as base, material formlessness. Amis maps his desires and fears about aesthetic form onto Nicola's body, thereby displaying an anxiety about the way art fixes and reifies while relying on a reifying connection between femininity and form.

Samson sees Nicola as both a muse and the raw material or content for his text. However, Nicola is an author figure, and her description as "a rivulet of black ink" suggests that she is the text itself. She embodies the disturbing, destabilizing effects of writing, down to her ambiguous name, variously heard as "sex," "sick" and "seeks." She is linguistic style, with its slippery, parodic qualities, as well as plot, with its structure: she therefore breaks down the distinction between form and content. As both plot and style, she incarnates textual form on its different levels. Although she likes danger, she avoids "vandal danger, with no form to it" (68). She compares herself to a sign on a derelict house: "DANGEROUS STRUCTURE. This was her body. This was her plan" (129). Here, as throughout the novel, the structure of textual form is specifically aligned with Nicola's body as "the female form shaped and framed, packaged and gift-wrapped" (71). This female form is contrasted with male formlessness, as Keith, who acts "in the name of masculinity" (24), is "formless – he had no form," while Nicola can "lend form to his chaos" (377).

Nicola is the form of the postmodern text, deconstructing the distinction between the real and the fictional to produce the hyperreal. When she presents herself to Guy, looking as though she just got out of bed, Samson comments: "Always the simulacrum, never the real thing. That's art" (131). She is always mediated, always "lit by her personal cinematographer" (69), and she experiences her life in mediated form, watching the televised aftermath of the plane crash which killed her parents. With her dress which is "man-made, drulon, trexcett, man-made in every sense, made by men with men in mind" (456–7), she illustrates Fredric Jameson's claim that "Postmodernism is what you have when the modernization process is complete and nature is gone for good" (ix). Amis's neologisms, the synthetic names of the synthetic fibres, imply that the disappearance of a stable linguistic norm is a corollary of the disappearance of nature, just as Keith's ridiculously reduced vocabulary ("innit") signals his status as the product of tabloids and television.

However, although Nicola is a representation of representations, a simulacrum emerging from the death of the real – as her link with on-screen, mediated death implies – she is also the real as death. She embodies the destructive forces of natural phenomena: *"That's what I am*, she used to whisper to herself after sex. *A black hole. Nothing can escape from me"* (66). Nicola is linked to the natural world through her description as "Miss World" (70) and her comment "I identify with the planet" (396); moreover, her crisis is mapped onto a global ecological crisis in which the distinctions between the natural and the unnatural are crumbling. Degraded criminality has infected the natural world, collapsing the differences between people, things, and animals: "People now treated themselves like telephone boxes" (94); pigeons wear "criminal balaclavas."

Blurring the boundaries between the natural and the unnatural, and between the real and the simulacrum, Nicola instantiates an ontological crisis. When Samson tells her, "And you know what the worst thing about everything is? About you. About the whole story. About the world. About death. This: it's *really happening*" (436), he shows himself to be "unreliably unreliable" (Wood, 8), simultaneously right and wrong, as Nicola is clearly a fiction but also bears witness to the reality of cultural traumas, including atomic destruction (she has an imaginary friend called "Enola Gay"). She exemplifies the competing strands that Hal Foster identifies in postmodern art: mediated self-referentiality, in which "reality is the effect of representation" rather than an underlying given; and the resurgence of the abject body, which he interprets as a reaction against simulacral art and a turn toward "the real as a thing of trauma" (*Return*, 146). Foster points out, nonetheless, that much contemporary art is both simulacral and drawn to the real, and this description applies also to Nicola's body. When Keith enters her bathroom, a place of "secretions" and "reflections," he notices "the small faecal stain on the cold white bowl" (73). We could read this referentially, as an image of abjection, because corporeal waste dissolves the boundary between the inside and outside of the body. It would therefore exemplify Kristeva's notion of the abject as "what disturbs identity, system, order. What does not respect borders" (4). But Nicola's shit should not be seen as the "abject-as-truth." Her abject body does not reveal the collapse of the female body as fetish, and the real behind the screen; nor does it literalize the trauma of castration which woman as fetish is supposed to hide.[4] These interpretations overlook the way this incident implicitly recalls Swift's "The Lady's Dressing Room," another satire about male fantasies of women, in which "Celia shits." Nicola's shit is therefore both abject (and referential) *and* simulacral, the representation of a prior representation. It does not expose the real behind the fetish but is itself a reality effect, the production of literary convention. Similarly, Nicola's desire for anal sex is abject in the way it complicates distinctions between "proper-clean and improper-dirty" (Kristeva, 72), but it is also simulacral because of its parodic relation to sodomy in twentieth-century literature, which the novel traces from Joyce and Lawrence onward (68).

In its ontological instability, Nicola's body is a figure for the post-modern novel. But she is an author as well as a text, "always [knowing] what was going to happen next" (15). She projects herself as a series of pornographic fantasies in order to manipulate Keith, before whom she appears in "electronic form" (427). In contrast to Keith, Guy, and Samson, she realizes the way in which fictional forms mediate the world, rather than mistaking the representation for reality itself. She not only recognizes the shaping power of fictional forms but also – like Amis – parodies literary and filmic forms for her own ends. While she parodies pornographic films for Keith, she mockingly plays up to Guy's Lawrentian fantasies of healthy sex and "real" women – he sees her as the answer to his search for "the thing itself" (35). Of course, neither Keith nor Guy recognizes her parodic ability, taking her perfor-mance for truth. Indeed, they consistently mistake representation for reality: Guy's dreams follow "adolescent storylines" (216) whereas Keith's view of the world is literally shaped by the media: "his eyes were television" (9). When he goes to a football match, "that misery of stringer's clichés *is what he actually sees*" (98). Similarly, Nicola is able to confound Samson, who thinks she provides him with the raw mate-rial he only needs to transcribe. Not until the novel's end – in a glori-ous rewriting of Agatha Christie's *The Murder of Roger Ackroyd* – does Samson realize that he is Nicola's murderer (rather than Guy or Keith). Only then does he recognize that Nicola is an artist, and that he too is a character in a story – her story: "She outwrote me. Her story worked" (466).

Nicola forces Guy and Keith into similar epiphanies. She frustrates Guy's desire by interrupting sex to send him on a trans-Atlantic wild-goose chase. This deflation is mirrored by the demystifying books she gives him for the plane: Stendhal's *Love*, about an untouchable beloved – which ends with the chapter "Concerning Fiascos" (440) – and *The Light of Many Suns*, from which Guy learns the true identity of Nicola's friend Enola Gay and her son Little Boy. Likewise, Nicola rubs Keith's nose into the distinction between reality and representation when she takes him behind the scenes of the televised darts championship. He asks, "Where's the pub then?" and is told, "We use cutaways and dub the pub later" (457). Nicola therefore combines the functions of both Martina Twain and the Martin Amis character in *Money*: like Martina, she educates Keith and Guy, teaching them how to interpret the relationship between text and world; like Martin, she reveals her role as the mastermind behind the elaborate, manipulative subterfuge of her plot.

Nicola's debunking here illustrates the tension throughout Amis's work that he destabilizes the boundary between the real and the virtual – the pub is simulacrum, a copy without an original, behind which there is only the revelation of the reality effect – while simultaneously reinforcing this boundary, reaffirming the distinction between the "real" of the set and the "image" of the television to puncture Keith's fantasies. Some critics assume that, because Amis destabilizes the distinction between reality and fiction, he is Baudrillard incarnated as a novelist. But Amis's novels also consistently ridicule the notion that images are indistinguishable from reality, and that we are left only with "models of a real without origin or reality" (Baudrillard, 166).[5] Keith's problem is that he cannot tell the difference between reality and fiction: the "riots in Kazakhstan were real [...] But so, to Keith was *Syndicate* and *Edwin Drood: The Musical*" (55). In contrast, Nicola easily discriminates between the two: "*Film, Keith*, she could have said. *Film. All that not real. Not real*" (190). The collapse in referentiality that characterizes the novel's apocalyptic world is depicted playfully, as a game (darts, rather than *Money*'s chess), but also as a potential catastrophe, linked to the destructive forces of entropy and nuclear war. The political and ecological crises of nuclear Armageddon and entropy that threaten the planet are mapped onto a crisis in representation, exemplified through the "disturbing literalism" in which signs increasingly resemble their referents, such as the five-foot toy baby elephant in Marmaduke's nursery (220). The "horrorday" of November 5, the eve of Nicola's death, when holocaust is narrowly averted, is mirrored by the collapse of language into "horrorfizz and horrorsquawk" (451).

London Fields maps a social crisis onto crime and onto a linguistic crisis, like its predecessor, *Bleak House*. J. Hillis Miller famously reads *Bleak House* as depicting a world in which crime and social malaise are symptoms of a crisis in signification, arguing that Dickens "locates with profound insight the causes of that sickness in the sign-making power, in the ineradicable human tendency to take the sign for the substance" (34) – a statement that could easily apply to *London Fields*. As a postmodern detective novel, *London Fields* explores a crisis in representation while participating in that crisis by confusing the relationship between signifiers, signifieds, and referents. However, although it is a novel about language, it is not *just* a novel about language. Raymond Williams offers an alternative explanation for the rise of the detective story, suggesting that crime figures as a trope for social relations (rather than Hillis Miller's linguistic relations): the mystery to be explored is "the opaque complexity of modern city life" (227). In the case of *London Fields*, it is impossible to decide whether Hillis Miller's linguistic crisis or Williams's social crisis is anterior, since the novel works on both anti-mimetic and mimetic levels simultaneously. In this respect the novel illustrates a central tension within metafiction, which can be seen as hyperrealism, more accurately reflecting the unreal, simulacral nature of the contemporary world, but also as a self-referential *mise-en-abîme*. The dartboard is the novel itself: Samson's pen is shaped like a dart (14), and it is also a trope for representation more broadly (a picture of the board appears on 98). However, the dartboard is also London – the "bull's-eye" of nuclear war (16) – and femininity: the center is a black hole, invoking Nicola. This suggests that analyses of the novel should attend to its status as social commentary as well as metafiction. A reading that reduces the novel to self-referential metafiction overlooks the way in which the novel is also "about" nuclear stockpiling, ecological crisis, gender, and the class system, and the way in which it insistently asserts the ineluctable presence of the real as trauma, particularly as death.

Sublimation and the *informe*

This point is crucial to my argument that although *London Fields* is an unstable text and deconstructs gender, it remains significant that Nicola is a woman. The text destabilizes the relationship between form and content, but it does not evacuate content, whether identified as plot or as mimetic referentiality. Many of the qualities associated with Nicola Six are also associated with *Money*'s John Self, who likewise undermines the boundaries between body and text, and the real and the simulacral. But these characters – the signifiers through which Amis explores a crisis in signification – differ dramatically, and it is the significance of this difference I seek to explain. The problem is not that Nicola is a figure of male fantasy, because such a reading overlooks how Amis's destabilized form knowingly satirizes this perception. Rather, the problem is the representation of her sexed body: the qualities associated with her female body position her as sublimation in contrast to the messy energies of formless masculinity. In other words, her deathly, death-producing, female body works against her function as the site of contradiction and aporia – just as Amis's desire to link femininity to form (and masculinity to formlessness) works against the

novel's own destabilizing energies. The novel's deconstructive operation is not consistent, and while Nicola complicates the distinction
between form and formlessness, Amis uses the gender of his authorial
doubles to simplify and reinscribe that distinction, and to align Nicola
with the female form.

I will first examine the evidence for what I consider the most powerful counterargument: the contention that both Nicola and the novel
destabilize the distinctions between form and formlessness, destruction
and creation. Although Nicola is associated with deathly, destructive
properties (the "unstable structure" with which she identifies is also
described as a "dead house" [129]), she may also be seen as creative. Far
from providing sterile closure, her death is described as a "feminine
ending" (15) that raises fresh uncertainty about the novel's author, for
after her death it is suggested that Mark Asprey may have written, mas-
terminded, or appropriated Samson's tale. (This ambiguity is enforced
by the initials "M.A." after the prefatory note.) Moreover, the end of
the novel renders phallic masculinity helpless: Samson is outwritten
and is forced to kill both Nicola and himself; Keith loses his darts
championship; and Guy does not come. There is no moment of climax
or resolution – no money shot – as there is no nuclear explosion on
November 5. These could all be seen as examples of the way Nicola's
destructive female form paradoxically deflects the phallic thrust of the
pen, the penis, the dart, and the bomb.

Like *Money*, *London Fields* constantly complicates stable distinctions between form and formlessness. Samson longs to capture the
formlessness of real life, but he constantly imposes form: as John
Dern points out, numerous inconsistencies appear in Samson's narration, revealing the gap between his story and any unvarnished truth
he claims to record (52–3). In *Money* John Self seeks form as the revelation of purpose and meaning that might compensate for his formlessness: "Our lives, they harbour form, artistic shape, and we want
our form revealed, even though we only move in our detail" (361).
However, in both *Money* and *London Fields*, plot is revealed as the
arbitrary imposition of form onto material, an authorial game rather
than the revelation of any moral, epistemological or aesthetic truth.
Form is therefore as random and arbitrary as formlessness, and the
baroque plot of *London Fields* merely reveals the absence of any
purpose, causality, or shape existing beyond the caprice of the author
(whoever he or she may be). In this manner Amis's novels erode the
distinctions between randomness and plot, shapelessness and shape,
and chaos and order.

Does *London Fields*, then, illustrate Bataille's notion of the *informe*? Bataille describes the *informe*, or formlessness, as: "a term that serves to bring things down in the world, generally requiring that each thing have its form. What it designates has no rights in any sense and gets itself squashed everywhere, like a spider or an earthworm … affirming that the universe resembles nothing and is only formless amounts to saying that the universe is something like a spider or spit" (31). The *informe* is connected to Bataille's concept of heterology, which he sees as the radical otherness or heterogeneity (social, aesthetic, or conceptual) that disrupts the sublimating forces of purity and homogeneity. Rosalind Krauss has influentially glossed the *informe*, describing it as "transgression against form" and an operation or process which disrupts "coherence, meaning, unity" (109). She differentiates between the informe as a structural operation and Kristeva's "abject," which she argues tends to fix the meanings of particular signifiers such as bodily waste, despite Kristeva's insistence that the abject "does not respect borders, positions, rules" (4). Krauss is wary of the way abjection becomes a means to produce the meanings of bodies and bodily fluids, rather than an operation that reveals the unstable working of language and signification. She moves away from the body in her analysis of transgressions against form, finding formlessness in highly abstract and shapely art (such as Giacometti's sculpture) in contrast to Bataille's own examples of base, shapeless matter – spiders and spit – drawn from the natural world. Her position is provocative for thinking about Amis since it suggests that formlessness can be found at the heart of a highly plotted novel, provided this form destabilizes oppositions. It provides a way of reading Nicola's destructive form as unstable formlessness.

Drawing upon Foster's critique of Krauss, however, I argue that this reading, although seductive, overlooks the way in which representational content – in particular, the signifiers of Nicola's corporeality – works against an interpretation of Nicola as *informe* and as pure trope. For Foster, Krauss's disdain for the literal content of an artwork erases the "materiality, bodiliness" of the *informe*. In her preoccupation with form and dismissal of content (or referentiality), Krauss is "resublimating, but in the guise of desublimating" ("Politics", 12) or purifying in the name of transgression. Foster argues that representational content, including that of the body, should not be dismissed as a naïve attempt to capture a referent or to fix signification. He defends both figurative art and the analysis of content alongside form, arguing that content should be considered a "network of signifiers" ("Politics", 16). This defence opens up a strategy for thinking about the content of *London*

Fields and the ways in which the network of signifiers that is Nicola's body works against the novel's deconstructive form. Amis's novels may destabilize signification, but they also deploy signifiers, imposing some categories while breaking down others.

The representation of Nicola's body reveals gender as a fictional, linguistic construct, but the meaning of her body does not stop there, as it also signifies the deathly nature of form. The signifiers attached to Nicola's body connote a sublimating and purifying version of aesthetic form. Her body sublimates base materiality, as when she rubs dirt on her dress: "You'd be surprised how eloquent a bit of dirt can be. Carefully applied" (455). Here she transforms a potentially chaotic or abject substance into a sign, bringing formless matter into the world of form and signs. Signs sublimate and purify, and Nicola's body, as both sign and form, links sublimation to death and sterility. We are told she is "the death of love" (19) and that "she welcomed and applauded the death of just about anything" (296). Her penchant for non-procreative anal sex indicates her sterility, though despite her sexual preferences, and further underlining her links with death, she has had seven abortions and lives on a "dead-end street" (402). Samson tells us that she insists on "Watertight Contraception. I'm not going to lose my figure and get up in the middle of the night" (284). This passage explicitly links the controlled perfection of Nicola's adult female figure or form to infertility.

If Amis links femininity to form, he also links working-class masculinity to formlessness. Formlessness has contradictory connotations for Amis. At times, he connects it to renewal and life, as in the case of the city's formlessness. The novel suggests that London's unrepresentable "illegible streets" (367) and "non-symmetrical" "lop-sided" (463) shape might offer "sudden eschatology" (271). London is the sublime, shapeless city that finally finds its voice and substitutes formless life for shapely destruction, uttering "pre-verbal" (404) cries that refuse the destruction Nicola represents. These descriptions suggest that formlessness is life-giving precisely because it resists the sublimating properties of aesthetic form and language. The same inference can be drawn from John Self's escape into the concluding, italicized monologue of *Money*, where he muses: "My life is losing its form. The large agencies, the pentagrams of shape and purpose have no power to harm or delight me now" (384). Here Amis is ambivalent about form, which both harms and delights, and similarly ambivalent about formlessness. For if formlessness is life's vital energy, it is also disturbing chaos, as in the lyrical description of Keith Talent's violent crime, where the absence of signification is linked to disarray and disharmony: "Meanwhile, in chaos's hiding place, what happens? Rocks and shells catch and grate in neither sea nor shore, and nothing is clean or means anything" (250). Keith Talent's formless chaos, John Self's formless new life: whether formlessness is chaotic muddle or vitality, it is clearly linked to working-class masculinity, which signals the energetic disorder which both threatens and potentially revitalizes aesthetic (female) form.[6]

The reductive question of whether Amis is a feminist is at best uninteresting and at worst unhelpful. But at the heart of Amis's work are questions about the relationship between art and life, between form and content, that are also at the heart of feminist criticism. The problem is how to read the significance of representational content while recognizing the ways that representation reveals itself to be unreliable and unstable. I have argued that *London Fields* associates Nicola with the power and danger of aesthetic form, which not only destabilizes and disrupts but also shapes and reifies. A reading of *London Fields* which focuses solely on its destabilizing metafictional qualities risks the act of sublimation and homogenization that Amis associates with Nicola's deathly form. By the same token, much post-Judith Butler gender criticism that locates performativity everywhere risks fixing and stabilizing the meaning of texts and bodies. *London Fields* portrays gender as performative and fictional, but it also makes Nicola's body mean as sublimating feminine form in contrast to base male formlessness. Although the novel and Nicola herself trouble the process of signification, the signifiers attached to her body nonetheless suggest she is form as cock-teasing, castrating, sterile sublimation. *London Fields* is haunted by the fear that art's shapely purposelessness renders it fundamentally sterile in the face of life's random energy, and it uses Nicola's female form to manage and contain that fear.

Notes

1 Amis concedes to Will Self, "I've got into terrible trouble over underwear." In his 24 April 1990 review of *London Fields* in the *Village Voice*, Graham Fuller suggests that "Amis himself is unable to resist Nicola's pornographic promise or the lascivious lexicon of sexism – which alone should offend many readers" (75). I would like to thank Jon Beasley-Murray, Peter Dickinson, Tom Grieve, Gavin Keulks, and Mark Little for their helpful feedback on this essay.

2 In *Gender Trouble: Feminism and the Subversion of Identity* (1989), Judith Butler describes performativity as a linguistic operation that constitutes identity, rather than a conscious set of choices by an agent. In Amis's novels, however, certain characters manipulate their own gender performances, although there is no stable self behind these performances.

3 In *Understanding Martin Amis* (1995), James Diedrick interprets Nicola as an "authorial alter ego – an instrument of the author's satirical aims"; she "is a literary character down to her linguistic bones" (148) who is "wrapped in all the metaphors men have used through the ages to express their fear of (and desire to control) female sexuality" (156).

4 In "A Phantasmagoria of the Female Body: The Work of Cindy Sherman" (*New Left Review*, 1991), Laura Mulvey offers these possibilities as ways of interpreting the abject female body in the photographs of Cindy Sherman.

5 In *The War Against Cliché* (2001), Amis also insists on a distinction between reality and representation: "I happen to like screen violence while steadily execrating its real-life counterpart. Moreover, I can tell the difference between the two. One is happening, one is not" (16).

6 Amis agrees with the suggestion that he sees working-class language as a source of vitality, as put to him in inimitable (and symptomatic) fashion by Self: "You want the proletarian cock to penetrate the bourgeois lexicon. You want it to push in there and spunk it up a bit."

Works cited

Amis, Martin. *Money*. London: Penguin, 1984.

——. *London Fields*. 1989. New York: Vintage, 1991.

Bataille, Georges. *Visions of Excess*. Minneapolis: U of Minnesota P, 1985.

Baudrillard, Jean. *Selected Writings*. Ed. Mark Poster. Stanford: Stanford UP, 1988.

Dern, John. *Martians, Monsters and Madonna: Fiction and Form in the World of Martin Amis*. New York: Peter Lang, 2000.

Foster, Hal, Benjamin Buchloh, Rosalind Krauss, Yves-Alain Bois and Denis Hollier. "The Politics of the Signifier II: A Conversation on the Informe and the Abject." *October* 67 (1994): 3–21.

——. *The Return of the Real: the Avant-Garde at the End of the Century*. Cambridge, MA: MIT P, 1996.

Jameson, Fredric. *Postmodernism, Or, the Cultural Logic of Late Capitalism*. Durham, NC: Duke UP, 1994.

Krauss, Rosalind. "Cindy Sherman: Untitled." *Cindy Sherman 1975–1993*. Eds. Rosalind Krauss and Norman Bryson. New York: Rizzoli, 1993.

Kristeva, Julia. *Powers of Horror*. Trans. Leon Roudiez. New York: Columbia UP, 1982.

Miller, J. Hillis. "Introduction." *Bleak House*. By Charles Dickens. Harmondsworth: Penguin, 1971. 11–34.

Mills, Sara. "Working With Feminism: What Can Feminist Text Analysis Do?" *Twentieth-Century Fiction: From Text to Context*. Eds. Peter Verdonk and Jean Jacques Weber. London: Routledge, 1995. 206–19.

Robinson, Sally. *Marked Men: White Masculinity in Crisis*. New York: Columbia UP, 2000.

Savran, David. *Taking It Like A Man: White Masculinity, Masochism and Contemporary American Culture*. Princeton, NJ: Princeton UP, 1998.

Self, Will. "An Interview with Martin Amis." *Mississippi Review* 7 (1995). <http://www.mississippireview.com/1995/07amis.html>

Thomas, Susie. "Posing as a Postmodernist: Race and Class in Martin Amis's *London Fields*." *Literary London* 1:2 (Sept. 2003).

Williams, Raymond. *The Country and the City*. London: Chatto and Windus, 1973.

Wood, James. *The Irresponsible Self: On Laughter and the Novel*. London: Jonathan Cape, 2004.

7
Martin Amis's *Time's Arrow* and the Postmodern Sublime

Brian Finney
California State University, Long Beach

Time's Arrow (1991) confronts a question that has consumed Amis from an early stage in his career: is modernity leading civilization to self-destruction? While his main concern remains the world's development of nuclear weapons, he sees the origins of the West's drive to implode not just in Hiroshima and Nagasaki but in the Holocaust (*Time's Arrow*) and the Soviet gulags (*Koba the Dread*). The Holocaust is, he has said, "the central event of the twentieth century" (Bellante, 16). As Dermot McCarthy observes: Amis's "generation suffers from an event it did not experience, and will expire from one it seems powerless to prevent" (301). James Diedrick has called *Einstein's Monsters* (1987), *London Fields* (1989), and *Time's Arrow* an "informal trilogy" (104). The first two focus on a nuclear holocaust that threatens postwar civilization, whereas *Time's Arrow* returns to the Holocaust, which cast its shadow over the rest of the century. *London Fields* and *Time's Arrow* complement one another in particular. In a prefatory note to *London Fields* Amis mentions that he even considered calling the novel by the latter's title. Indeed, Hitler remains at the heart of Amis's belief that we are living in the aftermath of disaster. In *London Fields* Nicola Six remarks that "it seemed possible to argue that Hitler was still running the century" (395), and in 2002 Amis confessed, "I feel I have unfinished business with Hitler" (Heawood, 18).

If the emancipatory view of modernity began with the Enlightenment, philosophers and historians have continuously questioned its assumptions. Many scholars contend that these questions took on a new urgency after the atrocities accompanying World War Two. Jean-François Lyotard epitomizes this skepticism towards the "grand narratives" of modernity to which he attributes those atrocities. He argues that modernity's pursuit of liberal humanist, universal standards led to

101

a lethal hostility to deviation or resistance. Lyotard defines as post-modern the large-scale postwar rejection of such metanarratives of rational progress – narratives concerned with truth, justice, and good-ness. Both Lyotard and Amis indict consensus as responsible for the German public's support for Nazi programs of racial purification. Both share Elie Wiesel's conviction that "at Auschwitz not only man died, but also the idea of man" – that is, the liberal humanist idea of "man" (Rosenfeld, 154).

As Lyotard wrote in *The Differend* (*Le Différend*), Auschwitz disproves that "[e]verything real is rational, everything rational is real: 'Auschwitz' refutes speculative doctrine. The crime at least, which is real, is not rational" (179). Yet as Zygmunt Bauman has clarified, the Holocaust did employ rationality to horrifying effect. Far from "an antithesis of modern civilization and everything … it stands for, … the Holocaust could merely have uncovered another face of the same society whose other, so familiar, face we so admire" (7). *Time's Arrow* gives fictional life to this Janus-faced modernity, to the fact that "there is no document of civilization which is not at the same time a document of barbarism" (Benjamin, 256).[1] The systematic extermination of six million innocent civilians, an act of the highest irrationality, relied on rational means for its implementation. This crucial event in modern history is a paradox that requires the use of paradoxical narrative techniques on the part of any novelist attempting to evoke it.

Amis's ambivalence towards modernity migrates to his novels, which present apocalyptic visions of what he calls "the toiletization of the planet." He informed Melvyn Bragg that this jaded view of modernity accounts for his characters' behavior – "as if they're heading towards an ending too" – but to Mira Stout he confessed that he is "trying to get more truthful about what it's like to be alive now" (35). Darkly comic, his novels attempt to undermine and embody the suicidal behavior of the contemporary world. He sees himself as representative of those who grew up in the shadow of the holocaust, telling Patrick McGrath that "We are like no other people in history" (194). He perceives himself, therefore, as modernity personified, split between ameliorative and pes-simistic versions. The same ambivalence appears in *London Fields* and *Time's Arrow*. Nicola Six, the anti-heroine of the former, exhibits a death-wish that parallels the planet's; yet only her personal death-wish is fulfilled. The planet lives on after the eclipse that substitutes for an apocalyptic big bang. Similarly, Odilo Unverdorben, the protagonist of *Time's Arrow*, lives out the ameliorative and degenerative versions of modernity in his two incarnations, which move in opposing temporal directions. Although *London Fields* is set in the near future and *Time's Arrow* returns to World War Two, both novels are irremediably tied to the present – and to modernity itself.

One can discern a further parallel between the novels' ameliorative and degenerative versions of modernity and Lyotard's distinction between two modes of (post)modernity – the melancholic and the jubilatory. For Lyotard these comprise an aesthetics of the sublime. The sublime entails a "combination of pleasure and pain, the pleasure that reason should exceed all presentation, the pain that imagination or sensibility should not be equal to the concept" (*Postmodern*, 81). According to Lyotard, postmodern art seeks the experience of freedom by staging a permanent crisis in representation. If such art is distinguished by its presentation of "the unpresentable in presentation itself" (81), then the postmodern mode is distinguished – and leant its jubilatory connotation – by its "invention of new rules" (80), of "allusions to the conceivable which cannot be presented" (81). Using Lyotard's distinction, both *London Fields* and especially *Time's Arrow* belong to the mode of the postmodern.[2] These two modes of modernity offer critiques of representation – what Lyotard calls "the 'lack of reality' of reality" (77). As in *Time's Arrow*, "they often exist in the same piece, are almost indistinguishable; and yet they testify to a difference (*différend*) on which the fate of thought depends ... between regret and assay" (80).

One could substitute "trial" or "test" for "assay," for either word accentuates the novelty and unrepeatability of such works. The point is that the first mode, like the chronological account of Odilo Unverdorben's life in *Time's Arrow*, induces feelings of regret (albeit extreme), whereas the second mode, like the chronologically reversed account of his life, produces feelings of jubilation – ones that derive from the radical critique of conventional representation inherent in the postmodern sublime. The two modes are separated by a *différend* that Lyotard defines as "a case of conflict ... that cannot be equitably resolved for lack of a common rule of judgment" (*Differend*, xi). Amis both knows about and admires the mode of the sublime which he considers the signature mark of Nabokov's early novels. In his 1979 essay, "The Sublime and the Ridiculous: Nabokov's Black Farces," Amis expresses surprise that Nabokov's work has so seldom been considered in this light: "the sublime directed at our fallen world of squalor, absurdity and talentlessness." "Sublimity replaces the ideas of motivation and plot with those of obsession and destiny," he continues. "It suspends moral judgements in favour of remorselessness, a helter-skelter intensity. It does not proceed to a conclusion so much as accumulate possibilities of pain and danger. The sublime is a perverse mode, by definition. But there is art in its madness" (76). This passage reads like a prophetic description of *Time's Arrow* in which destiny replaces plot, remorselessness moral judgment, and possibilities of pain and danger a conclusion. The novel perfectly demonstrates the art underlying its perversity.

This essay neither assumes conscious knowledge of Lyotard's theory on the part of Amis nor claims that *Time's Arrow* is postmodern simply because it conforms to Lyotard's definition of the postmodern within modernity.[3] But Lyotard does offer a useful definition of the way modern art critiques representational realism, a critique that assumes its most radical form through the postmodern sublime, which simultaneously evokes pleasure and pain in the reader. After Auschwitz and Stalinism, Lyotard insists, no one could maintain that modernity's hopes had been fulfilled. To write about the Holocaust is to risk estheticizing the unthinkable.[4] How then can such tragedy be incorporated, especially by a writer who often undermines concepts of tragedy and heroism? In structuring *Time's Arrow* Amis employed three interrelated techniques: a narrative form (temporal reversal), a narrative perspective (splitting the protagonist and narrator), and a narrative mode (irony that produces black humor). The narrative simultaneously embodies the pleasure of returning to a less appalling phase of modernity and the painful recollection of Western civilization's fall from innocence – a fall Lyotard attributes to those grand narratives of rationalist improvement that were invoked by Holocaust perpetrators.

Amis sheds light on his narrative form when he writes that the crisis facing our planet "is no longer spatial. It is temporal" (*War*, 33). Time, Nicola reflects in *London Fields*, "is always pulling us down" (297). It is appropriate that Amis employs temporal anticipation in *London Fields* and temporal reversal in *Time's Arrow*. In the former, Penny Smith writes, "the natural world is on fastforward, rushing towards catastrophe" (120). "We used to live outside history," Nicola reflects; "But now we're all coterminous. We're inside history now all right, on its leading edge" (197). Samson Young, the narrator of the novel, similarly reflects on the landscape of his childhood. "If I shut my eyes I can see the innocuous sky, afloat above the park of milky green" (463). But the London Fields that Sam remembers was the site of High Explosives Research where his father worked on "plutonium metallurgy" (161). Eden was already a fallen state.[5]

By contrast, *Time's Arrow* takes its readers back to an innocent, mythologized past. The order of narrated events regresses from the ugly and cruel present reminiscent of *London Fields* to a prelapsarian time when experience is exchanged for innocence. However, the chronologically restored story progresses inexorably through the horrors of concentration camps to the contaminated postlapsarian world of Ronald Reagan's America. The narrative temporally reverses the fortunes of the Nazi doctor, Odilo Unverdorben, who assists with the mass exterminations at Auschwitz. After escaping from the liberating Russians, he flees to Portugal where he assumes the name Hamilton de Souza. Using false papers he then emigrates to America as John Young and assumes the identity of an American physician, Tod Friendly. Reminders of earlier moments in this chronology repeatedly erupt into the inverted narrative – through his dreams or his wife's rejection of Nazism, for instance. From the opening page Amis plunges the reader into an inverted world where life begins at its end and death becomes a second birth. Through such temporal inversion Amis employs the postmodern sublime alongside his radical critique of the possibility of presenting so notorious a landmark of modernity as the Holocaust. Lyotard maintains that "[n]arrative organization is constitutive of diachronic time, and the time that it constitutes has the effect of 'neutralizing' an 'initial' violence" (*Heidegger*, 16). Inverting diachronic narrative organization attempts to avoid this danger.

Lyotard resorts to Kant's idea of "negative presentation" to elucidate how the modern artist can "make visible … something which cannot be seen": the "empty 'abstraction' which the imagination experiences when [searching] for a presentation of the infinite (another unpresentable)" that itself resembles "a presentation of the infinite, its 'negative presentation'" (*Postmodern*, 78). Lyotard specifically cites Auschwitz as an example of this "negative presentation of the indeterminate" because the Germans tried to erase its physical existence at the end of the War (*Differend*, 56). *Time's Arrow* uses this esthetic of the sublime to present the unpresentable as practiced at Auschwitz. Through temporal reversal Amis simultaneously evokes the unpresentable by invoking its negative presentation – a process which culminates in healing and renewal. "Almost any deed, any action, has its morality reversed, if you turn time's arrow around," Amis has remarked (DeCurtis, 147). Similarly, his Afterword acknowledges his debt to a famous paragraph in Kurt Vonnegut's *Slaughterhouse Five* (1970): the Dresden firebombing passage in which Billy Pilgrim watches backwards a late night movie of American bombers recovering their bombs from a German city in flames. (Compare the narrator of Amis's novel: "It just seems to me that the film is running backwards" [8]). Vonnegut's passage ends with Billy speculating, "Everybody turned into a baby, and all humanity, without exception, conspired biologically to produce two perfect people named Adam and Eve, he supposed" (54–5), and this brief inversion of chronology inspired Amis's own attempt to evoke a lost Eden. Amis's Afterword also acknowledges his debt to Robert Jay Lifton's *The Nazi Doctors: Medical Killing and the Psychology of Suicide* (1986). On reading this documentary account of an entire profession perversely adopting an ideology of killing as a means of healing, Amis realized that "[h]ere was a psychotically inverted world, and if you did it backward in time, it would make sense" (DeCurtis, 146).

Amis first utilized the idea of narrative inversion in the short story, "Bujak and the Strong Force, or God's Dice" (1985). Basing his idea on Einstein, Bujak is an "Oscillationist" who claims that the "universe would expand only until unanimous gravity called it back to start again" (*Einstein's*, 58). Bujak maintains that time would also be reversed, causing, the narrator speculates, all the events of the story to invert, concluding with Bujak "folding into" his mother's womb (59). In similar fashion the protagonist of *Time's Arrow* ends up entering his mother while she weeps and screams, only to be Oedipally murdered by his father's penis at the moment of conception (164). Amis also touches on these ideas in *London Fields*, as Nicola personifies the negative gravity of the black hole of astronomical theory into which the novel's world seems inextricably drawn backwards. The origins of the "death of love" which this novel takes for granted originate, for Amis, in the "negative gravity" of Nazi death camps.

Time's Arrow extends this conceit over its entire length, beginning with the protagonist's death (and narrator's birth) in America from a car accident. The book concludes in 1916 in Solingen, Germany, the birthplace of not only Amis's protagonist but also Adolf Eichmann, the man responsible for overseeing the Final Solution to which Unverdorben contributed (163). Amis's application of this unusual form to a fictional treatment of the Holocaust involved its own "assay," in other words, its own break with form.[6] Paralleling Lyotard's description of the postmodern within the modern, *Time's Arrow* "searches for new presentations, not in order to enjoy them, but in order to impart a stronger sense of the unpresentable" (*Postmodern*, 81). As Amis explains, the effects seem "philanthropic" – that is, life-giving – "if and only if the arrow of time is reversed" (Reynolds and Noakes, 21).[7] In reality, of course, that cannot happen, but fiction succeeds where reality – and modernity – fails.

Numerous elements make narrative inversion a particularly appropriate vehicle for such terrible subjects. First, its dual reversal of chronology and causality perfectly portrays the Nazis' reversal of morality. Certainly, it is less paradoxical to represent death as birth (and vice-versa) than for Nazi doctors to base their practice on "a manifest absurdity – 'a vision and practice of killing to heal'" (Easterbrook, 57). Using a wider perspective, Daniel Oertel suggests that *Time's Arrow's* "incoherent narrative structure" – incoherent to the narrator – "becomes a suitable metaphor for the incoherence of history" (132). The novel fulfils Amis's impossible fantasy that history could be reversed and the atrocities of the mid-twentieth century undone. As Dermot McCarthy argues, "the 'terrible journey' back into WWII and the Nazi Holocaust ... is a mirror inversion of the journey Amis sees his own generation taking *toward* nuclear holocaust" (303). Narrated in inverse order, the Holocaust is portrayed simultaneously as the end-product and the origin of contemporaneity. It reverts to an archaic time in Western history – "Germans ... have been preserved in ice from the beginning of time" (131) – and is also reimagined as progress: "But this was our mission, after all: to make Germany whole" (141). It is "a combination of the atavistic and the modern" (168) that produces what McCarthy, using a neologism, calls a "chronillogical world" (296) – precisely how Amis views post-Holocaust civilization.

"Invention," Lyotard insists, "is always born of dissension" (*Postmodern*, xxv), and indeed Amis aims to dissent from Nazi consensus about racial superiority. Amis's modern esthetic, like Lyotard's, "is based on a never-ending critique of representation that should contribute to the preservation of heterogeneity, of optimal dissensus" (Bertens, 133). Not just his argument but his entire narrative strategy stands opposed to consensus, especially Nazism. *Time's Arrow* negatively inverts temporality, rationality, and causality. The protagonist is characterized by his willingness to accept fascist ideology with what Lipton describes as its "promise of unity, oneness, fusion" (499). Even in later life the protagonist "sheds the thing he often can't seem to bear: his identity, his quiddity, lost in the crowd's promiscuity" (49).

The consequences of telling Unverdorben's story backwards are multiple, subtle and highly ironic. As Diedrick observes, the opening description of Unverdorben's/Tod Friendly's actions as a postwar American doctor "eerily anticipat[e] his eventual immersion in Auschwitz and intimat[e] the terrible secret of his ... past" (139). In reverse chronology a patient enters the operating room looking cured and emerges with a rusty nail planted in his head by the doctor (76).

From the opening pages doctors represent figures of authority "containing [...] above all power" (5). This "precognition," as Diedrick calls it, comes from the recurring dream of a figure from the "future": Uncle Pepi, modeled on Dr. Josef Mengele, Auschwitz's notorious "Angel of Death." As a "biological soldier" – a term first coined by the Nazis in a manual on eugenic sterilization (Lifton, 30) – Unverdorben joins the ranks of these doctors who "must wield the special power" (81). It is ironical, Amis writes, that as a doctor, "[y]ou have to harden your heart to pain and suffering" (82). Yet this is part of the rationale for the Hippocratic oath, which is excerpted in the novel: "I will abstain from all intentional wrongdoing and harm" (25). In Amis's inverted time scheme the protagonist deconstructs the oath by supposedly killing to heal; in exercising his *power* as a doctor he reinscribes the newly inferior term (healing) within the newly superior one of killing.

Power forms a recurrent motif in the novel, often becoming associated with sex. The first (and therefore last) time the protagonist has sex with Irene, the narrator says – as he "looms above her" – that he is "flooded by thoughts and feelings I've never had before. To do with power" (37). Power is equated with the ultimate authority over life, a fact literalized by the six figures in the photograph from Unverdorben's Auschwitz period who exercised power over their six victims (72). Sex makes Unverdorben feel like a lord: "you get everything on the first date. [...] Instant invasion and lordship" (51). It is as invasive (war-like) an act as surgery and becomes as perverted ("lording" it over the woman) in Unverdorben's hands. Power elevates its possessors to the status of gods: Lifton describes how the "Nazis saw themselves as 'children of the gods,' empowered to destroy and kill on behalf of their higher calling" (449). Perversion of power characterizes Unverdorben's sexual encounters with his wife, Herta, when she is "his chimpanzee required to do the housework naked, on all fours" (151). Herta is a young secretary when he meets her, and all his sexual partners occupy subordinate social positions. Ironically, this sexual power-play proves self-defeating when Unverdorben turns impotent. Perhaps this derives from his discovering an alternative outlet for exercising power in his role with the Waffen SS unit? Or perhaps it comments upon the dead-end where his cult of power terminates? He finds himself "omnipotent. Also impotent [...] powerful and powerless" (140). Amis appears to have adopted this paradoxical trait from Lifton's description of Nazi doctors who "called forth feelings of omnipotence and related sadism on the one hand, and of impotence and sometimes masochism on the other" (448). Amis's inverted narrative deconstructs Unverdorben's pursuit of power to reveal its attachment to its opposite. In adding his efforts to the consensual metanarrative of racial superiority, Unverdorben has multiplied zero by zero and still arrived at nothing, to adapt one heading of the novel (137).

Other critics have commented on the startling effects of this chronological and causal inversion. Such effects range from the bizarre (factories and automobiles effect an environmental clean-up [48]), through the perverse (Irene is blamed for her untidiness because the apartment is more messy when she leaves – that is, arrives [85]), to the tragic (the Nazis' purpose is to "dream a race" [120]). Amis never misses the opportunity to put these effects to use. For instance, he adopts the convention of reverse dialog. However, the conversations between Unverdorben and his lovers have an uncanny way of reading just as satisfactorily backwards as forwards, mirroring casual affairs which seem to work equally well recounted in reverse. After one such conversation the narrator comments: "I have noticed in the past, of course, that most conversations would make much better sense if you ran them backward. But with this man-woman stuff, you could run them any way you liked – and still get no further forward" (51). Amis's use of inverted dialog passes judgment on the power-induced encounters that Unverdorben pursues where the symmetry of the encounter reveals the termination of the affair in the opening exchange. Similarly, Unverdorben's journey by ship backwards across the Atlantic (from America to Europe) carries an ethical charge. The narrator observes, "we leave no mark on the ocean, as if we are successfully covering our tracks" (99). This is precisely what Unverdorben was doing in real chronological time – erasing his past. But in reality he was leaving indelible tracks in his wake that have vexed to nightmare the present age.

To effect this reversal Amis splits the narrating from the narrated subject. It appears that his strange narrator derives from Lifton's psychological concept of "'doubling': the division of the self into two functioning wholes, so that a part-self acts as an entire self" (418). Early in the novel the narrator describes feelings of estrangement from his body: "Something isn't quite working: this body I'm in won't take orders from this will of mine" (6). On the next page he explains, "I have no access to his thoughts – but I'm awash with his emotions" (7). The protagonist's mind therefore directs the actions of his body. But the protagonist must exclude his emotions from his part-self to perform his murderous procedures as a Nazi doctor. According to Lifton: "The requirements of conscience were transferred to the

Auschwitz self, which placed it within its own criteria for good (duty, loyalty to group), thereby freeing the original self from responsibility for actions there." This leads to "repudiation by the original self of *anything* done by the Auschwitz self" (421, 422), which leads in turn to an impaired narrating subject that, unlike the reader, is disabled from judging the narrated subject's actions with coherence. Deprived of life's experience, driven into a symbolic limbo from which to view his alter-ego's life in reverse, the narrator is unable to discern meaning and should be thought of as the doctor's soul, "the soul he should have had," according to Amis (DeCurtis, 146). This contrasts *London Fields* in that Keith Talent "thought of time as moving past him while he just stayed the same," but "in his soul he could tell what time was doing" (172). In *Time's Arrow* the narrator/soul stands outside time whereas the protagonist is the one who "didn't expect time to leave him alone" (*London Fields*, 172).

Paralleling Nabokov's fiction, most of Amis's narrators serve "as the malevolent force in the book" ("Sublime", 80). In *London Fields*, for instance Samson Young only understands at the end of the book that he has been callously manipulated – not by Nicola but by the ghostly M.A., the narrator's narrator, into murdering Nicola and taking his own life. But the narrator of *Time's Arrow* is the subject of – not the instrument for – "the spectacular humiliations that [the narrator] is obliged to undergo" (80). Richard Menke has called him "a supremely reliable narrator: he may be relied upon to get things diametrically, and often poignantly, wrong" (960). As Amis has observed, "If the trick is to work, the unreliable narrator must in fact be very reliable indeed: reliably partial" (*Experience*, 380). The narrator's partiality manifests itself in the sympathetic feelings he shows towards the disadvantaged and the marginalized in both American and German societies. In the States he is affronted at the protagonist's treatment of his patients and his women, while in Europe he applauds the dispersal of the Jews who are no longer victims of discrimination. In this sense the narrator aligns himself with Lyotard's stand against consensus in favor of heterogeneity – such as the Jewish minority in Europe. The narrator's exceptional stance parallels Lyotard's radical aesthetic of the postmodern sublime: one can only champion difference by stepping outside the rules governing consensus – both the rules of aesthetic practice (hence the inversion) and those of the postwar capitalist world that the narrator constantly condemns for its materialism and unfeeling practices. As Lyotard argues, the effect of the *Différend* is to turn those outside the consensus into victims because they lack common ground on which to argue their case. This is the case with the narrator, who becomes the victim of his exclusion from the master narrative that legitimated Unverdorben's wartime conduct in Germany. As Menke aptly puts it, the narrator "recast[s] genocide as genesis" (964). The narrator remains as ignorant of Unverdorben's criminal participation in the Holocaust as do many of those born since World War II.[8] The narrator is simultaneously deluded and the embodiment of a contemporary nostalgia for a reversal of the escalating horrors that constitute history after World War II.

What then should we make of the final paragraph in which the arrow of time reverts to its normal direction, point first? Few critics have attended to this crucial turning-point in the narrative. Michael Trussler claims that "ghosts can be said to spatialize time: their accusatory presence insists on infinite repetition over the irreversible loss of what we normally associate with the calendar" (28). Yet he fails to apply this insight to the predicament of the narrator at the novel's end. Is the narrator destined to relive his life in reverse – that is, historical – time, made to experience his life in real time? Or will he be again divided from the intellectual self that cannot feel the consequences of its actions? The hapless narrator embodies the barren fantasy that we could reverse the effects of history while illustrating the naïveté that such a forgetting would involve. He is the source of the inextricable combination of pleasure and pain that the postmodern sublime produces in the reader. In novels such as *Other People* and *London Fields* Amis stages a murderous act of narrative closure by killing off his narrator. But in *Time's Arrow* he rejects closure because this narrative should never be forgotten, only endlessly retold. Far from releasing readers in the final paragraph, the narrative condemns them to share with the narrator an endless oscillation between past and present, incorporating the past into our sense of modernity.

The reader is the missing third entity in the book. Confronted with two selves, each of which exhibits self-denial, the reader is constantly required to supply the historical events the protagonist seeks to forget and the narrator misunderstands. Witness the opening dialog, which offers the only instance of total speech reversal before the narrator learns to translate these words into conventional order:

"Dug. Dug," says the lady in the pharmacy.
"Dug," I join in. "Oo y'rrah?"
"Ald ul oo y'rrah?" (7)

The reader is compelled to work out the conventional order:

"How're you today?"
"Good," I join in. "How're you?"
"Good. Good," says the lady in the pharmacy.

To reach this understanding the reader must undergo three stages of comprehension. Read in reverse order, the dialog appears nonsensical: readers are presented with the unpresentable found in the postmodern sublime and experience the pain of incomprehension. But before they can reach the "translation" – offering, as Lyotard suggests, pleasure which "derives from pain" (*Postmodern*, 77) – they must first confront the intermediate stage in which "Good" reads as "Gud" and "How're you?" as "Harr'y oo?" The full "translation" situates the reader in the unpleasant world of modernity. But the intermediate language suggests an interspace between the repellant modern and the utopian pre-modern, an imaginary space detached from the poor "translation" of the narrator although nonetheless removed, like him, from the protag-onist's hellish experiences. The novel, in other words, instructs its implied reader in positioning himself in relation to *both* incarnations of Unverdorben. If the experienced protagonist becomes an unsympa-thetic anti-hero, the innocent narrator proves too naïve to be trusted. The narrative construction of *Time's Arrow* compels the reader to create meaning independent from the interpretations offered by either self.

Readers are made to vacillate between enjoying the conceits pro-duced by history's reversal and remembering with horror the disasters that – ironically – the narrator perceives in inverted and therefore cele-bratory form. An obvious instance is the narrator's reference to John F. Kennedy's assassination, a watermark in postwar Western history, mythologized as the downfall of a modern Camelot: "JFK: flown down from Washington and flung together by the doctors' knives and the sniper's bullets and introduced onto the streets of Dallas and a hero's welcome" (81). Readers enjoy the fantasy even as they remember the collective pain which arose as the unfolding event was transmitted over the airways. In Lyotardian terms, the pleasure of this imagined, impossible resurrection "derives from the pain" we experience in recol-lecting historical markers of decline. The reader must engage with the text in an unusually active way, because, as Trussler writes, "we as readers are party to, if not complicit with, a knowledge that the book desperately desires both to repress and expose" (37). At first, the narra-tor's naïveté anaesthetizes Unverdorben's actions from acceptable moral contexts. Yet as Amis explains, the narrator unconsciously urges readers to provide the missing history through his unease with aesthetics: "He keeps wondering why it has to be so ugly, this essentially benevolent action" (Reynolds and Noakes, 21). This entire strategy assumes a collective memory of recent Western history, especially the Holocaust, that raises important questions about the literary use of irony. Whereas in *London Fields* Nicola wagers that Guy won't recognize the names Enola Gay and Little Boy, in *Time's Arrow* Amis places the burden of knowing on the reader.

Amis's use of irony was attacked by some reviewers of the novel, but he maintains that it is entirely appropriate: "Nazism was a biomedical vision to excise the cancer of Jewry. To turn it into something that creates Jewry is a respectable irony" (Reynolds and Noakes, 20). Irony allows an alert reader to appreciate the fallible narrator's misunderstanding of his narration: such readers reconstruct an exactly opposite meaning. The final definition of irony in the Oxford English Dictionary is: "The use of language with one meaning for a privileged audience and another for those addressed or concerned." According to Lifton, the Nazis' misuse of language gave their doctors a "discourse in which killing was no longer killing" (445). He reveals how this practice of misnaming was firmly established at Auschwitz where "'Outpatient centers' were a 'place for selections'; and hospital areas, 'waiting rooms' before death" (186). In *Time's Arrow*, Amis effectively undermines Nazi misuse of language to rationalize mass murder, employing irony to assert an opposing ethic. Unverdorben's various name-changes further confirm the ways Amis reinforces morality through irony. When the novel's chronology is reversed, Tod Friendly becomes John Young: despite Tod's association with death (in German), he becomes a younger Jack-of-all-trades. John then transforms into the gold-rich Hamilton de Souza, who assumes his birth name of Odilo Unverdorben. His last name means "un-depraved" or "un-corrupt" in German. Thus he moves from death to innocence. The reader simultaneously transposes the narrative inversion, which shifts Unverdorben's journey: he becomes a bearer of death, mirroring the change in his ideology. As Diedrick observes, Unverdorben's name "contains both himself and his double" (138), just as Amis's use of irony offers both a literal fantasy (a journey to innocence) and a figurative dismissal of that fantasy (an impossible return to childhood or to pre-Holocaust history). The dual use of language parallels the dual time scheme and the dual codes of ethics. Irony, Amis concludes, "doesn't incite you to transform society; it strengthens you to tolerate it" ("Jane's", 35).

In *The Differend* Lyotard contends that although the Holocaust has robbed "grand narratives" of their legitimacy, it is still possible to legitimize less-sweeping narratives [*petit recits*]: "To learn names," he writes, "is to situate them in relation to other names by means of phrases. Auschwitz is a city in southern Poland in the vicinity of which the Nazi camp administration installed an extermination camp in 1940" (44). This might seem a modest claim within the realm of philosophy, but in the world of fiction such connections associate style with ethics. For Amis, naming, language, and style cannot be separated from morality. His essay on *The Adventures of Augie March* concludes by asserting that "style is morality. Style judges. [...] Things are not merely described but registered, measured and assessed for the weight with which they bear on your soul" (*War*, 467). In Nabokov's *Lolita* as well, Amis discerns a sublime "method of moral focus," one that allows Nabokov to invoke ethics through style: "rendering the imaginative possibilities as intensely, as open-endedly and as perilously as he can, and by letting his style prompt our choice" ("Sublime", 82). Amis does not offer a totalizing panacea to replace Holocaust horrors; instead he deconstructs such metanarratives to reinforce our capacity to confront modern contingency, irrationality and instability. In *Time's Arrow* he wages an ironic war of words on all users of clichés – "clichés of the mind and clichés of the heart" (*War*, xv) – who employ rationalist narratives to recount and account for the Holocaust and of the blood-dimmed tide that was loosed on the world after that crucial point in Western history.

Notes

1 In *Koba the Dread* (2002) Amis similarly aligns the Holocaust with modern technology – itself a product of rational progress: "The exceptional nature of the Nazi genocide has much to do with its 'modernity,' its industrial scale and pace" (83).

2 Although Amis has called postmodernism "a dead end," he confessed that it contained "comic possibilities" that he "hadn't exploited much" and called it "a theory or an idea with tremendous predictive power, because life became very postmodern, politics became postmodern" (Reynolds and Noakes, 16–17).

3 An earlier version of this essay appears in my book *English Fiction Since 1984: Narrating a Nation* (2006).

4 Of course the same danger made Theodor Adorno formulate his famous maxim in *Prisms* (1955) that "writing poetry after Auschwitz is barbaric," although he later withdrew it.

5 Elsewhere, Amis associates this Edenic state with his father Kingsley: "For his generation you were what you were, and that was that. It made you unswervable and adamantine. My father has this quality. I don't. None of us

does" (*War*, 170). He accuses that generation of getting it "hugely wrong" by endorsing the use of atomic weapons (*Einstein's*, 13).

6   Diedrick surveys other precedents for reverse narratives (264–5). To his list I would add Alejo Carpentier's *Viaje a la Semilla*; Carlos Fuentes's *Aura*; and Harold Pinter's *Betrayal*. Amis's Afterword also cites Isaac Bashevis Singer's "Jachid and Jechidah."

7   Menke is especially good on the novel's reversal of A.S. Eddington's image of the second law of thermodynamics (as time's arrow), seemingly defeating the entropic forces of history.

8   Instance Prince Harry of England, who attended a party wearing a Nazi uniform and swastika. A spokesman for the Board of Deputies of British Jews reported, "The whole event, the prince's choice of costume included, indicates a worrying trend of ignorance about the Holocaust that is reinforced by the results of a recent survey that 45% of U.K. residents have never heard of Auschwitz" (*Los Angeles Times*, 14 Jan. 2005: A8). In *Experience* Amis recounts his 1995 visit to Auschwitz, where his guide remarked, "We now have people coming here [...] who think that all this has been constructed to deceive them.[...] They believe that nothing happened here and the Holocaust is a myth" (369).

Works cited

Amis, Martin. *Einstein's Monsters*. New York: Vintage/Random, 1987.
——. *Experience: A Memoir*. New York: Talk Miramax/Hyperion, 2000.
——. Interview with Melvyn Bragg. *The South Bank Show*. 17 Sept. 1989.
——. Interview with Patrick McGrath. *Bomb Interviews*. Ed. Betsy Sussler. San Francisco: City Lights, 1992. 187–97.
——. "Jane's World." *New Yorker* 8 Jan. 1996: 31–5.
——. *London Fields*. New York: Vintage/Random, 1989.
——. "The Sublime and the Ridiculous: Nabokov's Black Farces." *Vladimir Nabokov: His Life, His Work, His World: A Tribute*. Ed. Peter Quennell. New York: Morrow, 1980. 73–87.
——. *Time's Arrow, or, The Nature of the Offense*. New York: Harmony, 1991.
——. *The War Against Cliché: Essays and Reviews 1971–2000*. 2001. New York: Vintage/Random, 2002.
Bauman, Zygmunt, *Modernity and the Holocaust*. Oxford: Polity, 1989.
Bellante, Carl and John. "Unlike Father, Like Son. An Interview with Martin Amis." *Bloomsbury Review* 12.2 (1992): 4–5, 16.
Benjamin, Walter. *Illuminations*. Ed. Hannah Arendt. Trans. Harry Zohn. New York: Schocken, 1969.
Bertens, Hans. *The Idea of the Postmodern: A History*. London and New York: Routledge, 1995.
DeCurtis, Anthony. "Britain's Mavericks." *Harper's Bazaar* Nov. 1991: 146–7.
Diedrick, James. *Understanding Martin Amis*. 2nd ed. Columbia: U of South Carolina P, 2004.
Easterbrook, Neil. "'I know that it is to do with trash and shit, and that it is wrong in time': Narrative Reversal in Martin Amis' *Time's Arrow*." *Conference of College Teachers of Studies* 55 (1995): 52–61.
Heawood, Jonathan. "It's the Death of Others that Kills You." *Guardian* 8 Sept. 2002: 18.

Lifton, Robert Jay. 1986. *The Nazi Doctors: Medical Killing and the Psychology of Genocide.* New York: Basic, 2000.

Lyotard, Jean-François. *The Differend: Phrases in Dispute.* Trans. Georgs van den Abbeele. Minneapolis: U of Minnesota P, 1991.

——. *Heidegger and "the Jews".* Trans. Andreas Michele and Mark Roberts. Minneapolis: U of Minnesota P, 1990.

——. *The Postmodern Condition: A Report on Knowledge.* Trans. Geoff Bennington and Brian Massumi. Minneapolis: U of Minnesota P, 1984.

McCarthy, Dermot. "The Limits of Irony: The Chronillogical World of Martin Amis's *Time's Arrow.*" *War, Literature and the Arts* 11.1 (1999): 294–320.

Menke, Richard. "Narrative Reversals and the Thermodynamics of History in Martin Amis's *Time's Arrow.*" *Modern Fiction Studies* 44.4 (1998): 959–80.

Oertel, Daniel. "Effects of Garden-Pathing in Martin Amis's Novels *Time's Arrow* and *Night Train.*" *Miscelánea* 22 (2001): 123–40.

Reynolds, Margaret, and Jonathan Noakes. *Martin Amis.* London: Vintage/ Random, 2003.

Rosenfeld, Alvin. *A Double Dying: Reflections of Holocaust Literature.* Bloomington: Indiana UP, 1980.

Smith, Penny. "Hell innit: The Millennium in Alasdair Gray's *Lanark*, Martin Amis's *London Fields*, and Shena Mackay's *Dunedin.*" *Essays and Studies* 48 (1995): 115–28.

Stout, Mira. "Down London's Mean Streets." *New York Times Magazine* 4 Feb. 1990: 32–6, 48.

Trussler, Michael. "Spectral Witnesses: Doubled Voice in Martin Amis's *Time's Arrow*, Toni Morrison's *Beloved* and Wim Wenders's *Wings of Desire.*" *Journal of the Fantastic in the Arts* 14.1 (2002): 28–50.

Vonnegut, Kurt. *Slaughterhouse Five.* London: Panther, 1970.

8
Under the Dark Sun of Melancholia: Writing and Loss in *The Information*

Catherine Bernard
University of Paris 7, Denis Diderot

"Every morning we leave more in the bed: certainty, vigour, past loves. And hair, and skin: dead cells" (*Information*, 197). In the third part of what he considers an "informal trilogy" (Fuller, 124), including *Money* and *London Fields*, Martin Amis writes once more as the "malcontent" (Mars-Jones, 156), the melancholy observer intent on outstaring fear and chaos. More than in *London Fields*, his subject in *The Information* is "the tiredness of time lived" (10), the fear and loathing induced by the relentless decay of a society hurtling towards self-destruction, doomed to meaninglessness and chaos. Like *London Fields*, the later novel should be defined as "an apocalyptic jeremiad about the world's decadence and exhaustion at the end of the century" (Diedrick, 128),[1] tapping the anxiety fuelled by the postlapsarian narratives of endings and disintegration. In that respect it can, like the other volumes of the trilogy and his latest novel *Yellow Dog*, indeed "be called distinctively postmodernist," "disjointed and fragmentary, disunified and mediated, entropic and dynamic" (Keulks, 193). More than *Money* or *London Fields*, however, *The Information* should also be defined as large-scale agony fiction in the sense that private, pitiful anxiety is both ruthlessly satirized and heeded for its paradoxical insurrectionary capacity to wreak havoc in a mediated universe, for its quirky responsiveness to worldwide entropy.

Confronted with ontological collapse, Amis both wallows in chaos and struggles to uphold the hermeneutic agenda of fiction precisely by making sense of – and out of – pain and *agon*. The characters' bodies may be beset by escalating pain; the body politic may be besieged by centrifugal, self-induced tensions; Amis still tries to gesture at a possible sublation of chaos, attempts to rethink the complex interdependence of

117

fiction's aesthetic and ethical agendas. The inquiry is all the more topical and crucial because in *The Information* Amis concurrently addresses the mechanics of popular fiction, this time by exploring literature's failed promise of universality, its pandering to the stratagems of the culture industry.

The risks of such a paradoxical enterprise are obvious enough: how can its mimetic negativity escape a counter-productive reintegration within the orbit of affirmative culture? How can literature outstare the dark sun of melancholy, anatomize the current sense of loss, while resisting the lures of reconciliation and preserving its force of impact? How, to put it more simply, can it help not being neutralized by its satirical intent?

"Saying bye"

With *The Information*, Amis continues his exploration of a world sub-mitting to the empire of simulacra. The same "thematic interplay of guilt, desire, and unattainable salvation" (Keulks, 57) prevails in his description of "an age of mass suggestibility, in which image and reality interact" (*War*, 16). He ruthlessly probes this "most vulnerable area in the common mind" (*ibid.*) in order to understand how our desperate yearning for meaning and redemption has been debased into mere con-sumption, whether the consumption of mass-mediated second-rate myths, mass-produced illusions, or mass-circulated information. The brief confrontation between Richard Tull, the protagonist of Amis's panoramic satire, and a "proselytizing Mormon" (173) is in itself reveal-ing: the man appears unaware of the Angel Moroni, the Book of Mormon Prophet. Like the mad speakers ranting "on all the other corners: every corner of London Town" (137), he strikes Tull as another messenger of madness and debilitating faith, inscribed, like the name of the Angel, in a telling paronomastic chain: "Big clue, that: Moroni. Moron with an *i* on the end of it. Moronic without the *c*" (173).

Tull's world is but an updated version of the "moronic inferno" Amis describes in his 1986 collection of essays. Focused more exclusively on the manufacturing of aura and the derealization of experience, *The Information* has rightly been defined as "a novel about the ways in which the late-twentieth century is ... an information age with an information culture driven by information technology down an in-formation highway" (Childs, 52), a tautological phrasing that catches the all-encompassing impact of the information and culture industry. As Theodor Adorno and Max Horkheimer anticipated, the triumph of a culture industry intent on the communication, the circulation and the consumption of transient depthless affects ultimately spells "the abolition of the individual" (154). Above all *The Information* mourns the liquidation of identity. It is thus befitting that the grand promotional tour that takes both Richard Tull and Gwyn Barry – the author "of TV fame" (17, 51) and Tull's closest friend and enemy – around the United States should include a party held in a circus. The allegory is telling: as Richard has sensed, individuality may have been irretrievably eroded:

> Even when he was in familiar company [...] it sometimes seemed to Richard that those gathered in the room were not quite authentic selves – that they had gone away and then come back not quite right, half remade or reborn by some blasphemous, cack-handed and above all inexpensive process. In a circus, in a funhouse. All flakey and carny. Not quite themselves. Himself very much included. (29)

Thus "nobody can just be somebody any more" (34); the self is endlessly processed by CCTV systems, video cameras, a whole array of lenses that frame the characters, ascribe them a place, subject them to a control that, for all its digitalization, is all too real. Most of the characters share in this process of derealization. At one point Richard is frozen inanely in front of the security camera barring him entry from Barry's Holland Park house (17). When Richard first encounters Steve Cousins, he describes him as looking "like a white-and-grey chessboard: like a forensic suspect on TV, his face smeared into squares" (158).[2] Metonymically Steve's flat is also protected by a series of CCTV systems and is ultimately "all for show, like a stage set – despite the fact that nobody ever [comes] here" (221–2). Like Barry's house, it is "a sham" (233), with its video corner predictably featuring "a depthless window-sized TV, the numb sleek blackness of the VCRs, the heap of remotes, plus a Canaveral of decoders and unscramblers" (222).

Barry's is also a world of "reality handler(s)" (355), fully wired like anthropomorphized droids out of a George Lucas film: "Richard sat down near the publicity boy, who, he saw, was not only on the phone but was physically attached to it: he had a thick wire circling his chin like a pilot's mouthmike, freeing both his hands to cope with his laptop E-mail and all the other light-speed technologies they had wired him into" (295). Ever more transient, insubstantial, and alienated, identity is caught in a whirlwind of information, as light and disposable as the junk mail in the "city cyclone" which Tull observes: "leaflike leaflets, flying fliers, circling circulars" (48). Amis's predilection for tautology captures the cultural logic of a world trading in depthless self-love, in media-produced images of interchangeable selves, a cultural logic that has turned Barry into a surrogate "video vicar" (141) "available for transference to the masses" (104)[3] and has reduced writers to marketable clichés – what Adorno and Horkheimer define as "a proficient apparatus, similar (even in emotions) to the model served up by the culture industry" (167). As Gal Aplanalp, a publishing agent, explains to Tull: "writers need definition. The public can only keep in mind one thing per writer. Like a signature. Drunk, young, mad, fat, sick" (130). Trapped in the entropic circulation of empty signs, man has become but a figment.

Part of the Borgesian intertext functions as a deceptive clue accentuating the exhaustion of meaning more than its replenishment. Ironically, Tull's plagiarism hoax to discredit Barry is unwittingly suggested by the failed poet Keith Horridge, whose lines for once strike Tull as "over-compressed [...] Like Yeats at his grandest and raciest" (422). However, Tull shortly realizes the words: "To be immortal / Is commonplace, except for man. / All creatures are immortal, being / Ignorant of death" (422) have been lifted from Borges's story "The Circular Ruins." The twist lends the issue of derealization greater focus. Like "The Aleph" alluded to earlier in the novel, "The Circular Ruins" is a tale of anxiety and loss in which the characters confront their insubstantiality. Far from being omniscient, Borges's protagonist eventually realizes that he is but the figment of another man's imagination. The text's dizzying effect is itself allegorical of the fear at the heart of *The Information*. Maybe the mysterious nightmares that haunt Tull's sleep bring "nothing" (494) with them but the disempowering news of man's final depletion, his ultimate subsumption into a system of simulacra and reflections spinning out of control.[4] The Borgesian melancholy is here tainted by the darker certainty that man's story is not only "the story of lost innocence" (151) but increasingly one of debased desires.

The Information's intertext systematically points to the postlapsarian theme of lost innocence, from Milton's *Paradise Lost* to Waugh's *Handful of Dust* and Marvell's "The Garden," whose titular motif haunts Amis's novel. Not only has the token patch of greenery in the Tulls' local park become a "Dogshit Park," where children are molested and raped, but even the countryside surrounding Demeter Barry's family estate strikes Tull as ominously acculturated:

> Richard felt that the land was being sculpted, was becoming, in fact, a garden, but on a sickening scale. Behold a sickening gardener, one

thousand feet tall, with his sickening scythe, his huge arrow, his reaping-tool, his mile-long trenchworks and earthworks, the terrible topiarist: those trees pregathered on the knoll, that planned plateau, those layered gouges to make the hillside frown or sneer. (263–4)

The well-known trope of fashioning nature to fit the preordained image of a garden – which in turn will become the matrix of Englishness – is here revisited in a melancholy vein more attuned to the deathly tonalities of the ancient pastoral mode. Man's unavowed desire to emulate God (the great gardener) strikes a chill in Tull's initially nostalgic trip down memory lane: "The road might have been taking him back down his central nervous system, to the past, to childhood and its green world, unfallen, where the lion lay with the lamb, and the rose grew without thorn" (263).[5]

Throughout the novel, the Miltonic and Arcadian theme is exploited in both melancholy and bathetic modes. Steve Cousins – the Barnado Boy – treasures a borrowed identity that is sadly ironic. He is no wild-child of Aveyron, but a dysfunctioning killing-machine. Similarly, every scrap of experience seems to tell Richard Tull "to stop saying *hi* and to start saying *bye*" (282). Not even a passing bee can assuage his repeated intimations of mortality and decay: "he was at the time of life when – sitting in a garden or a park – he was more pleased than vexed if a bee buzzed him, flattered that anything, however briefly and stupidly, could mistake him for a flower" (285). Even the final, unexpectedly upbeat, vision of spring seems to suggest a melancholy waning of affects more than a hypothetical reconciliation under the aegis of the rites of spring:

> More a breath sucked in than a breath expelled, up the street it hastened, shaking the trees until their teeth rattled and their pretty hair fell out. Soon the apple blossoms were everywhere, as an element.
>
> And that was the blossoms gone for another year. But for a little while longer they flew in festive and hysterical profusion, as if all the trees were suddenly getting married. (494)

The reader has been well and truly warned: the pastoral promise of redemption from chaos, the marriage of heaven and hell, is but a fantasy whose persistence makes it all the more poignant but no less deceptive. This epiphanic moment holds the antagonistic and agonistic forces of chaos at bay in a short-lived suspension that spells decay and death. The "festive" mood is "hysterical," strident. The apple trees seem suddenly aged – losing "their pretty hair" – even as they drown the city in the innocence of their blossoms.[6]

Barry and Tull's world is one of deadened utopias that have discarded their innocence and, like the Earl of Rievaulx's dynasty, seem to await "cancellation" (266) or, in the prophetic term that Adorno and Horkheimer used to describe the culture industry, "self-liquidation" (143). Even culture itself has become reified, petrified in the paradoxical process that neutralizes even as it sacralizes it. The transformation of Barry's metalanguage is itself allegorical of this exhaustion of culture that Adorno had anatomized in "Cultural Criticism and Society." Barry's well-rehearsed rhetoric, flourished to a bemused Demeter, is as petrified and predictable as the collective fantasy to which his pastoral novels *Amelior* and *Amelior Regained* pander: "The prose is given tautness and burnish precisely by what it deliberately excludes. Picasso's abstracts gain their force from the ... representational mastery he holds in check" (396).

The dissonance of genres

In a last crepuscular moment of anagnorisis, Tull eventually realizes that "all the time he used to spend writing he now spent dying. This was the truth. And it shocked him. It shocked him to see it, naked. Literature wasn't about living. Literature was about dying" (446). Such a negative epiphany is in keeping with the melancholy mood that was meant to preside over the composition of Tull's masterpiece, his *History of Increasing Humiliation*, intended to account for:

> the decline in the status and virtue of literary protagonists. First gods, then demi-gods, then kings, then great warriors, great lovers, the burghers and merchants and vicars and doctors and lawyers. Then social realism: you. Then irony: me. Then maniacs and murderers, tramps, mobs, rabble, flotsam, vermin. (129)

Ultimately, the archetypal non-hero for this archetypally debased novel seems to be Steve Cousins, the failed nemesis, the would-be Wild Boy of Aveyron, whose ineptitude Tull exposes in a mock-showdown at the Warlock, the seedy health club where the characters' destinies are locked in hate and self-loathing. "You think you're some kind of wild boy instead of a fucking dog who, for a while, stopped being a tramp in the city and started being a tramp in the country" (459).

Underlying *the Information*'s metafictional programme is a dark meditation on the logic of genres, on the exhaustion of the reliable calendar of modes and genres as established by Northrop Frye's *Anatomy of Criticism*. As Gavin Keulks has suggested (151), even the generously accommodating Menippean satire no longer seems flexible enough to account for the chaos that has overtaken fiction and subverts its hitherto neatly drawn frontiers. "The four seasons are meant to correspond to the four principal literary genres," Amis writes; "It's obvious, really. Once you've got comedy and tragedy right, the others follow" (52). But, as the intrusive narrator adds, "We keep waiting for something to go wrong with the seasons. But something has already gone wrong with the genres. They have all bled into one another. Decorum is no longer observed" (53). Even comedy seems to have lost its definition: "What genre did his [Richard's] life belong to? That was the question. It wasn't pastoral. It wasn't epic. In fact, it was comedy. Or anti-comedy, which is a certain kind of comedy, a more modern kind of comedy" (179).[7] Even the foray into the land of romance, on the Earl of Rievaulx's estate, takes place in the wrong season: "This was romance but they were doing it in the winter" (271).

In view of the prevailing uncertainty in the literary calendar, one may entertain doubts about the narrator's assurances regarding closure: "And this was spring. The season of comedy. But comedy has two opposites; and tragedy, fortunately, is only one of them. Never fear. You are in safe hands. Decorum will be strictly observed" (479). However, the novel does little to dispel the prevailing sense of generic ambiguity, if only because it eschews the heroic mechanics of tragedy. As Adorno and Horkheimer intuited, the same process of liquidation that engulfed culture has engulfed the tragic mode and symmetrically confirmed "the abolition of the individual" (154). Even Steve Cousins, one of Amis's most cold-blooded villains, fails to qualify fully as the intended nemesis, eventually meeting his fate at the hands of Barry's hired henchmen. Tull, for his part, qualifies as a tragic hero only in an ironical, possibly debased sense. Carrying his mailsack of *Untitleds* around the United States, he is a mock-Sisyphus, paying with a sore back and a bruised ego for his literary hubris. His is the lot of the *desdichado* figures Frye perceives at the hub of the sixth phase of satire, the mythos of winter, figures "of misery or madness, often parodies of romantic roles," condemned to "unrelieved bondage" (238). There may thus be some logic to this literary madness, although it is an ironical and degraded one which Frye already identified in the constant "humiliation" worked upon the fallen anti-heroes by this most modern of amenities: "the 'telescreen' device" (*ibid.*).

Tull's slow descent into hell gradually deprives him of all substance. From having been "a slave in his own life," he becomes "a ghost in his own life" (244), the ghost-writer of unpaid middles for *The Little Magazine*, the ghost-rewriter of inane biographies for Tantalus Press, and eventually the shadow mastermind behind the plot to convict Barry of plagiarism. He has literally become a paper figure: "much of [his life] *was* on paper, written words, memos to the self, scrawled on the corners of envelopes and on the backs of credit-card slips franked by Pizza Express" (250). His future novels also retreat into nothingness: "stacked against him in the future, he knew, were yet further novels, successively entitled *Unfinished, Unwritten, Unattempted* and, eventually, *Unconceived*" (12). Keith Horridge may again prove unexpectedly right when he writes, "Stasis is epitaph" (244), Tull's slow descent into insubstantiality finally threatening to "inhume him" (150).

The theme eventually coalesces around the paradigm of plagiarism. In that respect, *The Information* may be not so much a novel about writers as a novel about would-be/ex-/so-called writers all equally deprived of authority, all shaming inspiration, all signature-less; a pitiless *Künstlerroman* for our end-of-art age. Intertextuality is undoubtedly once more of the essence. Like Julian Barnes, A.S. Byatt, or Peter Ackroyd, Amis engages in an intertextual reflection on canon-formation and literary value, originality and the relation of individual talent to tradition. However what is here adumbrated is a probably darker truth than the one involved in the anxiety of influence syndrome. The Borgesian "circular ruins" may be those of literature, submitted to the same erosion as individual identity. Neither Barry nor Tull has produced a truly original word, and Tull's failed hoax to overshadow his friend may ultimately be but an indirect allegory clinching the novel's meditation on depleted identity. Marvell himself does not escape unscathed, so bathetically inane the words "Stumbling on melons" ("The Garden," line 39) suddenly seem, when decontextualized in the title of Barry's allegedly plagiarized novel.

The plagiarism hoax thus functions in a metafictional manner rather than as a revenge ploy. Its plot does not so much backfire as fail to commence in any effective way. Tull's impotence – in all senses of the term – is thus a far cry from the heroic sadness Julia Kristeva perceives as strategically essential to melancholy (113). In spite of his frantic exertions, Tull achieves nothing; his efforts are systematically debunked and bathetic, unravelling along a series of non-events, misunderstandings, anti-climaxes, missed opportunities to effect Barry's destruction. The general panic that overcomes Tull may thus prove to be an updated version of the hermeneutic energy of melancholy analyzed by Kristeva. However, Tull's activism is no modern *acedia*; it does not bring him nearer to truth, even the paradoxical truth disclosed by mystic revelation (18).

The saddest of truths may in fact be achieved ironically by what Julian Loose defines as the novel's "descent from black comedy to mechanical farce" (9), in which not only the body but also society and the universe exhibit immense dysfunction. In Tull's postlapsarian world physical integrity, like self-identity, seems absent. The electric appliances shop seems to offer a model for the universe: "Beyond, in the back, in a valved heap like the wet city, lay all the stuff that wasn't working and would never work again: the unrecompleted, the undescribed" (50). Disjointed, disconnected from reality, dysfunctioning, Tull's body is exposed as a sick machine in the "full realism" (219) of its entropic decay. Plagued by olfactory delusions that he smells of shit, consistently impotent, his body submits him, like his plummeting towards literary oblivion, to "a *Mahabharata* of pain" (41) that functions like an extended *Vanitas* portending his death: "From what he understood of these syndromes, the *copro* was closely aligned to the *necro* in its adoration of putrescence, waste and decay. Half the time, accordingly, in necromode, he thought he was smelling his own death, nosing it, getting wind of it" (237). His chronic sickness is literally that of the malcontent, the melancholic prone to sudden "liver attack[s]" (47). The already lethal "passions heat" of Marvell's poem (line 25) has become pornography. The inexorable decadence of protagonists in Tull's planned *History of Increasing Humiliation* dovetails into a symbolic descent from "Narcissus to Philoctetes – Philoctetes, whose wound smelled so bad" (197).

Although earlier in his career, Amis claimed to align himself with Fielding's "tradition of writing about low events in a high style" (Haffenden, 24), this influence has darkened to the extent that *The Information* eludes categorization into the Bakhtinian tradition of the carnivalesque grotesque. Far from liberating insurgent forces, the body is here the instrument of inglorious defeat. "Drenched in sweat," his "bowties and waistcoats [...] cratered with stains and burns," Tull is almost literally "falling apart" (40), in keeping with London, which "looked like the insides of an old plug" (11), and reflecting the decentered universe more widely. Tull's ailing body dysfunctions in synchrony with the body politic that London allegorizes at its most cataclysmic and loathsome, with its "bloodbath of sunset," its "red light spell[ing] arterial warning" (200), its bad humors and sad rejects:

> The doors were open to the evening traffic of Notting Hill Gate. Along with the seams of cigarette smoke, the pub vapours and pub humours, the pie waft and the yeasty burp of beer, there was also the breath of cars like a grey mesh of table height. Out on the pavement, only feebly stirred by the little cyclones of rubbish, the twisters of trex, lay several cartons of half-eaten food – meals abandoned in haste or disgust or outright vomitus. (214)

The same anxiously grotesque tone dominates and even triumphs over the bathetic glory of the flight from Boston to Provincetown, when the characters – caught in a hurricane – feel besieged by gods "who had put aside their bullwhips and their elemental rodeo and were now at play with their bowling balls clattering down the gutters of spacetime" (381), hurling these hypermodern Icaruses "to their own thing, the ground, the earth" (382). Nowhere in the novel does the body so forcefully intrude as during this ill-fated flight, when the passengers see a "patch of shit [appear] on the pilot's cream rump" (381) and the pilot eventually leaves the cockpit wearing a "voidance apron" (383). Whereas the culture industry imposes a cosmetic refashioning of identity to the point where it "scarcely signifies anything more than shining white teeth and freedom from body odor and emotions" (Adorno and Horkheimer, 167), the characters' intractable, obtuse bodies resist reification.

One should, however, be wary of aligning Amis's bathetic vision too closely with Adorno and Horkheimer's diagnosis of reified subjectivity. Amis's is in fact a degraded version of Adorno's and Benjamin's more high-minded, heroic plea for aesthetic disintegration or detotalization. Adorno's critique of the culture industry and defence of dislocation in "Trying to Understand *Endgame*" (1958) and *The Philosophy of Modern Music* (1948), Benjamin's anatomy of melancholy in *The Origin of German Tragic Drama* (1973), and Amis's fear and loathing may all tap the same millenarist anxiety; however, Amis offers a deliberately unheroic version of belatedness. In so doing he paradoxically comes closer to Adorno and Horkheimer's definition of the mass laughter exploited by the culture industry in its intimations of fear and its stand against beauty: "The triumph over beauty is celebrated by humor – the *Schadenfreude* that every successful deprivation calls forth. There is laughter because there is nothing to laugh at. Laughter, whether conciliatory or terrible, always occurs when some fear passes" (140).[8]

As Kristeva suggests in her analysis of Dostoevsky's melancholy vision, laughter may be but the flip-side of the green sickness produced by the *acedia* of mystics and writers (187). The dark, somewhat demonic laughter of *The Information* is symptomatic of the paroxystic, negative forces contained in a world which lacks a place for it, the world Barry has come to embody. Tull's intractable humors and those of the text are equalized in this anatomy of meaninglessness. Ultimately they become subsumed under a meta-allegorical structure that includes the cosmic irony of a universe gone awry.

As in his other London novels, Amis stretches pathetic fallacy to its limit. Nature does not merely provide an analogical backdrop to the characters' drama; it seems to emote with the characters, extrapolating their moods. Thus the fog engulfing the lonely fathers in the "loathed park and playground" (62) is not only an apt metaphor for the general despondency of the age; it is "sorry about it [...] wretched about the whole thing. Like the fathers the fog ha[s] nowhere to go" (63). Pathetic fallacy eventually becomes pan-allegorical in a desperate bid for meaning which is doomed to fail or yields even darker conclusions: "Richard sometimes tried to anthropomorphize the sun and the planets – or to solarsystemize his immediate circle. He never got very far with it" (230). Putting Richard's difficulties in "The context of the universe" (164) only brings more frightening intimations of "the great decline" (201), of "cognitive dissonance" (401). Amis's allegorical cosmogony of "red giants," "pulsars," "black holes," and "yellow dwarves" (125) revisits the allegorical matrix of *London Fields*, with its syzygy and impending ecological disasters. In keeping with the private cosmogony of melancholy's *desdichado* figures, it is harnessed onto the aesthetic paradigm and its counter-history of humiliation and loss. The history of fiction does not only chronicle the slow degradation of the protagonist. It is coincidental with the "progress of literature (downwards) [...] forced in that direction by the progress of cosmology [...] From geocentric to heliocentric to galactocentric to plain *eccentric*" (436).[9]

Even closer to the bone lies the demotion of motivation. As early as 1984 Amis was haunted by the certainty that "motivation has become depleted, a shagged-out force in modern life" (Haffenden, 5). The theme would prove central to *Time's Arrow*'s exploration of Nazism's "Nature of the Offense" against humanity. As Odilo Unverdorben explains: "*Hier is kein warum*. Here there is no why. Here there is no when, no how, no where" (128). Amis appropriates the words of a Nazi officer as reported by Primo Levi in *If this is a Man* – words which anticipate his later reflection on the destruction of innocence at the hands of serial killers in his autobiography *Experience*. Significantly, *The Information* is already dedicated to the memory of Amis's cousin Lucy Partington, one of Frederick West's victims. Although her ghostly presence is not as haunting as in Amis's memoir, it undoubtedly informs the novel's most excruciating pages, as when the novel dwells on the assassination of two boys in Washington State: "A contemporary investigator will tell you that he hardly ever thinks about motive. It's no help. He's sorry, but it's no help. Fuck the why, he'll say. Look at the how, which will give you the who. But fuck the why" (169).[10]

When the generic calendar, cosmogony, and causality fail, meaning itself becomes a "shagged-out force." The nature of the information "that comes at night" remains opaque throughout the novel. Its significance may lie in the mere fact of its haunting insistence. Intransitive, autotelic in its capacity to erase all certainties, it is no dark *aletheia*; it heralds no salvationary epiphanies, imparts solely an inchoate message, whose deciphering always eludes the characters, leaving them weeping in the dark.

From alienation to defamiliarization

Amis's paroxystic language largely contributes to the novel's senses of dissonance and doom. His trademark style of using redundancy, of emphasis through incremental repetition, may be defined as maximalist. It orchestrates saturation to achieve maximum effects and unleash maximum affects, producing that fusion of "meaning, motion and emotion" William Gass defines as already central to Robert Burton's language in *Anatomy of Melancholy* (xiv).[11] As Kristeva suggests, a new apocalyptic rhetoric may prove to be the hallmark of late-twentieth-century literature. Through it, writing attempts violently to disclose, uncover rather than reveal – as would be the case with progressive *aletheia* – the nothingness that underlies our belated condition (231) and, more widely, man's tragic fate. As Amis insists in his essay on nostalgia in Waugh: "The good is gone, the bad is all to come: this theme is as old as literature. What a writer does with it is simply a matter of style and tone" (*War*, 201).

In *The Information*, Amis intends not only to wage war on cliché through charged language, but also to emulate the "High-Style" (65) of cosmic chaos. With Tull he may indeed make his programmatic motto of Moloch's words in *Paradise Lost*, "My sentence is for open war" (II.51; Amis, *Information*, 62). In his interview with Alexander Laurence and Kathleen McGee, Amis explains that *The Information* tries to come as close as possible to the shifting vernacular of an age of "trex" and aggression:

> As I say in this book, I think that most books are written in a language thirty years out of date, a generation out of date. The rhythms of thought that are actually out there don't correspond [...] Maybe writing does lag behind the times. I wanted to suggest the new rhythms of thought which change all the time.

As John Nash suggests, "the information ... is apocalyptic: it's about death, local and universal. It is monstrous, the *telos* ... of life. The end of the 'terrestrial story' is the end of the act of reading (we'll no longer be reading Amis then), but not necessarily the end of language" (167). Paradoxically, language may be the only channel allowing the constructive discharge of "aggression" that Adorno contends "the new cultural matrix releases ... in at least equal measure to its release of desire" (*Culture*, 25) in its self-destructive libidinal energy. Undoubtedly the dialectical strength of Amis's writing lies in its capacity to be relentlessly confrontational. Adam Mars-Jones has accurately noted that "Amis's originality as a stylist has been to separate verbal beauty from the cause it has traditionally served, to detach lyrical language from the lyrical impulse" (155). Only in eschewing the comforts of harmony and self-identity, in waging war on the peace of language, can writing hope to resist the reification that has enslaved culture.

The limit between a rhetoric of resistance that would not accommodate "dominant currents of thought" (Adorno and Horkheimer, xii) and the controlled language of industrialized entertainment is more than tenuous. Sheer vigor, like the recourse to constant anathema, does not sufficiently create a truly oppositional idiom. As Adorno showed: "the entertainment industry determines its own language,... by the use of anathema. The constant pressure to produce new effects ... serves merely as another rule to increase the power of conventions" (*Dialectic*, 128). Amis's susceptibility to the new vernacular is in tune to the way the culture industry "forces together the spheres of high and low art" (Adorno, *Culture*, 98).

The inflationary quality of Amis's language testifies that he agrees with Adorno that the "task of art today is to bring chaos into order" (*Moralia*, 222) in order to resist its reification into a mere signature effect. Only thus may style be endowed with ethical power. Amis never tires of insisting with Nabokov that "style *is* morality" (*Experience*, 121; *War*, 467), and in order to defy neutralization and subsumption, Amis seems to heed the sirens' calls of the new, of entertainment culture. Complicity with the system may thus be of the essence in Amis's wintery satire. Perhaps the accusation of complicity is itself a cliché that the writer must appropriate in order to thematize and defamiliarize it. As Amis noted to Haffenden: "In my writing, yes, I am fascinated by what I deplore, or I deplore what fascinates me; it's hard to get it the right way round. But another equally reliable cliché is that you feel completely distinct as a writer and as a person" (3).

For Amis, the same degree-crisis that shook the Renaissance, when a new epistemological paradigm imposed itself, also prevails today. Paradoxically, this gives the age its peculiar energy.[12] With the demise of the inherited, stable generic taxonomy, the desuetude of authority and causality, comes the waning of the Modernist belief in the isolation of art from its nefarious environment. Amis seems to wallow deliberately in the effluvia of our mass-culture to sublate its Medusa-like allure. In spite of his sympathy for his anti-hero, Amis is no Richard Tull. He has moved beyond the pale of Modernism whereas he portrays his protagonist as stuck in a quasi-infant fixation that prevents him from coping with the rhythms of an age enamoured of its own degradation.

It is therefore only fitting that Amis should stage Tull's meeting with Gina – his wife and "mother-earth" figure (169) – in Nottingham, on the occasion of an exhibition commemorating D.H. Lawrence. Like Gina's endearing regionalisms, Lawrence's belief in the emancipating power of art seems out-of-place and out-of-date, inadequate before an abrasive age in which art has become complicit with the vices it intends to denounce. All too aptly, Gina's boyfriend – whom Tull succeeds in ousting – is named Lawrence.

Tull will, in his turn, be supplanted and abandoned by the gods of literature. The Nottingham episode finally strikes him as "an episode of reckless *nostalgie*: class, blood, the provinces, D.H. Lawrence, uncomplicated love" (329). He is a "marooned modernist" (170) out of synchrony with the present who belatedly worships at the altar of "tautly leashed prose" (67). As James Diedrick rightly remarks, referencing Tull's Läocoon-like entanglement in the hose of his vacuum-cleaner, Tull has failed to warn London – the modern Troy – against the impending invasion of (post)-modernity: "The gods of contemporary culture … embrace Gwyn's imagined new world order and reject Richard's vision of difficulty and asceticism" (157). Modernity, with its mute and obtuse appliances that refuse to submit to man's will, seems to have the final word. The irony is pat; Tull the modernist is nothing but a has-been who has overstayed his leave and should be vacuumed away. As Tull becomes trapped more tightly in the noose of his plot, he realizes that he will be defeated. As during their games of chess, he knows that "Gwyn [is] playing in the new notation while [he] toil[s] along in the old" (142).

Refusing to pander to his readers, Tull remains intent on "stretch[ing] them until they twanged" (170). And indeed they do, suffering from cataclysmic headaches, seizures and paralysis, Amis's comic hyperbole for modernist fidelity to intellectual art. Writing "in the wake of the *Wake*, [he] has missed the moment of unreadability" (Nash, 167). As Tull himself admits: "whatever [he] stood for – the not-so-worldly, the contorted, the difficult – had failed" (364). *Untitled*, with its "figment narrator pretend[ing] to attempt [a] series of decoy refocusings" (304) and other quirky mannerisms, fails to resist its own reification. It too becomes cliché.

What Tull fails to grasp is that, in his desperate bid for literary autonomy, he has fossilized, shed all individuality and, like Barry, turned into one of the hollowed-out, papery silhouettes that Adorno evokes in *Minima Moralia* – insubstantial husks deprived of personal truth. It is only too revealing that Tull's favorite narrative stratagems in *Untitled* should be the use of unreliable, surrogate narrators, of counterfeit travesty and "sham refocusings" (304). Such negative and ironic *ars poetica* indirectly confirms the liquidation of both writing and selfhood. Intending to oppose the forces of readability in the name of aesthetic autonomy, Tull may ironically have helped the final neutralization of writing, thus validating Adorno and Horkheimer's diagnosis that "throughout the whole history of the bourgeoisie [the artist's] autonomy was only tolerated, and thus contained an element of untruth which ultimately led to the social liquidation of art" (157). In a pat moment of allegorical dramatization, the novel clinches this meditation on the demise of artistic autonomy. Having narrowly survived their flight, Barry asks Tull to sign his copy of *Untitled*, failing to remember that he has already done so. Tull's signature thereby signifies nothing. His high-style fails to create a corresponding signature-effect that identifies Tull as an author. Thus two degraded figures of authorship confront one another across this unidentifiable signature, this signature that is no legible sign.

In order to avoid liquidation, writing must assume the risk of contradiction, and the writer must accept immersion in the society whose logic he exposes and which thereby alienates him, placing himself, as Adorno suggests, in Baron Münchhausen's position when he pulls "himself out of the bog by his pig-tail" (*Moralia*, 74). For criticism to be efficient, it must be immanent to its object yet literally remain in two minds and also stand aloof. Thus can it hope to be immune from the petrification of transcendent criticism which idealizes and fetishizes truth. Amis embraces the contradictions entailed by an immanent reading of contemporary society. He does not balk at the inconsistencies of the artist's status and eventually accepts the risks of aporia that ensue when artists do not "cover up the contradiction" but take it "into the consciousness of their own production" (Adorno and Horkheimer, 157).[13]

This is nowhere more obvious in *The Information* than in the instability of the narrative voice. Despite Amis's insistence that he did not intend *The Information* to be metafictional – that "there's no levels of reality or unreliable narrators" (Laurence and McGee) – the novel is fraught with self-awareness. As in *Money*, Amis features here between the lines. We see him giving his name in crooked sign-language to a boy in a London park, mistakenly assuming the child is deaf-and-dumb and realizing too late that he is merely giving him his name. His meta-literary reaction is symptomatic of the novel's overall anxiety: "how can I play the omniscient, the all-knowing, when I don't know *anything*?" (63). Throughout the text, the narrative voice intrudes during metafictional pauses to reflect on the increasingly risky business of fiction. Characters are admitted to have become unruly, particularly Steve Cousins, who can't be controlled (232). Language seems to offer little purchase on a reality too emotionally involved to be readable (68).

More important, the syntactic logic has spun out of control; personal pronouns have become expendable in a manic bid for transparency and opacity. As the intrusive narrator confesses, "the interior monologue now waives the initial personal pronoun, in deference to Joyce" (11). Although Amis still embeds himself in his own fiction, his position is not as clearly circumscribed as it was in *Money*. If he poses as a puppetmaster, this may be a mere posture to mask his lack of control and self-identity. No longer that of the omniscient mastermind, the voice has become estranged, ghostly, disembodied. Such deformation mirrors the dysfunctioning generic calendar and the "cognitive dissonance" previously analyzed. It may be the price one must pay to confront the "untruth" Adorno perceives at the heart of culture (*Prisms*, 28).

There is no end to melancholy. The information carried by *The Information* yields no certainty. The characters seem "poised between a destructive present and an even more terrible future; they face "massive contingency, entropic decay, and destabilization on both existential and ontological levels" (Keulks, 76). Instead of enlightenment Tull is offered the ambiguous solace of endless anxiety and longing. With Kristeva, Amis seems to concur that our postlapsarian condition calls for an *"esthétique de la maladresse"* (Kristeva, 233), an awkward art that is deliberately non-cathartic, an aesthetic both programmatically awkward (*maladroite*) and literally ill-addressed, missing its object in the very bid for recapture. Enamoured with the protracted experience of failure that "inhumes" it, writing may thus paradoxically assert itself as fully individualized by suffering and the empathy that comes from the sustained contemplation of loss (see Kristeva, 245).

For all its stridency, *The Information* is also, maybe equally, a novel susceptible to human vulnerability: the vulnerability of sleepers, children, broken things, and tattered memories. The numerous scenes describing characters asleep and adrift on the night waves of anxiety indicate a counter-sensibility, one in tune with the often imperceptible and suppressed rhythms of transient innocence. With Elias Canetti whose *Crowds and Power* is, one should remember, one of Steve Cousins's main inspirations, Amis empathizes with man at his weakest when, lying down, he appears unprotected.[14] Amis thus flouts the rule according to which "empathy is dilution and blunder" (Mars-Jones, 156). He deliberately blunders into the mined territory of sentimentalism to catch Demeter asleep with her hands "raised on either side of her fold of fair hair, as if in surrender" (234) or to portray Tull's twins, "their motive bodies reluctantly arrested in sleep, and reef-knotted to their bedware" (11).

Even more unashamedly and blunderingly (*"maladroitement"* in Kristeva's words), the text enlists the power of naked, albeit humorous, emotion through the character of Marco, the would-be victim of Steve's self-loathing, the child whose love for his father is as unfathomable as his fear that he may have disappointed him. Marco's song of love for his father – "I like Daddy. / He lives with me. / I like him. / And he likes me" – is "remarkable, really, for how little information it got across (and for its dud *rime riche*)" (120). It may be dissonant with the abrasive satirical tonality that prevails in the novel but indeed chimes with, rhymes with, the rampant nostalgia that underlies such satire.

The tonal hiatus between these antagonistic moods may be the key to understanding the novel, albeit a puzzling one. The "unsettling indeterminacy" (Diedrick, 147) that reigns supreme preempts any attempt at healing the rift between anger and sentimentalism. But maybe "the division itself is the truth" if one is to "express the negativity of the culture which the different spheres constitute" (Adorno and Horkheimer, 135). No dialectics seems possible or even relevant. One may object that contradiction may be yet another lure produced by culture to preempt implementing a new kind of praxis. One may object that such recourse to sentimentalism is but a crass ploy, an outdated Dickensian strategy tethering the reader's emotions and that, far from being critical, Amis here falls prey to the lures of mass culture. Amis would probably reply that neither realism nor experimentation is up to the task of coming to terms with our dark present if they are not pitted against each other. The contemporary writer, he has insisted, must therefore "combine these veins, calling on the strengths of the Victorian novel together with the alienations of post-modernism" (*War*, 79). The risk of fetishizing emotion is one of Amis's complex artistic gambles. The fact that the tripartite tensions between melancholy, hatred, and emotion that sustain *The Information* cannot be subsumed by totality is thus but another sign of Amis's resilient belief in the capacity of writing to confront aporia.

Notes

1 See Amis in Fuller: "*London Fields* is proclaimedly about the end of the millennium. You do feel that history is approaching a climax and that all over the world one is seeing the classical symptoms of millenarian anxiety and fever: fundamentalism, strange weather, et cetera."

2 The image recurs as Tull and Barry play chess: "The way the white pieces were configured, like a hairline, and the squares drifting in his milky gaze: the board resembled the image of a face, on TV; the smeared cubes of some wrongdoer, some child-murderer, pixelated – the face of Steve Cousins" (474). This moment paves the way for Cousins's assault on Tull's son Marco and locks him in the combined rhetoric of crime and TV culture.

3 Central to Barry's marketing are his posing as an amateur carpenter and his appearance on the TV program, "The Seven Vital Virtues: Uxoriousness," which depicts him strolling with his wife past "the squirrels and mazelets and mantled pools of Holland Park" and dining "at their 'local' French restaurant, [...] feeding each other dripping spoonfuls of goopy icecream" (92–3).

4 Diedrick insists on the centrality of "The Aleph" to *The Information*'s cosmological paradigm, contending Borges's vision of "a sphere whose center is everywhere and whose circumference is nowhere" is crucial to Amis's intuition of "the nothingness of the individual ego" and to Tull's "long lesson in his insignificance" (151).

5 The chill may indeed be deathly if one recalls a similar image in Amis's Afterword to *Time's Arrow*: "The National Socialists found the core of the reptile brain, and built an autobhan that went there. Built for speed and safety, built to endure for a thousand years, the *Reichautobahnen*, if you

remember, were also designed to conform to the landscape, harmoniously, like a garden path" (176).

6 See also Nash: "As with the ending of *Money*, the comedy that closes *The Information* is not tragic but melancholic" (167), and Luc Verrier's suggestion that "*eirene* is attained via agonistic negativity" (105).

7 See Amis in Fuller: "*The Information* is basically a comedy, and comedy in my view now has to do everything. It's as if all the other genres have collapsed, you're going to find some odd things in comedy these days, things that normally wouldn't have much business being in comedy."

8 Writing about *Lolita*, Amis returns to the ambiguity of laughter, to its close relation with darker affects: "What makes human beings laugh? [...] Human beings laugh, if you notice, to express relief, exasperation, stoicism, hysteria, embarrassment, disgust and cruelty" (*War*, 488).

9 In his essay "Sex, Violence and Complicity: Martin Amis and Ian McEwan" (1999), Kiernan Ryan insists on the "deadly reciprocity of domestic violence and the atomic violence in the international public sphere: the two realms feed[ing] off each other in a suicidal mockery of symbiosis" (209). For more on the climatics of *London Fields*, see Tredell (ch.7) as well as my earlier essays, "Dismembering/Remembering Mimesis: Martin Amis, Graham Swift" (1993) and "A Certain Hermeneutic Slant: Sublime Allegories in Contemporary English Fiction" (1997). The "dark sun of melancholy" is central to Verlaine's *Uhr* poem on melancholy, "El Desdichado," to which Kristeva devotes a chapter.

10 The waning of causality does not originate with *Time's Arrow*, as Haffenden's interview proves and Keulks explains: it is already programmatic to *Money* which "antagoniz[es] many of realism's classical conventions, [d]isbanding the classical segregation of author and text, rejecting motivation as an aspect of character, eliminating causality and linearity from the narrative frame" (189).

11 Amis understands the dangers of powerful signature effects. Witness his self-indicting comment about Tull's style: "he had just put *Untitled* away for the morning, after completing an hysterically fluent passage of tautly leashed prose" (67). Ryan argues that the experience of meaninglessness helps explain Amis's "swaggering verbal exorbitance and figurative overkill,... the sustained, speeding note of desperate excess" (209). On the link between loss and the rhetoric of objects, see Susan Stewart's *On Longing* (1993).

12 See Amis in Laurence and McGee: "one's place in the universe was an illusion till Copernicus came along. The earth was the center of the universe. Part of the energy of the Renaissance came from shrugging off that illusion."

13 On immanence, see Adorno, "Cultural Criticism and Society." Writing in 1986, Amis foregrounded Joyce's complex interweaving of longing and stylistic aggressiveness in an iconoclastic reading (that anticipates Tull's unreadability) by evoking the "reader-hostile; reader-nuking immolation of *Finnegans Wake*" (*War*, 442).

14 See the section "Aspects of Power" and the sub-section "Human Postures and Their Relation to Power. *Standing. Sitting. Lying. Sitting on the Ground. Kneeling.*"

Works cited

Adorno, Theodor W. *The Culture Industry. Selected Essays on Mass Culture.* Ed. J.M. Bernstein. London: Routledge Classics, 2001.
———. *Minima Moralia. Reflections from Damaged Life.* 1951. Trans. E.F.N. Jephcott. London: Verso, 1974.
———. *Prisms.* 1955. Trans. Samuel and Shierry Weber. Cambridge, MA: MIT P, 1983.
Adorno, Theodor, and Max Horkheimer. *Dialectic of Enlightenment.* 1973. Trans. John Cumming. London: Verso, 1979.
Amis, Martin. *Experience.* 2000. London: Vintage, 2001.
———. *The Information.* London: Flamingo, 1995.
———. *Time's Arrow, or, The Nature of the Offense.* London: Jonathan Cape, 1991.
———. *The War Against Cliché: Essays and Reviews, 1971–2000.* 2001. London: Flamingo, 2002.
Childs, Peter. *Contemporary Novelists. British Fiction Since 1970.* London: Palgrave, 2005.
Diedrick, James. *Understanding Martin Amis.* 2nd ed. Columbia: U of South Carolina P, 2004.
Frye, Northrop. *Anatomy of Criticism.* 1957. Princeton: Princeton UP, 1973.
Fuller, Graham. "The Prose and Cons of Martin Amis." *Interview* 25.5 (May 1995): 122–5.
Gass, William. Introduction. *Anatomy of Melancholy.* By Robert Burton. New York: New York Review, 2001. v–xiv
Haffenden, John. "Martin Amis." *Novelists in Interview.* London: Methuen, 1985. 1–24.
Keulks, Gavin. *Father and Son: Kingsley Amis, Martin Amis, and the British Novel Since 1950.* Madison: U of Wisconsin P, 2003.
Kristeva, Julia. *Soleil noir. Dépression et mélancolie.* 1987. Paris: Gallimard, 2002.
Laurence, Alexander, and Kathleen McGee. "Martin Amis is Getting Old and Wants to Talk About It." <http://www.altx.com/int2/martin.amis.html>
Loose, Julian. "Satisfaction." *London Review of Books* 11 May 1995: 9–10.
Mars-Jones, Adam. "Looking on the Blight Side." *Times Literary Supplement* 24 March 1995: 19–20. Tredell, 155–6.
Nash, John. "Fiction May Be A Legal Paternity." *English: The Journal of the English Association* 45.133 (1996): 213–24. Tredell, 163–72.
Tredell, Nicholas, ed. *The Fiction of Martin Amis.* London: Palgrave, 2000.
Verrier, Luc. "Sentimental Comedy in Martin Amis's 'State of England' and 'The Coincidence of the Arts'." *Miscelánea* 28 (2003): 97–108.

9
Mimesis and Informatics in *The Information*

Richard Menke
University of Georgia

In *The Information* (1995), fiction has entered a world whose dominant cultural form is named by its title. Martin Amis's darkly comic tale of literary rivalry does not merely anatomize authorial envy, midlife masculinity, or the high-octane literary scene of the 1990s, but ultimately views these subjects in relation to an era of information overkill, multimedia saturation, and the conversion of cultural expression into "content." More explicitly than Amis's earlier novels, *The Information* locates itself, and literature, within the contemporary media ecology – an information environment on the verge of the Internet Age. The novel treats successful authorship as a media phenomenon – a familiar insight to which Amis brings considerable wit and nuance as well as the inbuilt irony of his own celebrity. But the informatic orientation of *The Information* also operates more generally, shaping the novel on virtually every level, from its invocations of astrophysics to its self-reflexiveness and store of metaphors. Most strikingly, it enters the texture of the novel's mimesis, its stylized and self-conscious realism.[1]

The mode of fictional mimesis now called "classic realism" arose in a very different setting, one defined by the explosion of print rather than its looming eclipse. Histories of the novel have not yet fully come to terms with fiction's relationships to the changing media environment, but important critical accounts suggest we should read the English novel's rise and development against the cultural history of media. In *Orality and Literacy*, Walter Ong argues that the classic realist novel – with its norms of character development, linear plots, coherent point of view, and the quest for closure – represents the quintessential application of the norms of print literacy to imaginative storytelling (117–35). Lennard Davis's *Factual Fictions* rounds out Ong's general claims; it traces the genealogy of the English novel, including the "constitutive ambivalence towards fact and fiction" that Davis identifies as realism, through its development within the eighteenth century's surge of printed narrative prose (212).

Although not specifically concerned with fiction, Friedrich Kittler's *Discourse Networks 1800/1900* emphasizes the relationship of imaginative writing to dominant practices of inscription and data storage. Kittler contrasts the Romantic-era naturalization of writing with the modernist understanding of writing as a set of graphemic permutations, one medium among others. The first movement produces the *Bildungsroman*, which treats personal growth as narrative development and maps psychology onto print textuality; the second gives us the culture industry – and the novels of Woolf and Joyce. "[L]iterature as word art [...] this is [its] constellation in the purest art for art's sake and in the most daring games of the avant-garde," Kittler declares of the 1900 discourse network; ever since the Lumière twins opened their movie theater, "there has been one infallible criterion for high literature: it cannot be filmable" (248).

In an age of technical media for storing sight, sound, and movement more directly, modernist fiction grew wary of the mimetic techniques of classic realism. But as fiction becomes part of the discourse network of 2000, the old choice between the alternatives of mass culture and high modernism no longer functions similarly. Since Clement Greenberg, modernist works have been recognized for exploring the material conditions of their media. But what happens when fictional writing encounters a dominant cultural ideal defined by its opposition to media specificity – the concept of information? As John Johnston notes, information "is neither a language nor a medium" (*Information*, 2). Rather, *information* describes the idea of dematerialized data, equally unconstrained by context and by physical inscription in any medium – a kind of abstract factuality "disconnected from the situations that it is about" (Nunberg, 111). Information is knowledge apart from any knower; in information theory, it is "a probability function with no dimensions, no materiality.[...] a pattern, not a presence" (Hayles, 18).[2]

The oldfangled notion of postmodernism, which can turn the modernist quest for form into spiraling self-reference, often combined with an embrace of low culture, might offer one way of considering the change. From our position more than a decade after its heyday, we might take the term *postmodern* itself as memorializing the late-twentieth- century's vertiginous view of the cultural convergence that a rising norm of digital information would soon make inescapable. Fredric Jameson's magisterial *Postmodernism* (1991) argued for the "cultural logic" linking the arts and literature to an economic system defined by rapid global flows of finance capital – and by that capital's readiness to colonize every aspect of culture. Ultimately for Jameson, this logic works to abolish the former "semiautonomy of the cultural sphere" (48). Thanks to the growth of information technologies that were still emergent during the postmodern moment, today capital and cultural expression are ever more likely to move along the same channels, as coded digital information that is largely indistinguishable during its transit. In terms of Jameson's analysis, perhaps the flow of information further shortens the circuit between base and superstructure, art and economics. Which takes us to *The Information*.

Characterizing information

If modernist writing rejects classic realism's fabrication of a stable balance between mimesis and diegesis, or even the distinction between showing and telling, postmodern fiction can reengage realism by destabilizing that balance or highlighting its conventionality. Thus its procession of Ballardian or Baudrillardian simulations, of authors who appear as characters in their own works, of art novels that invoke the low mimesis of genre fiction. Clearly, none of this is foreign to Amis's oeuvre. Although they are less intrusive features than the arrival of the Martin Amis character in *Money* (1984) or the existential noir of *Night Train* (1997), *The Information* includes points at which the narrator identifies himself as "M [...] A" (42), in addition to Amis's customary incorporation of elements drawn from mystery novels, science fiction, and crime stories. Going further, *The Information* places such mimetic play in the framework not simply of textual self-consciousness but of a world of proliferating information.

Channeled by interconnecting forms of multimediation, such mimetic data raises issues not merely of verisimilitude or fidelity but of filtering, compression, and level of definition – even when it comes to an element as basic as characterization. After introducing us to the unsuccessful novelist Richard Tull and his nemesis Gwyn Barry, as well as Richard's twin sons, *The Information* brings in another male twosome as they distractedly surveil the authors. With a descriptive economy that recalls and exceeds the language of a police report or *roman policier*, the narrative presents the criminals Scozzy and 13, who will figure in the revenge plots between Richard and Gwyn: "13 was eighteen and he was black. His real name was Bently. Scozzy was thirty-one, and he was white. His real name was Steve Cousins" (8). Name, alias, age, ethnicity. The first extended description of Steve confirms the kind of media that have been reprocessed to invent this character; he is "reading a magazine called *Police Review*," a real publication for British police officers (14). More arrestingly, the passage represents Steve by invoking the manipulation of televisual data: "in certain lights his features seemed to consist of shifting planes and lenses, like a suspect's face 'pixelated' for the TV screen: smeared, and done in squares, blurred, and done in boxes" (14). A physical description of a character cites a technique from another medium, a moving image systematically reprocessed to give it lower definition, to decrease its informational content.

The typical use of video pixelation – to obscure the identity of a suspect who has not yet been convicted – makes it a fitting medium for Steve, as if he arrived with his own predestined video effect. But so do the mechanics of the process. Over a recognizable face, pixelation superimposes a large, virtual grid that replaces facial details with a color value derived from the hues contained in each square. The image becomes so dominated by its own averages that we can scarcely recognize the face as human. It is a commonplace to note the twentieth century's movement from a culture of the printed word to one increasingly centered on mass-circulated images. But here *The Information* highlights the status of the mediated image as information: how it has been mathematically transformed, what it leaves out. A kind of *reductio* of what Marshall McLuhan considered the "cool," low-definition medium of television, the pixelated image makes it clear that the television's screen is precisely that, with its grid of charged-up phosphors (22).

As a picture of the reptilian Steve Cousins, perhaps the most disquieting of Amis's urban sociopaths, the pixelated news video provides an apt figure for all of Steve's "features," not merely his mien; by invoking a modern medium, the passage at once concedes and transcends the character's lack of delineation, deliberate stylization, and origin in mass cultural stereotype (a word that itself records printing's passage from handset individual characters to large-scale uniformity). Like the blurred-out face with the sharpened edges, Steve appears in the novel as an uneven mosaic of transparency and opacity. The novel repeatedly defines him negatively, by the features it won't reveal in focus, the information that doesn't appear: his history (we learn only that Steve was a Barnardo boy, was abused, ran wild), his motive, his desire. Gwyn's wife, Lady Demeter, may be "blonde, rich, stacked. But she wasn't Steve's type. No human woman was. No, nor man, neither"

(15). Borrowing from *Hamlet*, the narrative places Steve's desires in a black box; we will learn that this box is opaque even to Steve himself.

"What you never wanted to do was fit the profile," muses Steve, as the novel offers a checklist of his damaged psyche (360). For Katherine Hayles, one hallmark of information culture and electronic media is their displacement of writing's Derridean dialectic of presence and absence for a new emphasis on the play of pattern and randomness (28). In its characterization of Steve Cousins, *The Information* seems to struggle to translate a version of such play into the terms of psychological fiction. The novel assures us that Steve is "not a type. Not an original, maybe; but not a type" (113). Reading *The Information*, it is not hard to notice that talk of *originals*, *types*, or even *characters* is the language of old media.

At the first meeting between Steve and a drunken Richard Tull, the novel recurs to pixelation, now augmenting the image – without increasing its resolution – by specifying Richard's role. Each man examines the other "quid pro quo," so that a narrative moment of shot-countershot focalization (Steve seen from Richard's viewpoint, Richard from Steve's) opens into a miniature mediascape of the criminal trial in an age of mass visuality:

> To Richard (who was "pixelated," and thoroughly, in the old sense), Steve looked like a white-and-gray chessboard: like a forensic suspect on TV, his face smeared into squares. To Steve [...] Richard looked like an artistic two-dimensionalization of himself, hollow, wavery, approximate, and rendered with minimum talent: the work of a court portraitist. (116)

An image from not a royal court but a legal one. If Steve is the suspect, Richard is "a witness.[...] a character witness," as hastily captured by the courtroom artist – and something of a daubed character himself (116). Richard has already recognized Steve's ferocity: "A violent manic who hated Gwyn's stuff," he thinks, "Why weren't there any more where he came from?" (114). Later, as he gingerly cancels his plan for Gwyn's brutalization by Steve and company, Richard comes to see the static-like storm within the pixelized image, "glimps[ing] the white-capped *tormenta* in the digital grid of the young man's face" (212).

The pixelated "chessboard" of Steve's face incorporates one of the real games played by the dueling novelists, proxies for their larger contest. Later the simile appears in reverse; the chessboard Richard and

Gwyn use in their final game "resemble[s] the image of a face, on TV; the smeared cubes of some wrongdoer, some child-murderer, pixelated – the face of Steve Cousins" (358). The chessboard suggests the pattern of rules behind the altered image, systems shaping not only the way a novel may picture a character but the way it imagines his consciousness. Surveying Gwyn's impressive house, Steve becomes not merely an image of filtered data but an information filter:

> Seeing it not as an architectural or even a real-estate phenomenon but as a patchwork of weaknesses. Bits of it seemed to flash and beep at him in outline – to flash and beep in his robot vision. Security-wise the first-floor terrace was a fucking joke. [...] Not that he'd be wanting to bring anything out of there except the information. (64)

In a sense, this passage employs two of classic realism's standard modes of representing thought: psychonarration (how Steve is "seeing"– an external account of mental events) and free indirect discourse (his inner monologue, presented in the narrative's grammatical tense and person). But here *The Information* shifts the language of mental narration from psychology to computing.

Technically, the passage comes closer to diegesis than mimesis, telling rather than showing, but it is a telling that derives from the mimetic code of another medium. Steve's "robot vision" owes much to the cyborg films of the 1980s and early 1990s; it is a prose pastiche of the cinematic cut from Technicolor Hollywood realism to the overtly machinic point-of-view shot attributed to a RoboCop, Terminator, or "Decimator" (which seems to be *The Information*'s fictitious version of such spectacles). After all, Scozzy and his abrupt, irrational violence come from the future: "Every day he pulled off the crime of the century. They didn't have to be completed or successful, because he didn't mean this century. He meant the *next* one" (140). But this appropriation of a science-fiction visual effect works in deeper ways to bring the representation of mental experience into a universe of information. Fracturing Steve's perceptions into flashing, beeping "bits" treats the absence of perceptual unity as a mode of digitization, via a half-pun that the novel makes several times. "13? 13 was in bits"; in response to Richard's question about what he does, Steve replies, "You know. 'Bit of this. Bit of that'" (50, 64). The treatment of the scene's visual bits as indifferent flashes and beeps represents them in the standard shorthand for electronic gibberish, but it also sustains their digital character. Digital information must be systematically converted to register in our senses; having no intrinsic tie to a particular sense modality, it can as readily be formatted for one sense as another – as flashes or as beeps.

Various bits in the perceptual field jump into salience without conscious attention or effort; Steve's thoughts suggest not the Freudian interplay of the conscious and unconscious so much as the coexistence of separate subroutines for mindfulness and basic pattern recognition. In this representation of a character's visual processes – as Johnston argues more generally of "machinic vision" – "perception has become a distributed function" ("Machinic", 45). Mentation gives way to data management, as the passage ends with one of the novel's many invocations of "information." The title of Richard's first novel, *Aforethought*, plays on the legal term for premeditation, but Steve's malice, while deliberate, seems almost like malice *before* thought, before awareness or intent. Reflecting on contemporary life, Richard, or the narrator, notes that "violence would come, if it came, from the individual, from left field, denuded of motive" (99), an idea soon echoed in the mystery plot of *Night Train* and a typical Amis stance.

A character's thoughts and intentions seem to emerge from local, parallel processes of data management that the novel screens out, limited by the properties of language, the exigencies of storytelling, or the seriality of an extended print narrative. The cyborgian Steve might seem a special case, with his isolation, his iciness, his "[a]nimal thermovision" (187). Yet *The Information* applies similar paradigms even to its protagonist. Much of the novel consists of representations of Richard's unspoken thoughts, and its narration of his consciousness is generally unmarked and transparent. In a revealing aside, however, the novel ventures a parenthetical recognition of its own invisible codes and processes:

> Richard was thinking, if thinking is quite the word we want (and we now do the usual business of extracting those thoughts from the furious and unceasing babble that surrounds and drowns them): you cannot demonstrate, prove, establish – you cannot know if a book is good. A sentence, a line, a phrase: nobody knows. (98)

In this account, what passes as "thought" becomes simply one component of a larger "babble." The brisk summary of narrative's pose of separating signal from noise at once acknowledges the convention and maintains a mimetic stance; it treats a character's thoughts as something pre existing and real, awaiting transcription As *The Information* presents Richard considering the problem of aesthetic judgment, the novel interrupts those thoughts with an acknowledgment of the lower-level subroutines at work in realist fiction and real cognition alike.[3] Between the character and his represented thoughts obtrudes a fleeting admission of mimetic convention that treats prose narrative as a fictional information processing – and which wryly consolidates the work of mimesis.

Mediating information

Information is not a medium. Indeed, invoking information is a way of treating knowledge or data as something prior to material instantiation, disconnected from *any* particular medium. Yet, in a particular media environment, a dominant medium may come to seem more general, more fundamental, than others. Such a medium seems almost to lose its materiality and therefore to model what a culture considers the ideal properties of information storage and communication. Within Kittler's 1800 discourse network, imaginative literature or "poetry" plays this part, offering a script for making dead letters into natural speech, for transforming a mode of data storage – alphabetic writing – into universal depth psychology. In offering a "reproducible" supplement for the senses, Romantic poetry "became the first medium in the modern sense," but it did this in part by ignoring or "liquidat[ing]" its materiality, its physical properties, the things that make it a medium (*Discourse*, 115, 114). For Kittler, digital information networks play a similarly central role in our information systems of 2000 – as the medium so foundational that it becomes the condition for other media and ceases to resemble a medium at all. "The general digitization of channels and information erases the differences among individual media. Sound and image, voice and text, are reduced to surface effects"; ultimately, Kittler predicts, "a total media link on a digital base will erase the very concept of medium" (*Gramophone*, 1, 2).

   The Information says little about computers or Kittler's fiber-optic networks. But the novel repeatedly emphasizes a medium to end all media, a universal font of information in a book preoccupied by the problem of the universal: television. The novel offers only a few scenes of television viewing, usually by Steve or the Tull twins. But it hardly need represent the medium directly; in *The Information*, television saturates culture far beyond any particular acts of watching.[4] The box can even provide information when it's off. As he creeps around during a late-night incursion into the Barrys' house, Steve finds himself "pleased, even flattered and moved, to see the television – proof of a shared humanity. Every household, be it never so mean, shared this square of dead gray" (171). Like Romantic poetry in Kittler's account, television is a medium that has been universalized into human nature – for Steve, at any rate.

Next to the Barrys' sleeping set, Steve also finds an anthology of coagulated and catalogued television: "There was a little bookcase for the videos" – the genus of the furniture is a subtle touch – "with a whole section devoted to the appearances of Gwyn Barry" (181). To Richard's astonished dismay, Gwyn's bland utopian novel *Amelior* has suddenly made him not only a bestselling author but a minor celebrity, a development consummated by appearances on television. Walking through the Warwick Sports Center, Gwyn now receives communal acknowledgment. He has entered "[t]he acceptance world. As if Gwyn was suddenly visible now [...] TV had democratized him, and made him available for transference to the masses" (74). The psychoanalytic overtones of "transference," as opposed to *transfer* or *transmission*, seem appropriate. Television becomes the essential mass-medium not merely because of its ubiquity but thanks to its carefully produced mass intimacy. Gwyn shows up on television not primarily as an author or intellectual but as a husband, acting as the spokesman for spousal devotion in "The Seven Vital Virtues, 4: Uxoriousness," a throwaway TV documentary (65). As we later learn, Gwyn's representation of uxoriousness is simply that – a representation, a media fiction. For all its feel of intimate proximity, television remains, as its macaronic name reminds us, a gawky fusion of sight and distance.

Richard believes that all authors "are competing for something there is only one of: the universal" (232). "Could it be that Gwyn had stumbled on the universal, that voice which speaks to and for the human soul?" he wonders, bewildered by *Amelior*'s popularity; "No, Gwyn had stumbled on the LCD" (86). With the acronymic efficiency of their common denomination, the lowest form of mass-appeal doubles as a video display technology. As the novel's informatic hub, television provides a switching station between media. Having come to television from print, Gwyn prepares to move into film. As Richard punches the buttons on an electronic pub game nicknamed "The Knowledge," he notes that television is the center and circumference of its knowledge. The game requires:

all the smatterings you could get of history, geography, etymology, mythology, astronomy, chemistry, politics, popular music – and TV.

> Most crucially TV: TV down through the ages. It was in TV form
> that the other stuff was meant to be propagated anyway [...] (176)

The medium that provides the subject and source for The Knowledge
has even become the game's medium; "the newer knowledge
machines, Richard had noticed, [...] actually *were* TVs: they fled the
written, and embraced the audiovisual" (176). In one of the final
minor indignities Richard endures in the novel – although major ones
still loom – he encounters a question on The Knowledge that includes
"Gwyn Barry" as a wrong answer, a distractor. Sanctified as electronic
trivia, the name so disconcerts Richard that he distractedly selects it.

Gwyn's unuxoriousness aside, it is not so much that television
creates false versions of reality as that it holds an inordinate ability to
shape and confirm the true ones. Steve "beat[s] up the man from the
Ten O'clock News: and, the next night, it was *on* the Ten O'clock
News! [...] Now that's the way the world's *supposed* to be run" (51). As
television channel-flips across any distinctions between medium,
viewer, and content, its shaping power comes to seem practically
literal. Visiting America to profile Gwyn during his high-powered book
tour, Richard spends much of his stint in Los Angeles drinking, watching *The Simpsons* in his hotel room, and nursing two epic toothaches.
When he emerges, "his face [i]s the shape of a television. He looks[s]
like one of the Simpsons. He look[s] like Bart" (272). As a medium,
television becomes an arena of representations that pass into reality,
sidestepping questions of mimesis.

More or less the same goes for pornography, which presents actual
sex as the least convincing of fictions. Richard in his L.A. hotel room is
also struck by *The Limpsons*, a pornographic parody of *The Simpsons*,
and a work whose name lampoons his own chronic impotence. But
pornography, he notes, seems to be moving from "the basements of
other genres (sex Westerns, sex space operas, sex murder mysteries)" to
a fixation on the dynamics of the porn trade itself – the same postmodern impulse that *The Information* remarks upon and exemplifies in
fiction (265).[5] Pornography figures as the video obsession of Steve
Cousins, "something [...] as interested in sex as he was" (308); he has
"watched so much pornography, and so little else, that he ha[s] some
mental trouble, watching normal videos" (150). "[N]aked in his black
leather chair," Steve views porn not for stimulation so much as for self-
knowledge, searching for something he wants in this dark repository of
information about human desire (360). More recently, in a piece published in *Talk* magazine and *The Guardian*, Amis expresses a similar

understanding of pornography. Its "danger," he asserts, is that it so faithfully "services the 'polymorphous perverse': the near-infinite chaos of human desire. If you harbor a perversity, then sooner or later porno will identify it. You'd better hope that this doesn't happen while you're watching a film about a coprophagic pig farmer – or an undertaker" ("Sex", 134). Video pornography, like Kittler's poetry, becomes a universal confirmation of psychological individuation. Steve goes to pornography for "information" but finds it not in the "[p]ornography of the visual spectrum: the red, orange, yellow," "[b]oy-and-girl or girl-and-girl and boy-and-boy" (360). Instead, he finds it in one video's random, nonsexual walk-on by a kitten. And what the creepily chaste Steve has looked for, what he finds at last in this pornography on another wavelength, is a readout on "what he want[s] to hurt" – the bit of information he has sought all along (360).

About the author

The editor who commissions Richard's profile of Gwyn asks that it include not simply "what every reader wants to know: what he's really like" but also a larger sense of "the pressures facing the successful novelist in the late 1990s" (180). But "[o]f the pressures facing the successful novelist in the mid-1990s Richard Tull could not easily speak. He was too busy with the pressures facing the unsuccessful novelist in the mid-1990s" (211). The quiet diminishment from the editor's overeager "late 1990s" to Richard's more immediate "mid" subtly fuses the novel's focus on Richard's daily struggles (the indignities of aging, the slipping marriage, a broken vacuum cleaner) with a sense of reflexive retreat. And the establishment here of an authorial theme with variations harmonizes the project of representing contrasting characters with a broader subject of authorship *tout court*. The treatment of the writing career as a formula with variables reminds us that one of the functions of *The Information*'s framework is to imagine the crosscutting logic of the literary arena, and the conditions of contemporary authorship, successful and unsuccessful alike. Within this field, literature functions less as a matter of art or news or even entertainment – nothing sounds less entertaining than the insipid and plotless *Amelior* – than of information.

Like Dickens's *Martin Chuzzlewit* (1843–44), *The Information* treats a central journey to America – Gwyn's trip to promote *Amelior Regained* and lobby for a genius grant called the "Profundity Requital" – as an intensification of themes established during its English action. Even the outbound transatlantic flight offers a comic chart of the literary field. Plodding from his seat in coach to Gwyn's in first class, Richard finds that, in literary terms, "his progress through the plane described a diagonal of shocking decline":

> In Coach the laptop literature was pluralistic, liberal, and humane: *Daniel Deronda*, trigonometry, Lebanon, World War I, Diderot, *Anna Karenina*. As for Business World, [...] [t]hey were reading trex: outright junk. Fat financial thrillers, chunky chillers, and tublike tinglers, escape from the pressures facing the contemporary entrepreneur. And then he pitched up in the intellectual slum of First Class, among all its drugged tycoons, and the few books lying unregarded on softly swelling stomachs were jacketed with hunting scenes or ripe young couples in mid swirl or swoon. [...] [N]obody was reading anything – except for a lone seeker who gazed, with a frown of mature skepticism, at a perfume catalogue. Jesus: what happened on the Concorde? (214)

This sparkling set-piece, a miniaturized book tour, also amounts to a parody of Pierre Bourdieu's account of the modern literary field. In the nineteenth century, Bourdieu finds an emerging logic that established the field of art and literature as "the economic world reversed," treating a work's aesthetic value as an inverse of its submission to the dominant values of the marketplace (29); this is the semi-separation between high culture and high commerce that, according to Jameson, postmodernism has collapsed.

Richard's "journey within a journey" from coach to first class literalizes Bourdieu's paradigm, modeling the inverse relationship between literary taste and the economic status so carefully laid out on the plane's seat map (214). The novel's treatment of the literary habits of violent criminals further extends the paradigm. "Beware the convict" absorbed in Kant's *Critique of Pure Reason*, it warns, and Steve is a devoted reader of Richard's rarefied novels – perhaps their only one (14). Aboard the plane, the reversal of values between economics and literature becomes so absolute that in the Elysium of first class, all books recede into dozy, satiated irrelevance. Meanwhile, waiting for Richard "[i]n the very nib of the plane," the famous author Gwyn Barry is "reading his schedule" (214).

Clearly, *The Information* – in contrast to Bourdieu's studies – "is not meant to be a sociological study of literary production and reception" (Moran, 312). But the structure of the literary field, as Bourdieu calls it, seems to have been much on Amis's mind, at least as a subject for satire. His story "Career Move" (1992), published as Amis worked on *The Information*, offers a pendant or antimasque to the novel; it imagines a world in which starving screenwriters vie to publish their scripts in obscure literary magazines, while poets are rewarded with three-sonnet development deals. "Career Move" and *The Information* even share minor reference points: *The Little Magazine*, the screenplay to *Decimator*, Calchalk Street. Whereas "Career Move" skewers the cultural field through a deftly surreal reversal, *The Information* seems carefully contrived to map it in greater satirical detail. Gwyn's successes and Richard's failures let the novel move from the glitzy world of P.R. synergies to the lowest reaches of publishing: wheezy low-circulation literary magazines, the "anti-literature" of the vanity press, book reviewing (54).

In the media environment anatomized by *The Information*, novels feature as the excuses for radio and television appearances, newspaper profiles and gossip columns, movie deals. Without the narrative distractions of wives or wide boys, *The Information*'s visit to America distills its theme of the informatic author-function, of authorship seamlessly looped from medium to medium. As one of Richard's first assignments in New York, he "listen[s] in on Gwyn being interviewed" and then "arrange[s] to interview the interviewer about what Gwyn was like to interview" (218). While "the *Post* guy" comes to watch Gwyn "doing the radio spot," "the guy from EF can listen to [him] do the TV spot – from the audio booth" (218). Gwyn plans to "get photographed while [he's] getting photographed" (219). For such purposes, the novels themselves need not actually be read. Although it is published only in America, Richard's last novel *Untitled* is no candidate for the media workup, "with its octuple time scheme and its rotating crew of sixteen unreliable narrators" (125). But as a book so entirely unreadable that – in an uproarious running joke – it induces neurological problems in any reader reckless enough to attempt it, *Untitled* parodies the wider situation. Even once Richard's book is published, it seems unclear whether anyone other than Richard and Steve has actually read it. Gwyn hasn't even opened his copy to see the dedication.

A rare fan letter – from the deranged Croatian (or possibly Serbian) plotter Darko – gets the punctuation wrong but the situation right: "Dear Richard You are the writer of a 'novel.' Aforethought. Congratulations! Hows it done. First, you get the topic. Next you package it. Then, comes the hipe" (34). For the successful novelist of the 1990s – Gwyn – authorship is "an operation, all fax and Xerox and preselect";

as the word "operation" indicates, the author-function becomes not only a collective business endeavor, but a mathematical or technical process, a function (10). Novelists themselves are more likely to be semi-famous "for being something else": "mountaineers. Comedians. Newscasters" (41). Or for inspiring literary gossip more than for producing literary texts – a situation crystallized by the media storm that would soon envelop Amis and his novel.

The notoriety surrounding *The Information* gave its reception an air of overdetermination and a diffuse sense of literary scandal.[6] Yet *The Information* is no *roman-à-clef*, despite some vague and halting attempts to see parallels between the inimical amity of Gwyn and Richard and the soured friendship of Amis and Julian Barnes. More than a decade after the novel's publication, what transcends the literary gossip and envy provoked by this novel of literary gossip and envy is the uncanny symmetry between *The Information*'s topic, package, and hype. The diffuseness of the scandal, the novel's solicitation and evasion of the connections between its theme and its history, suggest its engagement with information, that entity that presupposes the liberation of fact from context, matter, or embodiment. "I can't give up novels," Richard tells his wife, Gina, even as his work goes unpublished (60). Why? Because "then he would be left with experience, with untranslated and unmediated experience. Because then he would be left with life" (60). Authorship appears as a practice of translating between life and words, of mediating between experience and information.

"Essentially Richard was a marooned modernist," confirms *The Information* when giving us "a quick look at Richard's stuff – while the author stumbles, swearing, from Avenue to Crescent to Mews, in search of Darko" (125). "Modernism was a brief divagation into difficulty; but Richard was still out there, in difficulty"; as with his style, so with his life (125). Richard is "trying to write genius novels," for he is "too proud and too lazy and – in a way – too clever and too nuts to write talent novels. For instance, the thought of getting a character out of the house and across town to somewhere else made him go vague with exhaustion...." (125). Everyday external mimesis is not for him. Of course, Amis's novel supplies all of this diegetic information while within the plot of the novel Richard makes his way through town. The narrative echoes but deftly outstrips its protagonist's literary limitations and modernist mimeto-phobia. Were Amis to stop with exhaustion in the midst of the journey, Richard would be marooned indeed.

Given Richard's problems with quotidian novelistic realism, it should come as no surprise that his own plotting, his attempts at literary revenge, all end in failure or simply "go vague" (125). Often these plots too exploit the informatic situation of authorship. As a minor scheme against Gwyn, Richard sends a copy of the slab-like Sunday *Los Angeles Times* with an enigmatic note, trusting that Gwyn's curiosity and vanity will stimulate a maddening, fruitless search through its elaborate stratigraphy. Richard's plan seems to fail when Gwyn promptly finds his name in the Classifieds, along with an offer to buy his first, pre-*Amelior* novel. But by the end of *The Information*, the search of the *Times* seems to have grown into an entire campaign in which Gwyn obsessively scans an expanding range of print for the most casual mention of his name. "Pretty soon – and you could see this coming – he was reading everything about everything. Not in itself a bad idea, if information was what you sought. But we see accidents everywhere, on the information highway" (300). Gwyn starts seeing accidents too, even random versions of his name and initials, thanks to this informatic autoeroticism, a counterpart to Steve's pornographic self-searching. Every appearance of Gwyn's initials starts to rivet him: "George Balanchine," "George Bush," "Gutenberg Bible," "Great Britain" (300). Steve may come from the future, but Gwyn too is ahead of his time; by the real late-1990s, a self-Googling author would have had a more impressive database and silicon hardware to automate the search.

For a final plot against Gwyn, Richard attempts a form of authorial time travel, rewriting (or, mostly, retyping) *Amelior* and then commissioning a phony, yellowed first edition. Retroactively, Gwyn becomes a plagiarist, and Richard plans to expose him via a channel for gossipy literary journalism. Reworking Gwyn's novel raises Pierre Menardian possibilities: "Had he *become* Gwyn Barry? Was *this* the information?" (327). But Richard's earlier machinations have all been abortive or aborted, and this one is no exception, awkwardly abandoned when Richard suddenly learns that Gwyn has been conducting a crueler and more successful reprisal of his own.

Imagining information

Richard's redaction of *Amelior* seems likely to be his farewell to fiction. At the end of the novel (in several senses), Richard prepares to send the book back through time, but in sending it the wrong way, his action recalls the retrograde narrative of Amis's *Time's Arrow* (1991), written during a break from *The Information*. For literature orients itself towards the future, as *The Information* makes clear with its metaphors of paternity and deep time. This position becomes especially fraught, and urgent, at a time when literature seems less and less central as a part of our culture – even a sort of legacy form held over from the past. To adapt one of Richard's pet theories, literature may face a "history of increasing humiliation" not only in light of humanity's astronomical insignificance but because of the potential marginality of printed writing among multiple channels of mediated information (93).

"Whither the novel?" – as any number of hand-wringing symposia have put it, including one from which Richard once stormed when "he was the only panel member who [...] had not been offered a biscuit" (222). Literature, the novel, the codex book – the possibility that these may now be outmoded forms, occurs to Richard early on as he tries to write one of his interchangeable book reviews:

> What *was* it with *whilst*? A scrupulous archaism – like the standard book review. Like the standard book. It was not the words them-selves that were prim and sprightly polite, but their configurations, which answered to various old-time rhythms of thought. Where were the new rhythms – were there any out there yet? Richard sometimes fancied that his fiction was looking for the new rhythms. Gwyn sure as hell wasn't looking for them. (48–9)

Even the choice of "whilst" as the sign of literary obsolescence is telling. As a formal British *while*, it possesses a temporal sense of dis-crete duration and a contrastive sense of scrupulous, enlightened balance. Moreover, as a metonym for fiction, *whilst* echoes Benedict Anderson's description of the classic realist novel as a "complex gloss upon the word 'meanwhile,'" a literary expression of the social simul-taneity that linked nineteenth-century novels to the daily news (their etymological doublet) and to the nation-state (25).

If the rise of recorded sound and images in the analog era crystallized the modernist conception of writing as the inscription of graphemes, the digital age further refines its status. Literature, it occurs to Richard, would become "heavier and heavier, until it was all over and you arrived at *paperwork*. You arrived at *Amelior*" (141). In its success, *Amelior* becomes simply the paperwork for the show to follow. As Gwyn exclaims when Richard sneers about the surgically enhanced starlet who wants to play Gwyn's tomboyish heroine, "It's a different medium" (270). Amid a world of intersecting media, Richard's life remains paperbound – "on paper, written words, memos to the self, scrawled on the corners of envelopes and on the backs of credit-card slips" (184). That bit of information once came to him as he glimpsed a whirlwind of floating paper: "Once, in the street, on an agitated April afternoon, on his way back from lunch with some travel editor in some transient trattoria, he had seen a city cyclone of junk mail – leaflike leaflets, flying flyers, circling circulars – and had nodded, and thought: me, my life" (32). In a vivid encapsulation of Amis's fusion of low subjects and high style, waste paper comes to life as a subject worthy of Gerard Manley Hopkins. The sentence's alliterations build until they culminate in an explosion of simultaneous mimetic abjection and linguistic transcendence. Freed from the mundane circuit of their junk commerce, each paper thing speaks and spells itself; in a moment of grubby realism that is also an exercise in pure style, Amis's prose renews the mimetic possibilities in the very names of these objects, this fluttering paperwork. A description of physical disarray works to diminish information entropy, the randomness of any communication, by means of a verbal redundancy that remains mimetically significant.[7]

As James Diedrick notes, the title of *The Information* seems to hint at "some specific, ultimately clarifying revelation which never in fact materializes" (147). For there is no piece of information – not the exposure of Gwyn's perfidy, of Steve's particular perversity, of the plots that sink the would-be revenger Richard – that will bring everything together in this non-*roman-à-clef*, this novel without a key. A.O. Scott puts it more impatiently: "Not content to deliver the definitive study of literary envy in an age of postliterate celebrity, [Amis] festooned 'The Information' with cryptic ruminations on ... something." Likewise, the novel's response to the larger problem of assimilating cosmic information into "personal experience" remains indeterminate (81): "just by dropping his head like that Richard was changing his temporal relationship with the quasars by thousands and thousands of years" – "This is to put Richard's difficulties in context. The context of the universe" (120). So much context, so far outside human experience, becomes no context at all. What links the unmaterialized revelation, the satire on the literary racket, and the novel's cryptic night-thoughts is precisely information: information not as a particular item of data but as the concept of content freed of matter or context, the convergence of the media, knowledge without a knower.

Borges's story "The Aleph" (1945), an explicit intertext for the novel, describes a fictional instrument for such knowledge: "a magical device, the aleph, that knew everything" (*Information*, 165). As the aleph's owner puts it, "an Aleph is one of the points in space that contain all points," a "place where, without admixture of confusion, all of the places of the world, seen from every angle, coexist" (Borges, 126, 127). The aleph may be ancient, but its owner connects it to contemporary media; he envisions "modern man" "surrounded by telephones, telegraphs, phonographs, the latest in radio-telephone and motion-picture and magic-lantern equipment, and glossaries and calendars and timetables and bulletins" – equipped by "this twentieth century" to see the world from "his study" (120). "So witless did these ideas strike me as being, so sweeping and pompous," confides the story's narrator, "that I associated them immediately with literature" (120). Although in Borges's tale it inspires only "a terrible poem" that "wins a big prize, a big requital" (*Information*, 165), the all-containing aleph also dryly recalls the aspirations of classic realism, its dialogism, the simulated omniscience of its narrators. The aleph, like information, is both a terrestrial phenomenon (it seems to be destroyed upon the demolition of the poet's house) and a total vision of the world, a vision closely connected to a vision of modern media.

Instead of a revelation or a key or an aleph, *The Information* supplies only "the information, which is nothing, and comes at night," as its last line puts it: repeated "information" about cosmic humiliation, pain, mediocrity, death (374). This information has been there all along, from the first page of the novel, which gives us Richard crying in his sleep over "[n]othing," "[j]ust sad dreams," as he tells Gina (3). In strictly informatic terms, such recurrent information by the end of *The Information* indeed stands in danger of becoming "nothing" – noninformation, redundancy, or white noise – as opposed to the lively patterns of differentiation that have structured the novel's plot. From the cosmic perspective inserted with such memento-mori insistence into a comedy of literary revenge, perhaps such nothings are the real information in a world so full of media signals that they all seem on the verge of becoming noise.

A classic text published soon after "The Aleph" approached related problems of encoding, signal, and noise. Claude Shannon's epochal paper "A Mathematical Theory of Communication" described information in terms of entropy – and began with the gesture of freeing information from signification. "Frequently [...] messages have *meaning*," recognized Shannon; "that is they refer to or are correlated according to some system with certain physical or conceptual entities." But "[t]hese semantic aspects of communication are irrelevant" to information theory (379). Shannon's work helped initiate the age of digital computing, an age in which information has means bits and bytes, numerical patterns awaiting the transformation and transmission

made possible by mathematics. So defined, information has "no necessary connection to meaning" (Hayles, 18) – which, in *The Information*,
further increases its resemblance to the dreams that also come at night.
As Richard explains the title of his second novel, *"Dreams Don't Mean
Anything"*: "what I mean is dreams don't *signify* anything. Not exactly"
(93).

"What's your novel trying to say?" Richard is asked in a radio interview (252). "The contemporary idea seemed to be," he thinks, "that
the first thing you did, as a communicator, was come up with some
kind of slogan, and either you put it on a coffee mug or a T-shirt or a
bumper sticker – or else you wrote a novel about it" (252–3). "It's
saying itself," Richard replies, with a modernist view of art's resistance
to paraphrase; "I couldn't have said it any other way" (253). *The
Information* hardly endorses the view of fiction as bumper sticker, as
mere message transmitted on an arbitrary channel. Yet the novel also
satirizes Richard's penchant for painful unreadability. In a different
sense, this aesthetic too treats the novel as information, as data that
remains as hostile and inassimilable as the spatial void or the fate of
the universe. The nightly information often arrives by "jump-leads of
agony," just the sort of pain experienced by Richard's readers (110).

The Information suggests that some information remains out there,
resisting assimilation, but it also attempts a jagged fusion of that information with imitation, with characters moving across town, with a
tragicomic satire on the cultural circumstances that have launched the
novel into the universe. The refusal of revelation is not the refusal to
signify, not exactly. Juxtaposing information and experience – a
cosmos planning our ruin and a ruined writer whose plans come to
nothing – the novel challenges us to hold this entropic system together
as content and form, mimesis and style. Thus the novel's pixelation,
the sharp edges as it juxtaposes elements, a bit of this with a bit of
that. The title of the novel names not a discrete piece of data but information in the modern, aggregate sense, describing less anything the
novel contains than the book itself.

The novel frequently notes the information's arrival, and often its
receiver, but near the end, a more specific sense of its medium emerges:
"the information comes at night. The communications technology it
picks is not the phone or the fax or email. It is the telex – so its teeth
can chatter in your head" (340). A residual medium by the mid-1990s,
the telex is chosen here for its material properties, for the clacking
rhythms of its rapid, automated, serial transmission. The information,
which is to say the novel, comes clinging to the material of its

medium, offering experience at an informatic remove – its teeth in your head. Miming its name and saying itself, *The Information* becomes a telling telex or a coded codex, one whose account of culture as mediated information becomes all the more powerful for its incorporation of – and its uneven incorporation by – modern informatics.

Notes

1 On the "postmodern realism" or "meta-mimesis" of earlier Amis novels, see Catherine Bernard's and Amy J. Elias's essays in *British Postmodern Fiction* (1993). In his book on the Amises (2003), Gavin Keulks situates realism at the core of their literary conflicts.
2 Influential critiques of such visions of context-free, nonmaterial information include Hayles 192–221 (from the perspective of science studies and literary theory), and Brown and Duguid (from the viewpoint of business).
3 Amis's nonfiction reiterates such views. Without citing *The Information*, his preface to *The War Against Cliché* (2001) ends with the same reflections and comparison (here attributed to Richard) between two Wordsworth lines – a treatment of his novel as reusable "content."
4 Television plays a similar role in *London Fields* (1989): "TV came at Keith like it came at everybody else; and he had nothing whatever to keep it out. He couldn't grade or filter it. So he thought TV was real" (55).
5 A longstanding Amis theme before *Money* or the sex-murder-mystery *London Fields*, pornography becomes a central concern of *Yellow Dog* (2003). There porn, mimesis, and information technology come together most outrageously when Buckingham Palace denounces a pornographic video as a fake – then quietly commissions a computer simulation to test the plausibility of that lie. Courtesy of "isosurfaces and volumetric rendering" (200), mimesis attempts to reverse-engineer pornography as media spin.
6 These controversies included Amis's divorce, his move to a new agent, his payment for the novel, even his extensive dental surgery.
7 Extending the argument of my earlier essay, "Narrative Reversals and the Thermodynamics of History in Martin Amis's *Time's Arrow*" (1998), we might see Amis as progressing from physical entropy (in *Time's Arrow*) to informatic entropy in *The Information*.

Works cited

Amis, Martin. "Career Move." 1992. *Heavy Water and Other Stories*. New York: Harmony, 1999. 9–31.
——. *The Information*. New York: Harmony, 1995.
——. "Sex in America." *Talk* February 2001: 99–103, 133–5.
Anderson, Benedict. *Imagined Communities: Reflections on the Origin and Spread of Nationalism*. Rev. ed. London: Verso, 1991.
Borges, Jorge Luis. *The Aleph and Other Stories*. 1971. Trans. Andrew Hurley. New York: Penguin, 2004.
Bourdieu, Pierre. *The Field of Cultural Production*. Ed. Randal Johnson. New York: Columbia UP, 1993.

Brown, John Seely, and Paul Duguid. *The Social Life of Information*. 2000. Boston: Harvard Business School, 2002.

Davis, Lennard J. *Factual Fictions: The Origin of the English Novel*. New York: Columbia UP, 1983.

Diedrick, James. *Understanding Martin Amis*. 2nd ed. Columbia: U of South Carolina P, 2004.

Hayles, N. Katherine. *How We Became Posthuman: Virtual Bodies in Cybernetics, Literature, and Informatics*. Chicago: U of Chicago P, 1999.

Jameson, Fredric. *Postmodernism, Or, the Cultural Logic of Late Capitalism*. Durham: Duke UP, 1991.

Johnston, John. *Information Multiplicity: American Fiction in the Age of Media Saturation*. Baltimore: Johns Hopkins UP, 1998.

——. "Machinic Vision." *Critical Inquiry* 26 (Autumn 1999): 27–48.

Kittler, Friedrich A. *Discourse Networks 1800/1900*. 1985. Trans. Michael Metteer. Stanford: Stanford UP, 1990.

——. *Gramophone, Film, Typewriter*. 1986. Trans. Geoffrey Winthrop-Young and Michael Wutz. Stanford: Stanford UP, 1999.

McLuhan, Marshall. *Understanding Media: The Extensions of Man*. 1964. Cambridge: MIT P, 1994.

Moran, Joe. "Artists and Verbal Mechanics: Martin Amis's *The Information*." *Critique* 41 (2000): 307–17.

Nunberg, Geoffrey. "Farewell to the Information Age." *The Future of the Book*. Berkeley: U of California P, 1996. 103–38.

Ong, Walter. *Orality and Literacy: The Technologizing of the Word*. London: Routledge, 1982.

Scott, A.O. "Trans-Atlantic Flights." *New York Times Book Review* 31 Jan. 1999: 5.

Shannon, C.E. "A Mathematical Theory of Communication." *Bell System Technical Journal* 27 (1948): 379–423, 623–56.

10
W(h)ither Postmodernism: Late Amis

Gavin Keulks
Western Oregon University

Toward the end of *The Information* (1995), Richard Tull ponders a series of questions that have come to mirror Amis's own in the years following that novel's publication. Lamenting the enervation of literary form, Tull ruminates about the structural inversions of genre:

> [L]iterature, Richard said, describes a descent. First, gods. Then demigods. Then epic became tragedy: failed kings, failed heroes. Then the gentry. Then the middle class and its mercantile dreams. Then it was about *you* – [...]: social realism. Then it was about *them*: lowlife. Villains. The ironic age. And [...] Richard was saying: Now what? Literature, for a while, can be about *us* ... about writers. But that won't last long. How do we burst clear of all this? [...] Whither the novel? (328)

Since the end of the 1980s, Amis's investigations into a literary future beyond what Tull calls the "ironic age" have become increasingly insistent. His novels *Night Train* (1997) and *Yellow Dog* (2003) can be viewed in this regard as tentative forays toward constructing a post-ironic, "post-postmodern" voice. Correspondingly, and extending the trajectory of *The Information*, such a voice rejects the extremist claims of radical (or vulgar) postmodernism[1] and strives to recuperate select humanist themes. That *Night Train* and *Yellow Dog* are regarded as minor works within Amis's canon only confirms the obvious: that one of England's most celebrated writers has struggled to surmount the most onerous of postmodern crises: what to do when the techniques which animated such writing – reflexivity, metafiction, irrealism, temporal inversion, and problematized subjectivity – become themselves conventionalized and clichéd? How does Amis burst clear of all this? Whither his novels?

Beyond postmodernism: after theory/after-theories

The backlash against postmodernism has been exceptionally impassioned and self-congratulatory, easily counterbalancing the term's frenzied popularization in the 1980s and 1990s. Numerous voices have extended the moralist critiques of postmodernism's earliest opponents – John Gardner, Charles Newman, and Gerald Graff – or their fiercer reinforcements – Christopher Norris and Terry Eagleton. Writers, of course, preceded scholars: Thomas Wolfe's manifesto "Stalking the Billion-Footed Beast: A literary manifesto for the new social novel" (1989) is an important yet self-aggrandizing indictment, whereas David Foster Wallace's critique "E Unibus Pluram: Television and U.S. Fiction" (1990) attacks postmodern irony while soliciting a new generation of consumers who will "have the childish gall actually to endorse and instantiate single-entendre principles."[2] In 1998 Pope John Paul II indicted postmodern nihilism by name in his Encyclical Letter "Fides et Ratio," and in the early twenty-first century many of postmodernism's central theorists – especially Linda Hutcheon and Ihab Hassan – fled to safer ground, respectively bidding "Over to YOU" (12) or evolving an "aesthetic of trust" (3).

Rash judgments and lack of consensus aside, it is clear that the discourse surrounding postmodernism – regardless of its "death" or maturity – has irrevocably changed, begging the teleological questions what comes "after," what lies "beyond"? Recent scholarship has of course tendered answers, with the preferred approach stipulating a wistful return to realism, a critical mea culpa confirmed by the proliferation of rival "realisms" seeking to usurp postmodern terminology. Philosophy has offered "critical realism," spearheaded by Roy Bhaskar and Rom Harré. Literature has been far more effusive, suggesting "dirty realism," "postmodern realism," "neorealism," "deep realism," "spectacle realism," "fiduciary realism," "hyper-realism," and, most recently, "hysterical realism."[3]

Well-versed in literary theory, Amis has commented on these migrations himself. Reviewing Don DeLillo in 1991, he referred to postmodernism as clearly an "evolutionary" development, then bemoaned its tendency toward "huge boredom": "Why all the tricksiness and self-reflection? Why did writers stop telling stories and start going on about how they were telling them?" Delegating DeLillo the exemplary postmodernist, Amis forecasted that DeLillo would illuminate the path beyond, or after, postmodernism as well. Whereas his contemporaries had "been drawn to the internal, the ludic, and the enclosed," Amis wrote, "DeLillo goes at things the other way. He writes about the new reality – realistically" ("Thoroughly", 28). As recently as 2002 Amis reiterated that although postmodernism had proved "a dead end," it possessed "comic possibilities" that he "hadn't exploited much." It was, he concluded, a theory with "tremendous predictive power, because life became very postmodern, politics became postmodern" (Reynolds and Noakes, 16–17).

As has DeLillo, Amis has tried to mediate the dueling claims of humanism and textuality for the post-ironic, "post-postmodern" period, resulting in a lengthy phase (1995–present) that has produced his least successful novels, both artistically and commercially. These books remain divided between a postmodern perseverance and a realist accommodation. Their heavily contingent schemata problematize realist foundations, yet their structural modes confirm humanist precepts. When *Night Train* appeared in 1997, it seemed Amis's new direction was clear – a patent retreat to psychological realism. Six years later, however, *Yellow Dog* invalidated such hypotheses. In both works Amis attempts to resuscitate an experiential authenticity that can maintain representational fidelity, emotional sincerity, and satiric high-mindedness without foreswearing the hyperbolic themes and styles that have become his authorial hallmarks.

These forces have culminated in a humanist problematics in Amis's recent work, one that remains trapped between the opposing errors of a naïve return to realist universality and an equally naïve adherence to postmodern relativism or superficiality. Believing omniscient narration to be discredited yet recognizing that metafictional gamesmanship has failed to preserve humanist value, Amis has begun, I contend, to map an emergent form of late-phase postmodernism – one I will tentatively label "sanitized postmodernism." My use of this term is motivated not by a desire to add yet another label to an already expansive list; rather, I seek to correct a critical underestimation: those terms which labor to revitalize realism seem too eagerly to preclude postmodernism from evolving a late or secondary phase, contra the critical permissiveness afforded to feminism and Marxism, for instance. Amis's recent work cannot be considered postmodern in its first-phase or classical sense, but despite important swerves, these novels remain informed by the same postmodern sensibility that animated *Money*, a decidedly classical postmodern work. One of the most assimilative, polymorphic movements – which is its source of both weakness and strength – postmodernism seems supremely suited to immanent critique, revision from within. The term "sanitized postmodernism" acknowledges the difficulties of including Amis's work within realist frameworks, however expansive or experimental, and rejects the inherent "retreat to realism" implied by any *realism* moniker. My suggestion of second- or late-phase postmodernism seeks to mollify the extremism of its radical "first-phase" configuration – especially the "end of history" theories of Jean Baudrillard and Francis Fukuyama – as well as to recuperate, however problematically, essentialist concepts of agency, subjectivity, and authenticity. Embedded within this labeling are dueling impera- tives equally vital to Amis's art and to culture in general: a striving to *sanitize* postmodernism of its nihilist excess while restoring a degree of *sanity*, of emotional value and sincerity, to its fictional worlds.

In this framework, *Night Train* and *Yellow Dog* can best be viewed as Amis's attempts to reshape postmodernism to validate the competing claims of representation *and* self-representation, reality and the grotesque, rationalism and contingency. It is an artistry that endeavors to revive and rehumanize – or "re-hume," in more than one sense – the dehumanized subject while preserving epistemological indeterminacy. It maintains fatalist ironies within its depicted world but rejects, with decided moral fervor, the postmodern ironizing of the self. As Amis puts it in *Yellow Dog*, describing a hotel room in words that crystallize his comments on DeLillo: it "was postmodern, but darkly, unplayfully so" (163).

Journeys on the *Night Train*: postmodern crises and crossroads

The existential backdrop of *Night Train* remains as textualized, absur- dist, and bleak as any of Amis's earlier novels, marked by the dark energy of which Jennifer Rockwell, the novel's suicide-heroine, is an expert. Nor is the novel's absent center and shifting margins its only postmodern aspects. The novel should also be viewed as an instruc- tional revaluation – part extension, part-reversal – of at least two prev- ious postmodern works: *London Fields* (1989) and *Other People* (1981). (Connections to *The Information* abound as well, but in more derivative ways.)[4] *London Fields* begins with the epistemological confidence that *Night Train* erodes: "I know the murderer, I know the murderee. I know the time, I know the place" (1). The narrator even suggests the literary genre that *Night Train* will later inhabit, labeling the tale of Nicola Six "Not a whodonit. More of a whydoit" (3). In many ways Jennifer Rockwell is an extension of Nicola Six: both are fatalist femme fatales, suicidal earth-figures, swamped by astrophysics. Both are called *murderees*, and both separately orchestrate their deaths, asserting willpower over fate. Finally, their personal quandaries are dual extrapolations of the deep space, the universal dark energy, that suffuses their worlds and that Jennifer alone has mastered.

In addition, *Night Train* reimagines portions of *Other People*, which features another murderee, Mary Lamb, and a police*man* named Prince – versus the gender-neutral mannerism of *Night Train*'s opening line, "I am a police." Prince eventually confesses to being Mary's killer, claiming, "I am the policeman; I am the murderer" (222). If *Night Train* can be said to modernize *London Fields* for a post-ironic world, substituting Jennifer Rockwell for Nicola Six, then it should also be viewed as an updated *Other People*, one that eliminates that novel's temporal/ structural confinement. Although both works complicate closure, *Other People* remains far less deterministic than *Night Train*. Trapped in the novel's temporal loop, the heroine alternates between life and death. Following her murder, the novel ends with her awakening. By contrast, Amis extends no such amnesty, or authorial grace, to Jennifer Rockwell or Mike Hoolihan. The latter fails in her quest for answers, a search that Prince, lacking her self-awareness or agency, never undertakes. James Diedrick is correct to note that *Night Train* is a "palindromic narrative" that drives its readers back in the search for clues (161), and it is significant that Jennifer and Mike are denied the artistic consolations of repetitive time that *Other People* affords. In *Night Train*, time's arrow can never be reversed, regardless of Mike's determination or Jennifer's expertise in quantum physics.

It is therefore possible to view *Night Train* as a derivative work, and indeed such arguments would suitably bracket this slim novel's status in Amis's canon. Few readers would rank it among his finest work, and the numerous assessments – including my own – that forecasted an authorial mellowing now seem precipitate in light of *Yellow Dog*. However, it is also possible, and far more substantive, to view the novel as an illuminative signal, an artistic lesson that reveals the challenges Amis continues to face as he struggles to recuperate humanism, subjectivity, and agency in a world that seemed convincingly postmodern in 1997. Despite retracing old paths, *Night Train* does differ decidedly from previous work in its un-ironic, non-aesthetic treatment of human suffering – as related by Mike Hoolihan, related to Jennifer Rockwell. The book embraces traditional humanism in its orientation to questions of authenticity, sentimentality, and agency, but it also preserves postmodern indeterminacy and metafictional instability: through the mysterious triple bullet-wound in Jennifer's head; the numerous investigative false leads; the multiple references to astro-physics; Mike's subverted deductive reasoning; and the novel's deno-tative polyphony, which ranges from Mike's androgynous name to the intertextual allusions of other characters' names, which invoke analogues both literary and televisual. Far more complicated than a "straightforward narrative" (Nünning, 237) or a "post-human" scowl (Updike, 1), *Night Train* vacillates between surface and depth, contest-ing the hyper-textualized, multi-mediated world of postmodernism with the emotional sincerity of Mike's moral, humanist, reconstituted subjectivity.

The first step in this restitution involves stabilizing the narrative, which Mike's confessional, first-person narration paradoxically suc-ceeds in doing. Amis's decision to employ a female narrator is, however, a greatly overestimated facet of this achievement. As Adam Mars-Jones has explained about Ian McEwan's work, this only allows Amis "to smuggle himself across the border of gender" (33). Readers should also recall that *Other People* was written from a female point of view as were approximately 200 pages of *London Fields*. Each narrative dramatically differs from *Night Train*. Psychology and voice trump gender, mirroring a theoretical shift from Fredric Jameson to Henry James: Mike Hoolihan's nominal androgyny is less important than the fact that she becomes the novel's central consciousness and remains, above all things, reliable. Her voice grounds the narrative and becomes its emotional center, supplementing Jennifer's absence. From the opening page Mike is enlisted to "account" for Jennifer's suicide (11), and indeed Jennifer is a text that requires both spiritual reckoning and intellectual exegesis. She is both body and case number. Through the autopsy report as well as its accompanying video, through sundry explanations all designed to limit contingency, to restore metaphysical order, she is meticulously interpreted and endlessly textualized. But in this novel – as in literary theory, Amis knows – interpretation remains an arena of crisis and contention, not closure.

As in many of Amis's novels, postmodern elements complicate meaning and closure. Early in *Night Train* Mike relates that Jennifer's death was "definitely not a yeah-right suicide. This was a no-wrong suicide" (18), and indeed her death inspires a plethora of interpreta-tions, paralleling the eight different versions of the song "Night Train" on Mike's cassette. Perhaps too predictably, Jennifer's death is therefore deconstructive as well as destructive: it activates a familiar postmodern crisis of legitimacy, upsets binary orders of logic and meaning, and destroys the ordered moral worlds of other characters. It also furnishes

Amis yet another opportunity to meditate upon the "shagged out" state of motivation in the postmodern world.[5]

In my framework, Mike Hoolihan is best perceived as a realist contemplating and trying to contextualize radical postmodernism, symbolized by Jennifer's suicide, which acts as a quintessential vanquishing of Lyotardian grand narratives. Mike's world, by contrast, is one of emotional and economic determinism, cause and effect, discipline and punishment. Significantly, she tries to import improper, positivist analysis to Jennifer's postmodern quandary. She seeks a mimetic, rationalist universe containing answers, logic, and order, yet in the end, she symbolically – and ironically – inherits Jennifer's contingency and indeterminacy. Her crisis, in other words, becomes one that will resurface in *Yellow Dog*, where it is labeled, appropriately, as "category-error" (13).

Night Train aspires in this regard to Conrad's *Heart of Darkness*, an aspiration that precedes *Yellow Dog's* adoption of the Dickensian grotesque. Mike Hoolihan functions as an updated Marlow on at least two intertextual levels: Conrad's as well as Raymond Chandler's, whose chief detective was, of course, Philip Marlowe. The humanist horror that Mike confronts remains a muted Kurtzian cry, one that questions why, if Jennifer Rockwell would kill herself, those with less talent, less intelligence, less beauty should choose to live? Such lamentation both indicts and convicts the fatalist relativism of first-phase postmodernism, which Jennifer's suicide epitomizes and which Mike, the novel's realist questor, tries to resolve. When Mike questions the notably named Trader Faulkner, Jennifer's lover, their meeting devolves into farce. The interrogation scene subverts all conventions of television drama, as Trader refutes Mike's questions and breaks her resolve instead. Before the scene concludes with mutual handholding and weeping – which Amis presents without any comedy or irony whatsoever – Trader perfectly articulates the metaphysical void that Jennifer symbolizes:

> Mike, this is what happened: A woman fell out of a clear blue sky. And you know something? I wish I *had* killed her. I want to say: Book me. Take me away. Chop my head off. I wish I had killed her. Open and shut. And no holes. Because that's better than what I'm looking at. (71–2)

In this passage Amis not only manipulates cliché – including the obviously reflexive "Book me" – to mirror the artificial pacing and creative stagnation of television; he also critiques how conventionalized language emerges from a lazy response to crisis, diluting feeling and falsifying reality. Importantly, Trader's reference to a world with "no holes" opposes Jennifer's corollary: her binary opposite of "all hole" – pure indeterminacy – which dominates the novel, especially in its titular chapter (126–30). Crucially, however – and unlike in *Money* and *London Fields* – reflexivity in *Night Train* is directed toward absolution, not confession, a crucial marker of Amis's late swerve toward "sanitized postmodernism." The coroner "absolves" (74) Jennifer's body, and Mike similarly tries, but fails, to absolve her soul – and her story. Epitomizing the narrative's subverted closure, Mike reads the book *Making Sense of Suicide*, which Jennifer has annotated, and concludes that it makes no sense at all (133). Another section of the novel (93) appropriates the title of Frank Kermode's classic study *The Sense of an Ending* as a subheading, only to destabilize both sensibility *and* teleology.

Despite her thwarted hope for closure, Mike's attempt at existential reckoning accords with Amis's efforts to evolve a method beyond postmodernism. One person's relativism is another's compassion, one might suggest, and Amis centralizes Mike's episteme of moral longing. Unlike in earlier novels, however, no authorial trickery now undermines her authority, and although she fails to restore an orderly universe, Amis redeems her psychological autonomy, her quintessential un-ironic will-to-believe. The text foregrounds a plaintive, non-manipulative human voice that achieves levels of intimacy and sincerity that Amis usually lambastes. Mike's narrative voice remains less fragmentary than Jennifer's world; the subject, in other words, is less subjective. In short, *Night Train* depicts a crisis of signification within postmodernism itself – not realism – a crisis torn between a suffering humanist subject and its structural and thematic fidelity to postmodernism.

Indeed an important facet of the novel's critique of radical postmodernism lies in its opposition between authenticity and cliché, especially as regards multimedia. Hovering above any humanist depth, mocking it in fact, float levels of metafictional referentiality. As Daniel Oertel has shown, Mike Hoolihan's voice vies for legitimacy against a bulwark of other discourses, most deriving from, or constructed by, television. These competing voices epitomize the spectacle and sheen of radical postmodernism, inhibiting Mike's realist explanations, invading her speech. *Night Train* calls into question nearly every convention of the police procedural and hard-boiled detective story. Although its chief influences are James Ellroy's *My Dark Places* and especially David Simon's *Homocide*,[6] at least two American television dramas – *Homocide:*

Life on the Streets and *NYPD Blue* – influence Mike's diction as well. Early in the novel she teasingly remarks, "Homicide is the daddy. Homicide is the show" (13). Bax Denziger, the head of Jennifer's university department, is also "TV-famous" (106), and when Mike bemoans the exhaustion of motivation in her reality – but not popular media or art – she casts her words in the language of television: "They want reruns of *Perry Mason* and *The Defenders*. They want *Car Fifty-Four, Where Are You?*" (127), she laments before concluding, "This is plenty. This is practically tv" (128).

Character names similarly invoke popular films, books, or television programs of the 1980s, ranging from *The Rockford Files* to *Dallas*.[7] Indeed, the novel can be seen as an extravagant updating of a classic TV moment: Amis's own "who killed JR?" On one hand, Mike's language is a resonant "clash of linguistic registers" (Oertel, 133) that defies simplification. On another hand, her voice never defies *signification*, a key component of Amis's late work. As she informs the reader, justifying how she will address Colonel Tom, her former homicide squad supervisor and Jennifer's father:

> TV, etcetera, has had a terrible effect on perpetrators. It has given them *style*. And TV has ruined American juries forever. And American lawyers. But TV has also fucked up police. No profession has been so massively fictionalized. [...] But this was Colonel Tom I was talking to. So I spoke the plain truth. (29)

This mediated style, this re-stabilized, reconstituted subjectivity, elicits the emotional poignancy that many reviewers praised, and indeed it is where Amis's swerve, or retreat, from radical postmodernism can best be observed. Although the genesis of Amis's swerve can be located far earlier – gaining force in *London Fields* and flourishing in *The Information* – *Night Train*'s minimalist structure and style differentiate it from earlier texts. Mike's voice is pared and restrained, a deliberate subversion of Amis's usual hyperbolic exuberance. This streamlined narrative parallels Jennifer Rockwell's body, naked in death save for the turbaned towel around her head. "I've never seen one that sat with me like the body of Jennifer Rockwell, propped there naked after the act of love and life," Mike explains, confirming the novel's archetype of paradise *renounced*, not lost: "saying even this, all this, I leave behind" (172).

Importantly, Mike's voice proves incapable of contextualizing Jennifer's suicide. Realist discourse, in other words, cannot convey

Jennifer's postmodern world. Despite the fact that Mike is the novel's sole narrator, her multivocality conflates the high with the low, the grand with the gross, and derives equally – and problematically – from television, language-games, and the heart. This is another rationale for positioning the novel within a period of late-phase postmodernism rather than accommodated or over-assimilative forms of realism. Mike has no voice to express elevated thoughts. She is constituted, over-determined, by the "low" world of crime, instinct, and desire. The novel ends portentously, as she vows to depart – albeit a recovering alcoholic – for the "Battery and its long string of dives," contemplating "say[ing] goodbye" (175).

Unlike such analogues as Nicola Six or Mary Lamb, neither Jennifer Rockwell nor Mike Hoolihan eludes signification as a suffering human soul. In typical Amis fashion, they appear as doppelgangers, furnishing a final glimpse of the novel's emergent form of "sanitized postmodernism." In perhaps the most telling line of the book, Mike muses about changing her name to "Detective Jennifer Hoolihan" (125), and her moniker centralizes the hypothetical erasure of realism and radical postmodernism that the characters separately epitomize. Such implosion of opposites is also reflected in her discarded ruminations about the "ideational/organic" and "metaphysical" nature of Jennifer's disorder (92, 152). Although Mike is incapable of expressing her representational crisis as such, she craves precisely what Amis seeks: that the negotiation between these two implied subject-positions – between *Jennifer* and *Hoolihan* – can culminate in a rationalist acclimation that accepts contingency but preserves the quest for answers – for certainty, truth, and justice. She seeks, as does Amis, a mediated subjectivity to resuscitate the human, to reconfirm reality in the face of ontological dissolution and existential nihilism – two things that Jennifer's suicide and postmodernism itself confirm. Instead, however, the realist Mike – lashed to reality both professionally and narratologically – is forced to validate postmodern contingency and indeterminacy. This mediating trajectory, rooted in desire and denial, appears again near the end, as Mike prepares to meet Paulie No (Dr. No), the autopsy surgeon. "I will ask him two questions," she says. "He will give me two answers. Then it's a wrap. It's down. And again I wonder: Is it the case? Is it reality, or is it just me? Is it just Mike Hoolihan" (164).

This newly invigorated category of "just me" – of Mike Hoolihan, no longer a "category-error" and absent the metaphorical threat of *Jennifer* Hoolihan – expresses the thwarted transcendence, the muted yet decidedly essentialist voice of Amis's late-phase, revaluative, sanitized postmodernism. *Night Train* reveals his preservation of core postmodern themes and techniques – contingency/indeterminacy, absent centers, subverted closure, televisual simulacra, and metafictional referentiality – as well as his rejection of overeager realist retreats. Quite fairly, *Night Train* will never rank among his most famous works, but in some ways its relentless persecution of contingency and exhaustion attains a poignancy his grander novels lack. Whereas *Time's Arrow* opposed the limits of radical postmodernism to Nazi historical atrocities, *Night Train* indulges in what Stephen Baker calls the "relief of the postmodern..., silently implying regret for all that the celebration of textual play leaves unacknowledged" (148). Amis redeems the humanist subject as a wounded, suffering self, never fully acclimated but always cogently aware. Mike Hoolihan's voice accords with a liberal humanism that is outraged, horrified, and shocked into a dual crisis of representation and correspondence. Foreswearing his trademark caricatures and grotesques, Amis invests his own ideology critique into the character depths of Mike Hoolihan, who acts as our failed sibyl or deposed Marlow(e). The novel furnishes his only first-person female narrator, and her voice strives to counterbalance the horror of suicide and the ridicule of televisual simulacra. Jennifer's naked body leads to positivist exhaustion and then to reinvigorated humanism. In opposition to both John Barth and Ihab Hassan, Amis complicates issues of replenishment and rejects facile aesthetics of trust.[8] *Night Train* does not reject postmodernism in favor of realism but, rather, rejects only the extremist claims of radical postmodernism – those that would eradicate humanism through relativism, reflexivity, ahistoricity, or nihilism. A novelist who once famously claimed that he would sacrifice anything upon the altar of style, Amis arguably used *Night Train* to re-imagine the limits of radical postmodernism and realism both, mediating character, interiority, agency, and motivation. His conclusions were tentative and minimalist, and not surprisingly, he would be forced to revisit them in *Yellow Dog*, his most stentorian novel to date.

Yellow Dog: "One step behind, one step beyond" (299)

Whereas *Night Train* depicts realism pondering and failing to naturalize the postmodern, through Mike and Jennifer respectively, *Yellow Dog* dramatizes the humanizing (and sentimentalizing) of the postmodern. Despite Amis's contention that the novel should rank among his best,

Yellow Dog seems a spectacular misstep. It retreats to an ancillary post-modernism; commences with a relativist and ironic assault; progresses through amnesia and comic rage; and culminates in heavy-handed moralizing, as Amis proceeds to resensitize not only Xan Meo but the reader as well. Ultimately *Yellow Dog* stands as a heated rejection of all dehumanizing aesthetics, especially overdetermined linguistic notions about the presumptive death of the subject. In both *Night Train* and *Yellow Dog* Amis enlists his ideal reader – whom he has previously trained in postmodern tropes – to repudiate the false seduction of Barthesian erasure, which elevates textual titillation over satiric and humanist depth. Amis articulates this theoretical pivot early in *Yellow Dog*, contending that following Xan's assault his beleaguered wife Russia was, unmistakably, "leaving theory, now, and entering practice" (68).

As Amis has discussed, the novel's moral urgency stems directly from the September 11, 2001, terrorist bombings in the United States. Numerous sections of the novel depict the alterations in consciousness such events forged, and these sections are indicative of Amis's reconstruction of history and subjectivity from Baudrillardian/Fukuyamaian desuetude. Significantly, however, Amis's assessment of such "Horrorism" (150) remains rooted in postmodernism. As he told Jonathan Curiel during the novel's composition:

> Luckily, I know it will now be a novel about what it feels like to be living in our current era, which established itself on Sept. 11. It will be called the Age of Security, but now we'll feel it is the Age of Insecurity. Everything is qualified now. Everything is contingent. The verities that you depended on a few weeks ago are gone – and gone, I think, for our lifetimes." (2)[9]

One should also not forget that Amis's adoption of a voice of new sincerity originated much earlier, when a series of events in the mid-1990s culminated in personal as well as professional realignment. These emotional crosscurrents fueled the engines of *Night Train*, *Experience*, and *Koba the Dread*, and indeed *Yellow Dog* reads like an amplification of those works. However, *Night Train* and *Yellow Dog* contain numerous similarities that cannot be explained solely by 9/11. Dueling microcosms of exploitation and appeasement, both novels are haunted by vulnerability and violence; both feature mysteries involving identity; and both build upon the same analogues in Amis's canon – *Other People* and *London Fields*. In addition, androgyny figures prominently into both works – Mike Hoolihan in *Night Train* vs. He Zizhen (pro-nounced "her") and "k8" (a hermaphrodite) in *Yellow Dog* – as does polyphonic discourse: police-speak in *Night Train* vs. text messaging and pornographic idiolect in *Yellow Dog*. *Night Train* reinvests charac-ter, agency, and subjectivity, allowing Mike Hoolihan's voice to vocal-ize indeterminacy. By contrast, no such voice succeeds in surmounting the ceaselessly noisy world of *Yellow Dog*.

 Yellow Dog shares an emphasis on corruption and apocalypse with many Amis works, but *London Fields* is especially noteworthy, for it features sexism and child abuse, two prominent issues in *Yellow Dog*. Diedrick defines *London Fields* as a "mutant form" of "millen-nial murder mystery, urban satire, apocalyptic jeremiad, and domestic farce" (119), and such descriptions perfectly explain how *Yellow Dog* derives from the earlier book and independently fails. Lacking a central consciousness – suffering under the weight of its sliding perspectives, its stadium of characters, and its carnivalized "obscenification" (11, 335) – the novel originates in a politicized form of first-phase postmodernism (now decidedly more *vulgar* than *radical*) before over-correcting to an aggressive pietism, grounded upon love, family, and children. It is an unsteady stance that signifies that although the world may be ironic, the self decidedly is not. If *Night Train* allowed Amis to experiment with narrative com-pression and sincerity, then *Yellow Dog* must be seen as a rejection of those methods. Both novels share an artistic trajectory toward sane and sanitized postmodernism, and three things position *Yellow Dog* within this emergent form. The first is an expanded opposition between realism and postmodernism; the second is the reconfirma-tion of love in the face of pornography; and the third is the redemptive force of children.

 Similar to *Night Train*, *Yellow Dog* manipulates a binary opposition between realism and postmodernism to exhibit representational limits. These tensions center upon the character Joseph Andrews, a career criminal and pornography producer, whom Xan Meo accidentally exposes in his book *Lucozade*, prompting revenge. After Xan's assault, his world (and brain) divides. The most obvious form of such division is his regression to emotional primitivism, a schism between civilized and atavistic selves. However, a more theoretically significant schism emerges within the dialectic between realism and postmodernism, which pits Henry Fielding's comic realism against the novel's two-handed engine of postmodernism: absurdist death from above (a plum-meting comet and the doomed airliner 101 Heavy) and ubiquitous simulacra, crystallized by pornography's dehumanized subjects and manipulated surfaces.

Xan inherits a Fieldingesque realist world as a direct yet ironic conse-quence of his assault. In more ways than one, Joseph Andrews can be said to "order" Xan's attack. Unlike Mike Hoolihan, Xan eventually discerns the rationale for his punishment, and as he gleans this moti-vation, his assault becomes ironically reclaimed by – and reclassified as – realism, newly exiled from the provinces of radical postmodernism from which it derived. This is one of the clearest examples of Amis's efforts to revaluate postmodernism from within: Xan's assault migrates from postmodern amnesia, relativism, and absurdity to realist linearity, positivism, and causality, and in the process he becomes rationalized and humanized. The problem remains simply one of proportion. As Mal Bale informs Xan, "You've paid. And the punishment never fit the crime" (230).

Nor is violence the only psychological cage in which Xan is forced to spar. Nearly every character seeks definition through confrontation with the supreme postmodern simulacra – pornography. Hassan rightly affiliates pornography with the "ob-scenity" – the "empty scene" – of postmodern representations (220), and indeed it represents the point where high/low hierarchies become irrelevant, where the grotesque degenerates and undergoes a process of sentimentalizing. Central to Amis's discourse about pandemic "obscenification," pornography satu-rates characters such as Clint Smoker and Cora Susan (a.k.a Karla White), Xan's niece, who was abused as a child, now officiates over Karla White Productions, and assists Joseph Andrews in enacting vengeance against Xan. Whereas Andrews and his associates offer Xan realist order – once he (and Amis) re-establish motivation – Karla White offers him postmodern simulation and deceit. Significantly, radical postmodernism therefore tries to assault Xan twice: first through his beating, which appears initially senseless, then through Karla White, who represents postmodern seductivity. This seduction assumes direct and indirect forms, epitomized by Karla and Xan's incestuous fondling as well as their discussions of child molestation. In each instance, Xan must choose between solipsism and altruism, between self and family, or – adopting the logic of pornography – between masturbatory isolation and the liberation of love. It is the quintessential postmodern paradox.

As Tibor Fischer notoriously groaned, *Yellow Dog* flouts all moral limits.[10] Like Nabokov's *Lolita*, it enlists pedophilia within a larger cri-tique of aesthetics and morality. Child molestation functions in the novel as an obvious socio-literary litmus test. It is one of the oldest moral precepts, inviolable and austere, but in reality, Amis knows, it is overwhelmingly violable, quite frequently violated. Describing her victimization, Karla delivers a trenchant diagnosis of the fatalism implied in the act. In a disturbing passage, she plays upon Xan's nascent sexual attraction to his four-year-old daughter: "Look at the future. Us, us victims," Karla implores. "We're not so frightened and repelled by the way the world is now: the end of normalcy. We always knew there was no moral order. So sleep with Billie and introduce her to the void" (236). Pages later she reiterates these thoughts in diction that Amis aligns with "de-enlightenment" (252) and "category-error" (13): "if you wanted to sexualize your relationship with your daughter – she'd go along with it. [...] When it comes to Daddy, little girls are certainties" (244).

In brief, this is the most blatant invitation from the extreme environs of radical, *vulgar* postmodernism – amoral, relativist, and dehumanized. First-phase postmodernism solicits Xan *through* Karla, his mistress of the simulacrum, beckoning him to depthlessness. He therefore arrives at his crisis – his "cur moment" (275), possibly nodding to Conrad again (*Lord Jim*) – in a drastically different manner than Joseph Andrews or Karla White, who are porn-industry insiders; or Clint Smoker, who revels in superfluity; or even the novel's Royalists, King Henry IX and Princess Victoria, who contemplate abdication after a voyeuristic video of the princess surfaces. Indeed abdication is arguably the novel's overriding theme, for in the context of Amis's cleansing of radical postmodernism, it remains imperative that Xan reject Karla's solicitation, repudiating the void. As Xan's assault is domesticated under the rubrics of motivation and causality so too must the worlds of pornography and molestation undergo melioration. To Karla's invitation Xan responds with the consolations of domestic realism: he repairs the rift with his wife and resumes his role as family protectorate. He therefore restores a Fieldingesque moral order that can now, again ironically, be attributed to Joseph Andrews's violent game of symbolic tag that began the novel. Xan's regression to atavistic masculine states – to "magnified emotion" (81) and "Alien moral systems" (127) – operates also in this sense: he is beaten back to a primitive moral universe and tries to import displaced gender categories to the present. The fact that these retrograde codes fail only confirms the shifting morality of Amis's fictive worlds. Xan rejects vulgar postmodernism but succeeds only on a personal level. He cannot leverage his newfound realism against the *existential* void: both the comet and the doomed airliner 101 Heavy maintain their descents, and Xan's repudiation of pornography cannot unmake that world. In short, his metamorphosis, or re-humanization, remains localized, self-contained, dwarfed by the postmodern disorder that swirls about his re-constituted head.

Analyzing *The Information*, Vera Nünning clarifies how Amis rewrites Victorian conventions through parody and imitation, emphasizing the "lack of a common moral standard" by illustrating the differences between "traditional and contemporary ways of viewing the world and the inadequacy of older conventions" (251–2). Nearly a decade later in *Yellow Dog* – Amis's most darkly Dickensian book – his critique has become further defined. Although it would be easy to analyze the novel's Victorian structure – replete with tripartite plot and even including a bathing Princess Victoria, who is voyeuristically filmed in an act of postmodern assault – the far more dynamic facet of the novel is its dialectic between postmodernism and realism. *Yellow Dog*'s oppositions between love and pornography, children and childlessness, family and solitude strive to transcend literary confines. They conflate aesthetics and morality, assailing the divisions between realism and postmodernism as *literary modes* and as feuding *world orders*. Unfortunately, Amis's consideration of these themes remains underexamined in the novel: sentimental at best, sexist at worst. As in *Night Train*, love and family remain pivotal to closure. In *Yellow Dog*, however, Amis adds children to these themes, and although closure remains elusive, the novel furnishes his best effort to date at a positive ending.

Before Amis orchestrates the final scenes, he must rehabilitate Xan's ability to love. Rejecting the void that Karla White proffers is but one facet of this recuperation – and the easiest to achieve: because she resides only in pornographic simulacra. "One genuine smile and everything would disappear" (270). Even on cinematic sets, her tears can banish the performative and summon the reinvigorated real. During her aborted coupling with Xan, her tears also engender his anagnorisis. When he desists, she reveals herself as Cora Susan and stands before him significantly "wait[ing] with the keys" (299) – a postmodern ambassador officiating over Xan's deportation to the real. Only then does Xan repair his relationship with his family, which he attempts to do through textuality, composing a melodramatic letter that tests the limits of pathos.

This letter represents Amis's most prolonged attempt to square his fiction with his nonfiction writing about feminism and sexism. Unless sufficiently reworked, such efforts will court failure.[11] Like the video-tape of the bathing princess – the "apparently perfect simulacrum [... that] came up against its structural limits" (200) – Xan's thoughts lose their war against cliché. That does not diminish their significance, of course. His thoughts weigh upon the same "pan-inoffensiveness" (234) that underlies the novel's interrogation of "obscenification" – "loss of *pudeur*," loss of shame (12) – yet unlike pornography, Xan's letter does *not* exist in a state "without ontology" (159). Instead, it acts as a casuist imperative, a document of moral and spiritual reckoning. He mourns that his assault had "fucked up [his] talent for love" (306), then admits a gendered "deficiency of candour": "men miss women being tractable, and women miss men being decisive; but we can't say that" (307). The letter concludes by declaring its genre as a revisionist epithalamion, echoing his wife's earlier plea.

Unlike *The Rachel Papers*, which utilizes textuality to mediate romance and closure, *Yellow Dog*'s postmodern momentum overrides Xan's humanist clichés. His reconstituted realism cannot transfigure the novel. Importantly, however – and both mirroring and amplifying *Night Train* – the postmodern carves out space for the human: for agency, subjectivity, authenticity, and love. *Yellow Dog* proposes one set of epistemological values – grounded in postmodern simulacra, spectacle, relativism, and performativity – but it also validates an incompatible moral humanism – grounded in realism. That does not prevent Amis from trying to wrench a compromise. With its plaintive appeals and unchecked assumptions, Xan's letter exposes the dif-ficulties that any attempt to sanitize postmodernism will necessarily face. These difficulties culminate in the novel's use of children, which concludes its tripartite revaluation of radical postmodernism.

In contrast to *Night Train*, children are abundant in *Yellow Dog*, despite the fact that some of its locales – especially Lovetown – are "babyless place[s]" (286). Children redeem Xan's world through both presence and absence. In his degenerative state, Xan ponders failed parental duty: "They're mine, and I can't protect them," he laments, before veering toward perversion; "So why not rend them? Why not rape them? [...He] thought he knew, now, why an animal would eat its young. To protect them – to put them back inside" (217). Later, he refines his emotions into "pity and terror" (296), inspiring his plea that "the laws of motion could be redrafted more indulgently with infants in mind" (334). He therefore articulates two distinct versions of pedophilia: the reconfigured positivist form and its vulgar, obscene twin. Such dualism evades classification within the realist/postmodernist dialectic, however, which is one reason, I believe, that the ending becomes pietistic. Unlike other oppositions – identity/amnesia, pornography/love, authenticity/simulation – children and family exist in a rarefied, protected realm of the novel's ideological critique. And that is precisely the problem: its conclusions are foregone, as though the starkly real crises of the post-9/11 world banished not only irony and postmodernism but comedy and satire as well. Appropriating Mal Bale's words about disproportionality, Xan attempts to restore equilibrium, stating plainly (about children): "you have the right to retaliate. But with proportionality" (334). The Meo family welcomes back a "rehabilitated" (333) Xan, and as he ponders his return to "the thing which is called world," Amis redirects our attention to the "bare tress above his head" with its "furred" snow which would "soon melt" (336). The novel ends portentously, as Xan holds his child while watching the rogue comet fall, mourning their loss of innocence, the "project of their protection" (339).

The novel sounds the complementary notes of panic and consolation, terror and pity – the precise emotions that Xan rediscovered within himself and which wrought his recovery from postmodern egotism, relativism, and absurdity. The novel begins by dramatizing postmodern assault; evolves a sophisticated dialectic between realism and postmodernism; varies this analysis across multiple sub-plots and themes; then – in what seems like an act of artistic exasperation – swerves into mannered didacticism. *Night Train*, in other words, is not only the better novel, but the progression onward to *Yellow Dog* reveals Amis's attempt to define – and shifting levels of discomfort with – the artistic permutation I have chosen to call sanitized postmodernism.

Both novels seek a marriage of realism and postmodernism grounded in humanist depth. Both emphasize character and subjectivity, agency and absence, love and family. Both attempt to sanitize extremist postmodernism, whether radical (*Night Train*) or vulgar (*Yellow Dog*). Essentially, they act as critical correctives. A full decade before 9/11, writing about DeLillo, Amis had diagnosed the dangers of postmodern discontinuity. *Time's Arrow* attempted to redress such challenges within a hermetically postmodern frame. Four years later, he altered that form, describing *The Information* as "completely realistic" in his interview with Will Self. *Night Train* and *Yellow Dog* were the only novels to appear in the following eight years. Over time, scholars may choose to contextualize these works as part of Amis's "effortful decline," in Martin Cropper's memorable phrasing (6). But they seem far more significant and may confirm something other than decline. These novels comprise Amis's "sentimental education" (Diedrick, 244), but – more important – they exhibit his efforts to assimilate realist humanism and depth within metafictional and reflexive postmodern frameworks. They are certainly less saturated by postmodernism than *Money* or *London Fields*, but they pose too many problems for overt realist accommodation. To differing degrees they are overweighed by indeterminacy and contingency, suffused by self-reflexivity, simulacra (both televisual and pornographic), intertextuality, and polyphonic discourse. Importantly, both works resolve their epistemological crises through a resurrected moralism that struggles to cleanse and redeem. Their swerve into sanctimoniousness may reveal Amis's latest attempt to shock readers out of postmodern irony, detachment, and complacency.

Instead of describing a mass exodus to realism, variously qualified by modifiers such as *hysterical*, *grotesque* and the like, perhaps an intermediary scholarly position is advisable. No one now questions that the pinnacle of postmodernism has passed, but when considering landmark innovators like Amis one may wish to sound the death-knells more softly. *Night Train* and *Yellow Dog* invite the consideration of a late- or second-phase postmodern form, a critical metastasis that has been happily granted to other theories and movements. More than an authorial mellowing, a diminishment of talent, or a repudiation of values, these novels can still be viewed as extending the postmodern debate, an attempt to demarcate a method *beyond* postmodernism. That these novels do not rank as masterpieces only confirms the difficulty of evolving a voice that can articulate realist, post-ironic constructs of identity, love, agency, and family while preserving subjectivist postmodernist critiques of media, textuality, contingency, and motivation. "Postmodernism may not have led anywhere but it was no false trail," Amis explained in 1991 ("Thoroughly", 28). Six years later, he appended:

> the press-ganged children who wore the dog tags must live with a discontinuity in their minds and hearts. [...] In the end, death didn't triumph. It just ruled, for 50 years. I take DeLillo to be saying that all our better feelings took a beating during those decades. An ambient moral fear constrained us. Love, even parental love, got harder to do." ("Survivors", 13)

With building intensity, and to varying degrees of success, *Night Train* and *Yellow Dog* record the plaintive aftershocks of such deliberations.

Notes

1   Although the phrase "radical postmodernism" is used by many scholars, Hans Bertens defines it well in *The Idea of the Postmodern* (1995): "Radical postmodern theory must be regarded as a transitional phenomenon … After an overlong period in which Enlightenment universalist representationalism dominated the scene, and a brief, but turbulent period in which its opposite, radical self-representationalism, captured the imagination, we now find ourselves in the difficult position of trying to honor the claims of both, of seeing the values of both representation and anti-representation, of both consensus and dissensus. Postmodern or radicalized modern – this is our fate: to reconcile the demands of rationality and those of the sublime, to negotiate a permanent crisis in the name of precarious stabilities" (3).

2   See Gardner, *On Moral Fiction* (1978); Graff, *Literature Against Itself*, (1979); Newman, *The Post-Modern Aura* (1985); Norris, *What's Wrong with Postmodernism* (1990) and *The Truth About Postmodernism* (1993); and Eagleton, *The Illusions of Postmodernism* (1996) and *After Theory* (2004). Wolfe's essay appears in *Harpers* (Nov. 1989), Wallace's in *Review of Contemporary Fiction* (23 June 1993).

3   James Wood's "hysterical realism" only slightly improves on Jean Baudrillard's "hysteria of the hyperreal," Joseph Dewey's "spectacle realism," and Fredric Jameson's "technological sublime" or "high tech paranoia." Hassan speaks of "fiduciary realism" whereas "dirty realism" has been attributed to Bill Buford, in *Granta*. In the *Anchor Book of New Irish Writing* John Somer and John Daly coin the term "deep realism"; "Postmodern Realism" and "neorealism" are more ubiquitous. Those who, following Jürgen Habermas or Fredric Jameson respectively, prefer to theorize postmodernism as a terminal period of either modernism or capitalism might consider the term *hyper-modernism*, which is employed without controversy in professional chess.

4   *Night Train* mines *The Information* for its lingering astrophysics, which themselves build upon *London Fields*. More derivative are the twined abstractions "night train" and "the information." Compare "Suicide is the night train, speeding your way to darkness […] This train takes you into the night, and leaves you there" (83) with two passages from *The Information*: "the information came at night, to inhume him" (110) and the last line, "And then there is the information, which is nothing, and comes at night."

5   This has become commonplace in Amis's fiction but is central to *Money*, which famously declares that motivation is "shagged out" (331). Compare *Night Train*: "Motive might have been worth considering, […] half a century ago. But now it's all up in the fucking air. With the TV" (127).

6   Amis elevates these works above the "orgy of thrillers" and "couple of yards […] of True Crime" he consumed in "Books I Wish I Had Written: Martin Amis" (*Guardian*, 2 Oct. 1997: T18.). Discussing police language – which Updike and other reviewers lambasted – he calls Simon's work a "cathedral of illumination."

7   Among the more convincing allusions are Paulie No, the autopsy specialist or "state-cutter" (Dr. No) and Hi Tulkinghorn, Jennifer's physician, whom Diedrick attributes to Dickens (165). The minor character of Jennifer's grandmother, Rhiannon, pays homage to Kingsley Amis's *The Old Devils*

(1986), and devoted Amis scholars will note that an actor with the name of Trader Faulkner appeared with a 13-year-old Amis in the 1965 film *A High Wind in Jamaica*. Admittedly more tenuous connections exist between Mike Hoolihan and Major Margaret Houlihan, on *M.A.S.H.*, if only to accentuate their mutual opposition to death. Jennifer's case is also referenced as the "Rockwell File."

8   Barth's classic essays "The Literature of Exhaustion" and "The Literature of Replenishment" appear in *The Friday Book* (1984). Hassan proposes an aesthetic of trust in "Beyond Postmodernism."

9   Compare Amis to John Preston (*Sunday Telegraph*, 10 Sept. 2003): "I came back to *Yellow Dog* again after September 11 and I remember thinking, [...] let's make this a comic novel, because, as well as rationality and morality, the whole notion of comedy had been put at risk. To me it felt like the end of the Age of Normalcy."

10 Infamously, Fischer compared reading the novel to catching "your favorite uncle ... in a school playground, masturbating" ("Someone needs to have a word with Amis," *Daily Telegraph*, 4 Aug. 2003).

11 The sections on pornography directly parallel Amis's essay "Sex in America" (2001). Passages involving Princess Victoria, the disappearing princess (33 and 54), seem indebted to the Lucy Partington material in *Experience* and Amis's retrospective on Princess Diana, "The Mirror of Ourselves" (1997).

Works cited

Amis, Martin. *The Information*. New York: Harmony, 1995.

——. *London Fields*. 1989. New York: Harmony, 1990.

——. *Night Train*. 1997. New York: Harmony, 1998.

——. *Other People: A Mystery Story*. New York: Viking, 1981.

——. "Survivors of the Cold War." *New York Times Book Review* 5 Oct. 1997: 12–13.

——. "Thoroughly post-modern millennium." *Independent* 8 Sept. 1991: 28.

——. *Yellow Dog*. New York: Hyperion/Talk Miramax, 2003.

Baker, Stephen. *The Fiction of Postmodernity*. New York: Rowman & Littlefield, 2000.

Bertens, Hans. *The Idea of the Postmodern: A History*. New York: Routledge, 1995.

Cropper, Martin. "The Sisyphean treadmill of anguish." *Daily Telegraph Arts and Books* 31 Aug. 1996: 6.

Curiel, Jonathan. "Martin Amis: Working with words on all fronts." *San Francisco Chronicle* 4 Nov. 2001: RV-2.

Diedrick, James. *Understanding Martin Amis*. 2nd ed. Columbia: U of South Carolina P, 2004.

Hassan, Ihab. *The Postmodern Turn: Essays in Postmodern Theory and Culture*. Columbus: Ohio State UP, 1987.

——. "Beyond Postmodernism: toward an aesthetic of trust." *Angelaki* 8.1 (Apr. 2003): 3–11.

Hutcheon, Linda. "Postmodern Afterthoughts." *Wascana Review* 37.1 (2002): 5–12.

Mars-Jones, Adam. *Venus Envy: On the WOMB and the BOMB*. London: Chatto & Windus, 1999.

Nünning, Vera. "Beyond Indifference: New Departures in British Fiction at the Turn of the 21st Century." Stierstorfer 235–54.

Oertel, Daniel. "Effects of Garden-Pathing in Martin Amis's novels *Time's Arrow* and *Night Train*." *Miscellanea* 22 (2001): 123–40.

Reynolds, Margaret, and Jonathan Noakes. *Martin Amis*. London: Vintage/ Random, 2003.

Self, Will. "An Interview with Martin Amis." *Mississippi Review* 7 (Oct. 1995). <http://www.mississippireview.com/1995/07amis.html>.

Stierstorfer, Klaus, ed. *Beyond Postmodernism: Reassessments in Literature, Theory, and Culture*. Berlin: Walter de Gruyter, 2003.

Updike, John. "It's a fair cop." *Sunday Times Books* 21 Sept. 1997: 1–2.

11

J.G. Ballard's "Inner Space" and the Early Fiction of Martin Amis

James Diedrick
Agnes Scott College

In *Money: A Suicide Note* (1984), John Self visits a brothel called the Happy Isles soon after first meeting the character Martin Amis. One of the prostitutes asks for his name, and he answers "I'm Martin," confiding that he hates his real name: "I'm called John Self. But who isn't?" (97). One lie leads to another – Self then claims to be a fiction writer – and to a comic misunderstanding. The prostitute turns out to be a graduate student in English literature: "They call me Moby," she tells Self, alluding to the opening of *Moby Dick*. When she inquires about his writing, the verbally and aesthetically challenged Self hears her question as "John roar mainstream?" He's never heard the word "genre," so she clarifies her meaning: "are they mainstream novels and stories or thrillers or sci-fi or something like that?" (98). Self responds with another question – "what's mainstream?" – but instead of the mockery we might expect she replies, "That's a good question" (98). Self's mishearing of her question, which eliminates the conjunction "or" and thus collapses the distinction between ostensibly antithetical terms, enacts an erasure that Moby herself endorses with her final remark, which admits the difficulty of defining "mainstream."

As with nearly all of Self's experiences, this one comically limns Martin Amis's own – specifically, the ways in which his writing simultaneously asserts and undermines distinctions between "high" and "low" culture and their corollaries, "mainstream" and "popular" fiction. And "sci-fi" lies at the heart of these tensions. Amis's early enthusiasm for, and deep familiarity with, science fiction tropes continue to express themselves in his work – despite his various attempts to marginalize the genre and obscure his abiding affinity for its forms. The fact that he used the pseudonym "Henry Tilney" for 12 of the 26 "Science Fiction" review columns he wrote for the *Observer* from 1972 to 1974 is emblematic of this ambivalence. Henry Tilney, a character in Jane Austen's *Northanger Abbey*, is a parodist and opponent of genre fiction in a novel that burlesques two of the most popular eighteenth-century subgenres: sentimental and gothic novels. By adopting this pseudonym, Amis obliquely signals his disdain for mere genre fiction, particularly the science fiction he reviewed extensively throughout the 1970s.[1] The "creation story" that dominates Amis's self-mythologizing account of his artistic development hinges on a Copernican turn away from science fiction and toward "literature" during his teenage years, inspired by his novelist-stepmother Elizabeth Jane Howard's insistence that he read Jane Austen.[2]

Amis's omission of his science fiction review columns from *The War Against Cliché: Essays and Reviews 1971–2000* (2001) reinforces this narrative. In fact, he omits all the adulatory reviews of what he has called the "hard" science fiction of J.G. Ballard and Kurt Vonnegut, the two writers whose contributions to the genre he has most admired. Of Amis's five reviews of Vonnegut's work, only one – his review of *Galapagos* – appears in *The War Against Cliché*, and the novel is dismissed with the judgment that its second half "tends toward the formless, the random, the diffuse, the anecdotal" (305). Ballard fares somewhat better: five of Amis's eight notices of his work are included. But these concern Ballard's experimental novels, not his "hard" science fiction.[3] Moreover, they are placed in a section titled "Some English Prose" rather than "From the Canon" (which inexplicably groups P.G. Wodehouse, Evelyn Waugh, and Malcolm Lowry with Donne, Milton, Coleridge, Austen, and Dickens) or "Great Books" (which accommodates Cervantes, Austen, Joyce, Nabokov, and Bellow). The single work of pure science fiction Amis reviews in *The War Against Cliché* – Michael Crichton's *The Lost World* – is singled out for special derision: "Animals ... are what he is good at. People are what he is bad at. People, and prose" (222). Amis does include his review of Anthony Burgess's *1985*, but he avoids the term "science fiction" altogether, categorizing the novel as "futuristic" and "dystopian" (116–17).[4] For Amis, whose desire to be considered a serious novelist borders on the obsessive, genre fiction, with its appeal to special interests, is the enemy of "literature," which strives for the universal.[5]

Amis's marginalization of his many science fiction reviews creates a misleading impression of his early career and literary interests. In 1972, only a year out of Oxford, Amis returned to science fiction, reviewing hundreds of titles over a five-year period with the enthusiasm and deep familiarity of a fan.[6] Amis's essayistic interest in

science fiction continued well beyond the *Observer* column, extending to his 1982 book on video games (*Invasion of the Space Invaders*);
his 1982 essay in praise of Steven Spielberg's science fiction films; his
1990 report from the set of Paul Verhoeven's *Robocop II*; and his por-
tentous response to the 2001 terrorist attacks on America.[7] This
latter essay employs the apocalyptic mode of "New Wave" science
fiction, describing the glint of the second plane that slammed into
the World Trade Center as "the worldflash of a coming future" and
the collapse of both towers as "the apotheosis of the postmodern
era" ("Fear", G2). Amis also continued to review individual science
fiction novels and profile science fiction writers in subsequent
decades, especially Ballard, Vonnegut, and Ron Goulart. Even Amis's
fitful attempts at screenwriting testify to his ongoing fascination
with science fiction. In 1979 he wrote the script for the 1980 film
Saturn 3 (satirized obliquely in *Money*), and he contributed to the
screenplay for Tim Burton's *Mars Attacks!*. Amis has called his short
story "Career Move" – about a world in which poets are treated like
royalty and science fiction screenwriters toil away in oblivion – a
"revenge fantasy," telling interviewer Justin Bauer that "it was
written while I was a writer on *Mars Attacks!*, and of course, not a
word of my script was used in the eventual film."

Elsewhere I have written about Amis's appropriations of science
fiction themes in what I have called his "Apocalypse Now" fictions of
the mid-1980s to the early-1990s, including *Einstein's Monsters*, *London
Fields*, and *Time's Arrow*. These works, which draw on what Amis has
called the "apocalyptic-epiphanic" mode within the science fiction tradition (*War*, 95), have subsequently been analyzed in relation to
"hard" science fiction (David Moyle) as well as the history of science
(Richard Menke, Peter Rogers, Maya Slater). In this essay I want to
focus on Amis's reading of Ballard's work from the 1960s and 1970s to
demonstrate the importance of the science fiction genre to the development of his own hybrid fictions. Specifically, I want to show how
Ballard's example shaped the development of Amis's fictional voice
from the early 1970s to the early 1980s – especially his second novel,
Dead Babies (1975), his neglected poem "An American Airman Looks
Ahead" (1977), and his fourth novel, *Other People: A Mystery Story*
(1981).

Reviewing a collected uniform edition of Saul Bellow's works in
1985, Amis describes Bellow's "evolution as a novelist" in terms that
apply to his own early career. He writes that Bellow's first book of short
stories – "like most collections" – is "an assortment of voices, styles,

try-outs, mimicries." He then notes that in Bellow's next collection "we find a new invariance of tone. The voice is no longer interested in impersonation; it is settled in its authority, resolute in its inquiries and concerns (love, consanguinity, version of evil, death). Everything has come together. And this is a large part of what writers are really up to: finding the right voice, the right line, the right instrument" ("American Eagle", 17). By his own account, it took Amis two novels to audition various voices and develop "the right instrument." He has described *The Rachel Papers* (1973) and *Dead Babies* as apprentice works: "I am no great admirer of my first novel, or indeed of my second, regarding them as a mixture of clumsy apprenticeship and unwarranted showing off." He is especially critical of *Dead Babies*: "I'd give it a really blistering, unfavorable review. I can see what's contrived about it, what's plagiarized; I'm a great lifter of phrases, at least of how they're constructed" (Moritz, 21). Ironically, it was in his 1980 essay accusing Jacob Epstein of plagiarizing from *The Rachel Papers* in his novel *Wild Oats* that Amis admitted to his own smaller-scale plagiarism, revealing Ballard's importance to Amis's own developing voice:

> I am something of an idiom-magpie myself – to a reprehensible extent, perhaps ... I once lifted a whole paragraph of mesmeric jargon from J.G. Ballard's *The Drowned World*, and was reproved by the publisher via an alert Ballard fan. In fact, I had belatedly got verbal permission from Mr. Ballard, who is a friend and colleague. But the lapse was evidence of laziness, and a kind of moral torpor. ("Tale", 26)

Ballard published *The Drowned World* in 1962, too early for Amis to review in the *Observer*, but its hold on Amis's imagination has been considerable. Indeed, a careful reading of this novel alongside *Dead Babies* – the novel Amis declines mentioning above – suggests that more than a paragraph of "mesmeric jargon" found its way into Amis's second novel.

The Drowned World is Ballard's second novel also, and it prefigures many of the themes of his subsequent books: planetary/ecological disaster, entropy, the devolution of human nature, the roots of violence. On one hand, it is a conventionally admonitory narrative of global cataclysm; at the same time, it embodies the "New Wave" fiction that both Ballard and Vonnegut pioneered in the 1960s and 1970s. It appeared the same year as Ballard's manifesto "Which Way to Inner Space?," a guest editorial in the science fiction journal *New Worlds*, which calls for new work to emerge from the shadow of H.G. Wells and "turn its back on space, interstellar travel, extra-terrestrial life forms, galactic wars," as well as its "present narrative forms and plots." Ballard insists that the major developments of the immediate future will take place on earth: "it is inner space, not outer, that needs to be explored. The only truly alien planet is Earth" (James, 168). As Amis notes parenthetically in his review of Ballard's *Hello America* (1981), the holocaust rendered in *The Drowned World* is not imagined as a fearful visitation but "welcomed and embraced for the 'psychic possibilities'" it reveals (*War*, 104). Like the other novels in Ballard's "Global Disaster Quartet" – *The Wind from Nowhere*, *The Drought* and *The Crystal World* – *The Drowned World* ruminates on physical and psychological metamorphoses in the face of environmental apocalypse. Here, as in Ballard's subsequent fiction, the transformed physical world both engenders and registers transformations in the inner-world of the psyche – a representational strategy that Amis has employed from *Dead Babies* onward. This often produces haunting evocations of urban squalor or charged descriptions of the world rendered strange and malevolent by human perversity. *Other People, Einstein's Monsters, Time's Arrow, The Information*, and *Yellow Dog* are rich in such passages. At its worst, however, it takes the form of self-conscious metaphor-making, as when Mark Asprey, the doomed and despairing narrator of *London Fields*, links his own state to the entropic sky: "quite uncanny, the sun's new trajectory, and getting lower all the time. Seen from the rear, I must look exactly like I feel: a silhouette, staggering blind into the photosphere of an amber star" (309).

The Drowned World is set in an unspecified future when the world has been overwhelmed by catastrophic greenhouse effects. The resultant melting of the polar ice caps has drowned some parts of the world and landlocked others; at the same time, the increased radiation has produced freak mutations in Earth's flora and fauna, initiating a new biological era reminiscent of the Triassic period, in which reptiles and giant tropical plants dominated life on earth. Although the human population has drastically diminished, life does continue; the novel focuses on a survey expedition sent to map inundated areas for reclamation. This group of surveyors has been exploring the series of giant lagoons that were once Europe for so long that they have nearly forgotten their original purpose. They sink deeper into lassitude and indifference, and some of the members begin having strange dreams of a primeval swamp dominated by a huge, burning sun pulsing to the rhythm of their heartbeats. These dreams are revealed as intimations of a psychic process in which humans, responding to stimuli embedded in their genetic makeup, have begun to devolve. Their dreams are memories of the primeval ooze from which life emerged. As the Earth regresses through geophysical time, the dreamers retreat through "archaeopsychic time," recapitulating in reverse each of the stages of human evolution.

This new time is described by the biologist Bodkin, who identifies himself as an expert in "Neuronics," "the psychology of Total Equivalents": "Each one of us is as old as the entire biological kingdom, and our bloodstreams are tributaries of the great sea of its total memory. The uterine odyssey of the growing foetus recapitulates the entire evolutionary past, and its central nervous system is a coded time scale, each nexus of neurones and each spinal level marking a symbolic station, a unit of neuronic time" (44). Bodkin sounds like Ballard's aesthetic alter-ego when he describes the descent into the evolutionary past, for he describes a correspondence between inner and outer landscape that "Which Way to Inner Space?" proposes and *The Drowned World* enacts:

> The further down the CNS you move from the hindbrain through the medulla into the spinal cord, you descend back into the neuronic past. For example, the junction between the thoracic and lumbar vertebrae ... is the great zone of transit between the gill-breathing fish and the air-breathing amphibians with their respiratory rib-cages, the very junction where we stand now on the shores of this lagoon, between the Paleozoic and Triassic Eras. (44)

Bodkin extends this devolutionary analogy into the realm of the psyche. First, he asserts that in moving back through "geophysical time" we "move back through spinal and archaeopsychic time, recollecting in our unconscious minds the landscapes of each epoch, each with a distinct geological terrain, [...] as recognisable to anyone else as they would be to a traveller in a Wellsian time machine" (44). Then, he sharply distinguishes this journey from what he calls the "scenic railway" of Wells, noting that it engenders "a total reorientation of the personality. If we let these buried phantoms master us as they re-appear we'll be swept back helplessly in the flood-tide like pieces of flotsam" (45). By alluding to Wells while metaphorically appropriating his time machine, Bodkin also intimates the new directions in which Ballard is taking the science fiction genre.

Amis clearly found Bodkin's speculations compelling, since he puts some of his exact words into the mouth of Marvell Buzhardt, the character in *Dead Babies* who accelerates the moral devolution of his fellow debauchees. Buzhardt is an American, a "postgraduate in psychology, anthropology, and environment" (43), and author of *The Mind Lab*, which promotes the hedonistic use of psychoactive chemicals. He distributes these drugs to the weekend revelers at Appleseed Rectory, explaining that they will achieve in minutes something resembling the "total reorientation of the personality" that will take much longer for the characters in *The Drowned World*. In a chapter titled "The Lumbar Transfer," Buzhardt dispenses the following explanation along with a round of hallucinogens, borrowing liberally from Bodkin and Ballard:

> The further down the CNS you go – through the hind brain, the medulla, into the spinal track – gene activity increases and concentrates and you descend into the neuronic gallery of your own past, like your whole meteorologic personality going by in stills. As the drug enters the amnionic corridor it will start to urge you back through spinal and archaeopsychic time, reactivating in your mind screen the changing landscapes of your subconscious past, each reflecting its own distinct emotional terrain. The releasing mechanisms in your cytoplasm will be awakened and you will phase into the entirely new zone of the neuronic psyche. This is the real you. This is total biopsychic recall. This is the lumbar transfer. Come over here one at a time, please. (163)

Given the fact that *Dead Babies* is a coruscating satire on countercultural narcissism, it is not surprising that this "awakening" mandates a descent into moral atavism. Such themes are recurrent in Amis, from the bloody bacchanalia of *Dead Babies* to the "reptile mind" that dominates Keith Talent's thoughts and actions in *London Fields* (335) to Xan Meo's post-traumatic regression into the argot and attitudes of his criminal ancestors in *Yellow Dog*.

In terms of genre, most readers would associate *Dead Babies* with the country house comedies of P.G. Wodehouse, not the speculative futures of early Ballard.[8] But the correspondences with *The Drowned World* are striking. Set in an indeterminate future, *Dead Babies* explores the psychic degeneration of individuals stranded in a cultural landscape where narcissism is doing the work of the future floods that nearly drown Ballard's protagonists. Both novels employ what Amis, reviewing Ballard's *Concrete Island*, calls "the language of heightened, dislocated consciousness" in rendering the experiences of their characters (*War*, 99). Both novels also end with apocalyptic imagery intimating a post-humanist future. In *The Drowned World*, one of the male survivors heads south "through the increasing rain and heat, attacked by alligators and giant bats, a second Adam searching for the forgotten paradises of the reborn sun" (175). In *Dead Babies*, the murderous Quentin Villiers lies in wait for his next victim as "his green eyes flashed into the dawn like wild, dying suns" (206). It is as if Amis set out in *Dead Babies* to marry the comedy of manners (exceedingly ill manners, in this case) to the "apocalyptic-epiphanic" mode of science fiction. He acknowledged nearly as much in his contribution to a 1978 symposium in the *New Review* on the future of the novel – a symposium in which he shared space with Ballard.

Whereas Ballard champions the resurgence of "imaginative fiction and, paradoxically, a welcome end to moralizing" in his contribution to this symposium, proclaiming gleefully that "realist fiction seems finally to have run out of gas," Amis foresees a synthesis of the experimental and the realistic: "If I try very hard, I can imagine a novel that is as tricksy, as alienated and as writerly as those of, say, Robbe-Grillet while also providing the staid satisfactions of pace, plot and humour with which we associate, say Jane Austen. In a way, I imagine that this is what I myself am trying to do" ("State of Fiction", 18). If we substitute "J.G. Ballard" for Robbe-Grillet, this formulation helps account for the Ballardian notes that continue to sound even in the most urban and topical of Amis's novels.

Nor is *The Drowned World* the only Ballard fiction to haunt the margins of *Dead Babies*. In 1973, two years before he published *Dead Babies*, Amis reviewed two relevant works: a reprint of Ballard's 1971 short-story collection *Vermillion Sands* – surveyed in one of Amis's "Henry Tilney" columns – and *Crash*, published the same year as Amis's *The Rachel Papers*. The "Vermilion Sands" of the title seems in some ways a futuristic version of Appleseed Rectory, a resort whose visitors strikingly resemble the inhabitants of *Dead Babies*. In Amis's words, "the denizens of Vermilion Sands are sleepy playthings of their whims and desires, directionless, soulless, futile with the sullen corruption of boredom and affluence. Thus all the stories end on a note of withdrawal and suspension, of having got nowhere" ("Science Fiction", 23). As for the Appleseeders: "it seemed that everything they thought had already been done and done, and that everything they thought had already been thought and thought, and that this would never end" (*Dead Babies*, 120). Amis's detailed but distanced treatment of the grotesque extremes of sex and violence in *Dead Babies* calls to mind the clinical narrative viewpoint Ballard adopts in *Crash*, which Amis describes as a "mournful and hypnotic *tour de force*" (*War*, 101).

Crash is Ballard's most famous and influential work. His foreword to the 1974 French edition of the novel indicates the source of its influence and fascination for Amis: "The marriage of reason and nightmare which has dominated the 20th Century has given birth to an ever more ambiguous world. Across the communications landscape move the spectres of sinister technologies and the dreams that money can buy. Over our lives preside the twin leitmotifs of the 20th century: sex and paranoia.... The century's most terrifying casualty [is] the death of affect" (1). Ballard's fiction is emblematic of what postmodernist theorists variously describe as "the waning of affect" in postmodernism (Jameson, 10) or the eclipse of the real by "the cool universe of digitality" (Baudrillard, 149). For these theorists as for Ballard, new electronic technologies turn the world into a single global marketplace; universal commodity fetishism colonizes lived experience; the real becomes supplanted by its representations; and subjectivity breaks into fragments. This postmodern landscape is familiar to all readers of Martin Amis. The loss of the ability to feel or to empathize, a corollary of all these other losses, is a theme that echoes throughout his writing. It is registered in the post-nuclear dystopias of *Einstein's Monsters*, the eschatological drumbeat of *London Fields*, and the literal reference to "the deaths of feelings" in "Sex in America," which notes that "porno is littered – porno is heaped – with the deaths of feelings" (135).

Amis has returned to *Crash* almost obsessively since originally reviewing it in 1973 – perhaps appropriate to a novel he calls "both obsessive and obsessed, with a numb, luminous quality that loiters in the mind" (*War*, 105). Indeed, he reintroduces and reconsiders *Crash* in all seven of his subsequent reviews of Ballard's work. As he acknowledges in *The War Against Cliché*: "it took me a long time to get the hang of *Crash*, and of Ballard. My review, here, is so straitlaced that I hesitate to preserve it. But I do: readers should always be wrestling with the writers who feel intimate to them" (96). The anxiety of influence can be heard in Amis's original review, as he confronts a vision of sexuality that he later admits made his first novel seem "obsequiously conventional" (*War*, 110). While admiring the "deadpan singlemindedness of its attitudes," Amis faults the novel's "loose construction, perfunctory way with minor characters," and occasionally laughable overwriting, which makes the book seem "just an exercise in vicious whimsy." He concludes by rejecting Ballard's experimental mode in favor of his straight genre fiction: "in science fiction Ballard had a tight framework for his unnerving ideas; out on the lunatic fringe, he can only flail and shout" (*War*, 96–7).[9] Some six months later, reviewing *Vermillion Sands* as Henry Tilney, he concedes *Crash*'s stylistic brilliance, claiming that it has "the curious distinction of being at once rarefied, pornographic, tedious, puerile, and hauntingly well written" ("Science Fiction", 23). It is worth noting that these four adjectives – although not the final adverbial phrase – have been applied to *Dead Babies* itself, a novel written in the shadow of *Crash* and clearly determined to match Ballard's unflinching depictions of sexual perversity and violence.

By 1981, reviewing *Hello America*, Amis celebrates the prose texture of *Crash,* which he calls Ballard's "most mannered and literary book, its sprung rhythms and creamily varied vowel-sounds a conscious salute to Baudelaire, Rimbaud and Mallarmé" (*War*, 105). Ballard's militant aestheticism – what Amis in 1974 called his "creative narcissism" (101) – represents the extreme limit of Amis's own tendencies. Amis once told John Haffenden that he would "sacrifice any psychological or realistic truth for a phrase, for a paragraph that has a spin on it" (15), yet despite its stylistic bravado, *Dead Babies* is most notable for its moral disgust – a disgust directed both at the counterculture and at the experimental wing of fiction over which Ballard presided. As Amis wrote in a review of David Cronenberg's film adaptation, Ballard's novel "emerged from a background of surrealism, cultural activism, hyperpermissiveness and lysergic acid" (*War*, 110) – the same milieu Amis savages in *Dead Babies*. And it is Ballard's fictional illumination of the cultural *Zeitgeist* that reveals the deepest affinity between Britain's two leading postwar stylists. In 1987, reviewing *The Day of Creation* (which inevitably mentions and praises *Crash*), Amis reveals a fundamental similarity of subject matter that links his thematic concerns with Ballard's, labeling him "our leading investigator of the effects of technology, pornography and television" (108). This is a characterization many would apply to Amis himself.

One effect of technology that both Amis and Ballard explore is the "time sickness" it can engender. Sinking deeper into lethargy and ennui under the influence of hallucinogenic drugs, Amis's Appleseeders experience "lagging time," which "flopped down like an immense and invisible jelly from the ceiling, swamping the air with marine languor and insect speeds – lagging time, with its numbness and disjunction, its inertia and automatism, its lost past and dead future" (*Dead Babies*, 120). This description evokes the physically and psychically sodden landscape of *The Drowned World*; it also echoes a central theme of Ballard's "Cape Canaveral" stories of the late-1960s, some of which Amis reviewed when they were reissued in *Low-Flying Aircraft* (1976). These stories express Ballard's view that space exploration distorts humanity's relationship to time, a view he articulates in the 1981 story "News from the Sun":

> Each space-launch left its trace in the minds of those watching the expeditions. Each flight to the moon and each journey around the sun was a trauma that warped their perception of time and space. The brute-force ejection of themselves from their planet had been an act of evolutionary piracy, for which they were now being expelled from the world of time. (108)

In his December 1976 "Science Fiction" column, Amis praises Ballard's *Low-Flying Aircraft*, claiming that the stories represent "science fiction in a sense that the recent novels are not," and noting that "Ballard is far more relaxed and accessible when his unnerving ideas are held within the confines of the genre" (30). Amis singles out the 1968 story "The Dead Astronaut" for special note. The story focuses on Judith, whose astronaut-lover suffocates while orbiting in his space capsule. When she first learns of her lover's death, Ballard writes, her response was muted. Later, however, "after her miscarriage, the thought of this dead astronaut circling the sky above us re-emerged in her mind as an obsession with time. For hours, she would stare at the clock, as if waiting for something to happen" (69–70). After 20 years, Judith comes to Cape Kennedy, "waiting for the capsule to crash to earth, determined to memorialize her lover's life even though everyone else has forgotten both him and the others still in space" (70). She suffers from a temporal disorder engendered by technology, which Ballard describes in "News from the Sun": "the year-long flights ... had set off the whole time-plague, cracked the cosmic hourglass" (105). Significantly, Amis alludes to this concept in the title of his story "The Time Disease," set in a post-apocalyptic world that embodies the nuclear-age time Amis articulates in his essay "Thinkability": "the past and the future, equally threatened, equally cheapened, now huddle in the present" (*Einstein's*, 22). But as the example from *Dead Babies* indicates, his interest in "time sickness" began in the 1970s.

Six months after reviewing *Low-Flying Aircraft*, Amis published the poem "An American Airman Looks Ahead" in the *Observer* – a poem that alludes to W.B. Yeats's "An Irish Airman Foresees His Death." In certain respects it extends the ruminations on the relationship between technology and human consciousness that Amis encountered in "The Dead Astronaut." It is a dramatic monologue spoken by an "airman" who seems to be imagining his future in space – a thoroughly commodified future of diminished affect and temporal deformations. The poem begins:

> My outer wife sells darkness – it's
> Quite hard to come by on the flat
> Pink planet where she lives. I stay
> Inside her pod until the light hurts
> My eyes. (I get free darkness. She's
> Doing all right now. Darkness sells.)
> And then I coast the tides of space.

The speaker refers to a "wife" (line 1), "interior time girls" (8), and later a "milky mistress" (16), but his relationship to these women is fractured, tenuous, and mediated by money. His wife "sells" the "darkness" (1) that he needs; he has "fix[ed]" (14) the "concessions" (13) required by his "interior girls" (associated with the Fates of Greek mythology by way of a "creaking loom" [11]); and his mistress "deals / in distance" (16–17). In fact, the work of all these women pushes the speaker farther into space, where he clinches his teeth and shudders down warps that are "thin as dimes" (26).

"An American Airman Looks Ahead" employs the same language of "heightened, dislocated consciousness" that Amis praised in his 1974 review of Ballard's *Concrete Island* (*War*, 99). In this sense the poem looks ahead to Amis's fourth novel, *Other People*, his most Ballardian novel and the only Amis novel Ballard ever reviewed. *Other People* tells the story of Mary Lamb, a woman who suffers from amnesia. It depicts her encounters with a series of "other people," including her pre-amnesiac self, Amy Hide. As the novel opens, Mary is being discharged from the hospital; as she enters the urban mystery that is London, her perceptions transform both the cityscape and the skies:

> Not too far above the steep canyons there had hung an imperial backdrop of calm blue distance, in which extravagantly lovely white creatures – fat, sleepy things – hovered, cruised and basked. Carelessly and painlessly lanced by the slow-moving crucifixes of the sky, they moreover owed allegiance to a stormy yellow core of energy, so irresistible that it had the power to hurt your eyes if you dared to look its way. (18–19)

Here the things people take most for granted in the urban and natural realms (skyscrapers, clouds, jet airplanes, the sun) assume a heightened, numinous quality – just as they do in Ballard's fiction. Ballard's "real strength," Amis claimed in a review of *Hello America* during the same year *Other People* was published, is "the ability to invest abstract vistas with intense and furtive life" (*War*, 106). In *Other People* Amis marries this same quality to his own greater engagement with the contemporary social realm.

As I have written elsewhere, Amis's "defamiliarizing" perspective in this novel has much in common with the "Martian School" – a phrase coined by James Fenton to describe the poetry of Craig Raine and Christopher Reid (see Diedrick, ch. 3). Amis even wrote his own poem about the "Martian" perspective – "Point of View" – which was published in the *New Statesman* in 1979 and incorporated into the text of *Other People*. But "An American Airman" suggests an equally important imaginative example. The airman and his disorienting experience of time recall Judy's time sickness in "The Dead Astronaut," and both are echoed in Mary Lamb's shifting perceptions. In some ways, the narrator remarks, Mary "enjoys certain advantages over other people. Not yet stretched by time, her perceptions are without seriality: they are multiform, instantaneous and random, like the present itself" (55). But like Amis's airman, she quickly learns that time has been thoroughly commodified; subjective experience is hopelessly shaped by economic and social conditions. She tells her friend Trudy she wants a job, to which Trudy replies, "they take time, you know." Mary considers this: "You had to be out by nine. You couldn't come back until twelve. Time was slow on the streets when you had no money. Time took forever" (72). Earlier the novel declares, "Time – she needed more and more of it as time went by" (39).

Because of her amnesia, Mary has no memories and thus no emotions. She is a radical embodiment of the "death of affect" Ballard associates with the postmodern condition. Consider her musings on death: "She knew a little about death now. She knew that it happened to other people [...] It was a bad thing, obviously, and no one liked it; but no one knew how much it hurt, how long it lasted, whether it was the end of everything or the start of something else" (59). Her dreams, on the other hand, are where the emotional chaos of her former life resides, where "incredible things happen": "For hours in the darkness her mind struggled fiercely to keep the dreams away [...] But her mind wouldn't listen to her: it thrummed on its own fever, dealing her half-images of graphic sadness and fluorescent chaos, setting her hurtful tasks of crisis and desire" (59). As Mary muses on the source of these dreams, she imagines they come from her past: "She had never seen a red beach bubbled with sandpools under a furious and unstable sun. She had never felt a sensation of speed so intense that her nose could remember the tang of smoldering air. And the dreams always ended by mangling her; they came down like black smoke and plucked her apart nerve by nerve" (61). Here Amis powerfully renders the "inner space" of the "truly alien planet, earth" by means of science fiction-inflected imagery that evokes the haunting vistas of Ballard's "Global Disaster Quartet."

Ballard's review of *Other People* recognizes and celebrates Amis's stylistically daring exploration of "inner space," as this analogy makes clear: "[this] powerful and obsessive novel has all the electrifying conviction of a newsreel filmed inside our heads." Amis's achievement in stripping away this film of familiarity deeply impressed Ballard:

> With almost no surface, but with infinite depth, *Other People* resembles a geometric conundrum devised by a paranoid mathematician. In an extraordinary way it conveys the actual contours and texture of the uneasy realm wrapped around us by that ambiguous conspiracy between the universe and our own psyches – everyday reality. Reason attempts to rationalize that reality for us, but like the polite fictions of the bourgeois novel it somehow fails to convince, whereas *Other People* has the authority of a waking nightmare. ("First Things", 111)

This review also cunningly enlists *Other People* in Ballard's own anti-realist cause, employing a florid series of metaphors. He calls it "a remarkable achievement" that "hurls another spadeful of earth onto the over-ripe coffin of the bourgeois novel," a "metaphysical thriller," that "could not be further away" from the "true-to-life worlds" of such writers as John Updike or Anthony Powell, nor be "closer to our own." Ballard praises Amis for presenting the action from a woman's perspective: "He very skillfully constructs his portrait of this amnesiac woman who at the same time is re-inventing herself, literally from the toe-nails upwards" (111).

In his concluding remarks, Ballard also "re-invents" Amis, shuffling the chronology of his novels so Amis begins his career – in the manner of Ballard – with an experimental novel. In this revisionist chronology, Ballard consigns Amis's first two novels to a middle-period realm of holiday larks: "I believe that writers don't actually produce their books in their real order, and I regard *Other People* as Martin Amis's first novel, with *The Rachel Papers* and *Dead Babies* as perhaps his sixth and seventh, say, from his Monaco period. A great debut" (111). Given Amis's own dismissive remarks about his first two novels – and the fact that *Other People*, along with its predecessor (*Success*) and its successor (*Money*) represent Amis's major early achievements – Ballard sounds like one of Amis's ideal readers. He also demonstrates that he has given Amis's fiction the same kind of sustained, enthusiastic, engaged attention that Amis has given his own.

In the years since *Other People*, Amis's anxieties of influence have eased, especially concerning his early, half-concealed love of science fiction. The result has been a series of short narratives that embrace science fiction themes and strategies, most notably the anti-nuclear short story collection *Einstein's Monsters*.[10] By confining these genre experiments to short forms, however, Amis subordinates them to his longer, "mainstream" works, effectively reinforcing an imagined boundary separating the "popular" from the "literary." In his May 1973 "Science Fiction" review column, he defines the "SF story" as "a perfect miniature, a satisfying realization of a single idea" (37). By contrast, he claims "mainstream stories are oblique, tentative glimpses of small areas of life, deriving a good deal of their power from leaving much unsaid" and argues that this reveals a fundamental difference "between SF and mainstream fiction." While this tidy binary helps explain why Amis appropriated science fiction tropes for the single-issue *Einstein's Monsters*, its value as a generalization is questionable. Moreover, it deflects attention from the hybrid nature of Amis's own novels. As this essay has suggested, Amis's early and abiding interest in Ballard's haunting, often nightmarish explorations of inner space, alternate worlds, and possible futures played a formative role in shaping Amis's fictional imagination, a point he acknowledged in his June 1976 "Science Fiction" column concerning dystopias: "in fiction, nasty societies tend to be funnier, scarier and much more thought-provoking than nice ones" (27).

Notes

1 Amis makes exceptions for genre writers who are also superb stylists, as in his appreciation of Elmore Leonard (*War*, 225–8).

2 In an interview in *The Literary Review* (May 1987), Amis describes science fiction as "a kind of family hobby" (42). Kingsley Amis was famously fond of genre fiction and wrote the critical study *New Maps of Hell* (1960). In his *Paris Review* interview (spring 1998), Amis was asked if any writer's work "was pivotal or a turning-point"; he responded, "[t]he first literature I read

was Jane Austen" (119). As a novelist of "ill manners" and a keen observer of the human comedy, Amis understandably admires Austen, an early master of the "novel of manners." He has written four essays on Austen and in 2001 was hired by Miramax to adapt *Northanger Abbey* for the screen.

3 Amis's eight reviews of Ballard are exceeded only by his ten of Nabokov and nine of Roth. Reviewing Ballard's *Hello America*, Amis uses the phrase "hardcore science fiction" (later shortened to "hard sf") to describe the works of writers like Arthur Clarke and Isaac Asimov (*War*, 104). That category includes most of Ballard's short stories and his first novel *Wind from Nowhere* (1962).

4 In his 13 June 1976 "Science Fiction" review column, Amis identifies "the dystopia, or 'sick society,'" as "far and away the most popular theme in modern science fiction." Significantly, all of Amis's science fiction stories, from "Debitocracy" (1974) to "The Janitor on Mars" (1998), are dystopian.

5 Reviewing Thomas Harris's *Hannibal*, Amis writes that "the book-chat mediocrities have had it with the hierarchy of the talents. In promoting the genre novelist ... they demote his mainstream candidate, and doing this has long been their pleasure and solace" (*War*, 241).

6 Writing as Henry Tilney on 16 July 1972, Amis calls *Dimension X* a "dazzling collection of novellas,... definitive SF, which no fan ought to miss" (30). Significantly, Amis masked this enthusiasm by maintaining the "Tilney" pseudonym long enough to publish his first novel and have it judged a success.

7 See "Steven Spielberg: Boyish Wonder" in *The Moronic Inferno and Other Visits to America* (1986). In *Visiting Mrs. Nabokov and Other Excursions* (1993), Amis champions the prophetic satire of the original *RoboCop* film: "It wasn't just state-of-the-art. It was also state-of-the-science: when you see its twirling rivets and burnished heat-exchangers, [...] you suspect that the future really might feel like this – that it will act this way on your very nerve-ends" (164).

8 Reviewing *Sunset at Blandings* in 1978 Amis describes Wodehouse as an exponent of "the comic pastoral," adding that his imagined worlds are "devoid of all the baser energies" (*War*, 204–5). True to his dystopian sensibility, Amis systematically inverts this utopian vision in *Dead Babies*.

9 Commenting on his early reviews, Amis has remarked, "I am ... struck by how hard I sometimes was on writers who (I erroneously felt) were trying to influence me: Roth, Mailer, Ballard" (*War*, xv).

10 Amis did publish one science fiction story early in his career: "Debitocracy," a dystopian tale about a future of enforced sexual equality and opportunity. It was published in a non-literary venue (*Penthouse* [UK], Nov. 1974) and omitted from *Heavy Water and Other Stories* (1998). Like his most recent foray into the genre – "The Janitor on Mars" – "Debitocracy" recalls Vonnegut's *The Sirens of Titan* (1959). In addition to *Einstein's Monsters*, Amis's science fiction experiments include the "alternative world" novella *Time's Arrow* and the tales "Career Move" (1992) and "Straight Fiction" (1995), both collected in *Heavy Water*. In the first, science fiction screenwriters toil in penniless obscurity while poets bask in glamour; in the second, heterosexuals are an oppressed minority and homosexuality is the norm.

Works cited

Amis, Martin. "An American Airman Looks Ahead." *Observer* 5 June 1977: 28.

——. "The American Eagle." *Observer* 25 Aug. 1985: 17.

——. *Dead Babies*. 1975. New York: Vintage, 1992.

——. *Einstein's Monsters*. 1987. New York: Vintage, 1990.

——. "Fear and Loathing." *Guardian* 18 Sept. 2001: G2.

——. *London Fields*. 1989. New York: Vintage, 1992.

——. *Money: A Suicide Note*. 1984. New York: Penguin, 1986.

——. *Other People: A Mystery Story*. 1981. New York: Vintage, 1994.

——. Rev. of *1985*, by Anthony Burgess. *War*, 116–20.

——. Rev. of *Crash*, by J.G. Ballard. *War*, 95–7.

——. Rev. of *Crash*, by David Cronenberg. *War*, 109–12.

——. Rev. of *Concrete Island*, by J.G. Ballard. *War*, 98–101.

——. Rev. of *The Day of Creation*, by J.G. Ballard. *War*, 107–9.

——. [Henry Tilney]. "Science Fiction." *Observer* 23 Dec. 1973: 23.

——. [Henry Tilney]. "Science Fiction." *Observer* 20 May 1973: 37.

——. "Science Fiction." *Observer* 13 June 1976: 27.

——. "Science Fiction." *Observer* 5 Dec. 1976: 30.

——. "Sex in America." *Talk* Feb. 2001: 98–103, 133–5.

——. "A Tale of Two Novels." *Observer* 19 Oct. 1980: 26.

——. *The War Against Cliché: Essays and Reviews, 1971–2000*. 2001. New York: Vintage, 2002.

Ballard, J.G. *Crash*. 1971. New York: Vintage, 1985.

——. "The Dead Astronaut." *Memories of the Space Age*. Sauk City: Arkham, 1988. 65–78.

——. *The Drowned World*. London: Gollancz, 1964.

——. "First Things Last." *Tatler* Mar. 1981: 111.

——. "Low-Flying Aircraft." *Low-Flying Aircraft*. London: Panther, 1976. 88–107.

——. "News from the Sun." *Memories of the Space Age*. Sauk City: Arkham, 1988. 93–130.

Baudrillard, Jean. *Selected Writings*. Ed. Mark Poster. 2nd ed. Palo Alto: Stanford UP, 2001.

Bauer, Justin. "20 Questions." *Philadelphiapapercity.net* 11–18 Feb. 1999. 4 Oct. 2005 <http://citypaper.net/articles/021199/20q.shtml>.

Diedrick, James. *Understanding Martin Amis*. 2nd ed. Columbia: U of South Carolina P, 2004.

Haffenden, John. "Martin Amis." *Novelists in Interview*. London: Methuen, 1985. 1–24.

James, Edward. *Science Fiction in the 20th Century*. New York: Oxford UP, 1994.

Jameson, Frederic. *Postmodernism, Or, The Cultural Logic of Late Capitalism*. Durham: Duke UP, 1991.

Moritz, Charles, ed. "Martin Amis." *1990 Current Biography Yearbook*. New York: H.W. Wilson, 1990.

"The State of Fiction: A Symposium." *New Review* 5.1 (Summer 1978): 17–19.

12
A Reluctant Leavisite: Martin Amis's "Higher Journalism"

M. Hunter Hayes
Texas A&M University-Commerce

"Literature is, among other things," Martin Amis declares, "a talent contest, and every reader must his find his personal great tradition" (*War*, 78). One glimpse of Amis's own tradition begins to emerge from his first publication, a "Weekend Competition" entry in the *New Statesman*. An inauspicious way of breaking into print, this entry, edited to only sixteen words, is attributed to "M.L. Amis," a conscious echo of precursors such as T.S. Eliot, I.A. Richards, C.P. Snow and, aptly, F.R. Leavis. In fact, Leavis seems central to Amis's self-fashioning as a literary reviewer and critic – a position he held before attaining fame as a novelist. Leavis constitutes a strong presence in Amis's criticism, hovering implicitly and explicitly over much of Amis's literary journalism. He wavers between admiration for the elder critic's vigorous stance and repeated condemnations of Leavis's humorlessness, endorsement of D.H. Lawrence, and elitist posturing. In his two articles under the pseudonym of "Bruno Holbrook," for instance, Amis presents a tongue-in-cheek alternative to Leavis's dour rhetorical stance and intellectual snobbery. Moreover, Leavis at times appears in Amis's nonfiction as a kind of synecdoche, the totemic figurehead embodying all the judgmental errors Amis ascribes to Leavis and his followers – a figurative compaction that has led Amis to denounce Leavis *ad hominem*. Nevertheless, just as Amis has integrated into his fiction the influence of other novelists, most prominently Vladimir Nabokov and Saul Bellow, he has adopted in his "higher journalism" (*War*, 384) many of Leavis's critical strategies; by rebuking the Leavisite tradition Amis cleared the way for the cultivation of his own literary tradition and critical position.

On his 23rd birthday, 25 August 1972, Amis published in the *Times Educational Supplement* a dismissive review of Leavis's *Nor Shall My*

Sword. This marks the first of many occasions that Amis condemned Leavis in print; it also signals Amis's confidence as a critic by implying that he has acquired sufficient critical authority to join others in attempting to undermine Leavis's critical legacy. However, Amis's critical position was still at this stage a work-in-progress, and his eagerness to confront the formidable Leavis hints toward the reach of his critical ambition. Following his graduation from Oxford in 1971, Amis published reviews in various London newspapers and magazines, including the *Daily Telegraph, Spectator, New Society, Times*, and the *Observer* – for which he wrote a review-column of science fiction novels under another pseudonym, "Henry Tilney." From 1972–75 he served as an editorial assistant at the *Times Literary Supplement*, a position he resigned to work first as Claire Tomalin's deputy literary editor at the *New Statesman* and then as its literary editor. Until the publication of *The Rachel Papers* (1973), Amis therefore earned his literary credibility through journalism, developing his hermeneutic skills and expressive manner while working within the restrictive confines of column inches and house styles. He has written on a diverse range of cultural subjects, accommodating his exegetic goals to the requirements of form and content, gliding easily between conversational discussions of television programs to finely honed literary analyses. He has remained active in literary journalism, penning nearly four hundred articles and essays to date, and his nonfiction forms an important and influential aspect of his *oeuvre*. Although relatively ignored by scholars, the impact of Amis's journalism on his fiction has been demonstrable, allowing him to begin examining themes and preoccupations – particularly from the 1980s forward – that reemerge in his novels and short stories. A meticulous recycler of material, he efficaciously bridges the divide between the supposed "left-handed" requirements of journalism and the more autonomous nature of his fiction by transposing ideas, phrases, and perspective from his nonfiction to his fiction.

One of the more prominent factors linking Amis's literary journalism to his fiction is his evaluative confidence, a self-assurance that materializes in his early reviews and essays. As a young critic Amis squared up to his seasoned forerunners, exposing their respective strengths and weaknesses alike as he strove to position himself as their successor. As early as 1971, in a review of L.C. Knights's *Public Voices*, Amis already celebrates a rhetorical "high style" while deriding "the violence that cliché does to language" ("Language", 33) – two abiding aspects of Amis's conception of literary merit. In "Translucent Salamanders," the first of his half-dozen articles on William S. Burroughs, Amis makes the casual pronouncement that "the only time an educated and well-balanced person has any business being depressed by a book is when its author is simply a bore, nothing more sinister" (29). Subject matter and characterization, it follows, should not be held to the same rigorous standards as rhetorical execution, a perception that seems to confirm Amis's own narrative tendencies. Leavis is rarely far from Amis's frame of critical reference. When he claims that Lionel Trilling "is one of the few critics alive who can write sensibly" on literature *and* society ("Society and the Supergo", 18), the point targets what Amis considers to be Leavis's romantic desire for a "literary utopia" ("Corrective", 14).

In one of the copious footnotes that pepper his memoir, *Experience*, Amis recounts a gathering during the late-1970s. "I put to the table the following question," Amis writes:

> Who would you side with, if the choice were limited to Leavis or Bloomsbury? Everyone else said Bloomsbury. I said Leavis.... I had never been a Leavisite and I had written several attacks on his doctrines and followers. But I think I would cast the same vote, even today. What could be more antipathetic than Woolf's dismissal of *Ulysses* on the grounds of Joyce's *class*? No, give me F.R. and Q.D., give me Frank and Queenie, despite all the humuourlessness, the hysteria, and the Soviet gloom. (241)

Amis's companions for the evening comprised a notable group of writers and editors: Kingsley Amis, Julian Barnes, Mark Boxer, Russell Davies, James Fenton, Christopher Hitchens, Clive James, and Terence Kilmartin. The elder Amis and James would later contribute to the *New Statesman* symposium that Amis assembled to discuss Leavis's career and influence. An aside to a discussion of Philip Larkin, this passage in *Experience* is notable for several reasons: Amis's elimination of options, his willingness to counter consensus, and his desire to maintain his views nearly a quarter-century later. In effect, Amis sides grudgingly with the Leavis camp by adopting a version of the latter's most notorious critical standards. His remarks on Leavis in a 1975 *Observer* review encapsulate his own critical rigidity: "As in the literary utopias, the author's prescriptive vision of the world becomes an analogy for the disciplining of the well-tempered mind: authoritarian, inflexible, highly selective as regards art" ("Life", 25).

Amis's subjunctive qualification results in a dichotomy that by the 1970s would have reeked of quaintness, if not absurdity. By limiting the choice to Leavis or Bloomsbury, Amis proposes a choice between opposing factions of literary elitism. Perhaps because he has ruled out other alternatives simply for the sake of discussion, Amis achieves some recognition of his own allegiances to Leavis's literary and social critiques, regardless of how much he might have railed against Leavis in print. As a young critic Amis went to considerable effort to heap scorn on Leavis's literary and cultural judgments, an attack that continues through Amis's career to his 2002 essay "The Voice of the Lonely Crowd," in which he castigates Leavis as a "grizzled relic" (4). In this article, Amis associates Leavisism with such ideologies as Islamism and Political Correctness, striking a facetious tone toward Leavis and his adherents, particularly targeting the narrowness of Leavis's Great Tradition and his subsequent penchant for winnowing this canon:

> Left to itself, Leavisism might have ended up with a single text; and that sacred book would have been the collected works of a lone sociopath – DH Lawrence. It had all gone wrong: they were supposed to be judging literature, but literature was judging them, and raucously exposing their provinciality and humourlessness. When Leavis died, in 1978, his clerisy collapsed in a Jonestown of *odium theologicum*. It left nothing behind it. (6)

Despite Amis's aversion to what he sees as the Leavis ideology – one from which he has carefully attempted to distance himself – his writing contains at its core an enduring Leavisite kernel.

Much of Amis's fiction and nonfiction consciously bucks the parochialism of the Leavises and their adherents. Additional factors distinguish Amis from an identikit Leavisite. His Oxford background, his positions in London-based literary journalism – particularly at the *TLS* and *New Statesman* – and his taste in literature would all have likely elicited Leavis's stern condemnation, points that Ian Hamilton addresses in his contribution to the *New Statesman* symposium when discussing his own "acrimonious" interactions with Leavis (537). Having Kingsley Amis as his father – a man who infamously conflicted with Leavis at Cambridge – would likely have only exacerbated such scorn. But while Amis has not advocated an explicitly Leavisite position, he has advanced arguments with strong Leavisite affinities. Commenting on the anti-Leavisism in Amis's "The Voice of the Lonely Crowd," Howard Jacobson finds paradoxical Amis's failure to accept that Leavis possesses "an austerity comparable to his own." In this essay Amis discusses the position of the writer in the aftermath of the September 11, 2001, terrorist bombings, composing what Jacobson identifies as "a highly Leavisite argument for the ideological unrelated-ness of literature which paradoxically turned on Leavis midstream as though the author had to show he could make it to the shore unaided" (33). In response to Amis's *ad hominem* condemnation of Lawrence, Jacobson faults Amis for committing a critical lapse: "Allowing that, in the end, it is no more our business to like or dislike the character of the novelist than it is to dislike the novel's 'personnel,' as Amis calls them – he and Leavis are utterly one on this" (33). As Amis writes in "Thankless Tasker," his review of Leavis's *Letters in Criticism*: "criticism isn't to do with writers' personalities, isn't to do with despising (say) nursery rhymes for being insufficiently Laurentian, and isn't to do with ranking art like a mawkish schoolboy sorting out his conkers" (775). In "The Voice of the Lonely Crowd," Amis directs his comments to Leavis's critical "clerisy" (6), a role that advocates a quasi-religious role for literature, replete with its own canon and hierarchy. As Amis attacks what he sees as the ideological aspects of Leavisism he addresses the character traits of Leavis and his followers, deviating from his own critical standards – including a projection of his tastes and views onto those of the Leavisite tradition. In so doing Amis conflates Leavis, his followers, and his work into a straw-man argument.

Amis's comments on Leavis have not been entirely oppositional or disapproving. His writing demonstrates a clear familiarity with Leavis's work, including Leavis's style of arguments and evaluation as well as his polemics. "No other writer known to me commits his intelligence to his prose with the obtrusive, one-colour intensity of Dr Leavis," Amis writes in "Life, Literature and Leavis," ironically prefiguring many of the critiques on Amis's later work. "People complain about the impenetrability of his style but that tortuousness is functional: it reflects a genuinely complicated habit of thought, and one that has its eye on no object but its own inner consistence and conviction. Accordingly, even when his criticism is wrong-headed, tin-eared and purely rhetorical, it is always thrilling to read" (25). For much of his criticism of Leavis, Amis concentrates on the theoretical and method-ological aspects of Leavis's work rather than his style of expression. Amis's qualified respect for Leavis's style also conveys the value that Amis places on the avowedly literary as well as on literature.

One way to understand Amis's adversarial responses to Leavis and his followers is to bear in mind the differences between Leavis and T.S. Eliot. Although Leavis praised Eliot's poetry, their critical and cultural perspectives were antithetical, resulting in distinct traditions, as Robert Hewison explains. "The difference," he writes, "lay in the stricter definition of a tradition based on English literature, as opposed to Eliot's more catholic and cosmopolitan taste, and in their belief in the value of a university-based, critical clerisy, over against Eliot's metropolitan élite" (54). Hewison frames this division as a "cultural divide" entrenched in English history since the Civil War, not simply one confined to literature: "Both are authentic traditions, but while Eliot reflected an aristocratic, High Anglican taste Leavis was fundamentally a puritan. The difference might be described in terms of a cavalier pleasure in poetry, over against a reforming commitment to prose" (54). In other words, members of these competing traditions are analogously modernist Cavaliers and Roundheads, the very images that, coincidentally, Amis adopts to compare circumcised and uncircumcised penises in his short story "The Coincidence of the Arts," a work that marries Amis's critical and fictional perspectives with its attention to creative talent, innovation and aesthetic tradition. This division between Eliot and Leavis does not abrogate their similarities and common ground; indeed, the fact that they are competing *traditions* implies an inherent conservatism. Whether Amis rejected Leavis due in part to critical fashion seems less important than the possibility that by distancing himself from Leavis he began to distance himself from such a prominent and notorious conservative perspective. As Amis snubbed the Leavisite tradition, he forged one of his own – aligned more closely with what Hewison terms Eliot's "more catholic and cosmopolitan taste" than with Leavis's provinciality.

Rival views on matters of style and taste populate literary history. Such stylistic concerns indicate vital relationships to modes of thought as well as prose and poetic expressions. Rather than strict clashes, however, such dynamics usually produce competing views of the same essential premise or objectives, complements instead of contradictions. Matthew Arnold proposes in *Culture and Anarchy* an antithesis between Hebraism and Hellenism, between the strictness and the spontaneity of conscience. In his *Birth of Tragedy* Friedrich Nietzsche identifies competing Apollonian and Dionysian principles. The twentieth century witnessed the formation of several adversarial camps, each of which appears to be a variation on the same basic theme. In England Cyril Connolly's conception of the Mandarin and vernacular styles in his *Enemies of Promise* (1938) articulated dominant twin stylistic factions, while in the United States Philip Rahv argued for a division between "paleface" and "redskin" (1939), identifying a writer in terms of polarity. With her essay "Against Dryness" (1961), Iris Murdoch induced a choice between "crystalline" and "journalistic" modes of writing.

Keenly aware of this history and its concomitant traditions – including the venues of publication, *Horizon*, *Partisan Review* and *Encounter* respectively – Amis has cited each of these twentieth-century critics in his nonfiction. He reviewed the 1981 reissue of Connolly's novel *The Rock Pool* for the *Observer*, concluding with his personal speculations regarding the relationship between Connolly's creative and critical writing (*War*, 133–5). He cites Rahv's "Paleface and Redskin" early in his essay "The Supreme American Novelist." He even adopts Murdoch's title for the 2002 reprint of his review of Richard Eyre's *Iris* in Zachary Leader's *On Modern British Fiction*. By therefore establishing himself in opposition to the Leavisite tradition Amis carries forward this oppositional-cum-complementary strain in literary history, shrewdly positing a contemporary tradition to rival Leavis's.

Certainly one unavoidable aspect of Leavis's Great Tradition is its isolationist Anglocentrism. Leavis famously identified a select cadre of "great English novelists" (*Great Tradition*, 1) consisting of Jane Austen, George Eliot, Henry James, Joseph Conrad and D.H. Lawrence. Only the deracinated James and Conrad stretched the geographical boundaries of Leavis's version of Little Englandism. By contrast, Amis has keenly embraced writers from outside Britain, particularly those associated with the United States. Saul Bellow, Vladimir Nabokov, Philip Roth, John Updike, Norman Mailer, and Kurt Vonnegut have all significantly informed Amis's fiction, and almost one-fourth of his journalism focuses on American literature. Roth has proven to be an enduring subject for Amis; he has written extensively about Roth's work from *The Breast* (1973) to *The Dying Animal* (2001), and together these reviews indicate the importance that Amis ascribes to the American novelist in his own literary tradition. Moreover, the contemporary status of such writers stands in strong contradiction to Leavis's refusal to admit anyone since Lawrence into his tradition. By aligning himself with the contemporary American tradition – and also praising the virtues of Kafka, Borges, Zamyatin, Solzhenytsin and others – Amis rebuffs Leavis's Anglocentricism, forging his own countertradition and canon.

Not only does Amis's personal canon have a strong American bias; it also pays particular respect to Jewish-American novelists. Since first writing about Bellow in 1982 Amis has steadily elevated the author's importance – to Amis's own and even wider traditions. He declares that *The Adventures of Augie March* is "the Great American Novel" ("Why

Augie", T2) and predicts that Bellow "will emerge as the supreme American novelist," whose preeminence is threatened only by Henry James ("Supreme", 113). One of the ways that Amis supports this thesis is to follow a general truth with a pair of personal suppositions presented as indisputable certainties: "The American novel, having become dominant, was in turn dominated by the Jewish-American novel, and everybody knows who dominated that: Saul Bellow" (111). In order to reinforce his argument regarding Bellow's "incontestable legitimacy," Amis contends that "to hold otherwise is to waste your breath" (111). This argument is Leavis-like in its assumption of critical authority and its militant tenor. Moreover, Amis attempts to preclude all disagreement by declaring that contradictory opinions could not withstand this reasoning, a strategy Amis has noted in Leavis's writing. Herein lies the irony: in constructing his counter-Leavisite canon Amis often resorts to Leavis's rhetorical strategies.

In rejecting Leavis, Amis seems intent on overthrowing one of the twentieth century's most significant scholars, positioning himself as a successor. Amis's critical hierarchy, equally informed by considerations of personal taste, uses "talent" as an instrument to measuring greatness. In his introduction to *The War Against Cliché*, Amis identifies his own "Age of Criticism," which spans the publication of Leavis's *The Great Tradition* and Eliot's *Notes Towards the Definition of Culture* (1948) and culminates with the oil crisis in the mid-1970s. This era predates Amis's birth by one year and terminates after he published his first novel, confirming that his experiences and education are products of this critical age. It is fitting in this regard that *The Rachel Papers* provides both a *Bildungsroman* of a young critic (rather than the more typical *Künstlerroman* of a young novelist) and what might be perceived as an elegy to a vanished era. As Amis writes in the novel, speaking through its narrator Charles Highway, who fantasizes about publishing a "long-awaited open letter" in *The Times*: "I should like to point out, for the last time, to Messrs Waugh, Connolly, Steiner, Leavis, Empson, Trilling, *et al*, that the argument of my *The Meaning of Life* was *intended* to be anti-comic in shape" (93–4).

In his introduction to *The War Against Cliché*, Amis proclaims assuredly that "literary criticism was inherently doomed. Explicitly or otherwise it had based itself on a structure of echelons and hierarchies; it was about the talent elite. And the structure atomized as soon as the forces of democratization gave their next concerted push" (xii). This introduction extends the views that Amis first set forth in "Life, Literature and Leavis," his review of *The Living Principle* (1975), demonstrating that the depth of his conviction is akin to Leavis's unwavering dedication to his critical principles. Once again, however, Amis fails to recognize the inherent critical similarities between himself and Leavis. "Style," he writes, "is morality. Style judges" (*War*, 467). Conversely, style also serves as a standard for judgment, a factor for ascertaining talent. In his notorious riposte to C.P. Snow, Leavis exposes Snow's presumed reliance on clichés: "We think of cliché commonly as a matter of style. But style is a habit of expression, and a habit of expression that runs to the cliché tells us something adverse about the quality of the thought expressed" (*Nor Shall*, 50). Indeed, the fact that clichés stem from habituated expression runs counterintuitive to thought as well as originality. Later in the same volume, targeting a hypothetical "'humanist' intellectual" who is given to speaking in hackneyed expressions, Leavis avows boldly that the "defence of humanity entails their reclamation for genuine thought" (163). However reductive and logically fallacious this premise might seem – and it provides a fair example of the types of remarks that brought Leavis so much scorn in the 1960s and 1970s – the vigor with which he condemns clichés is a view that Amis shares. The conclusion to Amis's introduction similarly notes the absences of thought and feeling that characterize commonplace expressions: "To idealize: all writing is a campaign against cliché. Not just clichés of the pen but clichés of the mind and clichés of the heart. When I dispraise, I am usually quoting clichés. When I praise, I am usually quoting the opposed qualities of freshness, energy, and reverberation of voice" (*War*, xv). Although their views differ regarding what constitutes "style," Amis's opinions on the adverse nature of clichés accord with Leavis's.

In "Corrective Force," his review of Leavis's *Nor Shall My Sword*, Amis remarks that "Leavis's obsequious allegiance to Lawrence continues to have its mischievous effect" (14), most notably Leavis's penchant for ignoring certain of Lawrence's preposterous views such as the conviction that "masters ought to get round to beating up their servants again in order to restore their precious bond of blood reciprocity" (14). Amis also wrenches out of context Leavis's praise for Lawrence's evaluation of Wyndham Lewis, resulting in the parenthetical proclamation that "Leavis's shaping embarrassment, however, was to nominate as his model of sanity the person of D.H. Lawrence" (xiii). But Leavis's original remarks were more tempered than Amis suggests: "The Lawrence who thus places Wyndham Lewis seems to me the representative of health and sanity," Leavis writes (*Great Tradition*, 238). Amis's strongest complaints about Leavis – the latter's "stultifying humour-lessness, the lack of any sense of irony or self-doubt," his "shrewish polemic" and "dilapidated moral arrogance" ("Corrective", 14) – are promptly set aside in this review without significant elaboration. Had Amis explored these objections further he might have been able to for-mulate a pre-emptive reply to his own critics, who have laid similar charges against him, beginning with his attention to nuclear weapons and other political issues.

Like his literary criticism, Amis's social critiques include stringent quasi-Leavisite considerations of moral value, akin to what Leavis terms a promotion of "human awareness ... of the possibilities of life" (*Great Tradition*, 2) as well as the proper study of literature – "an inti-mate study of the complexities, potentialities and essential conditions of human nature" (*Common Pursuit*, 184). This becomes most apparent in Amis's writings on the sex industry, a topic that he has examined throughout his career as a novelist and journalist. Although Amis's fiction permits him to range more liberally through comic and satiric depictions of mediated sex and its onanistic province, his assorted reviews, columns, and other nonfiction works concerning pornography inform the moral pitch of his novels and short stories. For Amis, pornography induces an erosion of social empathy, and his critiques of the sex industry register the moral and human expenditure of this mer-ciless capitalist system. At the same time, pornography educes Amis's indignation at imaginative impotence, especially through its visual clichés, the prefabricated visual imagery on which the industry trades. Together, the moral and aesthetic aspects of Amis's recurrent critiques of pornography reveal the sincerity of his social engagement with what he terms "the deaths of feelings" ("Sex", 135) in a jaded, industrialized culture that elides personal and intellectual probity in favor of an impotent literalism.

As the title of *The War Against Cliché* implies, Amis denigrates such automatism as the manifestation of stunted creativity. When he moves from literary criticism to social critiques, Amis applies a similar ana-lytical method, compounding the difficulty of distinguishing his views on society from those on literature. In both areas Amis confronts pertinent issues involving a Leavisian notion of "human awareness" by offering a critical corrective to Leavis's restrictive parameters. By addressing avowedly "lowbrow" subjects such as popular fiction, rock music, television, sports and, most significantly, pornography and the sex industry, Amis implicitly rejects Leavisite elitism and high-art tran-scendentalist pretensions. Writing under the pseudonym of "Bruno

Holbrook," Amis satirically examines a seedier side of London: "the pathetic vulnerability of nakedness" in the city's sex industry ("Fleshspots", 362). He has long been attracted to the satirical possibilities of pornography, most obviously in his novels *Money, London Fields* and *Yellow Dog*, but in the Holbrook pieces he develops a persona that heightens his satirical edge. Yet despite the facetious comments that Amis expresses through his Holbrook persona, his reaction in these articles is that of a moralist shocked and embarrassed by the degenerating condition of contemporary urban society. The Holbrook persona provides a counterblast to Leavis's stern social sermonizing – as well as to other commentators including David Holbrook, Frank Longford and Mary Whitehouse – by first adopting a pose of awkward sympathy and then subverting the performative medium to out-burlesque the burlesque.

In "Fleshspots," the first Holbrook review, Amis writes that "My own dominant emotion, settling down for my first ever body revue, was profound embarrassment – not for myself but for the girls I had paid to see" (362). This embarrassment stems from Holbrook's presumed naïveté, his confronting a stark, carnal actuality in the Soho clubs rather than some male idea of feminine seductiveness and eroticism:

> Instead of the zeppelin-breasted harridans that striptease lore gears one to expect, a succession of gawky little waifs wandered on to the stage, seemingly as nervous about the flimsiness of their routines as they were ashamed of the rickety state of their bodies. Appendix scars gleamed tranquilly in the subdued purple light; mottled thighs, punctured breasts and caved-in behinds formed a patchy mosaic against the dank silk backdrop; lascivious wiggles and enamel grins collapsed all too readily into distracted shrugs, apologetic smiles. (362)

Through this faux-naïf sensibility, Amis's Holbrook persona pokes fun at the men who frequent the Soho strip clubs rather than the performers. His target audience for these articles – young males, predictably – is made explicit through a parenthetical reassurance where he refers to his readers as "chaps." Self-consciously laddish, "Fleshspots" parodies its very form as a way of rhetorically underscoring the inherent vulgarity and sexual travesty of these clubs.

For men, Amis implies, sexual desire and gratification have degenerated to "a telling parody of awkward bedroom moments, a shrewd evocation of the pathetic vulnerability of nakedness" (362). These clubs trade in performances that reflect the sexual frailties of the male audience, suggesting a communal impotence through the lack of genuine response incited by the women's physical unattractiveness: "Certainly one could be stirred neither to desire nor distaste by something so unlike life" (362). Conversely, according to this formulation, a Leavis-like "awareness to the possibilities of life" could affect one's emotions and sensibilities. In his second (and final) Holbrook review Amis surveys sex magazines, commenting on the magazines' textual failings as well as their pictorials. Summarizing his survey, Amis draws attention to these magazines' dehumanizing natures:

> Some readers may opt for the seamy mags because of the occasional shaved vagina or Sapphic snap but my guess is that they just like sex to seem monochrome, furtive, unreal. Some readers may opt for the dinkier mags because they prefer fantasy girls to everyday ones but my guess is that they just like sex to seem brisk, throwaway, unreal. The only moralistic line one can take against these magazines is that they are *malum per se*: they cheapen and dehumanise; although they may not be corrupting, they are corrupt. ("Coming in Handy", 922–3)

Amis returns to this peroration in "The Bodies in Question," a "Private Line" editorial for the *Observer*, where he employs a rhetorical strategy akin to Leavis's method of social critique: the prompt dispatching of a counter viewpoint.

After terming the "feminist case" against pornography "obviously unanswerable," he continues by asserting that "even the most complacent citizen of the permissive society will have doubts about its effect on the pre-adolescent psyche." Amis again employs Leavis's shrewd rhetorical tactic of inflating personal conviction into universal truth. When he next contends that "its new-found ubiquity and intrusiveness raise further points" (11), one gleans the potential genesis of such themes in *Money*, *London Fields* and *Yellow Dog*. While Amis's tone appears on the verge of venturing into the hyperbolic reactionary domain of Lord Longford or Mary Whitehouse in their campaigns against pornography during the 1970s, it is in spirit and content a continuation of the final Holbrook column. "We are told that there is no evidence that pornography corrupts," Amis writes, demolishing opposition by declaring that the absence of empirical evidence results from an ongoing decadence that is not consciously perceived. To suggest otherwise, he implies, would be to ignore the obvious: "Well, there wouldn't be. As the word suggests, it is a long-term process, and people aren't always aware that it is happening to them. We do not know that pornography is corrupting; we know that it itself is corrupt. We know, too, that the more of it there is, the more of it there will have to be; and we have already learnt to deal with it ("Bodies", 11).

Amis's columns under his own byline and especially as Bruno Holbrook critique pornography as escapist, banal fantasy, trash entertainment for the imaginatively impoverished that exacerbates a disengagement from society and relationships. By satirizing the view of women as an amalgamation of body parts, as in "Fleshspots," Amis draws attention to the pathetic fantasies that have replaced emotional desires and intellectual expressions, a quest for fulfillment through passive voyeurism. This dreary inversion of exhibitionism requires a partner only for physiological arousal; gratification becomes onanistic, a fact that pornography commodifies and that Amis uses as a source for his fictional caricatures. Moreover, the Holbrook reviews comprise only one aspect of Amis's writing about "lowbrow" activities and media. He has also written extensively about film, television, sports (especially soccer and tennis), and music performances. Together these articles enhance Amis's cultivated air of anti-superciliousness, which his comments on literature frequently belie and which scholarship on Amis has too often overlooked.

Amis's "higher journalism" demonstrates a remarkable diversity in its subject matter and tone that his three volumes of collected journalism unfortunately fail to convey. While there remains the inevitable and expected bias towards literature, these reviews, essays and columns display other areas of Amis's interests and preoccupations. More significantly, through his journalism Amis provides a textual barometer of his professional life, an eclectic bio-bibliography. Music and television reviews follow his literary essays and reviews – articles on poetry, fiction, and biography that vary in their rhetorical and critical objectives as well as in their subject matter, ranging from a thoughtful exegesis of a single text to a terse rundown of a dozen or so volumes of science fiction. Profiles, interviews, and travel pieces appear intermittently by the late-1970s and regularly by the mid-1980s, providing most of the copy for his first two nonfiction collections. Similarly, Amis's fiction profits immeasurably from his journalism. Although he had completed and submitted the manuscript of his third novel, *Success* (1978), by the time he published his guest editorial "Green with Envy," the latter's discussion of envy and social class links directly with an underlying theme of that novel. At the end of 1985, Amis published the first of his articles concerning nuclear weapons, "Kilotons of Human Blood," followed by seven other similarly oriented reviews and essays in just over two years. These works indicate Amis's concern with nuclear weapons beyond what he writes in *Einstein's Monsters* (1987) and *London Fields* (1989). They also help to chart the evolution of Amis's discursive authority in the political as well as literary arenas. Underlying much of his journalism is a firm sense of re-evaluation: a stock-taking of literary eminence or insignificance; of social customs, diversions, excesses and follies; and of political policies, personalities and consequences. Amis's writings as a literary critic and social commentator provide a forum, in short, for his occasional discourses on contemporary culture. Throughout them he displays a complicated relationship to the Leavis contingent, a critical parallax that precludes his recognition of the frequent similarities between his perspective and theirs.

Works cited

Amis, Martin. "Bodies in Question." *Observer* 18 Feb. 1979: 11.
——. [Bruno Holbrook]. "Coming in Handy" *New Statesman* 14 Dec. 1973: 922–3.
——. "Corrective Force." *Times Educational Supplement* 25 Aug. 1972: 14.
——. *Experience: A Memoir.* New York: Talk Miramax/Hyperion, 2000.
——. [Bruno Holbrook]. "Fleshspots." *New Statesman* 14 Sept. 1973: 362.
——. "Green with Envy." *Observer* 19 June 1977: 13.
——. "Kilotons of Human Blood." *Observer* 29 Dec. 1985: 21.
——. "Language, Truth and Politics." *Observer* 14 Nov. 1971: 33.
——. "Life, Literature and Leavis." *Observer* 14 Sept. 1975: 25.
——. "Sex in America." *Talk* Feb. 2001: 98–103, 133–5.
——. "Society and the Supergo." *Times Educational Supplement* 1 Dec. 1972: 18.
——. "The Supreme American Novelist." *Atlantic Monthly* Dec. 2003: 111–14.
——. "Thankless Tasker." *New Statesman* 31 May 1974: 774–5.
——. "Translucent Salamanders." *Observer* 11 June 1972: 29.
——. "The Voice of the Lonely Crowd." *Observer Review* 1 June 2002: 4–6.
——. *The War Against Cliché: Essays and Reviews 1971–2000.* New York: Talk Miramax/Hyperion, 2001.
——. "Why Augie Has it All." *Guardian* 4 Aug. 1995: T2.
Hewison, Robert. *Culture and Consensus: England, Art and Politics since 1940.* 2nd ed. London: Methuen, 1997.
Jacobson, Howard. "Don't Shoot the Critic." *Evening Standard* 30 Dec. 2002: 33.
Leavis, F.R. *The Common Pursuit.* London: Chatto and Windus, 1952.
——. *The Great Tradition.* London: Chatto and Windus, 1948, 1955.
——. *Nor Shall My Sword.* London: Chatto and Windus, 1972.
"Symposium: F.R. Leavis, 1895–1978." *New Statesman* 21 Apr. 1978: 537.

13
Nonfiction by Martin Amis, 1971–2005

Compiled by James Diedrick and M. Hunter Hayes

The following is an annotated bibliography of the nonfiction written by and attributable to Martin Amis though 2005. Included are eight unsigned reviews written for the *Times Literary Supplement*; three unsigned essays written for the *New Statesman*; and 14 pieces written under a pseudonym. The latter include 12 of the 26 "Science Fiction" review columns Amis wrote for the *Observer* using the pseudonym "Henry Tilney" (a character in Jane Austen's *Northanger Abbey*), and the two essays he wrote for the *New Statesman* under the byline "Bruno Holbrook." Amis also contributed frequent unsigned pieces to the "Commentary" column in the *Times Literary Supplement* from 1972–74, which the *TLS* Centenary Archive has not yet attributed; we have included two of these based on statements by Amis himself and Kingsley Amis.

To indicate the breadth of Amis's nonfiction and make the material more accessible, we divided the list into five sections: Book Reviews; Other Reviews (film, television, concert, miscellaneous); Profiles and Interviews; Essays and Columns; and Original Contributions to Books. Each section is organized chronologically. Of the nearly 400 entries, only 155 have been collected; we indicate reprinted selections using the following abbreviations: *TMI* for *The Moronic Inferno and Other Visits to America* (1986); *VMN* for *Visiting Mrs. Nabokov and Other Excursions* (1993); and *WAC* for *The War Against Cliché: Essays and Reviews 1971–2000* (2001).

Book reviews

"What the People Sing." *Daily Telegraph* 4 Nov. 1971: 8. Geoffrey Grigson, ed., *Faber Book of Popular Verse*.

"Language, Truth and Politics." *Observer* 14 Nov. 1971: 33. L.C. Knights, *Public Voices.*

"Believe it or Else." *Spectator* 11 Dec. 1971: 855. *Guinness Book of World Records. WAC* 359–61.

"Reviews in Brief." *New Society* 2 Mar. 1972: 461–2. Abraham Rothberg, *Aleksander Solzhenitsyn: The Major Novels.*

"Science Fiction." [as "Henry Tilney"]. *Observer* 16 Apr. 1972: 32. Ron Goulart, *What's Become of Screwloose?*; Joseph Green, *Conscience Interplanetary*; Clifford Simak, *Out of their Minds*; André Norton, *Dread Companion*; Damon Knight, ed., *Orbit 6.*

"Science Fiction." [as "Henry Tilney"]. *Observer* 28 May 1972: 33. James Blish, *The Day After Judgement*; Robert Silverberg, *Nightwings*; A.E. Van Vogt, *Children of Tomorrow*; John Brunner, *Timescoop.*

"The Shrug of Resignation." *Times* 8 June 1972: 10. James Hanley, *Another World.*

"Translucent Salamanders." *Observer* 11 June 1972: 29. William S. Burroughs, *The Wild Boys. WAC* 299–300.

"Generation Gap." *Observer* 2 July 1972: 31. C.P. Snow, *The Malcontents. WAC* 129–31.

"The Dragon." *Times* 13 July 1972: 10. Yevgeny Zamyatin, *The Dragon.*

"Science Fiction." [as "Henry Tilney"]. *Observer* 16 July 1972: 30. Robert Sheckley, *You Feel Anything When I Do This?*; Bob Shaw, *Other Days, Other Eyes*; Damon Knight, ed., *Dimension X*; Roger Zelazny, *Nine Princes in Amber*; Eric Temple Bell, *The Time Stream.*

"Organ Duets." [unsigned]. *Times Literary Supplement* 4 Aug. 1972: 909. Alan Friedman, *Hermaphrodeity.*

"Corrective Force." *Times Educational Supplement* 25 Aug. 1972: 14. F.R. Leavis, *Nor Shall My Sword.*

"Science Fiction." [as "Henry Tilney"]. *Observer* 3 Sept. 1972: 33. Edmund Cooper, *Who Needs Men?*; John Rackham, *Ipomea*; Paul Anderson, *Un-Man*; Kurt Vonnegut, *Welcome to the Monkey House*; Jimmy Miller, *The Big Win.*

"Circling Around." *Observer* 5 Nov. 1972: 38. Alan Sillitoe, *Raw Material*; John Knowler, *Trust an Englishman.*

"Science Fiction." [as "Henry Tilney"]. *Observer* 12 Nov. 1972: 37. Arthur C. Clarke, *Of Time and Stars, The Wind from the Sun,* and *Lost Worlds of 2001*; Isaac Asimov, *The Gods Themselves, An Isaac Asimov Double, The Space Merchants*; John Brunner, *The Dreaming Earth.*

"The Deviousness of STC." [unsigned]. *Times Literary Supplement* 1 Dec. 1972: 1463. Norman Fruman, *Coleridge, The Damaged Archangel.*

"Society and the Superego." *Times Educational Supplement* 1 Dec. 1972: 18. Lionel Trilling, *Sincerity and Authenticity.*

"Guilty Rimer." [unsigned]. *Times Literary Supplement* 15 Dec. 1972: 1524. William Empson and David Pirie, *Coleridge's Verse: A Selection.* WAC 178–81.

"Second Thoughts." *New Statesman* 19 Jan. 1973: 96. Jennifer Johnston, *The Gates*; Caradog Prichard, *Full Moon*; Helen Yglesias, *How She Died.*

"Science Fiction." [as "Henry Tilney"]. *Observer* 28 Jan. 1973: 35. Harry Harrison, *A Transatlantic Tunnel, Hurrah!*; Walter Harris, *Mistress of Downing Street*; Pierre Boulle, *Clone*; Ron Goulart, *Broke Down Engine*; Lester del Rey, *Pstalemate.*

"Precious Little." [unsigned]. *Times Literary Supplement* 2 Feb. 1973: 113. Richard Brautigan, *The Abortion.*

"MacPosh." *New Statesman* 9 Feb. 1973: 205–6. J.I.M. Stewart, *Mungo's Dream*; Ernest J. Gaines, *Autobiography of Miss Jane Pittman*; Violette Leduc, *The Taxi*; Frank Norman, *One of Our Own*; John Banville, *Birchwood.*

"Alas, Poor Bradley." *New Statesman* 23 Feb. 1973: 278–9. Iris Murdoch, *The Black Prince*; Shaun Herron, *Through the Dark and Hairy Wood*; Natsume Soseki, *Botchan.* Murdoch in *WAC* 83–5.

"Beautiful Diseases." *New Statesman* 23 Mar. 1973: 426–8. John Cornwell, *Coleridge.* WAC 175–8.

"A Big Boob." *Observer* 25 Mar. 1973: 36. Philip Roth, *The Breast.*

"Formidable Wit." *Times Educational Supplement* 6 Apr. 1973: 27. W.H. Auden, *Epistle to a Godson and Other Poems.*

"Board Meeting." *New Statesman* 13 Apr. 1973: 552–4. George Steiner, *The Sporting Scene.* WAC 342–4.

"Educated Monsters." *New Statesman* 20 Apr. 1973: 586. Shiva Naipaul, *The Chip-Chip Gatherers.* WAC 403–5.

"Science Fiction." [as "Henry Tilney"]. *Observer* 10 May 1973: 37. Bob Shaw, *Tomorrow Lies in Ambush*; Larry Niven, *Inconstant Moon*; Keith Roberts, *Machines and Men*; John W. Campbell, *The Best of John W. Campbell*; Isaac Asimov, *The Early Asimov*; Amabel Williams-Ellis and Michael Pearson, eds, *Out of This World*; Thomas Disch, *The Ruins of Earth*; Lindsay Gutteridge, *Killer Pine*; William Hjorstberg, *Grey Matters*; Dick Morland, *Heart Clock*; Christopher Hodder-Williams, *Panic O'Clock.*

"Nabokov in Switzerland." *Spectator* 12 May 1973: 591. Vladimir Nabokov, *Transparent Things.*

"Kith of Death." *New Statesman* 1 June 1973: 811–12. Angus Wilson, *As If By Magic.* WAC 73–5

"Auto-Perversion." *Observer* 1 July 1973: 33. J.G. Ballard, *Crash*; J.M.G. le Clézlo, *War*. *WAC* 95–7.

"Cultivating a Cult." *Observer* 15 July 1973: 33. Kurt Vonnegut Jr., *Breakfast of Champions* and *Happy Birthday, Wanda June*.

"Eliot Made Easy." [unsigned]. *Times Literary Supplement* 17 Aug. 1973: 950. T.S. Pearce, *George Eliot*; Patrick Swinden, ed., *George Eliot: Middlemarch*.

"Science Fiction." [as "Henry Tilney"]. *Observer* 2 Sept. 1973: 35. Arthur C. Clarke, *Rendezvous with Rama*; Ian Watson, *The Embedding*; Richard Cowper, *Time Out of Mind*; John Brunner, *Age of Miracles*; James Blish, *Star Trek 7*.

"Coleridge in Malta." *Observer* 16 Sept. 1973: 37. Aleth Hayter, *A Voyage in Vain*.

"The Coming Thing." *New Statesman* 28 Sept. 1973: 438. Albert Z. Freedman, ed., *The Best of Forum*. *WAC* 57–8.

"The Dialect of the Tribe." *New Statesman* 19 Oct. 1973: 564–5. Ian Robinson, *The Survival of English*.

"Science Fiction." [as "Henry Tilney"]. *Observer* 11 Nov. 1973: 36. Harry Harrison, *Stainless Steel Rat Saves the World*; Brian Aldiss, *Frankenstein Unbound*; Stanislaw Lem, *The Invincible*; Michael Moorcock, *The Oak & the Ram*; James Blish, *Midsummer Century*; Robert Conquest, ed., *Robert Sheckley Omnibus*; *Best of Arthur C. Clarke*; *Best of Isaac Asimov*; *Best of Robert Heinlein*; Donald Wollheim, ed., *1973 World's Best SF*; Lester del Rey, ed., *Best SF Stories of the Year*.

"Entertainment Guide." *New Statesman* 23 Nov. 1973: 776–7. John Carey, *The Violent Effigy: A Study of Dickens' Imagination*. *WAC* 191–5.

"Verse Vocation." [unsigned]. *Times Literary Supplement* 23 Nov. 1973: 1452. C.B. Cox and Michael Schmidt, eds, *Poetry Nation*.

"Science Fiction." [as "Henry Tilney"]. *Observer* 23 Dec. 1973: 23. J.G. Ballard, *Vermillion Sands*; Michael Rogers, *Mindfogger*; Edmund Cooper, *The Tenth Planet*; Isaac Asimov, ed., *Where Do We Go From Here?*

"Rhetoric of Ghosts." *Observer* 3 Mar. 1974: 37. William Burroughs, *Exterminator!*.

"Science Fiction." [as "Henry Tilney"]. *Observer* 17 Mar. 1974: 37. Richard Cowper, *The Twilight of Briareus*; Robert Silverberg, *Dying Inside*; Kit Pedler and Gerry Davis, *Brainrack*; Thomas Disch, ed., *Bad Moon Rising*; A.E. Van Vogt, *The Darkness on Diamondia*; Roger Zelazny, *Guns of Avalon*; *SF Monthly*.

"Queasy Rider." *New Statesman* 22 Mar. 1974: 414. Iris Murdoch, *The Sacred and Profane Love Machine*. *WAC* 85–7.

"For His Pains." *New Review* 1.1 (Apr. 1974): 91–2. Denis Donoghue, *Thieves of Fire*.

"Isadora's Complaint." *Observer* 21 Apr. 1974: 37. Erica Jong, *Fear of Flying*.

"Hard Shoulder." *New Review* 1.2 (May 1974): 92. J.G. Ballard, *Concrete Island*. *WAC* 98–101.

"Science Fiction." [as "Henry Tilney"]. *Observer* 5 May 1974: 37. Richard McKenna, *Casey Agonistes*; Brian Aldiss, *The 80-Minute Hour*; Robert Heinlein, *Time Enough for Love*; Michael Coney, *Friends Come in Boxes*; Thomas Page, *The Hephaestus Plague*; James Herbert, *The Rats*.

"Thankless Tasker." *New Statesman* 31 May 1974: 774–5. F.R. Leavis, *Letters in Criticism*.

"Science Fiction." *Observer* 18 Aug. 1974: 28. Christopher Priest, *Invented World*; D.G. Compton, *The Continuous Katherine Mortenhoe*; Brian Stableford, *Halcyon Drift*; Barry Malzburg, *Beyond Apollo*; John Brunner, *The Sheep Look Up*.

"Getting Hitched." *New Statesman* 1 Nov. 1974: 625–6. Philip Roth, *My Life As a Man*. *WAC* 285–7.

"Catcher in the Sty." *New Review* 1.9 (Dec. 1974): 64–5. Joseph Heller, *Something Happened*.

"Science Fiction." *Observer* 8 Dec. 1974: 31. Philip K. Dick, *Flow My Tears, The Policeman Said*; Richard Cowper, *Worlds Apart*; Harry Harrison, *Star Smashers and the Galaxy Rangers*; Dick Morland, *Albion! Albion!*; Ian Weekley, *The Moving Snow*; Michael Coney, *Winter's Children*; Peter Macey, *Stationary Orbit*; Robert Wells, *The Parasaurians*; Brian N. Ball, *Singularity Station*; Arthur Herzog, *The Swarm*; Kate Wilhelm, ed., *Nebula Award Stories 9*; Harry Harrison, ed., *John W. Campbell Memorial Anthology*; Isaac Asimov, ed., *Before the Golden Age*.

"Each Dawn They Die." *Times Literary Supplement* 17 Jan. 1975: 48. Reg Gladney, *The Last Hours Before Dawn*.

"Tour De Farce." *New Statesman* 21 Feb. 1975: 250. Peter De Vries, *The Glory of the Hummingbird*; John Hawkes, *Death, Sleep and the Traveler*; Bruce Jay Friedman, *About Harry Townes*.

"Science Fiction." *Observer* 23 Feb. 1975: 28. Bob Shaw, *Orbitsville*; Robert Silverberg, *Unfamiliar Territory*; Christopher Priest, *Real-Time World*; Brian Stableford, *Rhapsody in Black*; Anne McCaffrey, *To Ride Pegasus*; Harry Harrison, *The Men from PIG and ROBOT*.

"Fellow Fans." *New Statesman* 7 Mar. 1975: 315–16. Giles Gordon, ed., *Beyond the Words*; *Farewell, Fond Dreams*.

"Left-Handed Backhand." *Observer* 6 Apr. 1975: 30. Kurt Vonnegut, *Wampeters, Foma and Granfalloons*; Gore Vidal, *Myron*.

"Out of Style." *New Statesman* 25 Apr. 1975: 555–6. Vladimir Nabokov, *Look at the Harlequins!*.

"Science Fiction." *Observer* 18 May 1975: 30. Ian Watson, *The Jonah Kit*; James Blish, *The Quincunx of Time*; Robert Silverberg, *To Live Again*; James Tiptree Jr., *10,000 Light Years from Home*; Philip Strick, ed., *Antigrav*; John Wyndham, *The Man from Beyond*.

"Science Fiction." *Observer* 8 June 1975: 26. Brian Aldiss and Harry Harrison, eds, *Hell's Cartographers*; Brian Aldiss, ed., *Space Odysseys*; Philip K. Dick, *The Man in the High Castle*; Curt Slodmak, *City in the Sky*; Clifford Simak, *Cemetery World*.

"Tinkering with Jane." *Observer* 20 July 1975: 23. *Sanditon: A Novel by Jane Austen and Another Lady*. WAC 183–5.

"Life, Literature and Leavis." *Observer* 14 Sept. 1975: 25. F.R. Leavis, *The Living Principle*.

"Being Serious in the Fifties." *New Statesman* 7 Nov. 1975: 577–8. Philip Roth, *Reading Myself and Others*; Alan Sillitoe, *Mountains and Caverns*.

"Up!" *New Statesman* 14 Nov. 1975: 618. J.G. Ballard, *High-Rise*; Douglas Hurd, *Vote to Kill*; Clive Murphy, *Freedom for Mr. Mildrew and Nigel Someone*. Ballard in *WAC* 102–3.

"Science Fiction." *Observer* 16 Nov. 1975: 30. Ron Goulart, *After Things Fell Apart*; Alfred Bester, *Extro*; Larry Niven and Jerry Pournelle, *The Mote in God's Eye*; Arthur Clarke, *Imperial Earth*; Charles Logan, *Shipwreck*; Chris Boyce, *Catchworld*; *The Best SF Stories*; *The Dynostar Menace*; Patrick Tilley, *Fade-Out*; Lloyd Biggle Jr., *Monument* and *The Light That Never Was*.

"Science Fiction." *Observer* 8 Feb. 1976: 27. Jack Dann, ed., *Wandering Stars*; Bob Shaw, *Night Walk*; Michael Coney, *Charisma*; Roger Zelazny, *To Die in Italbar*; Peter Edwards, *Terminus*; Dan Morgan, *High Destiny*; *Best of E.E. 'Doc' Smith*; *Best of SF Monthly*.

"Soft Cor." *New Statesman* 13 Feb. 1976: 199–200. Richard Wortley, *Erotic Movies*.

"Life Class." *New Statesman* 19 Mar. 1976: 368–9. John Updike, *Picked-Up Pieces*. WAC 369–72.

"Science Fiction." *Observer* 4 Apr. 1976: 27. Isaac Asimov, *Buy Jupiter, Earth is Room Enough,* and *The Foundation Trilogy*; Ursula Le Guin, *The Wind's Twelve Quarters*; Michael Moorcock, *A Cure for Cancer*; Christopher Priest, *The Space Machine*; *Early Writings in Science and Science Fiction by H.G. Wells*; Jack Vance, *The Brains of Earth* and *The Moon Moth*; A.E. Van Vogt, *The Wizard of Linn*; Robert Heinlein, *Glory Road*.

"Cover Up." *New Statesman* 21 May 1976: 690. E.W. Hildick, *Louie's Snowstorm*; S.E. Hinton, *Rumble Fish*; Evan H. Rhodes, *The Prince of Central Park*; Clive King, *Me and My Million*; Anders Bodelsen, *Operation Cobra*.

"Here Comes Everybody." *Observer* 6 June 1976: 29. Martin Seymour-Smith, *Who's Who in Twentieth Century Literature*. WAC 391–3.

"Science Fiction." *Observer* 13 June 1976: 27. Robert Sheckley, *The Status Civilisation*; Robert Silverberg, *The Stochastic Man*; Richard Cowper, *The Custodians*; Christopher Hodder-Williams, *The Prayer Machine*; Lester del Ray, *Badge of Infamy*; Robert Holstock, *Eve Among the Blind*; Norman Spinrad, *No Direction Home*.

"Tom Cojones." *Observer* 25 July 1976: 21. Brian Aldiss, *The Malacia Tapestry*. WAC 131–2.

"Science Fiction." *Observer* 8 Aug. 1976: 22. Bob Shaw, *A Wreath of Stars*; John Robert King, *Bruno Lipshitz and the Disciples of Dogma*; Michael Coney, *Bronotomek!*; *The Book of Philip Jose Farmer*; Keith Roberts, *Anita*; Ward Moore, *Bring the Jubilee*; Philip K. Dick, *Martian Time-Slip*; Naomi Mitchison, *Memoirs of a Spacewoman*; Brian Aldiss, ed., *Galactic Empires*.

"Science Fiction." *Observer* 3 Oct. 1976: 24. Harry Harrison, *Skyfall*; Frank Herbert, *Children of Dune*; Robert Silverberg, *The Feast of St Dionysus*; Robert Silverberg, ed., *New Dimensions 6*; Harlan Ellison, *The Beast that Shouted Love at the Heart of the World* and *Again, Dangerous Visions*; Vonda McIntyre, *The Exile Waiting*; J.B.S. Haldane, *The Man with Two Memories*; Keith Roberts, *The Grain Kings*.

"The Jokers in the Pack." *Observer* 7 Nov. 1976: 27. Kurt Vonnegut, *Slapstick*; Peter De Vries, *I Hear America Swinging*.

"Nice and Nasty." *New Statesman* 26 Nov. 1976: 760–1. *Four Crowded Years: The Diaries of Auberon Waugh 1972–1976*; *The Book of Bores*; *Lord Gnome of the Rings*.

"Science Fiction." *Observer* 5 Dec. 1976: 30. J.G. Ballard, *Low-Flying Aircraft*; Bob Shaw, *Cosmic Kaleidoscope*; Frederik Pohl, *Man Plus*; Colin Wilson, *The Space Vampires*; Steve Wilson, *The Lost Traveller*; Brian Ash, *Who's Who in Science Fiction*; Peter Nicholls, ed., *Science Fiction at Large*.

"A Girl in Winter." *New York Times Book Review* 26 Dec. 1976: 2, 16. Philip Larkin, *A Girl in Winter*. WAC 149–51.

"Science Fiction." *Observer* 13 Feb. 1977: 35. Ian Watson, *The Martian Inca* and contribution to *festschrift J.G. Ballard*; Isaac Asimov, *The Bicentennial Man*; Ron Goulart, *The Hellhound Project*; Olaf Stapleton, *Nebula Maker*; Brian Stableford, *The Paradise Game*; *Best of Harry Harrison*; *Best of Fred Pohl*.

"The Bad Bits." *New Statesman* 18 Mar. 1977: 359–61. Eric Mottram, *William Burroughs. TMI* 144–6.

"Science Fiction." *Observer* 8 May 1977: 26. Bob Shaw, *Medusa's Children*; Larry Niven, *Out of Time*; Robert Silverburg, *Shadrach in the Furnace*; Joe Haldeman, *Mindbridge*; Alexander Thynn, *The King is Dead*; William Nolan, *Wonderworlds*; Ray Bradbury, *Long After Midnight; Frights*.

"A?" *New Statesman* 17 June 1977: 821–2. Anthony Burgess, *Abba Abba. WAC* 113–16.

"Stranger Than Fiction." *Observer* 7 Aug. 1977: 28. Andrew Field, *Nabokov: His Life in Part. WAC* 245–7.

"Prose is the Leading Lady." *New York Times Book Review* 2 Oct. 1977: 13, 52. Fay Weldon, *Words of Advice. WAC* 135–8.

"In a State of Emergency." *New Statesman* 21 Oct. 1977: 543–4. V.S. Naipaul, *India. VMN* 121–6.

"No Satisfaction." *New Statesman* 13 Jan. 1978: 50–1. Philip Roth, *The Professor of Desire. TMI* 42–5.

"Electric Ladyland." *New Statesman* 14 Apr. 1978: 503. Ron Goulart, *Crackpot*.

"A Stoked-Up 1976. *New York Times Book Review* 19 Nov. 1978: 3, 60, 62. Anthony Burgess, *1985. WAC* 116–20.

"One Wodehouse, Two Hanleys, One Green." *New York Times Book Review* 10 Dec. 1978: 10, 46. P.G. Wodehouse, *Sunset at Blandings. WAC* 204–6.

"Joan Didion's Style." *London Review of Books* 2.2 (7 Feb. 1980): 3–4. Joan Didion, *The White Album. TMI* 160–9.

"In Praise of Pritchett." *London Review of Books* 2.10 (22 May–4 June 1980): 6–7. V.S. Pritchett, *The Tale Bearers; On the Edge of the Cliff. WAC* 65–71.

"Getting Laid Comfortably." *Observer* 29 June 1980: 28. Gay Talese, *Thy Neighbour's Wife. TMI* 184–6.

"More Bones." *New Statesman* 4 July 1980: 19–20. V.S. Naipaul, *The Return of Eva Peron. WAC* 418–23.

"Fall from Graceland." *Observer* 17 Aug. 1980: 28. Dee Presley et al., *Elvis, We Love You Tender. WAC* 37–9.

"Let's Fall in Love." *Observer* 7 Sept. 1980: 29. Iris Murdoch, *Nuns and Soldiers. WAC* 88–90.

"Kool-Aid and Cyanide." *Observer* 2 Nov. 1980: 29. Shiva Naipaul, *Black and White. WAC* 405–7.

"Burgess at his Best." *New York Times Book Review* 7 Dec. 1980: 1, 24. Anthony Burgess, *Earthly Powers. WAC* 121–3.

"The 'Me' Machine." *Observer* 21 Dec. 1980: 26. Tom Wolfe, *In Our Time.*

"Stay, Gentle Reader. *Observer* 25 Jan. 1981: 28. Vladimir Nabokov, *Lectures on Literature. WAC* 249–51.

"Shatter Day Night Fever." *Observer* 29 Mar. 1981: 32. William S. Burroughs, *Cities of the Red Night. WAC* 300–2.

"The World, the Flesh, the Poet." *Observer* 10 May 1981: 32. John Carey, *John Donne. WAC* 197–9.

"Journey Without Maps." *Observer* 7 June 1981: 32. J.G. Ballard, *Hello America. WAC* 104–6.

"In the Hot Seat." *Observer* 19 July 1981: 28. Jorge Luis Borges and Adolfo Bioy-Casares, *Six Problems for Don Isidro Parodi.*

"Scrambled Egos." *Observer* 30 Aug. 1981: 20. Philip Roth, *Zuckerman Unbound. WAC* 287–9.

"Young, Gifted and Funny." *New Statesman* 2 Oct. 1981: 21–2. Adam Mars-Jones, *Lantern Lecture.*

"The Art of Snobbery." *Observer* 25 Oct. 1981: 28. Evelyn Waugh, *Brideshead Revisited.* Rpt. "Revisiting Brideshead." Donald Trelford, ed., *Sunday Best* 2, 1982. *WAC* 201–4.

"The Manqué Puzzle." *Observer* 29 Nov. 1981: 26. Cyril Connolly, *The Rock Pool. WAC* 133–5.

"The King in His Diapers." *Observer* 6 Dec. 1981: 26. Albert Goldman, *Elvis. TMI* 50–2.

"Football Mad." *London Review of Books* 3.22/23 (3–16 Dec. 1981): 23. Desmond Morris, *The Soccer Tribe. WAC* 345–50.

"We are all not guilty." *Observer* 17 Jan. 1982: 30. John Updike, *Rabbit is Rich. TMI* 155–7.

"The Game of Kings." *Observer* 7 Mar. 1982: 32. Andrew Waterman, ed., *The Poetry of Chess*; W.R. Hartston, *Karpov v Korchnoi: The World Chess Championship 1981.*

"In the Jungle, the Mighty Jungle." *New York* 8 Mar. 1982: 84–5. Paul Theroux, *The Mosquito Coast.*

"The Moronic Inferno." *London Review of Books* 4.6 (1–14 Apr. 1982): 3, 5. Saul Bellow, *The Dean's December. TMI* 1–8.

"Laughter in the Dark." *Observer* 20 June 1982: 31. Norman Page, ed., *Nabokov: The Critical Heritage.*

"Unpatriotic Gore." *Observer* 15 Aug. 1982: 30. Gore Vidal, *Pink Triangle and Yellow Star and Other Essays. TMI* 106–8.

"Advertisement for Himself." *Observer* 22 Aug. 1982: 28. Norman Mailer, *The Essential Mailer. WAC* 267–70.

"Room with a Viewer." *Observer* 16 May 1982: 31. Peter Conrad, *Television*; Frank Pike, ed., *Ah! Mischief.*

"The Magus and His Muse." *Observer* 10 Oct. 1982: 31. John Fowles, *Mantissa. WAC* 138–40.

"Bringing Bech to Book." *Observer* 16 Jan. 1983: 47. John Updike, *Bech is Back. TMI* 157–9.

"Sticking Up for Milton." *Observer* 23 Jan. 1983: 46. A.N. Wilson, *The Life of John Milton. WAC* 187–90.

"Don't Leave 'Em Laughing, Just Leave." *New York* 24 Jan. 1983: 56. Richard Price, *The Breaks.*

"The D.M. Thomas Phenomenon." *Atlantic Monthly* Apr. 1983: 124–6. D.M. Thomas, *Ararat. WAC* 141–5.

"A Slowcoach in Slaka." *Observer* 3 Apr. 1983: 29. Malcolm Bradbury, *Rates of Exchange.*

"Kafka Renewed." *Observer* 24 Apr. 1983: 30. Franz Kafka, *Stories 1904–1924.*

"To the Nth Degree." *Observer* 1 May 1983: 28. Iris Murdoch, *The Philosopher's Pupil. WAC* 91–3.

"Trekking the Void." *Atlantic Monthly* July 1983: 100–4. Andrew Harvey, *A Journey in Ladakh. WAC* 409–14.

"Through the Pain Barrier." *Observer* 10 July 1983: 29. *Complete Short Stories of Franz Kafka; Complete Novels of Franz Kafka. WAC* 399–402.

"The School of Doyle." *Observer* 11 Sept. 1983: 31. A. Alvarez, *The Biggest Game in Town. WAC* 355–7.

"Christian Gentleman." *Observer* 15 Jan. 1984: 48. John Updike, *Hugging the Shore.*

"Ghost at the Feast." *Observer* 22 Jan. 1984: 53. Roman Polanski, *Roman.*

"Song of Himself." *Observer* 26 Feb. 1984: 26. Philip Roth, *The Anatomy Lesson. TMI* 46–9.

"American Nightmare." *Observer* 29 Apr. 1984: 23. William S. Burroughs, *The Place of Dead Roads.*

"Before Taste Was Outlawed." *Atlantic Monthly* May 1984: 112–15. Angus Wilson, *Diversity and Depth in Fiction. WAC* 76–81.

"Areas of Darkness." *Observer* 6 May 1984: 20. V.S. Naipaul, *Finding the Centre. WAC* 415–18.

"Saul's December." *Observer* 24 June 1984: 20. Saul Bellow, *Him With His Foot in His Mouth. TMI* 8–11.

"No Laughing Matter." *Observer* 8 July 1984: 20. Mordecai Richler, ed., *The Best of Modern Humour. WAC* 363–6.

"Not Un-Macho." *Observer* 14 Oct. 1984: 25. Norman Mailer, *Tough Guys Don't Dance. WAC* 270–2.

"Russian Ghost." *Observer* 4 Nov. 1984: 26. Yevgeny Zamyatin, *Islanders* and *The Fisher of Men. WAC* 395–7.

"Book of David." *Observer* 18 Nov. 1984: 29. Joseph Heller, *God Knows. TMI* 125–8.

"Chequered Careers." *Observer* 23 Dec. 1984: 28. David Spanler, *Total Chess*; Richard Eales, *Chess*; David Hooper and Kenneth Whyld, *Oxford Companion to Chess*.

"The Bottom Line." *Observer* 24 Feb. 1985: 27. Vladimir Nabokov, *The Man From the USSR and Other Plays. WAC* 253–6.

"He Likes it There." *Observer* 16 June 1985: 22. Paul Theroux, *Sunrise with Seamonsters. TMI* 181–5.

"Norman and the Women." *Observer* 28 July 1985: 25. Peter Manso, *Mailer. TMI* 70–3.

"The Little Tease." *Observer* 4 Aug. 1985: 23. Lawrence Grobel, *Conversations with Capote. TMI* 39–41.

"The American Eagle." *Observer* 25 Aug. 1985: 17. Uniform collection of Saul Bellow's work.

"Kurt's Cosmos." *Observer* 3 Nov. 1985: 25. Kurt Vonnegut, *Galapagos. WAC* 305–7.

"Broken Lance." *Atlantic Monthly* Mar. 1986: 104–6. Cervantes, *Adventures of Don Quixote. WAC* 427–32.

"Impossible Love." *Observer* 20 Apr. 1986: 24. William Burroughs, *Queer. WAC* 302–4.

"Californian Lifeniks." *Observer* 22 June 1986: 23. Vikram Seth, *The Golden Gate*.

"Teacher's Pet." *Atlantic Monthly* Sept. 1986: 96–9. James Joyce, *Ulysses. WAC* 441–6.

"A Bolt Out of the Blue." *Observer* 7 Sept. 1986: 26. Joseph Heller and Speed Vogel, *No Laughing Matter*.

"Designer Universe." *Observer* 12 Oct. 1986: 26. John Updike, *Roger's Version. WAC* 373–5.

"A Handful of Dust." *Observer* 9 Nov. 1986: 29. Truman Capote, *Answered Prayers. WAC* 309–11.

"Lolita's Little Sister." *Observer* 4 Jan. 1987: 22. Vladimir Nabokov, *The Enchanter. WAC* 261–3.

"Nukesville USA." *Observer* 11 Jan. 1987: 25. A.G. Mojtabai, *Blessed Assurance. WAC* 48–50.

"Found in Jerusalem." *Atlantic Monthly* Feb. 1987: 89–91. Philip Roth, *The Counterlife. WAC* 289–93.

"Jack be Nimble, Jack be Quick." *Observer* 22 Feb. 1987: 28. Anthony Burgess, *Little Wisdom and Big God. WAC* 123–7.

"Dangerous Dream." *Observer* 21 June 1987: 25. Robert McNamara, *Blundering into Disaster*. WAC 45–7.

"Water Diviner." *Observer* 13 Sept. 1987: 27. J.G. Ballard, *The Day of Creation*. WAC 107–9.

"The Latest Bad News." *Observer* 25 Oct. 1987: 26. Saul Bellow, *More Die of Heartbreak*.

"Apocalypse 2000." *Observer* 31 Jan. 1988: 27. Robert Scheer, *With Enough Shovels*; Alun Chalfont, *Defence of the Realm*; William Kimber, *Star Wars in a Nuclear World*; William Broad, *Star Warriors*. WAC 51–5.

"In the Boiler-Room of the Self." *Observer* 14 May 1989: 49. John Updike, *Self-Consciousness*. WAC 375–8.

"'Ugly People Are Just as Hard to Get as Pretty People'." *New York Times Book Review* 25 June 1989: 9. Pat Hackett, ed., *The Andy Warhol Diaries*. WAC 40–4.

"The Winners Who Are Losers." *Times Literary Supplement* 30 June–6 July 1989: 709–10. Fred Waitzkin, *Searching for Bobby Fischer*. WAC 331–5.

"Maggie the Iron Man." *Elle* (US) Oct. 1989: 202, 204. Hugo Young, *The Iron Lady*. WAC 19–23.

"Hikers' Guide to the Death of Everything." *Independent on Sunday* 28 Jan. 1990: Review, 21. Bill McKibben, *The End of Nature*. WAC 33–6.

"Miss Jane's Prime." *Atlantic Monthly* Feb. 1990: 100–2. Jane Austen, *Pride and Prejudice*. WAC 433–9.

"Seryozha, Shikochka and Mityusha." *Independent on Sunday* 11 Feb. 1990: Review, 16. Dmitri Nabokov and Matthew J. Bruccoli, eds, *Vladimir Nabokov: Selected Letters 1940–1977*. WAC 257–60.

"Death of the Typical American Heart." *Independent on Sunday* 28 Oct. 1990: Review, 32. John Updike, *Rabbit at Rest*. WAC 379–83.

"Sin Has Come a Long Way Since 1939." *New York Times Book Review* 27 Jan. 1991: 9. Robert B. Parker, *Perchance to Dream*. WAC 215–18.

"Thoroughly Post-Modern Millennium." *Independent on Sunday* 8 Sept. 1991: Review, 28. Don DeLillo, *Mao II*. WAC 313–16.

"Adventures of Bovver Boy Bill." *Independent on Sunday* 27 Oct. 1991: Review, 33. Bill Buford, *Among the Thugs*. WAC 350–3.

"Magnanimous in a Big Way." *New York Times Book Review* 10 Nov. 1991: 12. John Updike, *Odd Jobs*. WAC 384–8.

"Return of the Male." *London Review of Books* 5 Dec. 1991: 3. Robert Bly, *Iron John*; Liam Hudson and Bernadine Jacot, *The Way Men Think*; *Men, It's Time to Pull Together*. WAC 3–9.

"Poet of Thingies." *Independent on Sunday* 8 Mar. 1992: Review, 21. Nicholson Baker, *Vox*. VMN 189–96.

"What He Learned in Bed." *New York Times Book Review* 30 Aug. 1992: 1, 21. Richard Rhodes, *Making Love*. WAC 59–62.

"Lolita Reconsidered." *Atlantic Monthly* Sept. 1992: 109–20. Vladimir Nabokov, *Lolita*. WAC 471–90.

"The Fuck-It Generation." *Esquire* (UK) Nov. 1993: 92–5, 220. Roger Graef, *Talking Blues; Living Dangerously*.

"Transformation of the Nerds." *Independent on Sunday* 7 Nov. 1993: Review, 10. Vladimir Nabokov, *The Real Life of Sebastian Knight* and *The Defence*; Fred Waitzkin, *Searching for Bobby Fischer* and *Mortal Games*; Viktor Korchoi, *Chess Is My Life*. WAC 336–41.

"Demons Under the Volcano." *Independent on Sunday* 12 Dec. 1993: Review, 38. Gordon Bowker, *Pursued by Furies: A Life of Malcolm Lowry*. WAC 207–11.

"Junk Souls." *New York Times Book Review* 14 May 1995: 7. Elmore Leonard, *Riding the Rap*. WAC 225–8.

"Why Augie Has it All." *Guardian* 4 Aug. 1995: T2. Rpt. "A Chicago of a Novel." *Atlantic Monthly* Oct. 1995: 114–27. Saul Bellow, *The Adventures of Augie March*. WAC 447–69.

"Fatally Flawed." *Sunday Times* 10 Sept. 1995: 7.1–7.2. Norman Mailer, *Oswald's Tale*. WAC 273–7.

"Over-Sexed and Over Here." *Sunday Times* 24 Sept. 1995: 7.3. Philip Roth, *Sabbath's Theater*. WAC 294–7.

"Jurassic Larks." *Sunday Times* 1 Oct. 1995: 7.1–7.2. Michael Crichton, *The Lost World*. WAC 219–23.

"A Talent to Abuse." *Sunday Times* 22 Oct. 1995: 7.1–7.2. Gore Vidal, *Palimpsest*. WAC 279–83.

"A Capital President." *Sunday Times* 7 Jan. 1996: 7.1. David Herbert Donald, *Lincoln*. WAC 24–8.

"First Lady on Trial." *Sunday Times* 17 Mar. 1996: 7.1–7.2. Hillary Clinton, *It Takes A Village*. WAC 28–32.

"Hitting His Stride." *Los Angeles Times Book Review* 8 June 1997: 3. Saul Bellow, *The Actual*. Rpt. "Don't Call Him Mellow Bellow." *Observer* 18 Aug. 1997: 14. WAC 323–7.

"Survivors of the Cold War." *New York Times Book Review* 5 Oct. 1997: 12–13. Don DeLillo, *Underworld*. WAC 316–21.

"High for a Time." *Guardian* 7 Nov. 1998: 10. Tom Wolfe, *A Man in Full*. WAC 229–32.

"Hannibal, the Camus of Carnage." *Talk* Sept. 1999: 222, 224–6, 247. Thomas Harris, *Hannibal*. WAC 233–41.

"The Breasts." *Talk* May 2001: 111–12. Philip Roth, *The Dying Animal*

"All Together, Please." *Times Literary Supplement* 18 Jan. 2002: 10. Mark D. Steinberg, *Voices of Revolution, 1917.*

Other reviews (film, television, concert, miscellaneous)

"Unisex Me Here." *New Statesman* 6 July 1973: 28–9. Concert: David Bowie, 2 July 1973.

"Fleshspots." [as "Bruno Holbrook"]. *New Statesman* 14 Sept. 1973: 362. Strip clubs.

"Coming in Handy." [as "Bruno Holbrook"]. *New Statesman* 14 Dec. 1973: 922–3. Pornographic magazines.

"Whisper Who Dares." *The Listener* 21 Feb. 1974: 250–1. Television: *Tuesday Documentary; Click; Play for Today, Joe's Ark; Kung Fu; Visitors.*

"Fewer Means Prettier." *The Listener* 14 Mar. 1974: 346. Television: *Miss England 1974; Look, Stranger; For the Love of Triumph; Play for Today, Easy Go; Monty Python's Flying Circus.*

"Family Operatics." *The Listener* 11 Apr. 1974: 479–80. Television: *Shoulder to Shoulder; The Family; Philpott File; Just a Nimmo; Russell Harty Plus; Eurovision Song Contest.*

"Miss Emmanuelle." *New Statesman* 23 Aug. 1974: 264–5. Film: *Emmanuelle.*

"Television." *New Review* 1.12 (Mar. 1975): 68–9. Television: *Emmerdale Farm; General Hospital; Rooms; Crown Court; Zodiac; Pebble Mill; Camberwick Green; Good Afternoon; Mr. and Mrs.*

"Infra Dog." *New Statesman* 1 Aug. 1975: 150–1. Television: *Johnny Go Home; Royal International Horse Show; Once Bitten; The Policewoman; Beyond the Crowd; Murrain; Our Terry; Film Night.*

"Beating People is Wrong." *New Statesman* 8 Aug. 1975: 178–9. Television: *The Jay Interview; A Fall Like Lucifer; Beneath the News.*

"Pot Luck." *New Statesman* 15 Aug. 1975: 208–9. Television: *Horizon: Cannabis;* Gore Vidal, *Success Story; The Likes of; The Jay Interview.*

"Footer Mouth." *New Statesman* 22 Aug. 1975: 232–3. Television: *Football Focus; On the Ball; Match of the Day; The Big Match; The Editors; Ten Years of Man Alive.*

"Summer Hols." *New Statesman* 29 Aug. 1975: 261–2. Television: *The Disney Adventure; Living on the Land; The Liver Birds; The Squirrels; The Policewoman; The Kojak Movie; Seaside Special; Vienna 1900; Crown Court; Wheeltappers and Shunters Social Club; 2nd House 2nd Run; Match of the Day; That's Life; Ghost Story, Circle of Fear; Barbarella; Kojak; Understanding Ourselves; Love is the Answer; Something to Sing About; In*

Every Corner Sing; Sunday Cinema; Facets of Bruce Forsyth; Orson Welles; Benny Hill; Horizon; The Water-Baby; The Spinners in Blackpool.

"Bless Me." *New Statesman* 5 Sept. 1975: 288–9. Television: *Network; Quiller; Oliver Twist.*

"Your Good Elf." *New Statesman* 12 Sept. 1975: 316–17. Television: *Tonight; World in Action; This Week; Angels; The Stars Look Down.*

"Bias Will Be Bias." *New Statesman* 19 Sept. 1975: 348. Television: *The Other Half of the Sky; Joining Up; Panorama; Richard Dimbleby; Explorers.*

"Potter Platter." *New Statesman* 9 Apr. 1976: 481–2. Television: *Play for Today; Double Dare; Edgar Wallace; Play for Britain; Top of the Pops; Mrs Ghandi's India.*

"Legs." *New Statesman* 16 Apr. 1976: 517–18. Television: *The World About Us; The Burke Special.*

"I Didn't Get No..." *New Statesman* 28 May 1976: 712–13. Concert: The Rolling Stones. *VMN* 94–8.

"The Mild Bunch." *New Statesman* 18 June 1976: 823–4. Films: *The Last Hard Men; The Human Factor; What's Up Tiger Lily?*

"Socket To Her." *New Statesman* 27 Aug. 1976: 286–7. Films: *The Tenant; Murder by Death.*

"X to Grind." *New Statesman* 3 Sept. 1976: 321. Film: *From Noon Till Three.*

"Crassroads." *New Statesman* 24 Sept. 1976: 427–8. Television: *The Crezz; The Duchess of Duke Street; Dorian Gray,* adapted by John Osborne.

"Capitalism and the Camera-Angle." *Sunday Times* 16 Jan. 1977: 35. Television: *The Age of Uncertainty; Eleanor Marx; World in Action; Wildlife on One.*

"Till The Ratings Do Us Part." *Sunday Times* 23 Jan. 1977: 38. Television: *Man Alive Report; Panorama; Top of the Pops; The Old Grey Whistle Test; Sportsnight;* "The Kennedy Interview"; *Tonight; The Age of Uncertainty; Moses – The Lawgiver; Warship.*

"The Week Rape Came Into Its Own." *Sunday Times* 30 Jan. 1977: 38. Television: *Act of Rape; Moses – The Lawgiver; Warship; Robin's Nest; Benny Hill; Eleanor Marx.*

"Tyrannical Whims." *Observer* 18 Sept. 1977: 27. Television: *Tonight; Race; Star-Spangled Banner; The Show.*

"Punchbags." *New Statesman* 30 Sept. 1977: 454–5. Television: *Pilger Report; World of Pam Ayers; Tonight;* Tom Stoppard, *Professional Foul.*

"Madder and Madder." *Observer* 5 Mar. 1978: 29. Television: *Panorama; A Change in Mind; Tonight; Man Alive; Americans.*

"In the Fast Lane." *Observer* 12 Mar. 1978: 35. Television: *Elvis – Aloha from Hawaii; Panorama; Pennies from Heaven.*

"The Sporting Week." *Observer* 27 Aug. 1978: 20. Television: *Football Focus; Match of the Day; The Big Match; Taste for Adventure.*

"Somebodaddy." *New Statesman* 8 Sept. 1978: 307–8. Films: *Heaven Can Wait; The Silent Partner.*

"Unideal Olympics." *Observer* 27 July 1980: 44. Television: *Olympic Grandstand; Vodka-Cola; Guyana Tragedy.*

"Trials of Strength." *Observer* 28 Dec. 1980: 32. Television: *World's Strongest Man; Christmas Star Games; Billy Smart's Christmas Circus; World Land Speed Record.* Broadcast films: *Midnight Cowboy; The Front Page; Earthquake; The Towering Inferno; Airport 1975; The Secret Life of an American Wife; Digby; The Man with the Golden Gun.*

"An Inside View." *Observer* 19 Sept. 1982: 40. Television: *Living in Styal; The Gathering; That's Life; Lady Sings the Blues; The Deep.*

"Daylight Robbery." *Observer* 26 Sept. 1982: 40. Television: *Midweek Sports Special; King Lear; Animal Passions; Smiley's People.*

"Chicken Raunch." *Observer* 3 Oct. 1982: 40. Television: *Chicken Ranch; Clive James on Television; Ivanhoe; Panorama; Futures; Couples.*

"Mother Nature and the Plague." *Observer* 1 May 1983: 36. Television: *"Killer in the Village"; The World About Us; Brideshead Revisited; Wise Man at the Wheel; The Falklands Factor – 1770; Eurovision Song Contest;* World Snooker Championship.

"A Bowl of Catfood for Breakfast." *Observer* 8 May 1983: 40. Television: *Inside China; Sportsnight; South Bank Show.*

"A Rich Week for the Rough Stuff." *Observer* 11 Sept. 1983: 48. Television: *The Godfather; Reilly – Ace of Spies; The Gathering Seed; Killer; Out.*

"The War According to Supersoap." *Observer* 18 Sept. 1983: 48. Television: *Winds of War; Der Stürmer; Propaganda with Facts; All for Love; US Open; The Gathering Seed; Killer; Barry at Blenheim; A Frame with Davis.*

"O, The Enterprise is Sick." *Observer* 29 July 1984: 22. Television: *Star Trek; Crime Inc.; Case on Camera; The Groundling and the Kite; Cricket.*

"The Wimbledon Shower." *Observer* 30 June 1985: 24. Television: Wimbledon.

"Inside Charles's Marriage." *Observer* 27 Oct. 1985: 28. Television: Prince and Princess of Wales; *Whicker's World; Queens'; Midweek Sport Special.*

"Ronbo and the Arms Habit." *Observer* 13 Apr. 1986: 28. Television: *Kenny Everett Show; Magnum; Miami Vice; Film 86; MOD; Viewpoint 86; Our Bomb.*

"Cronenberg's Monster." *Independent on Sunday* 10 Nov. 1996: Review, 8–9. Film: *Crash. WAC* 109–12.

"Remembering A Life." *Talk* Dec. 2001: 131–3. Rpt. "Age Will Win." *Guardian* 21 Dec. 2001: G2, 2–4. Rpt. "Against Dryness." Zachery Leader, ed., *On Modern British Fiction*, 2002. Film: *Iris*.

Profiles and interviews

"Harold Robbins." [unsigned]. *Times Literary Supplement* 14 July 1972: 819. Interview.

"Brainewaves." [unsigned]. *Times Literary Supplement* 26 Apr. 1974: 444. Profile: John Braine.

"The Boy from Bingley." [unsigned]. *New Statesman* 21 Mar. 1975: 368–9. Profile: John Braine. *VMN* 231–7.

"The Three-D Man." [unsigned]. *New Statesman* 24 Oct. 1975: 496–7. Profile: Peter Parker.

"Joseph Heller in Conversation with Martin Amis." *New Review* 2.20 (Nov. 1975): 55–9.

"Celebrity Square." [unsigned]. *New Statesman* 15 Apr. 1977: 489–90. Profile: Esther Rantzen.

"Then There Were Three." *Telegraph Sunday Magazine* 18 June 1978: 28–30, 32, 34. Profile: music group Genesis.

"Shower of Gold." *Observer* 22 Apr. 1979: 34. Profile: Joseph Heller.

"Kevin Keegan's Success at Home and Away." *Telegraph Sunday Magazine* 6 May 1979: 35–41. Profile: football star K. Keegan.

"Roman á Clef." *Tatler* Apr. 1980: 61–2. Profile: Roman Polanski. *VMN* 246–54.

"Fame on his Own Terms." *Telegraph Sunday Magazine* 20 July 1980: 23–4, 27. Profile: filmmaker Alan Parker.

"Burgeoning Burgess." *Observer* 12 Oct. 1980: 13. Profile: Anthony Burgess. *VMN* 241–5.

"Is Capote Kaput?" *Tatler* Nov. 1980: 63–5. Profile: Truman Capote. *TMI* 33–8.

"Mailer. Coming on Strong." *Observer* 22 Feb. 1981: 29–30. Profile: Norman Mailer. *TMI* 57–65.

"Speaking Memories from Montreux." *Observer* 20 Sept. 1981: 33. Profile: Véra Nabokov. *VMN* 113–19.

"A Critic in the Courtroom." *Observer* 2 May 1982: 27. Profile: Diana Trilling. *TMI* 53–6.

"Beyond the Slaughterhouse." *Observer Magazine* 6 Feb. 1983: 17–18. Profile: Kurt Vonnegut. *TMI* 132–7.

"Claus and Sunny: An American Tragedy." *Observer Magazine* 18 Sept. 1983: 18–25. Profile: Claus von Bulow affair. *TMI* 22–31.

"Saul Bellow's December." *Observer* 11 Dec. 1983: 25. Profile. *TMI* 199–208.

"The Utopian Woman." *Observer Magazine* 15 Apr. 1984: 54–5. Profile: Gloria Steinem. *TMI* 138–43.

"Ballard's Worlds." *Observer Magazine* 2 Sept. 1984: 50, 53. Profile: J.G. Ballard. *VMN* 76–82.

"Graham Greene at Eighty." *Observer* 23 Sept. 1984: 7. Profile. *VMN* 1–6.

"Brian De Palma in Two Takes." *Vanity Fair* Nov. 1984: 14, 19. Profile. *TMI* 79–88.

"Mr Hefner and the Desperate Pursuit of Happiness." *Observer Magazine* 22 Sept. 1985: 12–16. Profile: Hugh Hefner. *TMI* 170–80.

"Updike's Version." *Observer* 30 Aug. 1987: 15–16. Profile: John Updike. *VMN* 47–59.

"Rendezvous with Rushdie." *Vanity Fair* Dec. 1990: 160–3. Profile: Salman Rushdie. *VMN* 170–8.

"An Ear Open to the Stories We All Tell Ourselves." *Independent on Sunday* 16 Dec. 1990: Review, 24. Profile: V.S. Pritchett. *VMN* 265–74.

"In search of Dieguito." *Guardian* 1 Oct. 2004: G2, 2–5. Profile: Diego Armando Maradona.

Essays and columns

"Chalk and Cheese." *Times Educational Supplement* 21 Sept. 1973: 58. Thom Gunn; Ted Hughes.

"How Awful Goodness Is." *Times Educational Supplement* 21 Sept. 1973: 61. Charles Dickens, *Bleak House*.

"Enigma and Variations." *Radio Times* 13–19 Dec. 1975: 7–9. Jane Austen.

"One Man's Week." *Sunday Times* 25 Jan. 1976: 32. Diary of Amis's week.

"Problem City." *New Statesman* 6 Feb. 1976: 156. New York City.

"On the Wagon." *Sunday Times* 22 May 1977: 35. Cannes film festival.

"Hollywood-by-the-Sea." *Sunday Times* 29 May 1977: 33–4. Cannes film festival. *VMN 207–16*.

"Green With Envy." *Observer* 19 June 1977: 13. "Private Line" column: class.

"Dark Laughter." *New Statesman* 8 July 1977: 55–6. Vladimir Nabokov.

"Blackpool Diary." *New Statesman* 14 Oct. 1977: 504. Blackpool Tory conference.

"The State of Fiction: A Symposium." *New Review* 5.1 (Summer 1978): 18. One paragraph contribution.

"Books of the Year." *Observer* 17 Dec. 1978: 33. Craig Raine, *The Onion, Memory*; Peter Porter, *The Cost of Seriousness*; James Fenton, *A Vacant Possession*.

"Action at Sea." *Telegraph Sunday Magazine* 21 Jan. 1979: 46, 50. Travel essay: cruise ship *Oriana*.

"The Bodies in Question." *Observer* 18 Feb. 1979: 11. "Private Line" column: pornography.

"Five-Star People." *Tatler* Feb. 1980: 91–2. Travel essay: Marbella.

"Reagan Bids for his Biggest Role." *Telegraph Sunday Magazine* 13 July 1980: 24–5, 27–8. *TMI* 89–96.

"Out of the Pews, Into the Polls, Amen." *Observer* 21 Sept. 1980: 25, 27; Rpt., with revisions, "Born-Again America." Donald Trelford, ed., *Sunday Best*, 1981. US Presidential elections. *TMI* 109–19.

"A Tale of Two Novels." *Observer* 19 Oct. 1980: 26. Accusations of plagiarism against Jacob Epstein.

"A New Sheriff Rides in from the West." *Observer* 9 Nov. 1980: 11. Rpt. "The New Sheriff." Donald Trelford, ed., *Sunday Best*, 1981. Ronald Reagan's presidential campaign.

"Books of the Year." *Observer* 7 Dec. 1980: 27. Evelyn Waugh, *Letters*; V.S. Naipaul, *The Return of Eva Peron*; Anthony Burgess, *Earthly Powers*.

"Lennon – from Beatle to 'Househusband.'" *Observer* 14 Dec. 1980: 25. Elegiac essay: John Lennon. *VMN* 182–85.

"Christmas Quiz: Books." *Observer* 21 Dec. 1980: 23, 30.

"The Killings in Atlanta." *Observer* 5 Apr. 1981: 25–6. Child murders. *TMI* 12–20.

"London Literary Life: Let Me In, Let Me In!" *New York Times Book Review* 5 Apr. 1981: 9, 28. Literary Obsession.

"The Library of Babel." *Observer* 2 Aug. 1981: 22. Richard Booth; Hay-on-Wye.

"Frankfurt Follies." *Observer* 18 Oct. 1981: 26. Frankfurt Book Fair. *VMN* 127–31.

"Books of the Year." *Observer* 6 Dec. 1981: 25. V.S. Naipaul, *Among the Believers*; Nirad Chaudhuri, *Hinduism*; Adam Mars-Jones, *Lantern Lecture*.

"Back Behind Bars." *Observer* 24 Jan. 1982: 27. Jack Henry Abbott. *TMI* 65 9.

"Gore and Jerry (and the Lesson of Lynchburg)." *Observer* 7 Feb. 1982: 27. Gore Vidal in Virginia. *TMI* 120–4.

"The Novelist Cast as Mendacious Wrecker." *Times* 8 Sept. 1982: 9. Vladimir Nabokov, *Despair*.

"Tabloid Tactics: Martin Amis in New York." *Observer* 12 Sept. 1982: 28. Tabloids.

"Tough Nut to Crack." *Observer* 31 Oct. 1982: 27. Rpt. "Why I was Expelled–1." Donald Trelford, ed., *Sunday Best 3*, 1983. Academic Expulsion. *VMN* 186–8.

"The World According to Spielberg." *Observer Magazine* 21 Nov. 1982: 16–19. Rpt. Donald Trelford, ed., *Sunday Best 3*, 1983. Steven Spielberg. *TMI* 147–54.

"Books of the Year." *Observer* 5 Dec. 1982: 25. Gore Vidal, *Pink Triangle and Yellow Star*; J.G. Ballard, *Myths of the Near Future*; Saul Bellow, *The Dean's December*; Christopher Reid, *Pea Soup*; James Fenton, *The Memory of War*; *Penguin Book of Contemporary British Poetry*.

"Vanity Fair." *Observer* 6 Mar. 1983: 27. *Vanity Fair* relaunch. *TMI* 129–31.

"The Long March from Vicarage Road." *Observer Magazine* 10 July 1983: 8–13. Watford Football Club. *VMN* 34–45.

"Books of the Year." *Observer* 4 Dec. 1983: 25. Clive James, *Glued to the Box*; Ian Hamilton, *Robert Lowell*; Peter Porter, *Collected Poems*.

"Books of the Year." *Observer* 2 Dec. 1984: 19. Craig Raine, *Rich*; Redmond O'Hanlon, *Into the Heart of Borneo*; Peter Porter, *Fast Forward*; Julian Barnes, *Flaubert's Parrot*; Saul Bellow, *Him With His Foot In His Mouth and Other Stories*; V.S. Pritchett, *Collected Stories*; Yevgeny Zamyatin, *Islanders*.

"Oh, for Pitty's Sake!" *Observer* 27 Jan. 1985: 49. Literary competition for 16- to 25-year-olds. *VMN* 197–200.

"Letter from London." *Vogue* (US) Apr. 1985: 216, 221–2. Prince Andrew; tabloids.

"Making Sense of AIDS." *Observer* 23 June 1985: 17–18. *TMI* 187–96.

"A Talent for Warmth." *Observer* 18 Aug. 1985: 19. Elegiac essay: Shiva Naipaul. *WAC* 407–8.

"Wishing for Milton's Power and Tolstoy's Zaniness." *New York Times Book Review* 8 Dec. 1985: 47. Response to query, "If Santa Clause were the muse, what would you ask for?"

"Kilotons of Human Blood." *Observer* 29 Dec. 1985: 21. Literature of nuclear weapons.

"The Great American Mix." *Observer* 16 Feb. 1986: 29. Sex, drink, and celebrity.

"Memento Mori: Other People are Hell, Philip Larkin 1922–1985." *Vanity Fair* Apr. 1986: 46–7. Elegiac essay. *VMN* 201–6.

"A Blast Against the Bomb." *Observer* 19 Apr. 1987: 17. Nuclear weapons.

"Reasoning That's Easily Exploded." *Times* 23 May 1987: 20. Response to Bernard Levin (11 May 1987).

"Women We Love: Joan Collins." *Esquire* (US) June 1987: 166.

"Nuke City." *Esquire* (US) Oct. 1987: 97–111. Nuclear defense. *VMN* 13–33.

"*Goodfellas*: Blowing Away the Romantic Myth of the Mobster." *Premiere* Oct. 1987: 76, 79. Martin Scorsese.

"Darts Fly High and Handsome." *Observer Magazine* 17 Jan. 1988: 34–5, 37–8. Championship darts. *VMN* 223–30.

"Ronnie and the Pacemakers." *Esquire* (US) Nov. 1988: 132–6. US Republican convention. *VMN* 99–112.

"The Worst Review." *New Statesman & Society* 31 Mar. 1989: 29. Contribution to symposium on Salman Rushdie.

"Hotel California." *Condé Nast Traveler* Oct. 1989: 64. Chateau Marmont.

"Who's Reading Whom." *Sunday Times* 5 Nov. 1989: G2. Don DeLillo.

"Relative Values: Deux Amis." *Sunday Times Magazine* 3 Dec. 1989: 11, 14. Kingsley and Martin Amis on their relationship.

"Robocop Redux." *Premiere* July 1990: 62–5. *Robocop II*. *VMN* 159–69.

"Second Thoughts: Crying for the Light." *Independent* 29 Sept. 1990: Books, 29. Composition of *London Fields*.

"Books for Christmas." *Independent* 2 Dec. 1990: 31. John Updike, *Rabbit at Rest*; V.S. Pritchett, *Complete Short Stories*.

"The Grudge Match: Amis v. Barnes." *Esquire* (UK) Nov. 1991: 78–83. Rpt. Greg Williams, ed., *The Esquire Book of Sports Writing*, 1995. *VMN* 154–8.

"Books of the Year." *Independent on Sunday* 1 Dec. 1991: 28. Will Self, *The Quantity Theory of Insanity*; Nicholson Baker, *U and I*; Jung Chang, *Wild Swans*.

"The Coming of the Signature." *Times Literary Supplement* 17 Jan. 1992: 18. Amis's tenure at *TLS*.

"Madonna Exposed." *Observer Magazine* 11 Oct. 1992: 22–37. Madonna, *Sex*. *VMN* 255–64.

"A Defence of the Writer's Realm." *Sunday Times* 4 Apr. 1993: 7.7. Acceptance speech, Award for Excellence in Writing (28 Mar. 1993).

"Don Juan in Hull." *New Yorker* 12 July 1993: 74–82. Philip Larkin. *WAC* 153–72.

"The Heat of Wimbledon." *New Yorker* 26 July 1993: 66–70.

"Cover Story." *Guardian* 21 Aug. 1993: Weekend, 6. Philip Larkin.

"At the Wide-Open Open." *New Yorker* 4 Oct. 1993: 173–8. US Open.

"The Thugs Have Taken Over." *Evening Standard* 25 Oct. 1993: 27. Crime.

"Mark Boxer." *Sunday Times Magazine* 7 Nov. 1993: 20–4. Elegiac essay.

"A Hero's Welcome Amid the Myths of Time." *Mail on Sunday* 24 Apr. 1994: 60, 61. Travel essay: Ithaca.

"The C-Note Project." *Esquire* (US) May 1994: 84. Contribution, 100 words for $100.

"Blown Away." *New Yorker* 30 May 1994: 47–9. Rpt. "Acts of Violence." *Observer* 3 July 1994: Life, 20. Film violence. *WAC* 11–17.

"Tennis Personalities." *New Yorker* 5 Sept. 1994: 112. Rpt. "A 'Personality'? You Cannot Be Serious!" *Observer* 29 June 1997: 24.

"Travolta's Second Act." *New Yorker* 20 & 27 Feb. 1995: 212–18. Rpt. "Look who's Smirking." *Sunday Times Magazine* 26 Feb. 1995: 16–22. John Travolta.

"Buy My Book, Please." *New Yorker* 26 June–3 July 1995: 96–9. *The Information*'s US book tour.

"Who's Reading What: Turning Over Some New Leaves." *Sunday Times* 6 Aug. 1995: 7.6.

"The Games Men Play." *New Yorker* 14 Aug. 1995: 40–7. US Open.

"Let the Real Tennis Begin." *New Yorker* 21–28 Aug. 1995: 54. Monica Seles.

"Favourite Lines." *Sunday Telegraph* 5 Nov. 1995: Books, 13. John Keats, "Bright Star."

"Pick of the Year." *Sunday Times* 19 Nov. 1995: 7.1. Norman Mailer, *Oswald's Tale*; Gore Vidal, *Palimpsest*; Salman Rushdie, *The Moor's Last Sigh*.

"Jane's World." *New Yorker* 8 Jan. 1996: 31–5. Jane Austen.

"Heaven on a Stick." *Sunday Times* 10 Mar. 1996: 4.1–4.2. Travel essay: Mauritius.

"In the Land of a Million Mobiles." *Evening Standard* 26 June 1996: 10. Wimbledon.

"Henman, A Master of Passionate Calm." *Evening Standard* 28 June 1996: 19. Wimbledon.

"Farewell to Edberg Champion of Grace." *Evening Standard* 1 July 1996: 13. Wimbledon.

"How Sampras Met Krajicek and the Wind." *Evening Standard* 5 July 1996: 7. Wimbledon.

"My Ad." *New Yorker* 9 Sept. 1996: 98. Tennis.

"My Secret Plan to be Wimbledon Champion." *Evening Standard* 14 Oct. 1996: 23.

"Unembarrassable." *New York Times Magazine* 8 June 1997: 44. America.

"The Sporting Scene." *New Yorker* 16 June 1997: 38. Tim Henman.

"The Mirror of Ourselves." *Time* 15 Sept. 1997: 64. Elegiac essay: Princess Diana.

"Books I Wish I'd Written." *Guardian* 2 Oct. 1997: T18. Research for *Night Train*.

"Of Cars and the Man." *The Republic of Letters* 3 (Mar. 1998): 2–3. Rpt. "Road Rage and Me." *Guardian* 7 Mar. 1998: Features, 1.

"The Shock of the Nou." *Observer* 30 May 1999: Review, 1–2. Football crowds.

"Sex in America." *Talk* Feb. 2001: 98–103, 133–5. Rpt. "A Rough Trade." *Guardian* 17 Mar. 2001: Weekend, 8–14. Pornography industry.

"Fear and Loathing." *Guardian* 18 Sept. 2001: G2, 2–5. Terrorism.

"The Queen's Heart." *New Yorker* 20 May 2002: 106–10. Queen Elizabeth II; Robert Lacey, *Monarch*; Deborah Hart Strober and Gerald S. Strober, *The Monarchy*.

"The Voice of the Lonely Crowd." *Guardian Review* 1 June 2002: 4–6. Rpt. *Harper's* Aug. 2002: 15–18. Terrorism.

"Restoration." *The Sunday Telegraph* 2 June 2002: Review, 1–2. Revised *New Yorker* essay (20 May 2002), Queen Elizabeth II.

"Window on a Changed World." *Daily Telegraph* 11 Sept. 2002: 17. Terrorism.

"The Palace of the End." *Guardian* 4 Mar. 2003: 23. War in Iraq.

"The World: An Explanation." *Daily Telegraph* 8 Mar. 2003: 29. Global politics.

"The Supreme American Novelist." *Atlantic Monthly* Dec. 2003: 111–14. Rpt. "Capo di Capi." *Guardian* 4 Mar. 2004: 4. Saul Bellow.

"We Have to Face It: English Football is Just No Good." *Guardian* 28 June 2004: 14.

"Authors in the Front Line: Martin Amis." *Sunday Times Magazine* 6 Feb. 2005: 21–7. Violence in Colombia.

Original contributions to books

Untitled contribution. Ann Thwaite, ed., *My Oxford*. London, 1977. 203–13. Experience at Exeter College.

"The Sublime and the Ridiculous: Nabokov's Black Farces." Peter Quennell, ed., *Vladimir Nabokov: His Life, His Work, His World*

London: Weidenfeld and Nicolson; New York: William Morrow, 1980, 73–87. *Despair; King, Queen, Knave; Laughter in the Dark; Lolita.*

"H is for Homosexual." Stephen Spender, ed., *Hockney's Alphabet: Drawings by David Hockney.* London: Faber; New York: Random House, 1991. 23–4. Childhood homosexual encounter.

"My Imagination and I." Anthony Barnett, ed. *Power and the Throne: The Monarchy Debate.* London: Vintage, 1994. 79–80. "Sex dream" about Sarah Ferguson.

["In adolescence..."] *Contemporary Writers: Martin Amis.* London: Book Trust, 1994. 1. Brief comment on authorial inspiration.

"Peter Porter." Anthony Thwaite, ed. *Paeans for Peter Porter.* London: Bridgewater, 1999. 13–15. Brief appreciation.

Index

Adorno, Theodor
  analysis of culture industry, 118,
    120, 122–3, 126, 129, 132, 134
  Culture Industry, The, 122, 129
  Dialectic of Enlightenment, 118, 120,
    122, 123, 126, 129, 131, 132,
    134
  immanent critique, 81, 132, 135n,
    160
  Minima Moralia, 129, 131, 132
  Philosophy of Modern Music, The, 126
  Prisms, 132
  "Trying to Understand Endgame",
    126
  on writing after the Holocaust, 114
  see also Max Horkheimer
"An American Airman Looks Ahead"
  (M. Amis), 190–2, 196
  influence of J.G. Ballard upon, 191–2
  invocation of W.B. Yeats, 190
  relationship to *Other People*
    (M. Amis), 182, 192
angry young men, 12, 76
Amis, Kingsley
  Lucky Jim, 13, 77
  as novelist, 77, 177n, 194n, 199, 211
  relationship with M. Amis, 2, 114n,
    200, 231
Amis, Martin
  awards, 1, 88, 231
  and J.G. Ballard, 8, 139, 180–94,
    195n, 230
  and Saul Bellow, 2, 55, 57, 181–3,
    197, 203–4
  as "Bruno Holbrook", 8, 197,
    207–10, 211, 224
  and Don DeLillo, 159–60, 161, 175,
    176, 222, 223, 231
  education at Oxford, 181, 198, 200,
    233
  as film actor, 61, 178n
  and gender portraiture, 1, 55–69,
    71 85, 87 100, 160, 173

as "Henry Tilney", 7, 180–1, 187,
  189, 195n, 198, 211, 212, 213,
  214, 215
and F.R. Leavis, 8, 197–210
as literary reviewer, 180–94,
  197–210
London in the novels of, 22, 24, 26,
  46, 79, 95, 98, 118, 125, 127,
  130, 132, 207
and Nabokov, 55, 103, 110, 114,
  129, 135n, 171, 195n, 197, 203
and Lucy Partington, 128, 178
poetry of, 190–2, 196
pornographic themes in the novels
  of, 44, 46, 51, 58, 63, 66, 87,
  125, 146–7, 156, 170–5, 178,
  189, 206–9
relationship with K. Amis, 2, 114n,
  200, 231
and science fiction, 181–2, 183,
  185, 186, 188–9, 190, 192,
  195n
television in the novels of, 10, 56,
  62, 89, 91, 93–4, 144–6, 149,
  156n, 164–7, 189, 198, 206,
  209, 211, 224–6
on terrorism, 3, 169, 178n, 182,
  201, 233
and United States, 17, 65–6, 80, 90,
  105–7, 110, 146–7, 149, 165–6,
  182, 188–92, 203–4
and Evelyn Waugh, 83–4, 120, 128,
  181, 204
see under individual novels
Aristotle, 49, 54
Arnold, Matthew, 202
Austen, Jane, 181, 187, 195n, 203,
  211, 216, 222, 228, 232

Bakhtin, Mikhail, 125
Ballard, J.G., 8, 139, 230, 180–95
  aestheticism, 185, 189, 193, 194
  Concrete Island, 186, 191, 215

Ballard, J.G. – *continued*
  Crash, 188–9, 214
  Crystal World, The, 184
  Drowned World, The, 183–7
  film adaptations of his novels, 189
  Hello America, 184, 189, 192, 219
  influence upon M. Amis, 182–4,
    186–91, 193, 195n
  literary reviews by, 189, 191, 193–4
  Low-Flying Aircraft, 190, 217
  reviewed by M. Amis, 181–2, 186,
    188–9, 192, 195n, 214–17, 219,
    222, 228
  science fiction, 181–2, 183, 185, 190
  Vermillion Sands, 187, 189, 214
  "Which Way to Inner Space", 183,
    185
  Wind from Nowhere, 184
Barnes, Julian, 124, 150, 199, 230, 231
Barthes, Roland, 47, 49, 54, 89, 169
Bataille, Georges, 47, 49, 54, 88, 97,
  100
Baudrillard, Jean, 37, 48, 94, 139, 161,
  169, 177n, 188
Bellow, Saul
  influence upon M. Amis, 34n, 55,
    57, 181–3, 197, 203–4
  as literary mentor, 55, 181–3, 203
  as novelist, 2, 181–3
  reviewed by M. Amis, 219, 220,
    221, 222, 223, 228, 230, 233
Benjamin, Walter, 43, 52, 54, 102,
  115, 126
Booker Prize, The 1, 88
Borges, Jorge Luis
  "The Aleph", 134, 153–4, 156
  "The Circular Ruins", 120, 124
  influence upon M. Amis, 120, 203,
    219
Bourdieu, Pierre, 75, 148, 156
Burgess, Anthony, 181, 196, 218, 221,
  227, 229
Burroughs, William, 198, 212, 214,
  218, 219, 220, 221
Butler, Judith, 55, 69, 77, 84, 85, 99

Christie, Agatha, 98
Conrad, Joseph, 164, 172, 203
Connolly, Cyril, 202, 203, 204, 219
Cronenberg, David, 189, 196, 227

Dead Babies (M. Amis, 1975), 23–4,
  28–9, 183–90
  as apprentice work, 183, 194
  characterization in, 28–9, 34, 186–7
  comedy, 1, 187
  country house genre, 186
  doubles/doubling, 24, 32
  influence of J.G. Ballard upon, 8,
    182–3, 186–9
  intertextuality, 183, 186–7
  morality, 186
  narcissism, 186–8
  narrative strategies, 23, 28–9, 32,
    184, 189
  postmodern elements, 23, 32
  satire, 1, 186–7, 189
  thematic concerns, 24, 28, 186–8,
    189–90, 195n
DeLillo, Don, 159–60, 161, 175, 176,
  222, 223, 231
de Man, Paul, 46, 51, 53n, 54,
Derrida, Jacques, 36, 47, 54, 141
Dickens, Charles, 82, 94, 100, 134,
  147, 164, 173, 177n, 181, 214, 228
Diedrick, James, 4, 5, 7, 8, 13, 32, 33,
  46, 47, 56, 71, 80, 83, 84, 101,
  107, 108, 113, 115n, 117, 130,
  133, 153, 162, 170, 176, 192
Dostoevsky, Fyodor, 46, 80, 127

Einstein's Monsters (M. Amis, 1987), 2,
  101, 106, 115n, 182, 184, 188,
  190, 194, 195n, 210
  "Bujak and the Strong Force", 106
  "Thinkability", 190
  "The Time Disease", 190
Eliot, T.S., 201–2, 204
Ellis, Brett Easton, 17
Epstein, Jacob, 183, 229
Experience: A Memoir (M. Amis, 2000),
  2–3, 4, 110, 115n, 128, 129, 169,
  178n, 199

Fenton, James, 192, 199, 229, 230
Fielding, Henry
  character Joseph Andrews in *Yellow
    Dog* (M. Amis), 170–2
  thematic concerns, 125, 170–1, 172
Fitzgerald, F. Scott, 65
Fitzgerald, Zelda, 67

Flaubert, Gustave, 65
Fowles, John, 17, 220
Frye, Northrop, 123, 136
Fukuyama, Francis, 161, 169

Haffenden, John, 10, 11, 14, 15, 21,
    28, 30, 33, 55, 66, 125, 127, 130,
    135n, 189
Hassan, Ihab, 159, 168, 171, 177n,
    178n
Hawthorne, Nathaniel, 65
Heavy Water and Other Stories
    (M. Amis, 1998), 2
"Career Move", 149, 156, 182, 195n
High Wind in Jamaica, A, 61, 178n
Hitchens, Christopher, 199
Hopkins, Gerard Manley, 153
Horkheimer, Max
    analysis of culture industry, 118,
        120, 122, 123, 126, 129, 132,
        134
    Dialectic of Enlightenment, 118, 120,
        122, 123, 126, 129, 131, 132,
        134
    see also Theodor Adorno
Howard, Elizabeth Jane, 181
Hutcheon, Linda, 159, 178

Information, The (M. Amis, 1995),
    117–35, 137–56
    characterization in, 118–22, 130,
        139–43, 145–8, 150–3
    and cliché, 128–9, 133
    comedy, 125, 127
    influence of Jorge Luis Borges upon,
        120, 124, 151, 153–4
    influence of D.H. Lawrence upon,
        130
    influence of science fiction films
        upon,
    and information theory, 137–42,
        154–6
    intertextuality, 120, 123–5, 142,
        149, 151, 153–4
    literary envy/rivalry, 147–8, 150
    and literary tradition, 123–5, 127–8,
        130, 150, 152–3, 158, 173
    narrative strategies, 25, 127–8, 130,
        132–3, 143
    pixelation, 140–3, 144

and pornography, 146–7
postmodern elements, 119–20, 132,
    138, 140–2, 145–6, 149, 158
realism, 127–8, 137–9, 144, 150–1,
    155, 158, 175
televisual aesthetic, 119–20 124,
    137–9, 141–6
thematic concerns, 117–18, 120–2,
    124–5, 127–8, 130–4, 145–6,
    152–5

James, Henry, 163, 203, 204
Jameson, Fredric, 91, 100, 138–9, 148,
    157, 163, 177n, 188
Joyce, James, 93, 132, 135n, 138, 181,
    199, 221

Kafka, Franz, 203, 220
Keulks, Gavin, 4, 6, 11, 13, 37, 46, 48,
    55, 56, 62, 71, 82, 83, 84, 117,
    118, 123, 133
Kilmartin, Terence, 199
Kittler, Friedrich, 138, 144–5, 147,
    157
*Koba The Dread: Laughter and the
    Twenty Million* (M. Amis, 2002), 3,
    101, 114n, 169
Kristeva, Julia, 92, 97, 100, 124, 125,
    127, 128, 133, 135n, 136

Larkin, Philip, 199, 217, 231, 232
Lawrence, D.H., 6, 13, 53n, 89, 93,
    130, 197, 200, 201, 203, 205
Leavis, F.R., 197–210
    critical legacy, 8, 197–9, 210,
        215–16
    critical values, 200–1, 203–4, 205,
        206–8
    contrasted to Bloomsbury ethos,
        199–200
    contrasted to T.S. Eliot, 201–2
    Great Tradition, The, 200, 203, 204,
        205
    Letters in Criticism, 201
    Nor Shall My Sword, 198, 205
Lessing, Doris, 56
Levi, Primo, 127
Lewis, Wyndham, 205
Lifton, Robert Jay, 106, 108, 109, 113,
    116

London Fields (M. Amis, 1989), 71–85,
    87–100
  Booker Prize controversy, 88
  characterization in, 72–6, 80–2,
    87–96, 98, 101, 102, 169, 184
  class issues in, 71–5, 79–82, 98
  comedy, 78
  doubles/doubling, 73–4, 76–7, 90–1,
    93–5
  gender portraiture in, 5–6, 56, 71–3,
    75–6, 82, 87–92, 95–6, 98–9
  narrative strategies, 77–8, 81–2,
    104, 113, 163, 184
  and literary tradition, 77–8
  pornography and sexuality in, 87,
    98, 170, 207
  postmodern elements, 73, 81, 88,
    91–4, 98–9, 103, 161–2, 166
  thematic concerns, 2, 56, 75, 79–80,
    87, 90–4, 96, 98–9, 101–4, 105,
    106, 110, 117, 127, 161–2, 170,
    182, 186, 188, 210
Lyotard, Jean-François, 10, 101–7,
    110–11, 112, 114, 164
London, 4, 18, 198, 200
  in the novels of M. Amis, 22, 24,
    26, 46, 79, 95, 98, 118, 125,
    127, 130, 132, 207

Mailer, Norman, 61, 195n, 203, 219,
    220, 221, 223, 227, 232
Mars-Jones, Adam
  commentary on M. Amis, 25, 34,
    35, 56, 60, 69, 117, 129, 133
  as novelist, 163, 219, 229
Marx, Karl, 36, 39, 40, 41, 43, 54
"Martian" school of poetry, 29, 34n,
    192
  see also Craig Raine, Christopher Reid
McLuhan, Marshall, 140, 157
Melville, Herman, 65, 180
Miller, Karl, 23, 32, 34n, 35, 58, 82
Miller, J. Hillis, 94–5, 100
Milton, John, 120, 121, 181, 220, 230
Money: A Suicide Note (M. Amis, 1984),
    23–8, 36–53, 55–69, 71–85
  allegory, 5, 36–42, 44–7, 49–52
  characterization in, 10, 14, 22–3,
    25–8, 36–7, 39–41, 45, 48–52,

    55–60, 62–4, 66–8, 72, 74–6,
    80, 82, 84–5, 95, 180
  class dynamics in, 5, 71, 73–4,
    77–80, 82
  doubles/doubling, 5, 22–3, 25–8,
    36, 37, 47, 51, 53n, 68, 87
  gender portraiture in, 5–6, 42–4,
    55–9, 61–3, 71–6, 82–3, 85
  intertextuality, 45, 51, 52, 53n, 57,
    62–3, 65, 66–7, 117, 194
  irony in, 51, 62
  literary reputation of, 1–2
  narrative strategies, 22–3, 24, 28,
    33, 42, 45–6, 52, 55–7, 59–60,
    78–9, 83, 84–5, 96, 98, 132,
    135n, 165, 177n
  pornographic or sexual themes,
    40–4, 50, 57–8, 63–4, 83 156n,
    207, 208
  postmodern elements, 23, 48, 73,
    79, 81, 135n, 160, 176
  queer theory in, 55–6, 61, 63–9, 72
  role of Martin Amis character, 14,
    28, 47, 68, 80, 82, 85, 90, 93,
    139, 180
*Moronic Inferno and Other Visits to
    America, The* (M. Amis, 1986), 2,
    118, 195n, 211
Murdoch, Iris, 34n, 203, 213, 214,
    218, 220, 227

Nabokov, Vladimir
  influence upon M. Amis, 34, 55,
    103, 110, 114, 129, 171, 181,
    195n, 197, 203
  narrative strategies, 45, 114, 129,
    171
  Lolita, 45, 114, 135n, 171, 181, 223,
    233
  reviewed by M. Amis, 181, 211,
    213, 216, 218, 219, 221, 222,
    228, 230
Nietzsche, Friedrich, 202
Night Train (M. Amis, 1997), 158–79,
    233
  characterization in, 161, 162, 164,
    166–7
  doubles/doubling, 161, 164
  gender portraiture in, 61, 169–70

intertextuality, 158, 161–2, 163, 165–6, 177n
humanist themes, 7, 162–3, 168, 174
narrative strategies, 61, 139, 143, 161–4, 165, 166, 168, 170, 177n
political contexts, 2, 169
postmodern elements, 160–1, 163–4, 165, 167–8, 169, 170, 174–6
and realism, 160, 163, 164
televisual aesthetic, 165–6, 168
Nuclear weapons, 2, 81, 94–6, 107, 190, 222, 230, 231
in the work of M. Amis, 2, 81, 94–5, 96, 101, 107, 188, 190, 194, 206, 210

Ong, Walter, 137, 157
Orwell, George, 27, 37–8, 39
Other People: A Mystery Story (M. Amis, 1981), 28–32, 191–4
characterization in, 1, 28–30, 162, 191
doubles/doubling, 28–31
influence of "Martian School" upon, 29, 192
influence of J.G. Ballard upon, 182, 184, 191–2, 193–4
narrative strategies, 28, 31, 34n, 111, 161–3
and nonfiction of M. Amis, 8, 182, 184
and poetry of M. Amis, 182, 191–2
postmodern elements, 161, 193
thematic concerns, 1, 28–30, 111, 162, 169, 184, 192

Partington, Lucy, 128, 178
pornography
critical contextualization of, 146–7, 171
in the fiction of M. Amis, 42, 44, 46, 51, 58, 63, 66, 87, 125, 146–7, 156, 170–1, 173–5, 178, 189, 206–9
reviewed by M. Amis, 229, 233
see also Martin Amis, *Money*, *Yellow Dog*

postmodernism
characteristics of, 9, 73, 102–5, 117, 138–9, 158–61, 162–3, 165–6, 168, 170–1, 172–4, 188
cultural contexts, 102–5, 107, 110, 158–60, 173, 182, 192
as literary period, 6–7, 81, 102–5, 138–9, 158–61, 165, 167, 169–70, 172–3, 174–6, 182
and M. Amis, 1, 6–7, 14–15, 81, 91–2, 93, 94, 101–14, 114n, 117, 146, 148, 156n, 158–77, 188
narrative strategies, 9, 15, 92, 103–5, 110–11, 112, 117, 138–9, 160, 162–3, 170–1, 174, 188
reaction against, 7, 138, 159–60, 168, 176
and the sublime, 101–7, 110–11, 112
see also Jean, Baudrillard, Ihab Hassan, Linda Hutcheon, Fredric Jameson, Jean-François Lyotard

Rachel Papers, The (M. Amis, 1973), 9–21, 23–5
as apprentice work, 183, 194
characterization in, 4, 9–12, 14, 16–20, 22, 23, 24, 27–8
doubles/doubling, 23, 27
gender portraiture in, 11, 12, 14, 16, 18, 55
intertextuality, 13, 17, 24
and literary tradition, 4, 11, 13, 21, 204
love and sexuality in, 12, 14, 16–18, 19–20, 55, 174
narcissism in, 9, 11–12, 18–19, 25
plagiarism of, 183
self-reflexivity/reflectiveness, 24
thematic concerns, 1, 2, 9, 14–15, 24, 27, 30, 174, 187, 194, 198
Rahv, Philip, 202, 203
Raine, Craig, 192, 229, 230
"Martian" school of poetry, 29, 34n, 192
Reid, Christopher, 192, 230
Roth, Philip, 195, 203
reviewed by M. Amis, 213, 215, 216, 218, 219, 220, 221, 223

Salinger, J.D., 17
Sartre, Jean Paul, 31, 50, 54
science fiction
  influence upon M. Amis, 7, 139,
    142, 180–95, 198, 209
  thematic concerns, 180, 182, 183–6,
    187, 190, 193
  see also J.G. Ballard
Sedgwick, Eve Kosofsky, 65, 66, 70
Self, Will, 12, 89, 99n, 175, 231
Shakespeare, William, 40
  allusions in the work of M. Amis,
    26, 63, 65, 141
Shannon, Claude, 154, 157
Showalter, Elaine, 57, 60, 70
Simmel, Georg, 39–41, 43, 53n
Snow, C.P., 197, 205, 212
Steinem, Gloria, 61, 228
Stevenson, Robert Louis, 23, 24, 32
Success (M. Amis, 1978), 23–4, 32–3
  doubles/doubling, 23–4, 32–3
  narrative strategies, 23–4, 32–3
  thematic concerns, 1, 194, 209

Television, 140, 144, 145, 159, 219
  critical contextualization of, 7,
    144–5, 164–7
  in the novels of M. Amis, 10, 56,
    62, 89, 91, 93, 94, 144, 145–6,
    149, 156n, 164–7
  reviewed by M. Amis, 189, 198,
    206, 209, 211, 224–6
Terrorism, 3, 169, 178n, 182, 201, 233
Time's Arrow, or, The Nature of the
  Offense (M. Amis, 1991), 101–15
  characterization in, 102–5, 108–9,
    112–13
  doubles/doubling, 108–9
  influence of Robert Jay Lifton, 106
  intertextuality, 105–6, 110
  narrative techniques, 2, 34n, 104,
    106, 109, 110, 111–13, 151
  and modernity, 101–2, 103–4, 106
  political contextualization, 2, 6,
    101–2, 103, 104–7, 111,
    112–13, 114, 127, 134n, 168
  postmodern elements, 6, 101,
    103–4, 106, 110–11, 114, 168,
    175

relation to novels of M. Amis, 22,
  29, 30, 101–2, 106, 110, 111,
  127, 168, 182, 184, 195n
role of the reader, 111–13
temporal inversion in, 104, 107,
  109, 111–12, 151
thematic concerns, 22, 29, 30, 104,
  106–7, 108–9, 111, 135n, 151,
  156n
Tolstoy, Leo, 56, 230
Trilling, Lionel, 199, 204, 213

United States, 90, 220, 222, 228, 229,
  230, 233
  in the work of M. Amis, 3, 17, 62,
    65–6, 80, 105–7, 109–10, 119,
    123, 146–7, 149, 156, 165–6,
    169, 178n, 182–3, 186, 188,
    190–2, 203–4
  politics of, 65, 80, 105
  select writers of, 8, 17, 184, 189,
    192, 195n, 202–4
Updike, John, 163, 177n, 179, 193,
  203
  reviewed by M. Amis, 216, 219,
    220, 221, 222, 228, 231

Vidal, Gore, 61, 216, 219, 223, 224,
  230, 232
"Voice of the Lonely Crowd, The"
  (M. Amis), 200–1, 233
Vonnegut, Kurt, 105, 116, 181–3,
  195n, 203
  reviewed by M. Amis, 212, 214,
    216–17, 221, 227

War Against Cliché: Essays and Reviews,
  1971–2000, The (M. Amis, 2001),
  3, 56, 63, 60, 66, 69, 104, 114,
  115n, 118, 128, 134, 181–2, 184,
  187–9, 191–2, 197, 203–6
Waugh, Evelyn
  influence upon M. Amis, 83–4, 120,
    128, 181, 204
  Handful of Dust, 120
  reviewed by M. Amis, 219, 229
Williams, Raymond, 94–5, 100
Wodehouse, P.G., 181, 186, 195n,
  218

Yellow Dog, The (M. Amis, 2003), 1, 2, 3, 7, 158–79
    characterization in, 170–2, 186
    intertextuality, 169, 170
    and humanism, 158, 169, 171, 174
    narrative strategies, 158, 160–1, 162, 170, 171, 173–4, 186
    political contextualization, 169, 178n
    pornographic themes, 156n, 170, 173–4, 207

    postmodern elements, 7, 158, 160–1, 168–9, 170, 174, 175–6
    and realism, 7, 160, 170
    role of Joseph Andrews character, 170–2, 186
    thematic concerns, 164, 168, 170, 171, 173–4, 184, 208

Žižek, Slavoj, 38, 42, 54, 77, 86